epic!

CAT NINJA

CAT'S CLAW

Written by
Matthew Cody
Jadzia Axelrod
Dan Nordskog
Kurtis Scaletta
Chris Schweizer
Chad Thomas

Illustrated by
Chad Thomas
Eduardo Medeiros
Brett Bean

Colors by
Warren Wucinich
Cindy Zhi
Maarta Laiho

Andrews McMeel
PUBLISHING®

Cat Ninja created by Matthew Cody and Yehudi Mercado

Cat Ninja: Cat's Claw text and illustrations copyright © 2023 by Epic! Creations, Inc. All rights reserved. Printed in China. No part of this book may be used or reproduced in any manner whatsoever without written permission except in the case of reprints in the context of reviews.

Andrews McMeel Publishing
a division of Andrews McMeel Universal
1130 Walnut Street, Kansas City, Missouri 64106

www.andrewsmcmeel.com

Epic! Creations, Inc.
702 Marshall Street, Suite 280
Redwood City, California 94063

www.getepic.com

23 24 25 26 27 SDB 10 9 8 7 6 5 4 3 2 1

Paperback ISBN: 978-1-5248-8228-0
Hardback ISBN: 978-1-5248-8230-3

Library of Congress Control Number: 2023932660

Design by Dan Nordskog and Carolyn Bahar

Made by:
King Yip (Dongguan) Printing & Packaging Factory Ltd.
Address and location of manufacturer:
Daning Administrative District, Humen Town
Dongguan Guangdong, China 523930
1st Printing — 5/15/23

ATTENTION: SCHOOLS AND BUSINESSES
Andrews McMeel books are available at quantity discounts with bulk purchase for educational, business, or sales promotional use. For information, please e-mail the Andrews McMeel Publishing Special Sales Department: sales@amuniversal.com.

Table of Contents

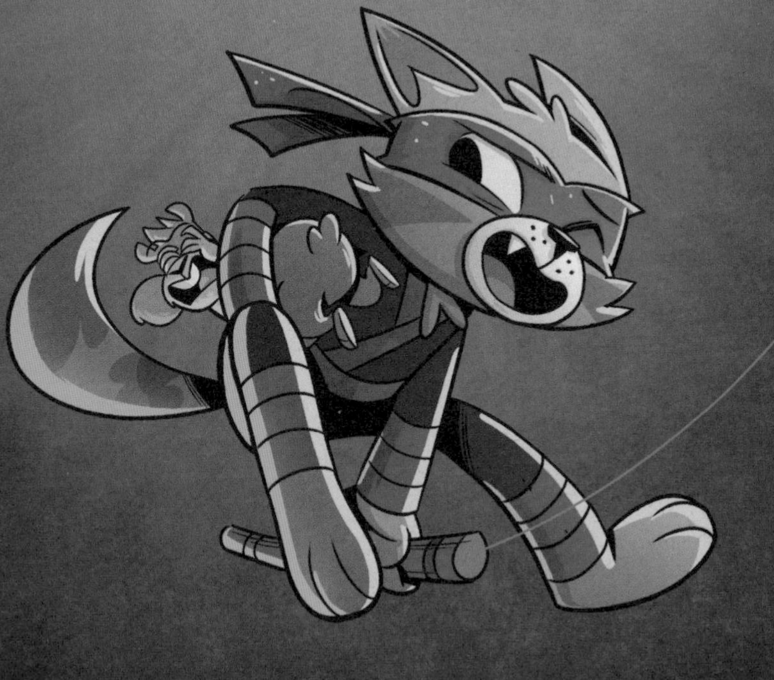

Matthew Cody

Illustrated by
Chad Thomas

Colors by
Warren Wucinich

Mystery of the Cat's Claw
Part 1

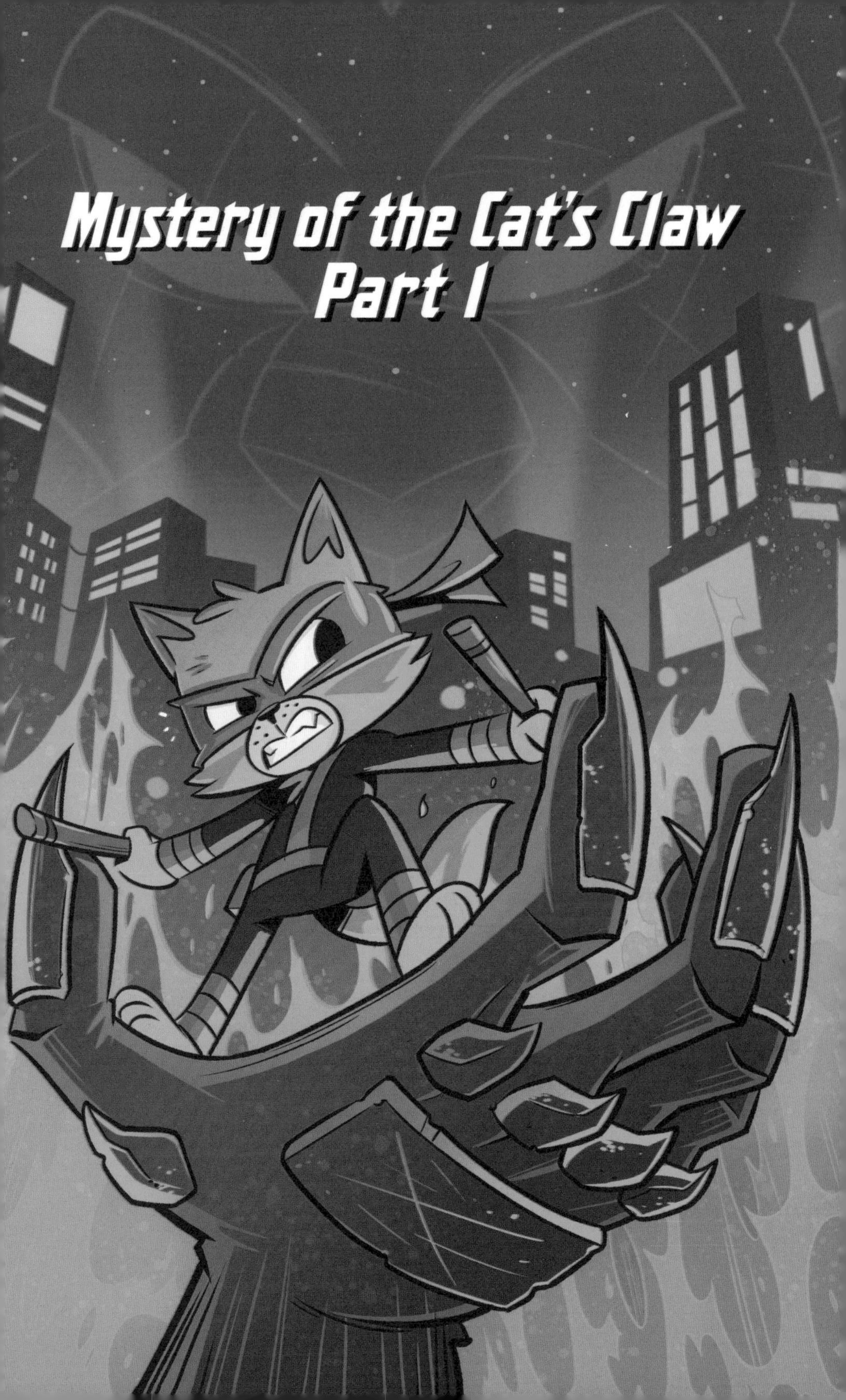

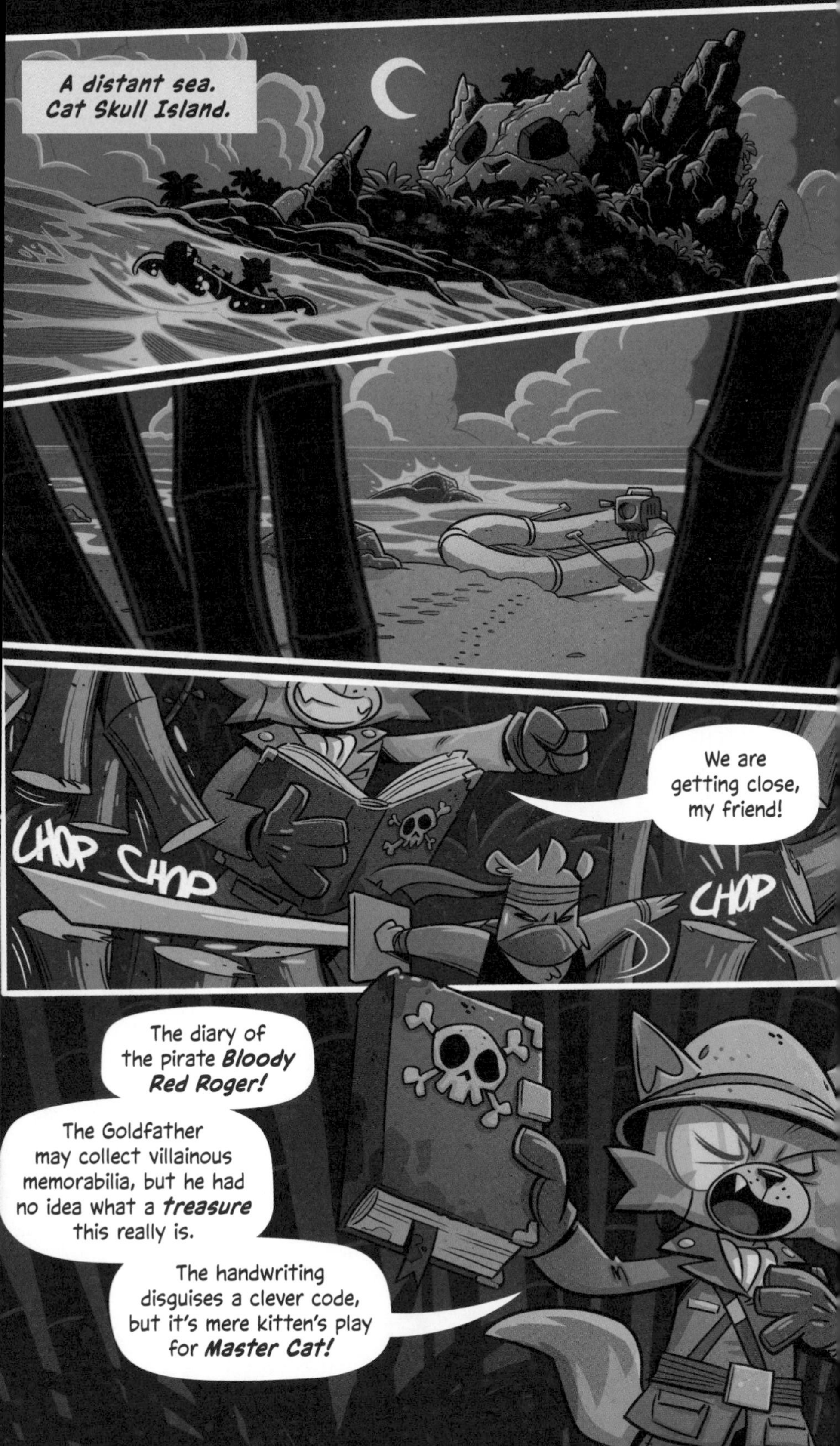
A distant sea. Cat Skull Island.
We are getting close, my friend!
CHOP CHOP
CHOP
The diary of the pirate ***Bloody Red Roger!***
The Goldfather may collect villainous memorabilia, but he had no idea what a ***treasure*** this really is.
The handwriting disguises a clever code, but it's mere kitten's play for ***Master Cat!***

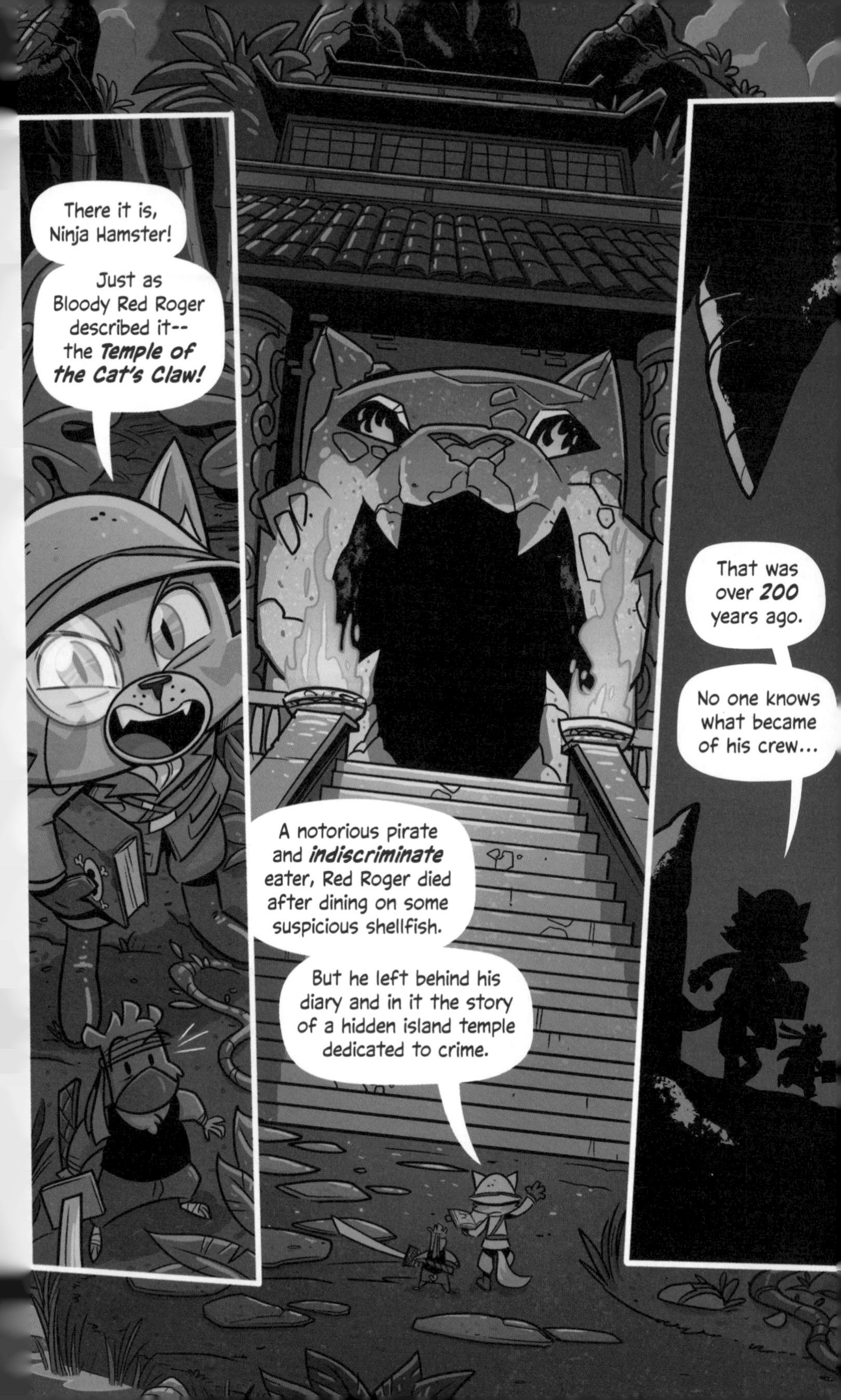
There it is, Ninja Hamster!
Just as Bloody Red Roger described it-- the *Temple of the Cat's Claw!*
A notorious pirate and *indiscriminate* eater, Red Roger died after dining on some suspicious shellfish.
But he left behind his diary and in it the story of a hidden island temple dedicated to crime.
That was over *200* years ago.
No one knows what became of his crew...

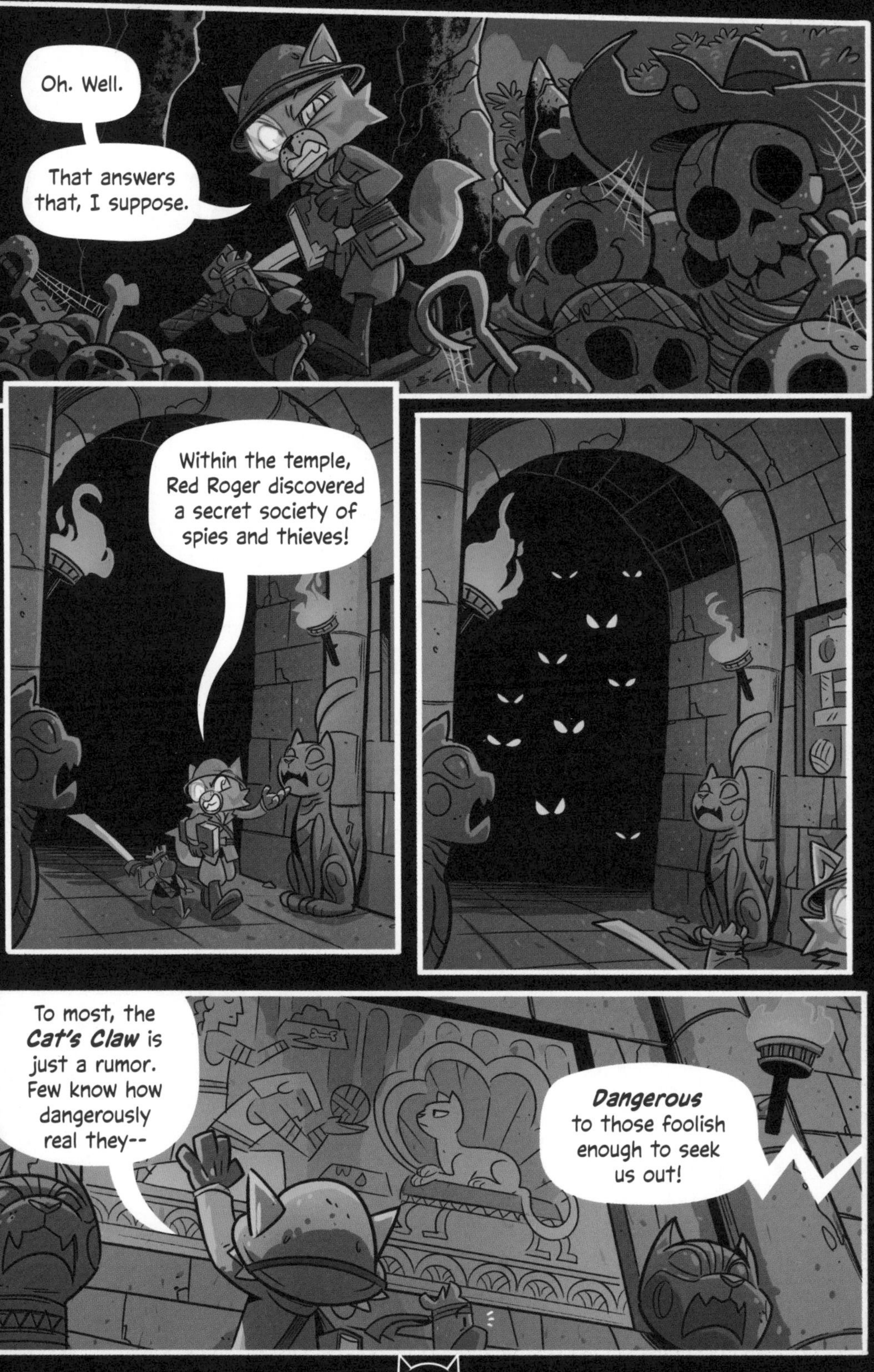
Oh. Well.
That answers that, I suppose.
Within the temple, Red Roger discovered a secret society of spies and thieves!
To most, the *Cat's Claw* is just a rumor. Few know how dangerously real they--
Dangerous to those foolish enough to seek us out!

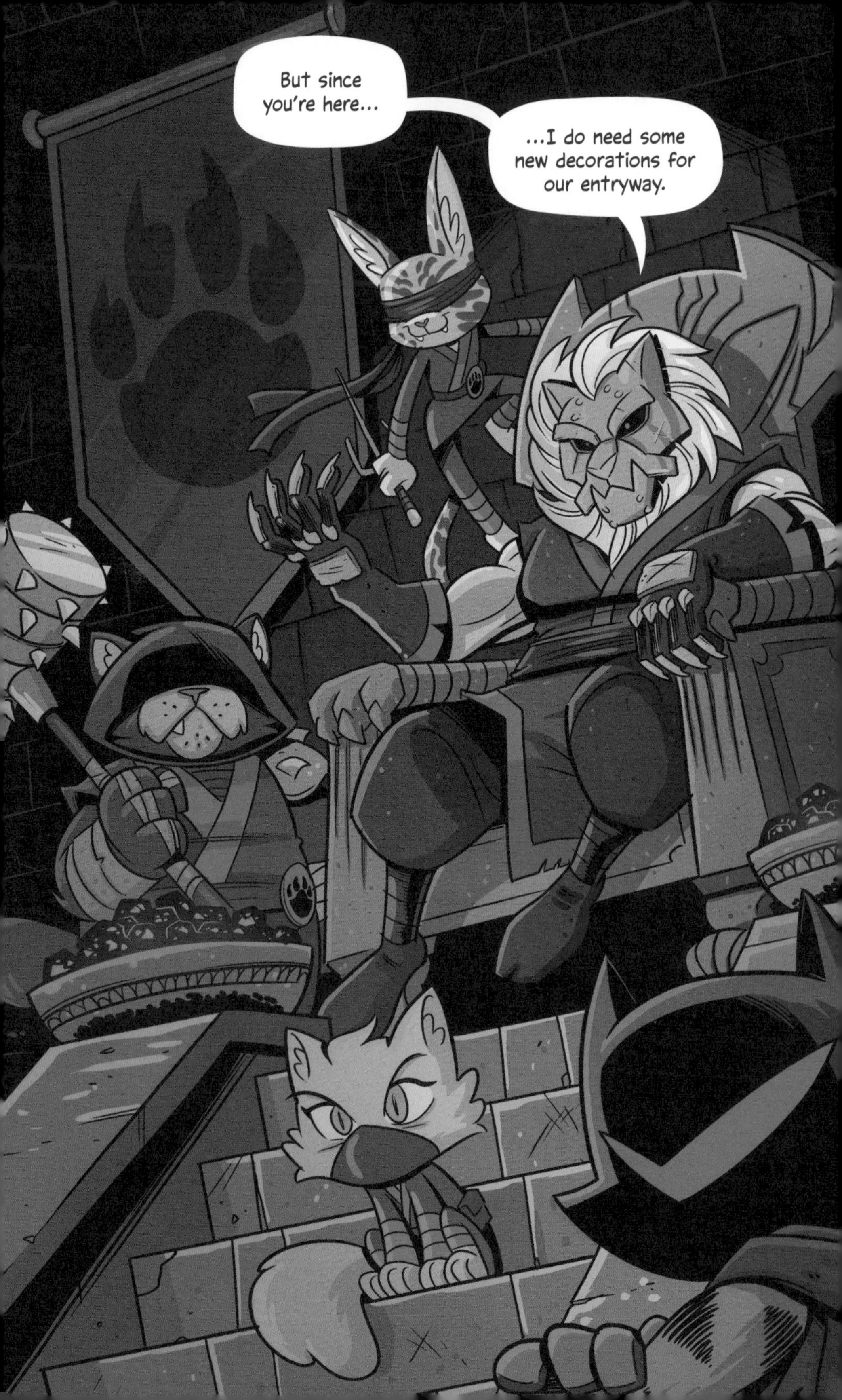

But since you're here...
...I do need some new decorations for our entryway.

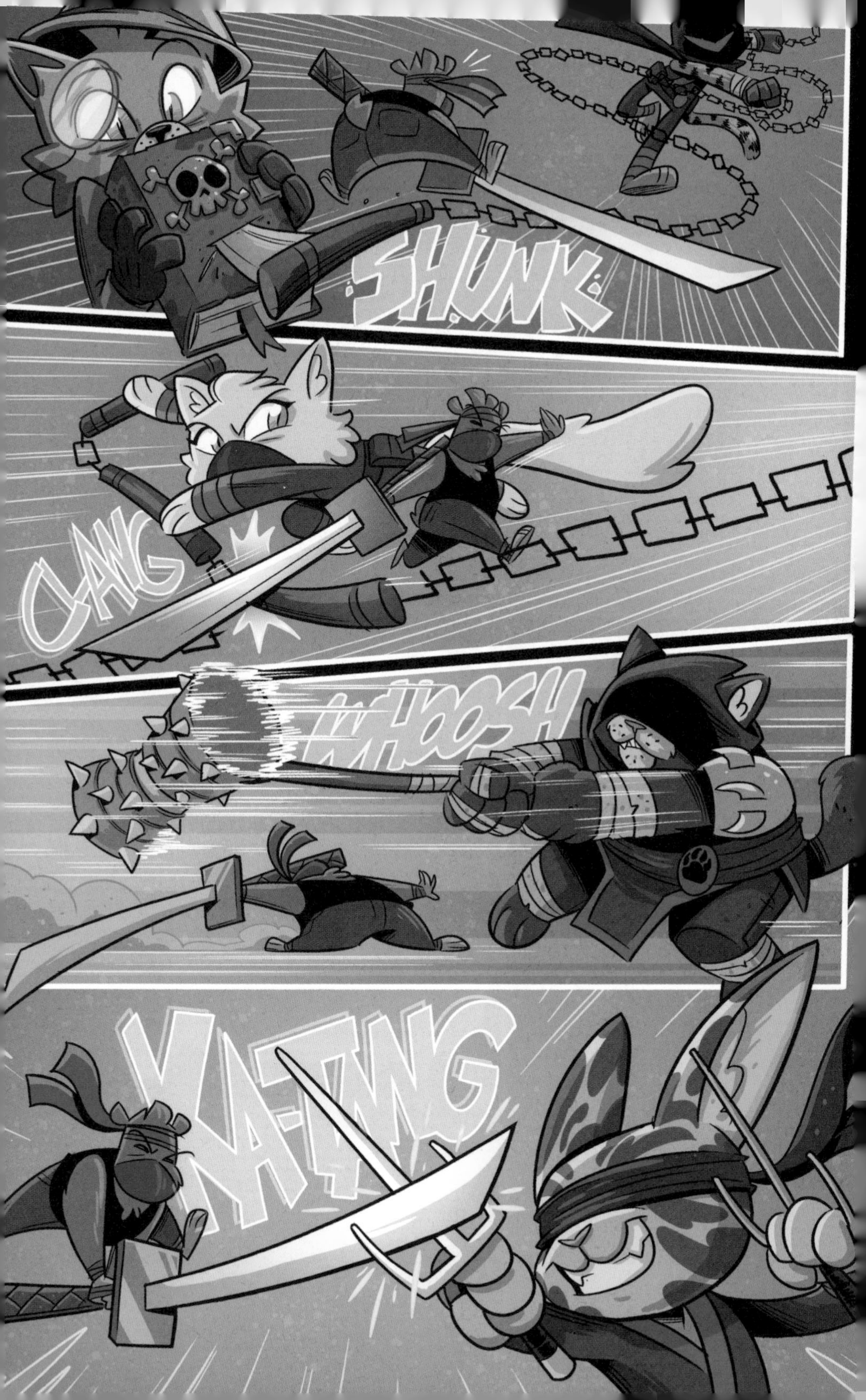
SHUNK
CLANG
WHOOSH
KA-TWANG

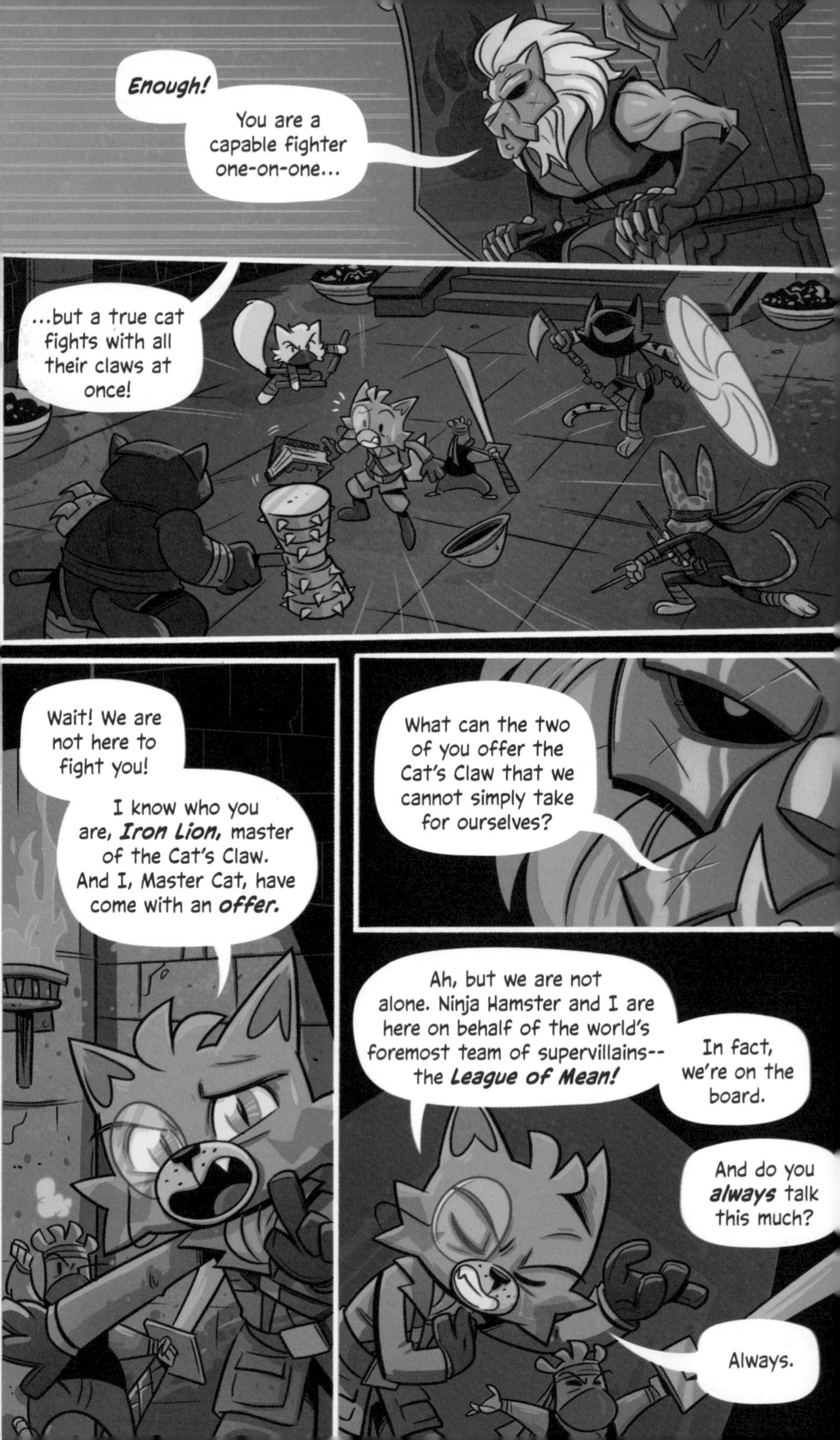
Enough!
You are a capable fighter one-on-one...
...but a true cat fights with all their claws at once!
Wait! We are not here to fight you!
I know who you are, Iron Lion, master of the Cat's Claw. And I, Master Cat, have come with an offer.
What can the two of you offer the Cat's Claw that we cannot simply take for ourselves?
Ah, but we are not alone. Ninja Hamster and I are here on behalf of the world's foremost team of supervillains--the League of Mean!
In fact, we're on the board.
And do you always talk this much?
Always.

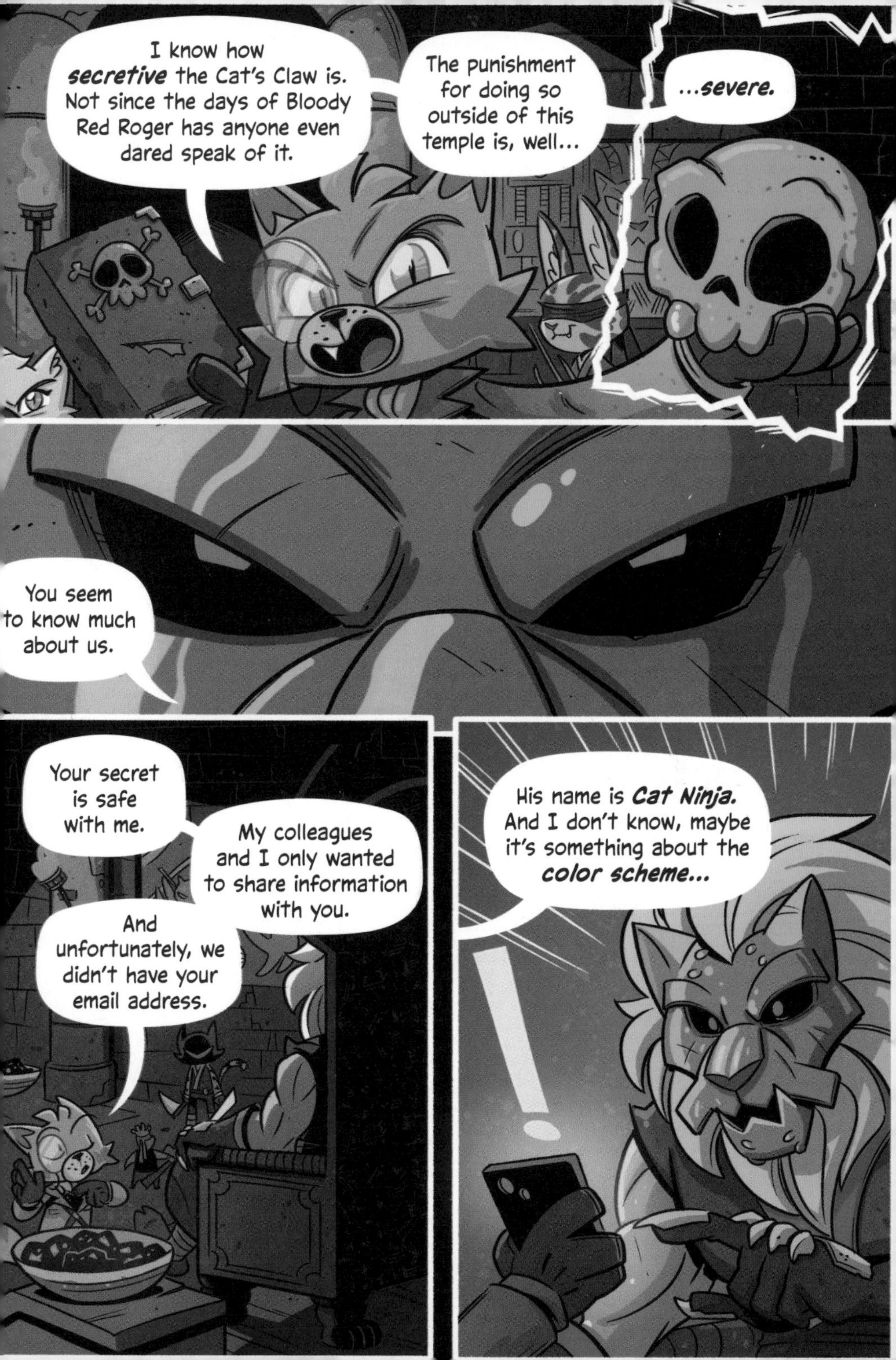

I know how *secretive* the Cat's Claw is. Not since the days of Bloody Red Roger has anyone even dared speak of it.
The punishment for doing so outside of this temple is, well...
...*severe.*
You seem to know much about us.
Your secret is safe with me.
My colleagues and I only wanted to share information with you.
And unfortunately, we didn't have your email address.
His name is *Cat Ninja.* And I don't know, maybe it's something about the *color scheme...*

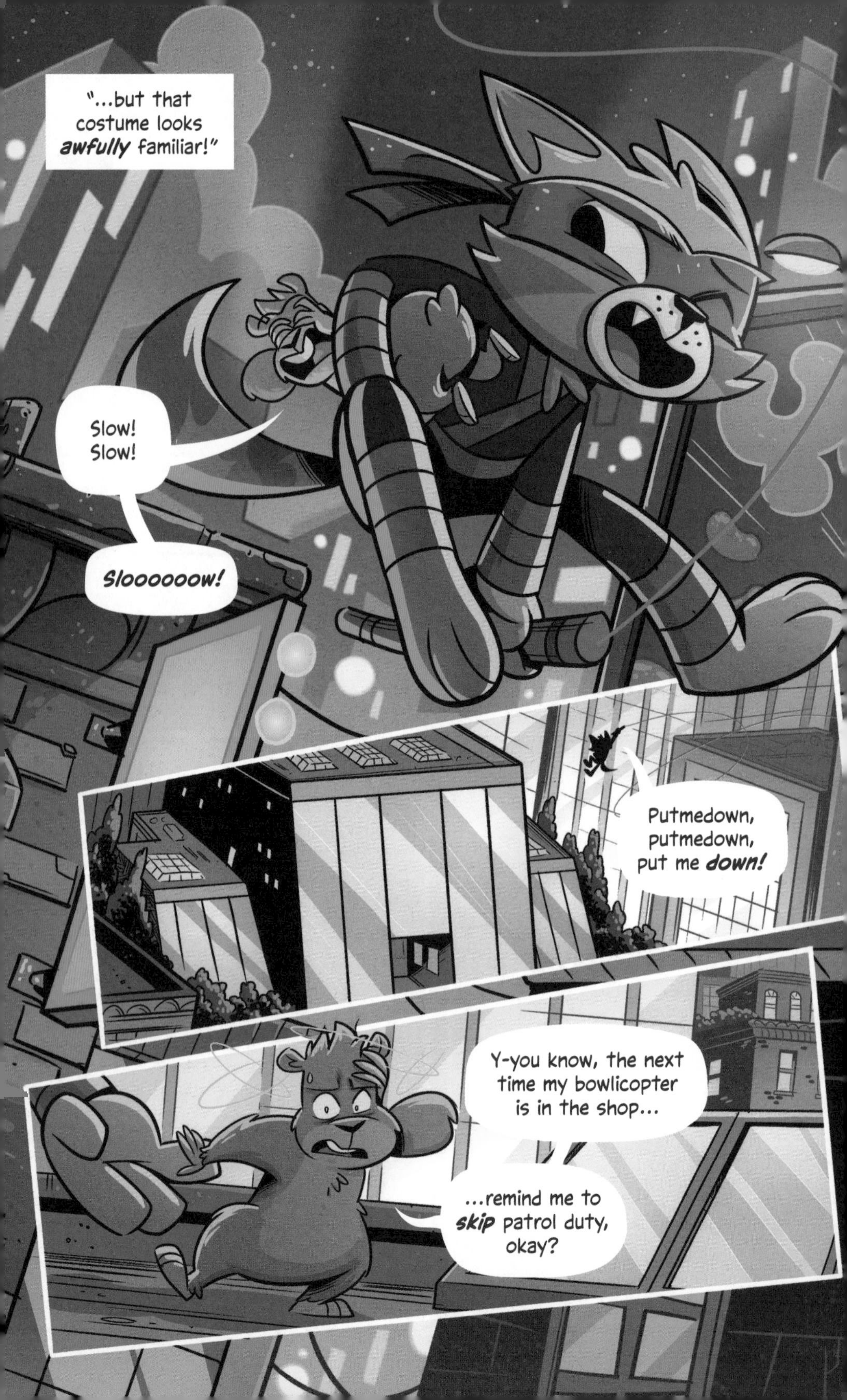
"...but that costume looks *awfully* familiar!"
Slow! Slow!
Slooooooow!
Putmedown, putmedown, put me *down!*
Y-you know, the next time my bowlicopter is in the shop...
...remind me to *skip* patrol duty, okay?

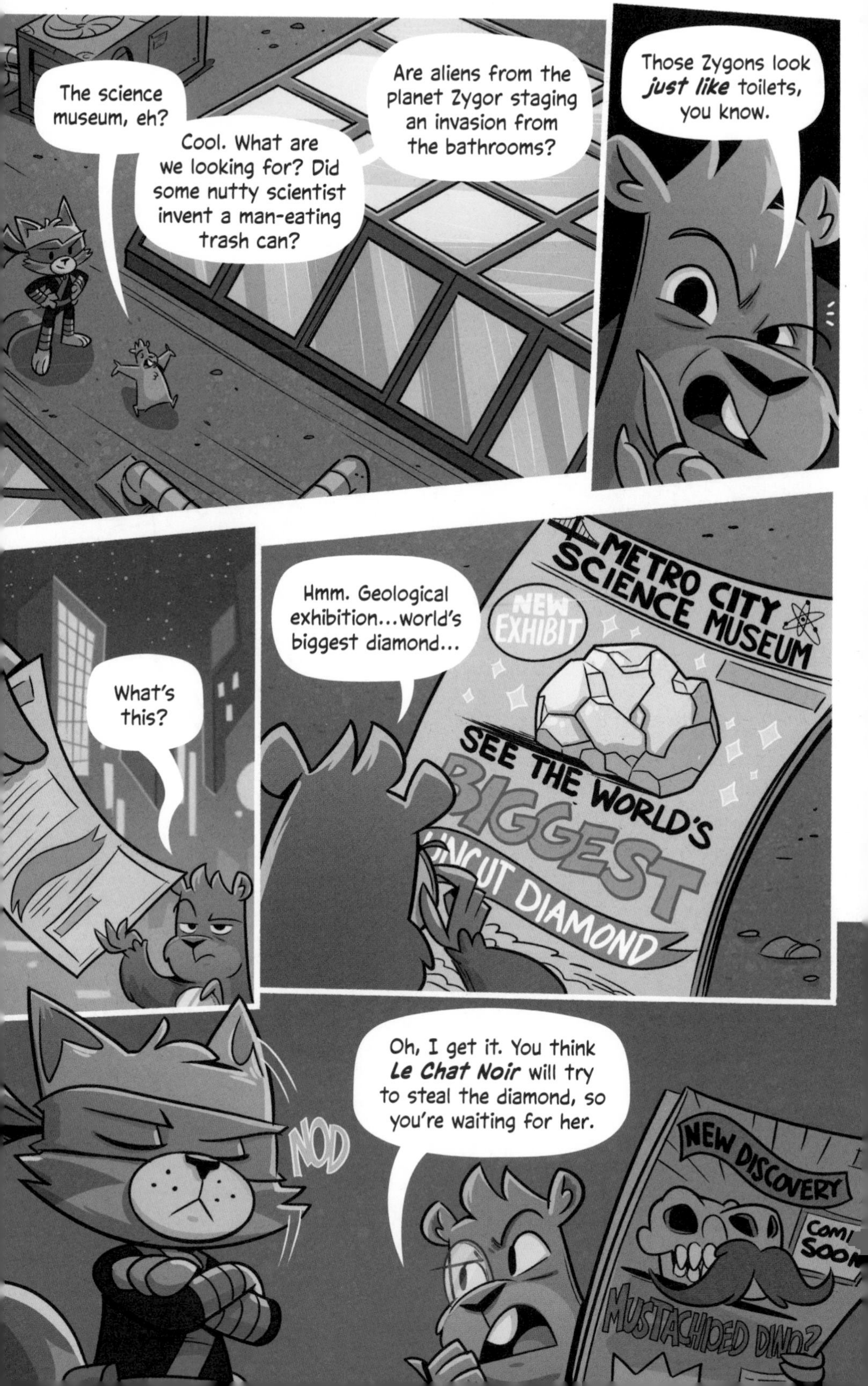
The science museum, eh?
Cool. What are we looking for? Did some nutty scientist invent a man-eating trash can?
Are aliens from the planet Zygor staging an invasion from the bathrooms?
Those Zygons look *just like* toilets, you know.
What's this?
Hmm. Geological exhibition...world's biggest diamond...
METRO CITY SCIENCE MUSEUM
NEW EXHIBIT
SEE THE WORLD'S BIGGEST UNCUT DIAMOND
NOD
Oh, I get it. You think *Le Chat Noir* will try to steal the diamond, so you're waiting for her.
NEW DISCOVERY
MUSTACHIOED DINO?

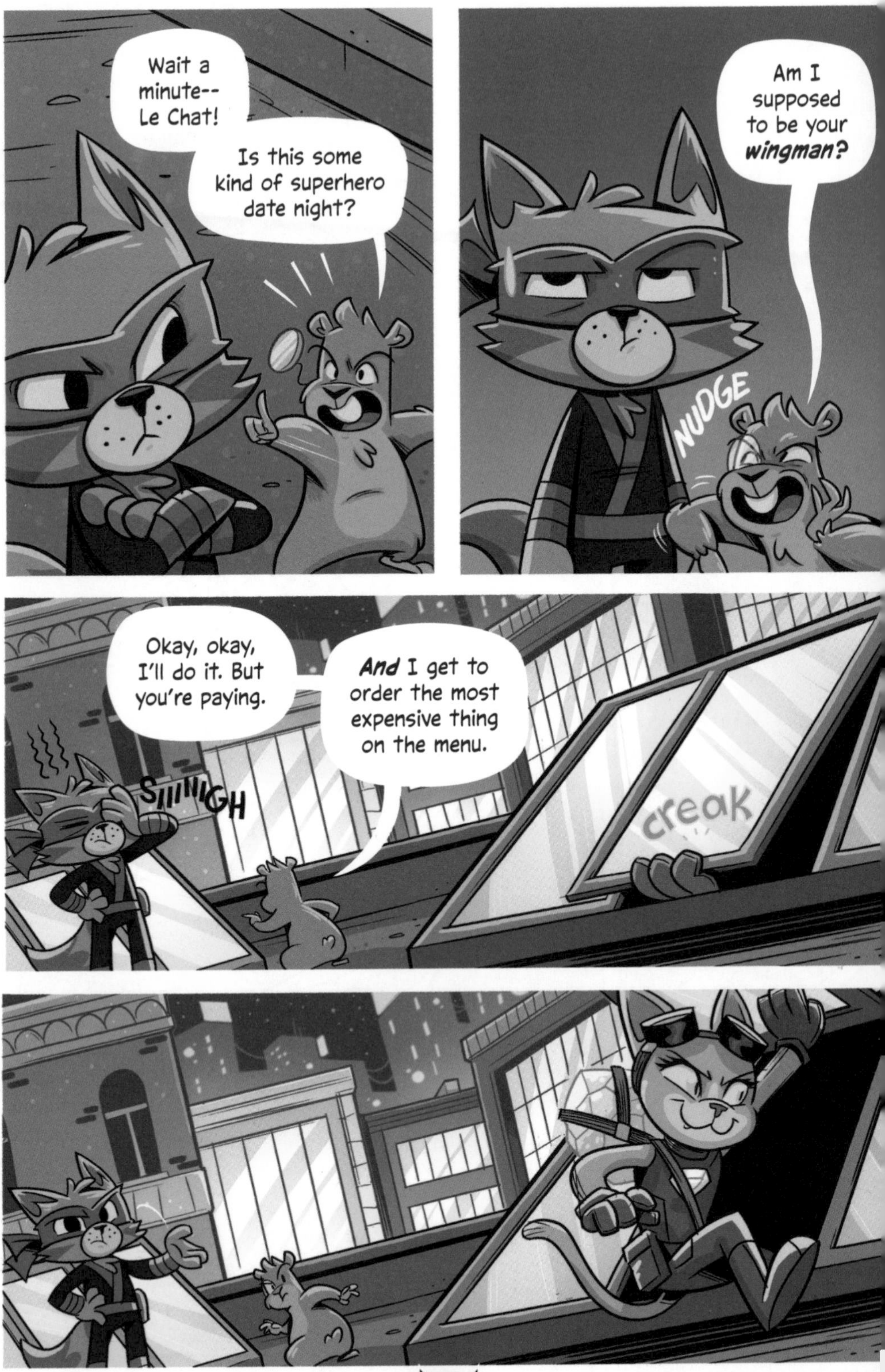
Wait a minute-- Le Chat!
Is this some kind of superhero date night?
Am I supposed to be your *wingman?*
NUDGE
Okay, okay, I'll do it. But you're paying.
And I get to order the most expensive thing on the menu.
SIIIIIGH
creak

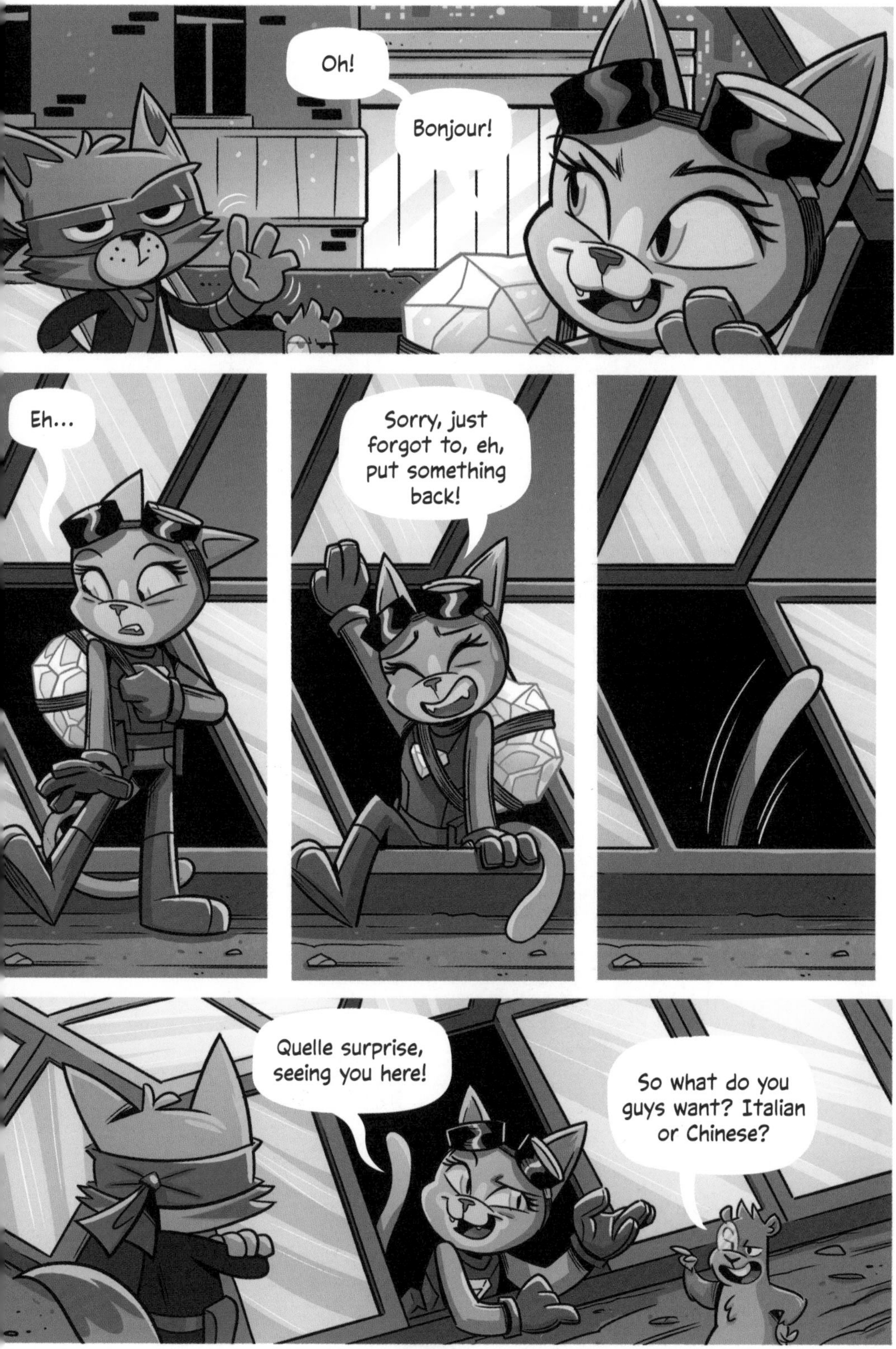
Oh!
Bonjour!
Eh...
Sorry, just forgot to, eh, put something back!
Quelle surprise, seeing you here!
So what do you guys want? Italian or Chinese?

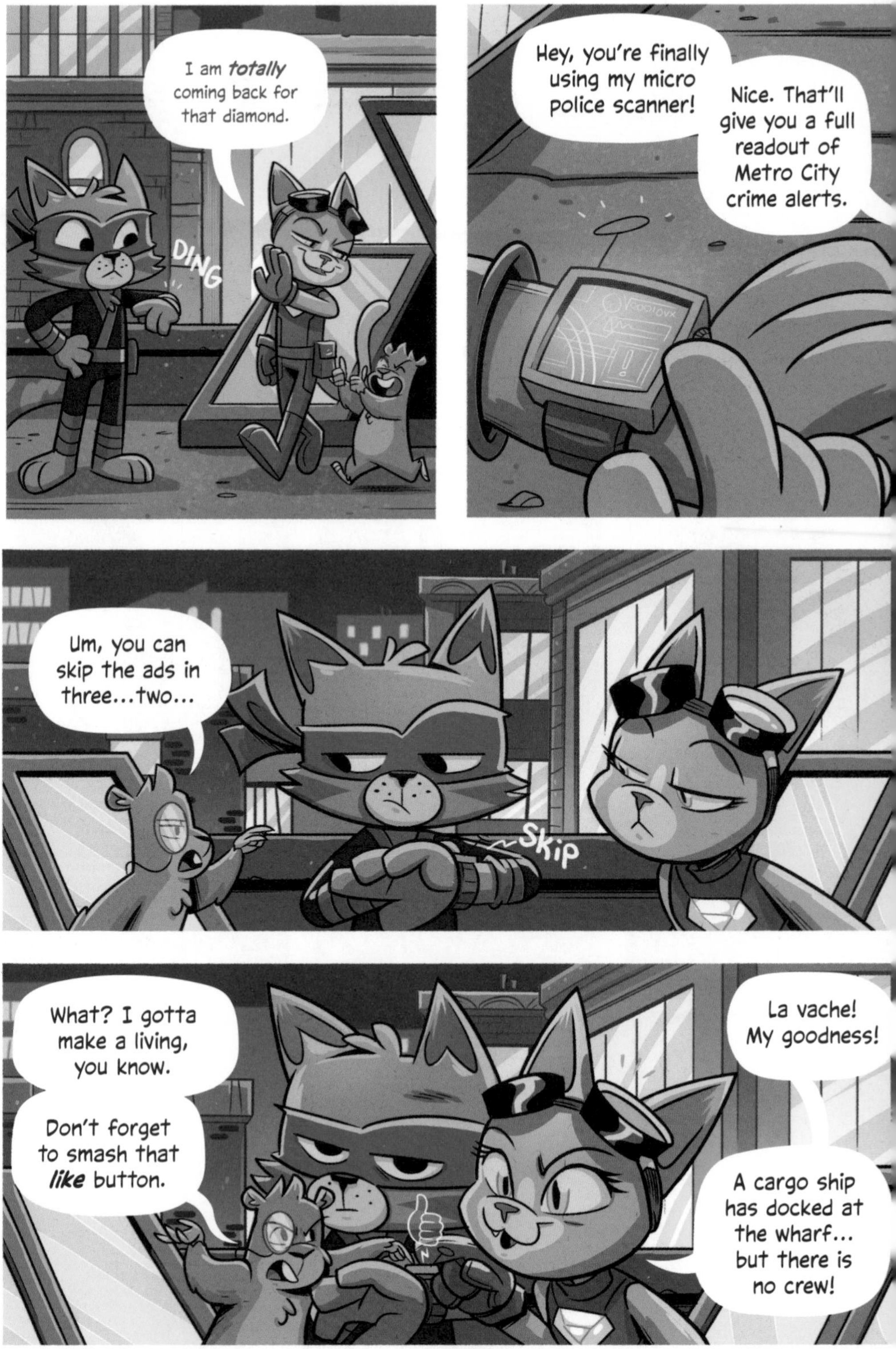

I am *totally* coming back for that diamond.
DING
Hey, you're finally using my micro police scanner!
Nice. That'll give you a full readout of Metro City crime alerts.
Um, you can skip the ads in three...two...
SKIP
What? I gotta make a living, you know.
Don't forget to smash that *like* button.
La vache! My goodness!
A cargo ship has docked at the wharf... but there is no crew!

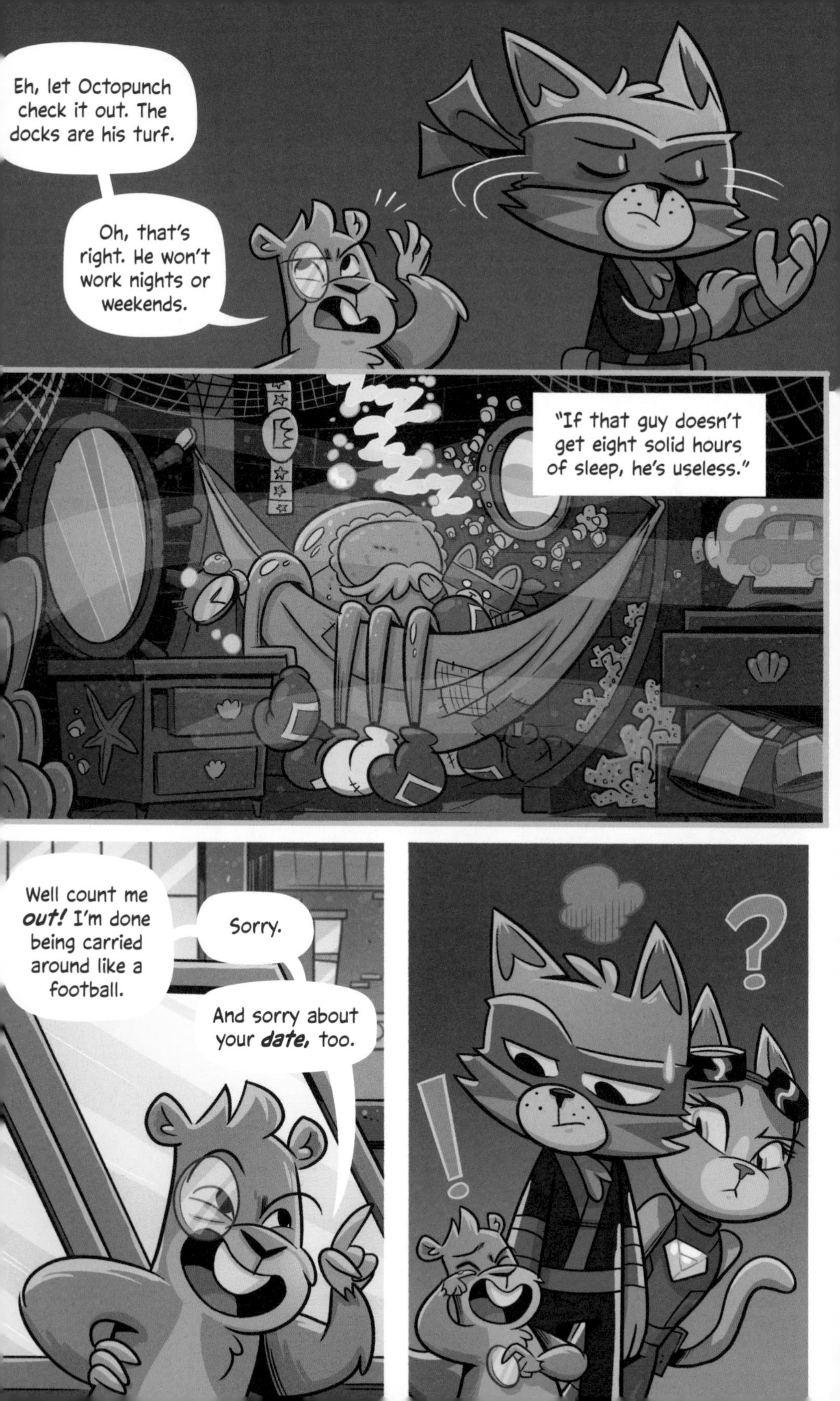
Eh, let Octopunch check it out. The docks are his turf.
Oh, that's right. He won't work nights or weekends.
"If that guy doesn't get eight solid hours of sleep, he's useless."
Well count me *out!* I'm done being carried around like a football.
Sorry.
And sorry about your *date,* too.
?
!

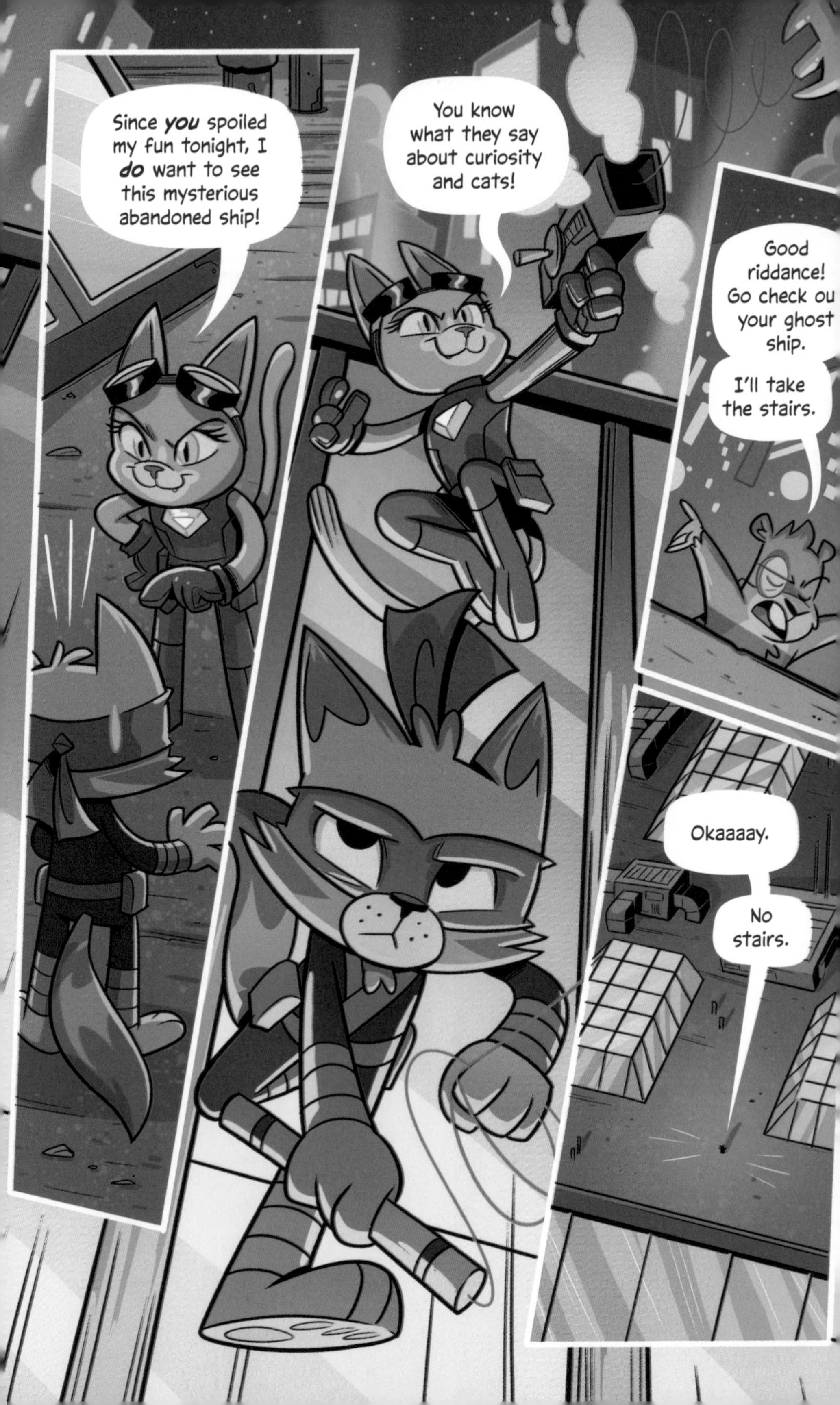
Since *you* spoiled my fun tonight, I *do* want to see this mysterious abandoned ship!
You know what they say about curiosity and cats!
Good riddance! Go check ou your ghost ship.
I'll take the stairs.
Okaaaay.
No stairs.

Mystery of the Cat's Claw
Part 2

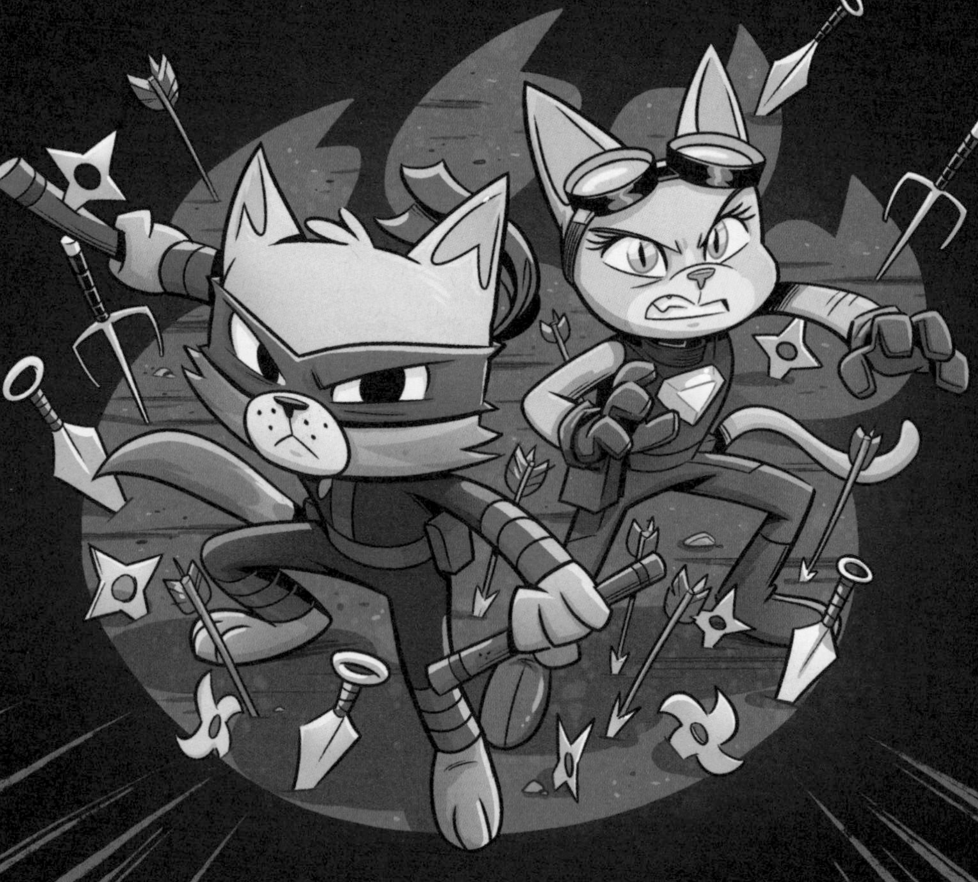

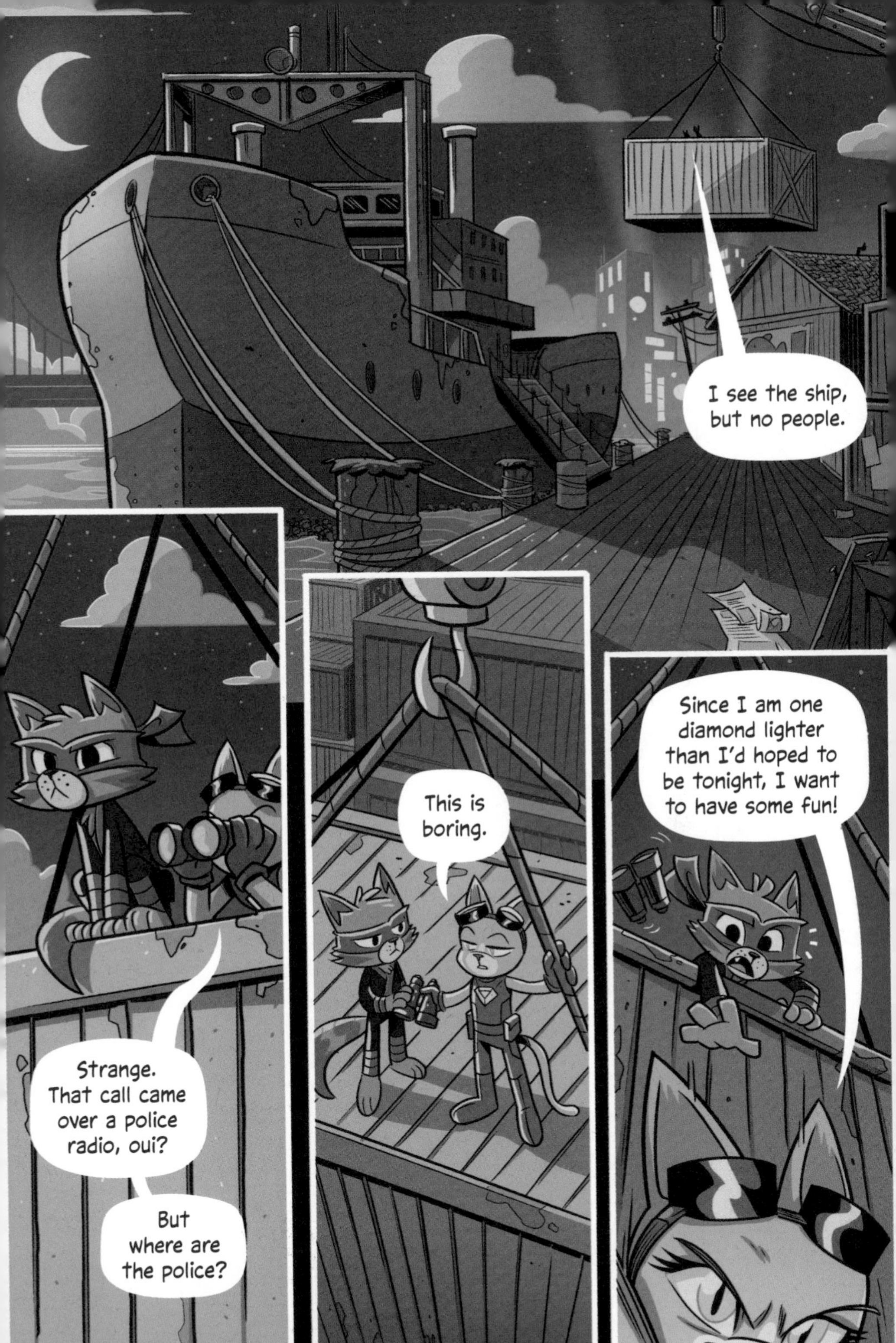
I see the ship, but no people.
Strange. That call came over a police radio, oui?
But where are the police?
This is boring.
Since I am one diamond lighter than I'd hoped to be tonight, I want to have some fun!

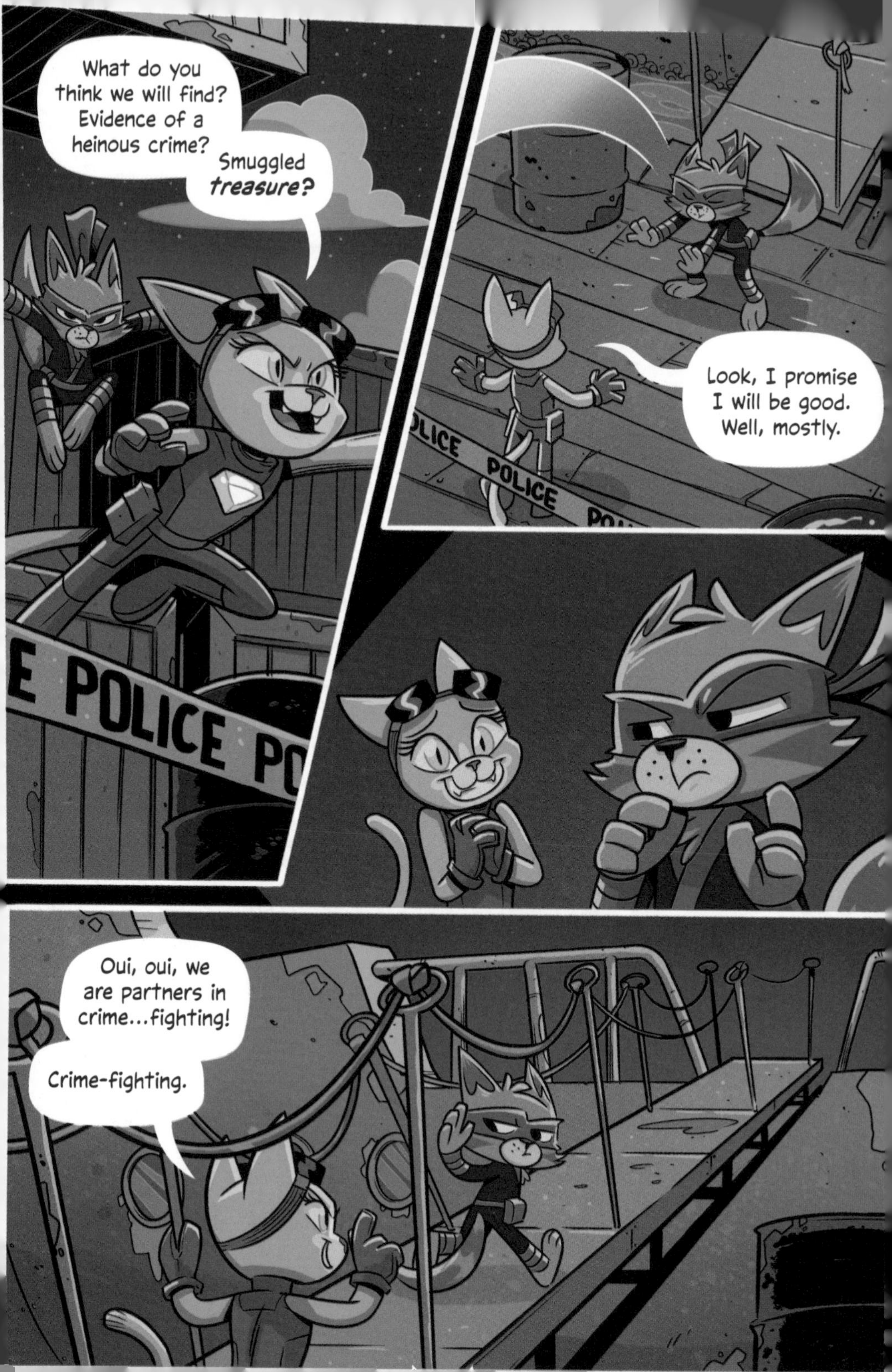
What do you think we will find? Evidence of a heinous crime?
Smuggled *treasure?*
POLICE
Look, I promise I will be good. Well, mostly.
Oui, oui, we are partners in crime...fighting!
Crime-fighting.

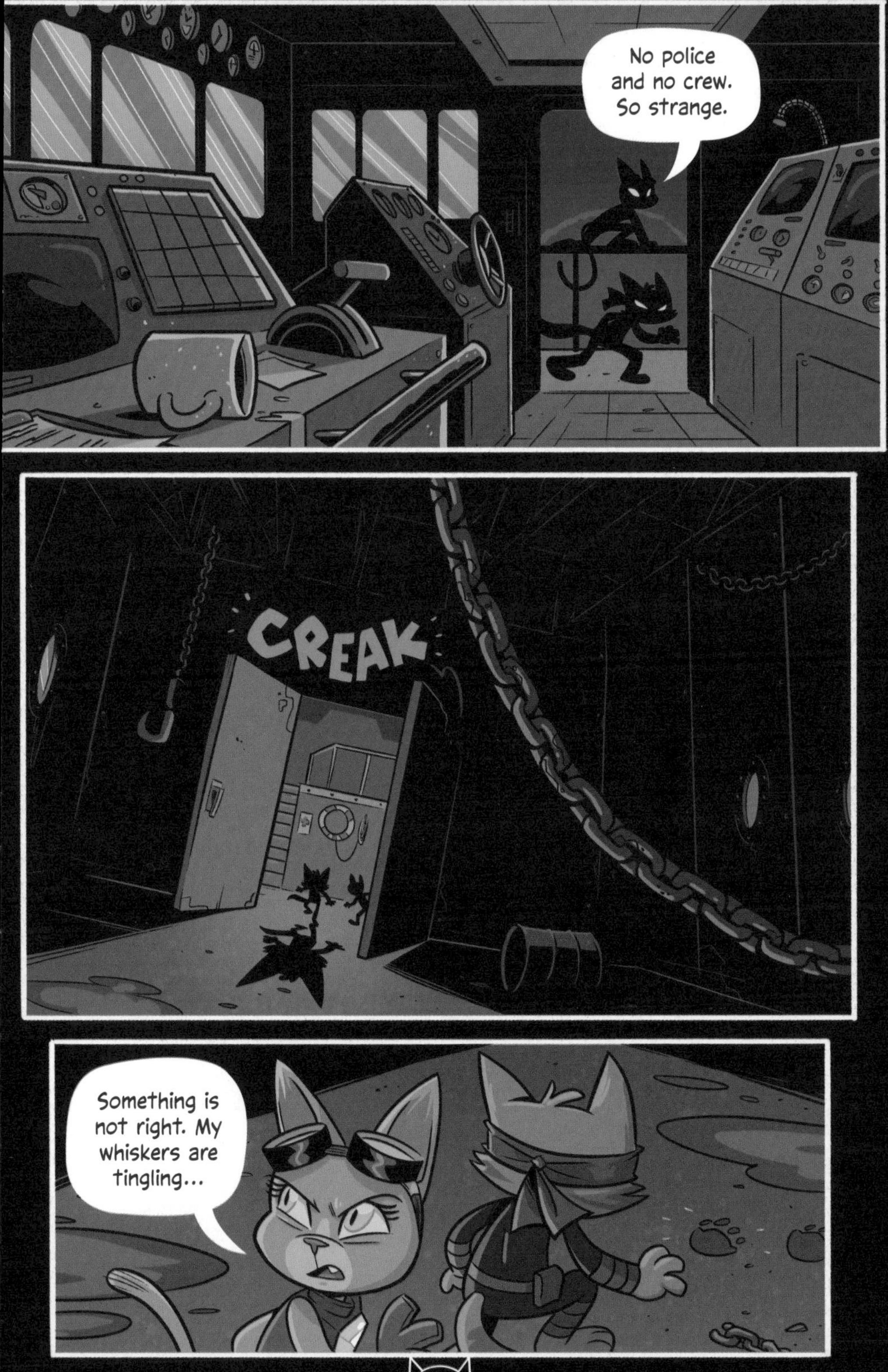
No police and no crew. So strange.
CREAK
Something is not right. My whiskers are tingling...

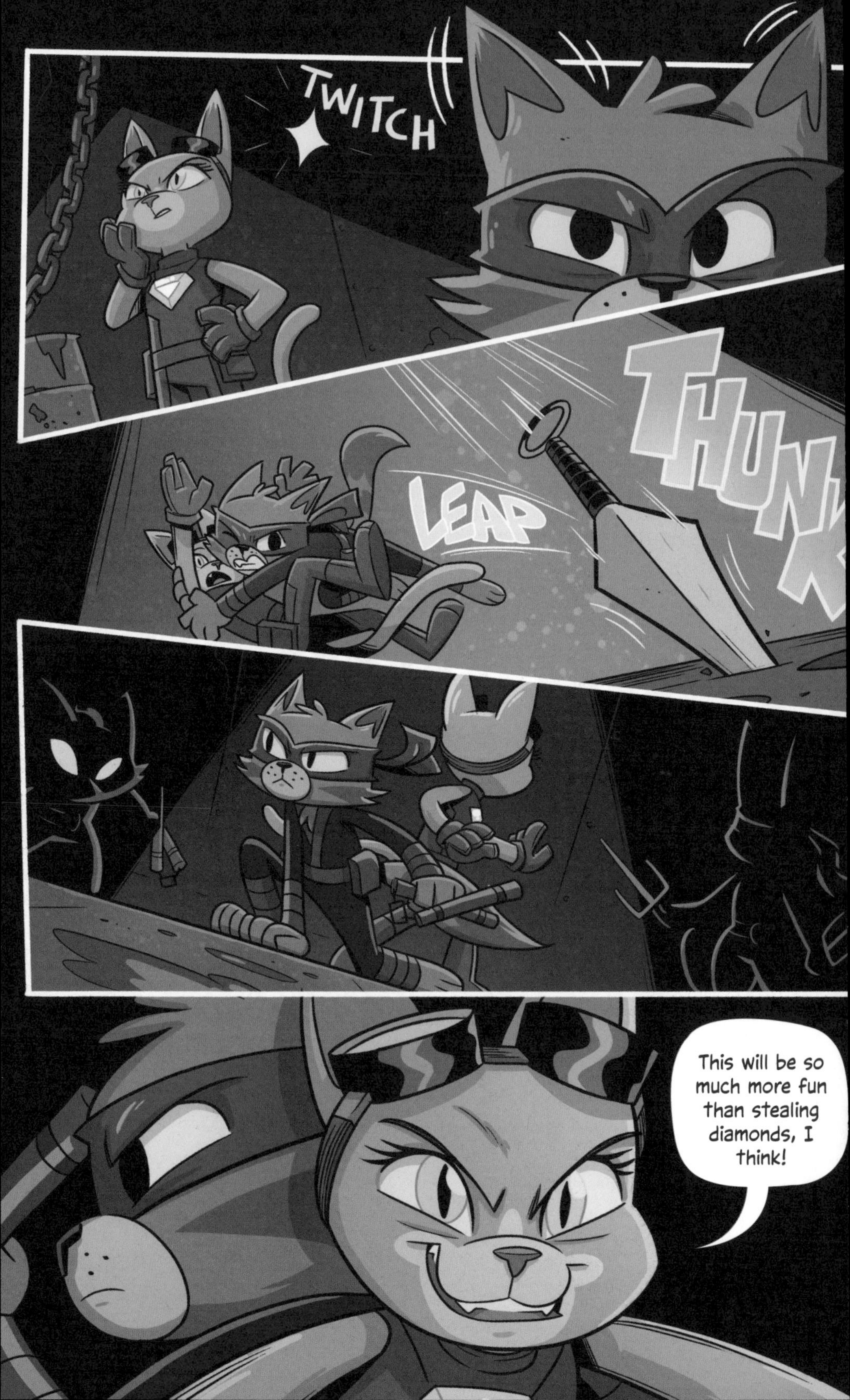
TWITCH
LEAP
THUNK
This will be so much more fun than stealing diamonds, I think!

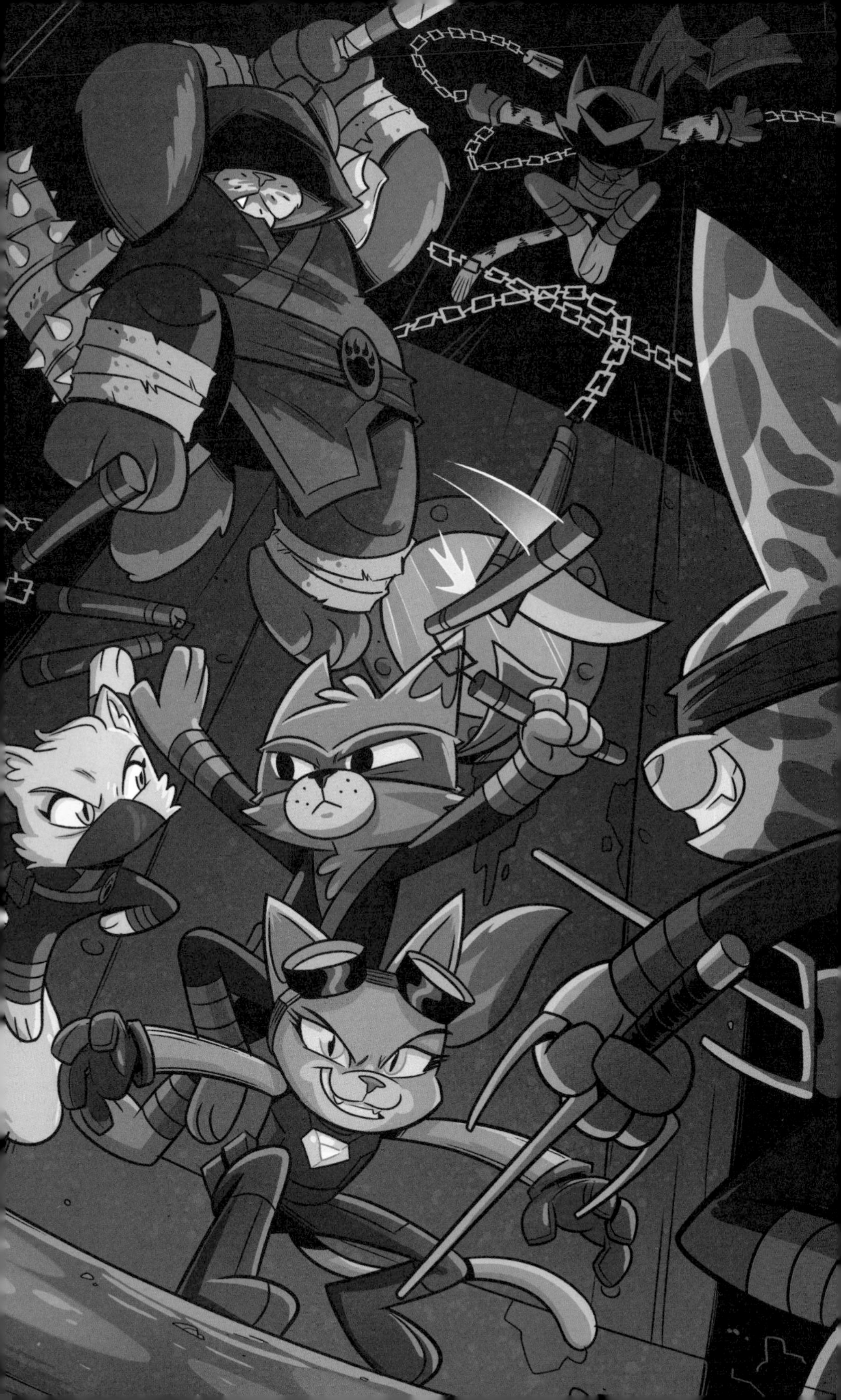

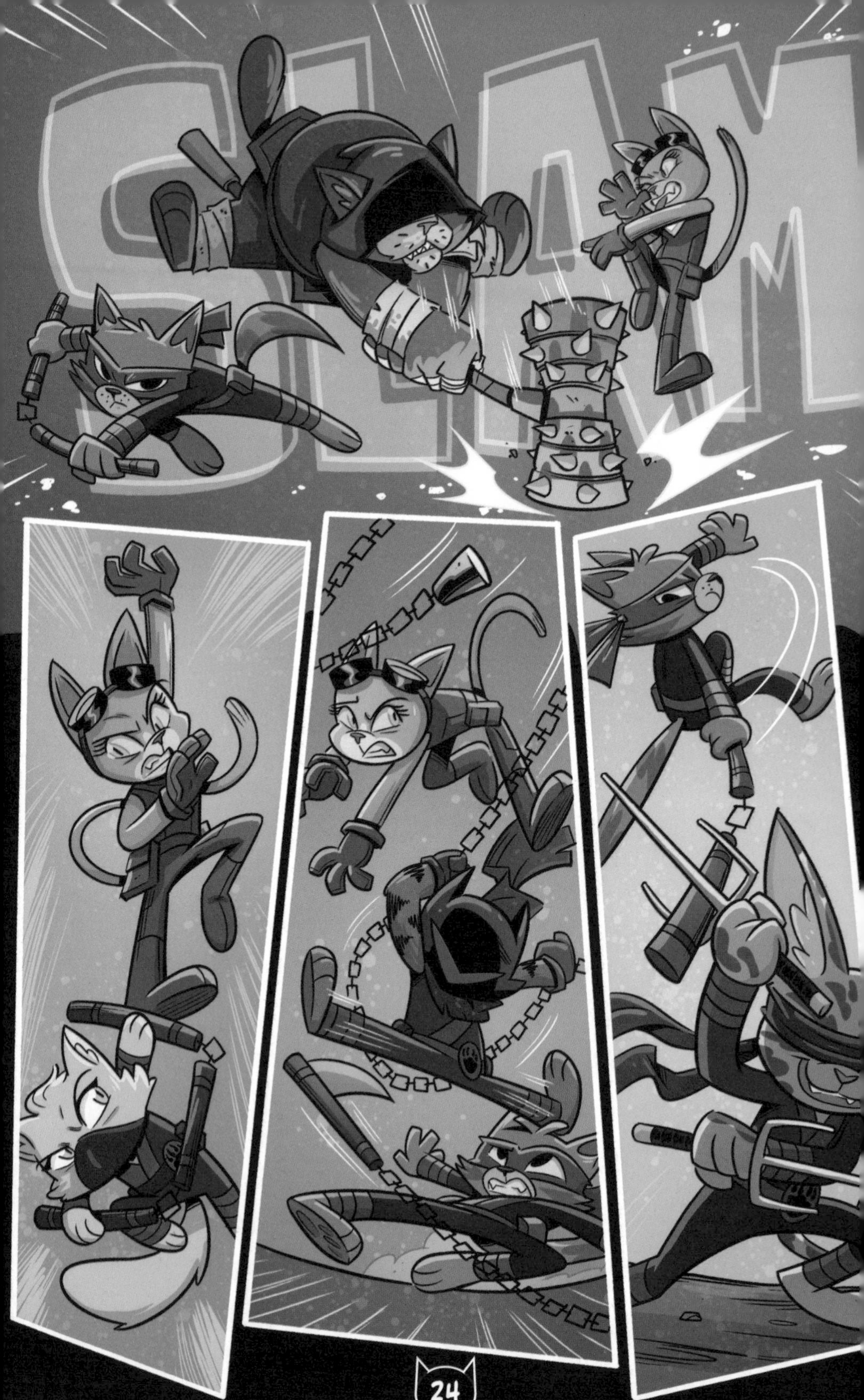
SLAM

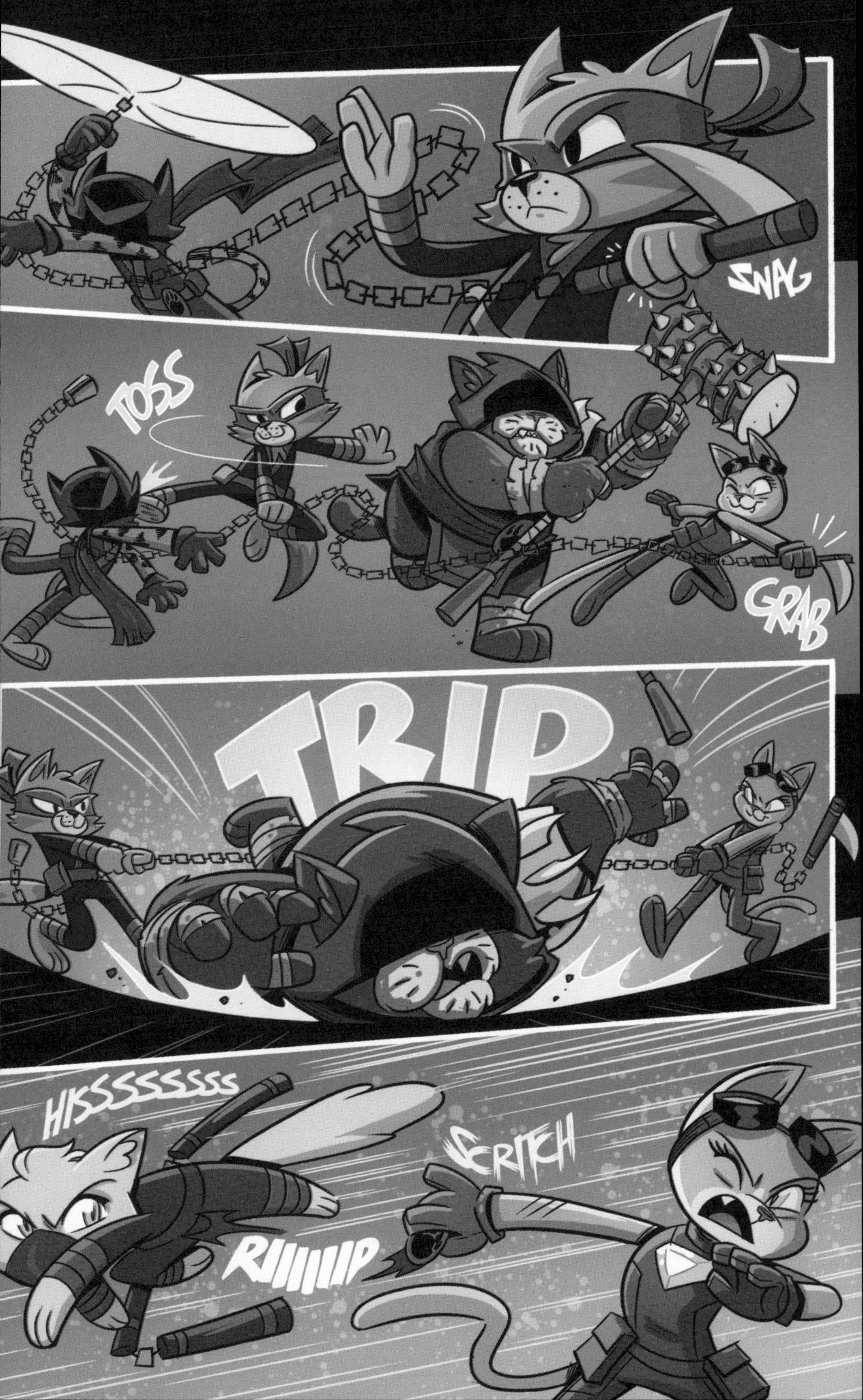
SNAG
TOSS
GRAB
TRIP
HISSSSSSSS
SCRITCH
RIIIIIIP

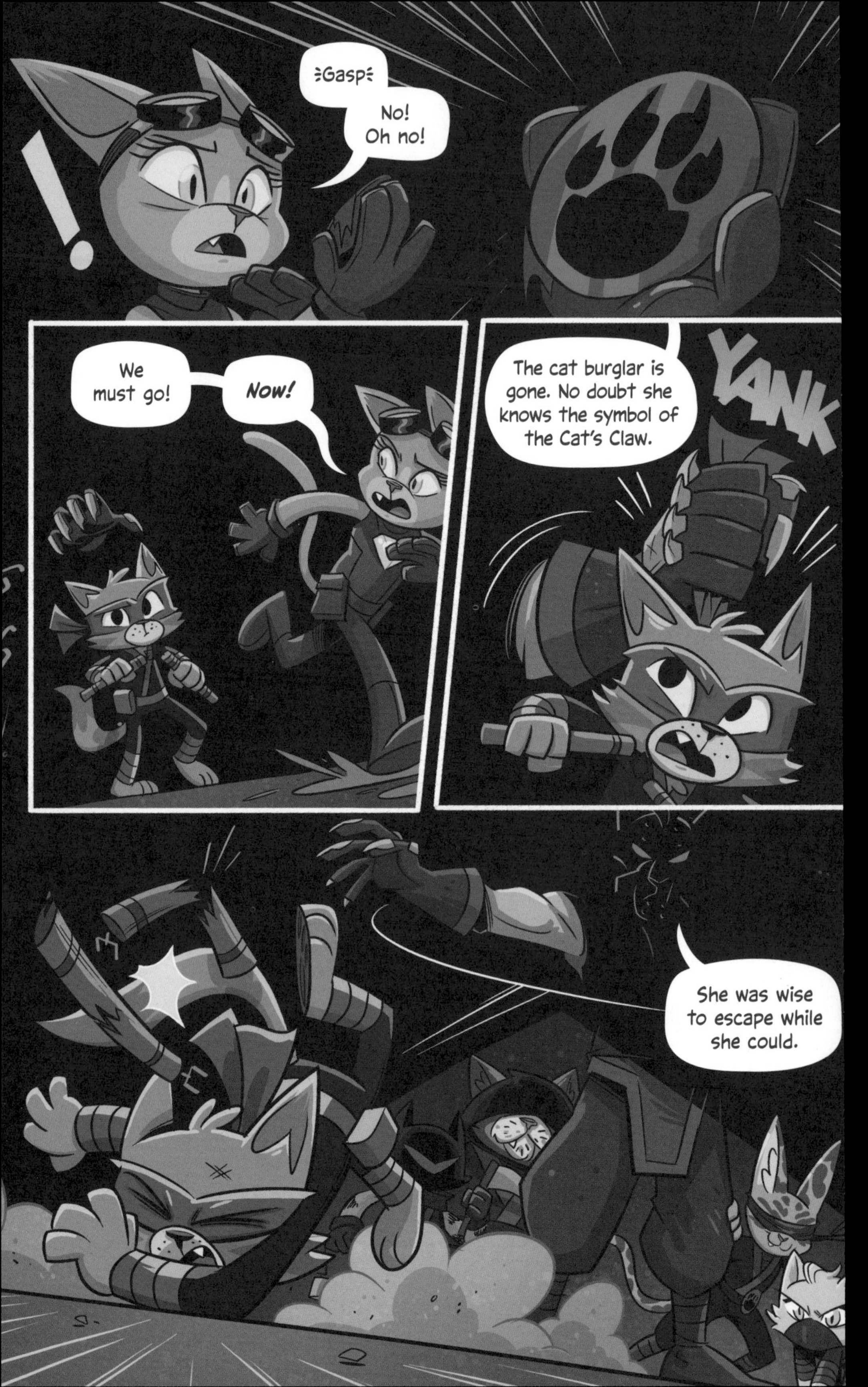

=Gasp=
No! Oh no!
We must go!
Now!
The cat burglar is gone. No doubt she knows the symbol of the Cat's Claw.
YANK
She was wise to escape while she could.

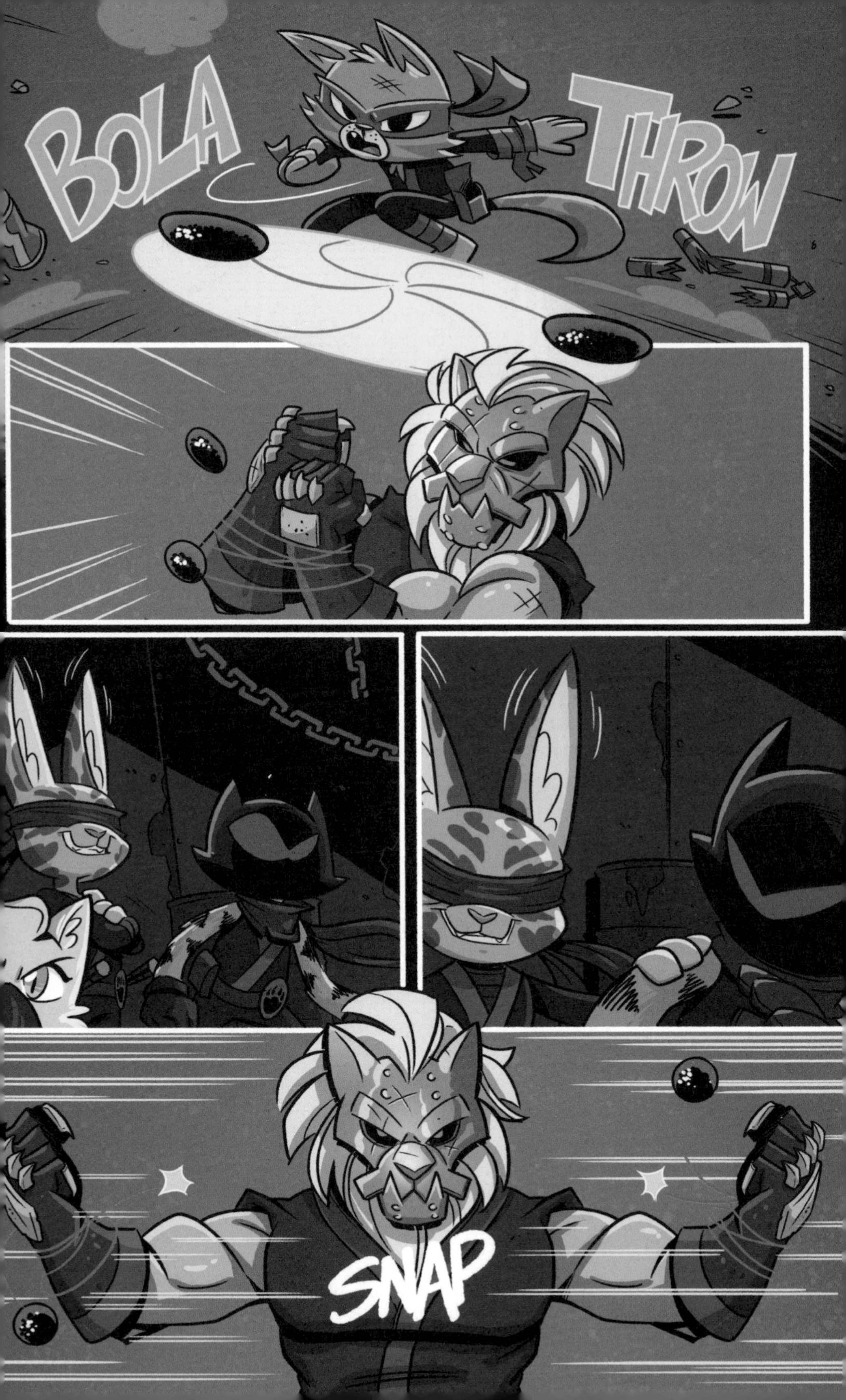
BOLA THROW
SNAP

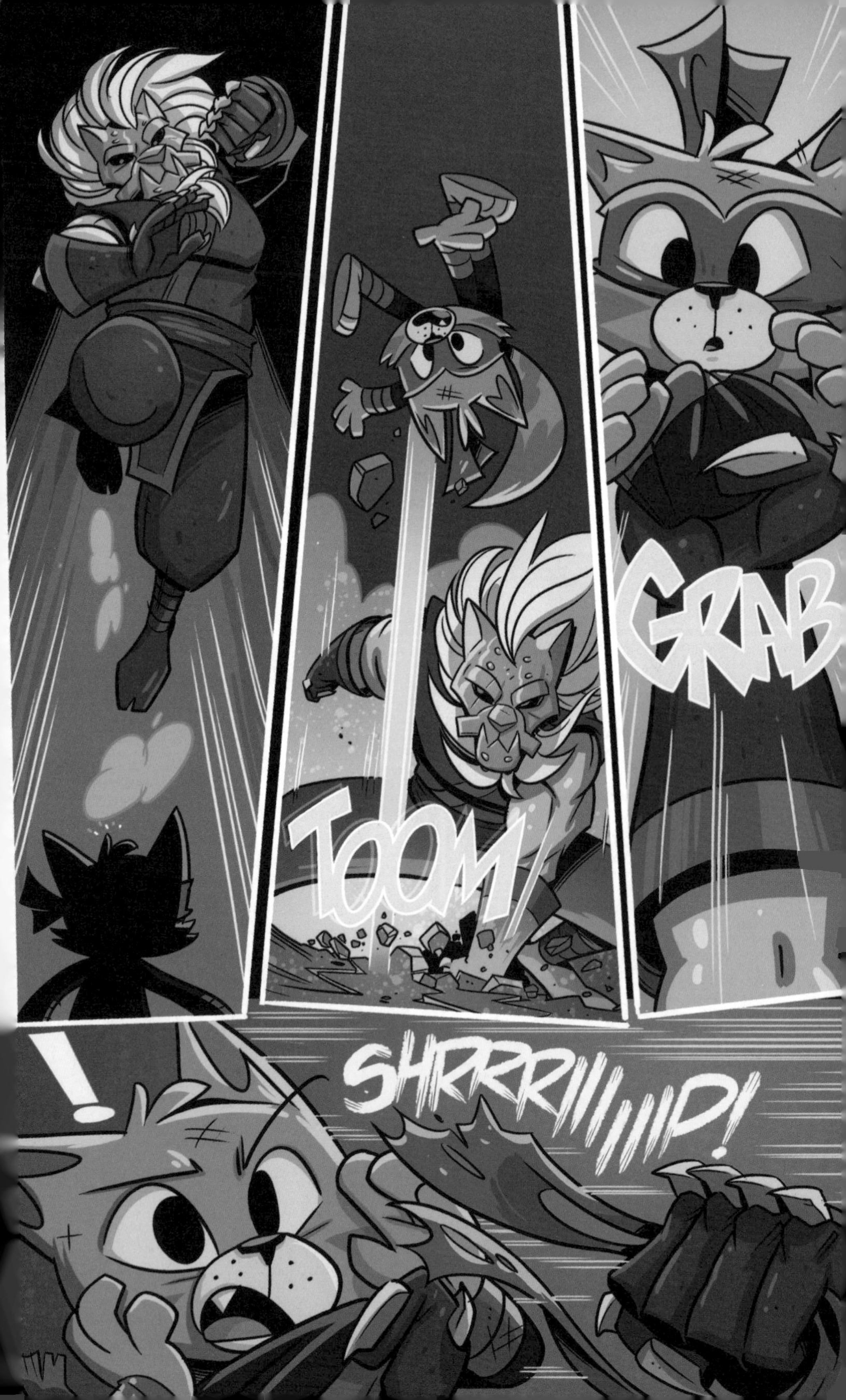
TOOM
GRAB
!
SHRRRIIIIIP!

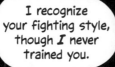

I recognize your fighting style, though *I* never trained you.

I recognize your colors, though you never *earned* the right to wear them.

Cat Ninja, is it? How imaginative.

Tell me, where did you train?

Who was your master?

Where. Is. *She?*

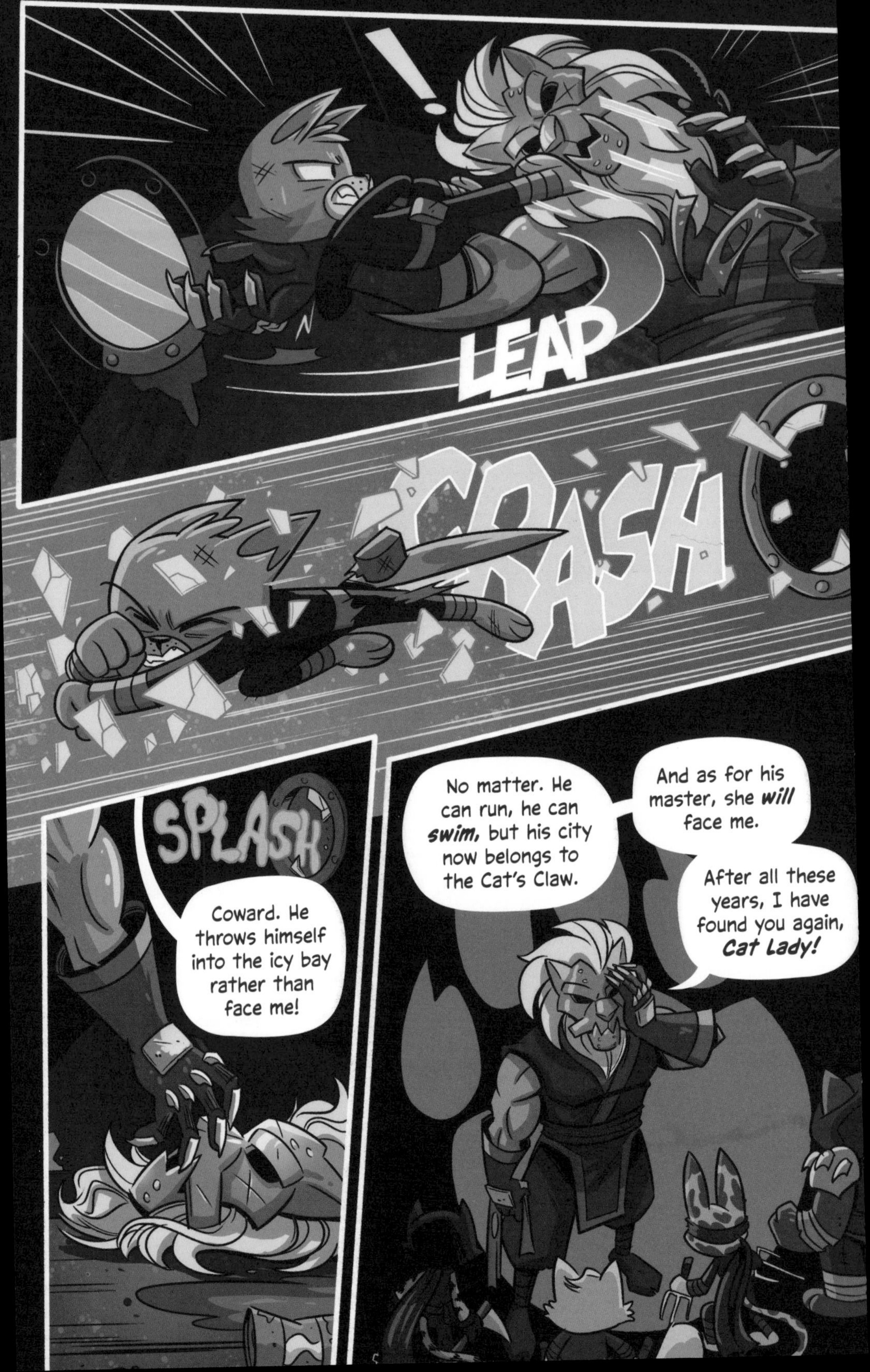
!
LEAP
CRASH
SPLASH
Coward. He throws himself into the icy bay rather than face me!
No matter. He can run, he can *swim,* but his city now belongs to the Cat's Claw.
And as for his master, she *will* face me.
After all these years, I have found you again, ***Cat Lady!***

Mystery of the Cat's Claw
Part 3

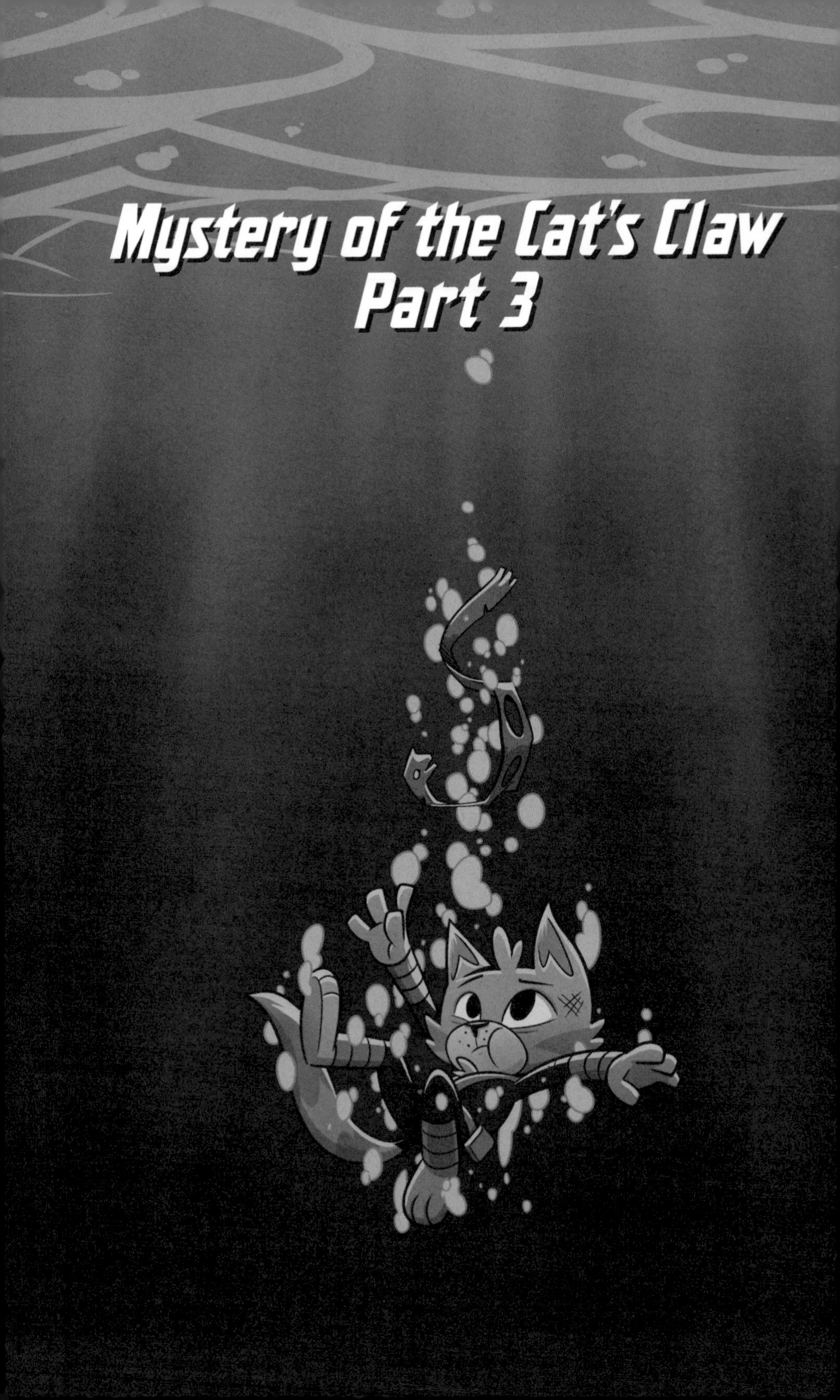

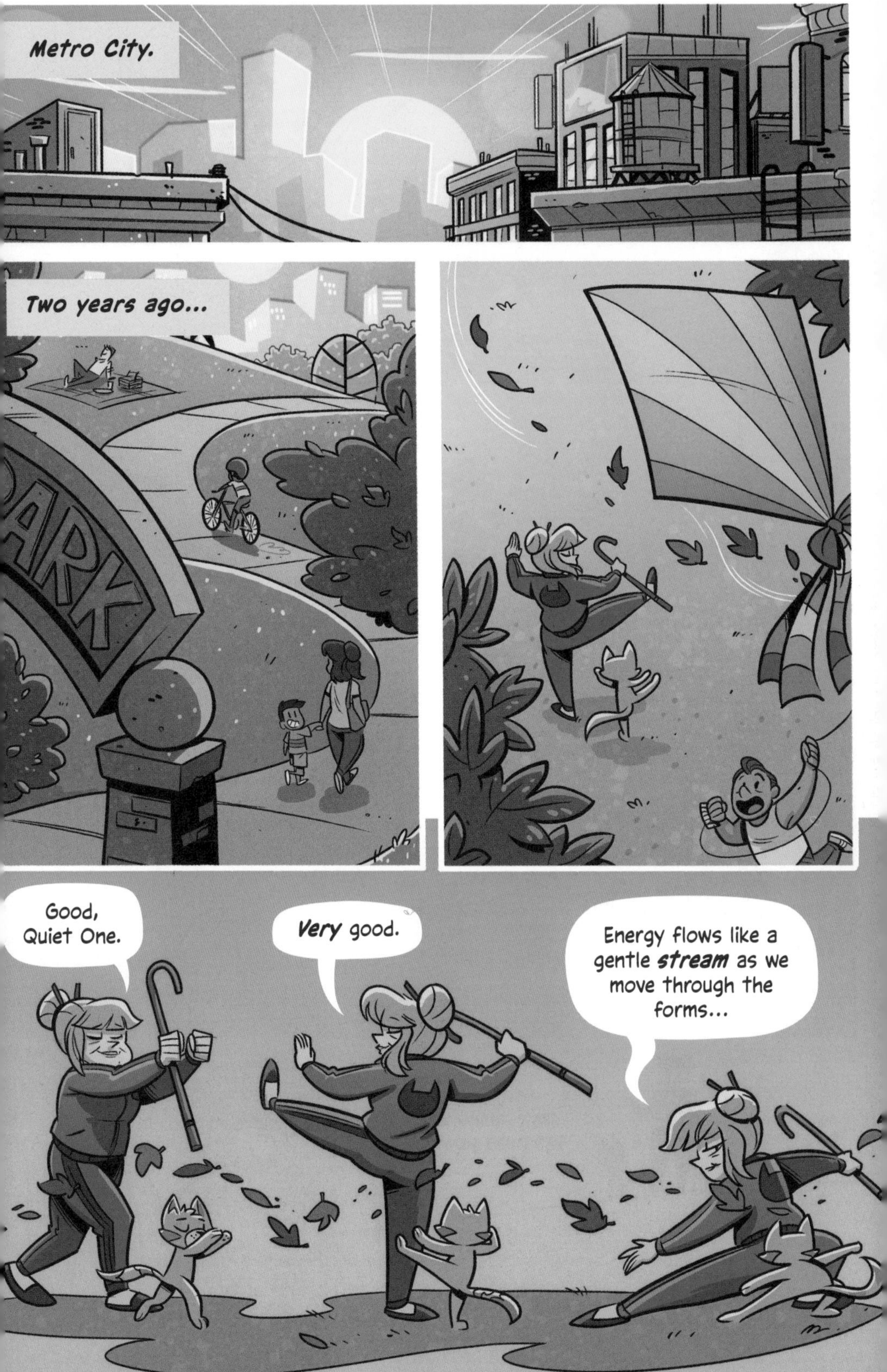
Metro City.
Two years ago...
PARK
Good, Quiet One.
Very good.
Energy flows like a gentle stream as we move through the forms...

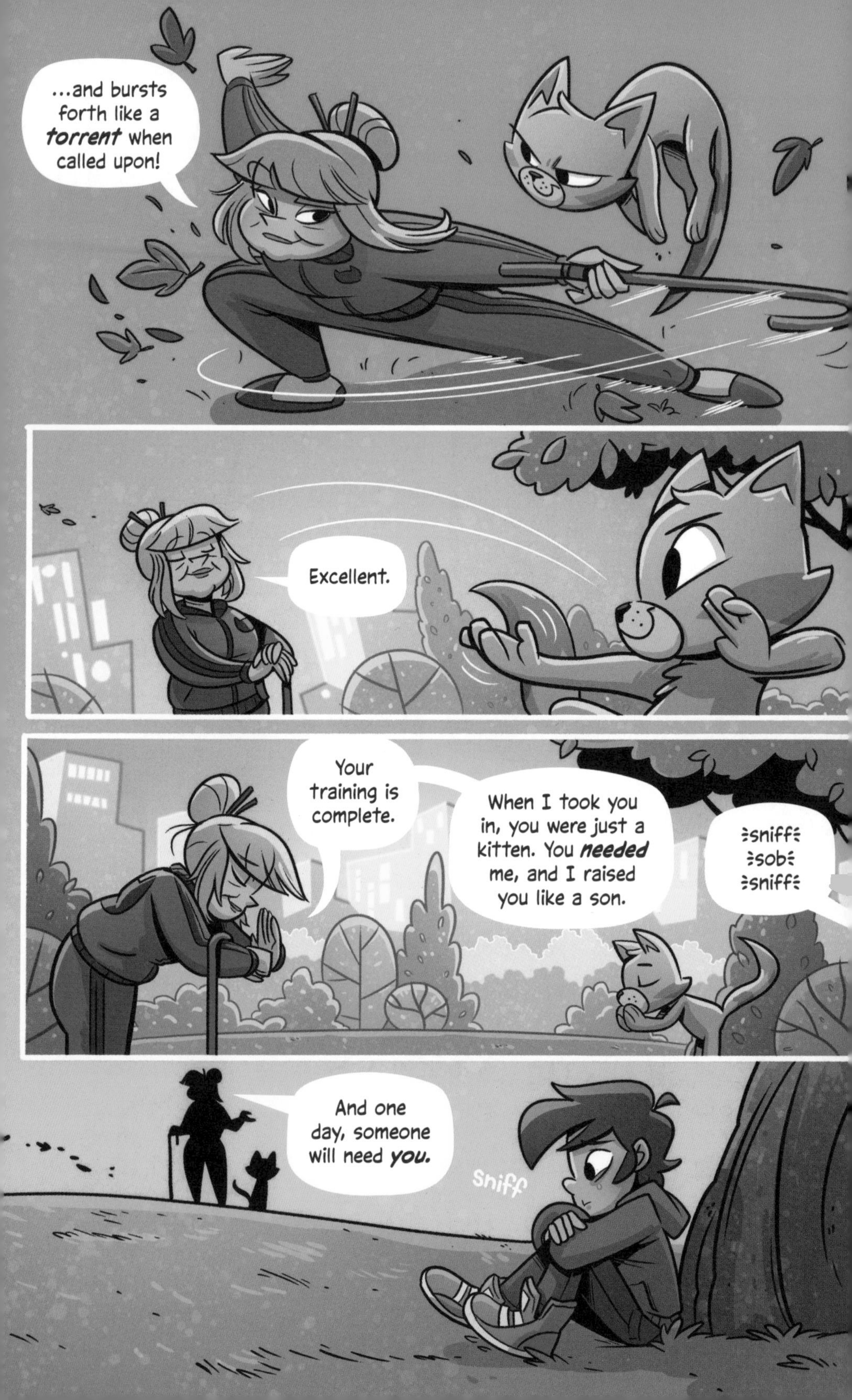
...and bursts forth like a *torrent* when called upon!
Excellent.
Your training is complete.
When I took you in, you were just a kitten. You *needed* me, and I raised you like a son.
sniff sob sniff
And one day, someone will need *you.*
Sniff

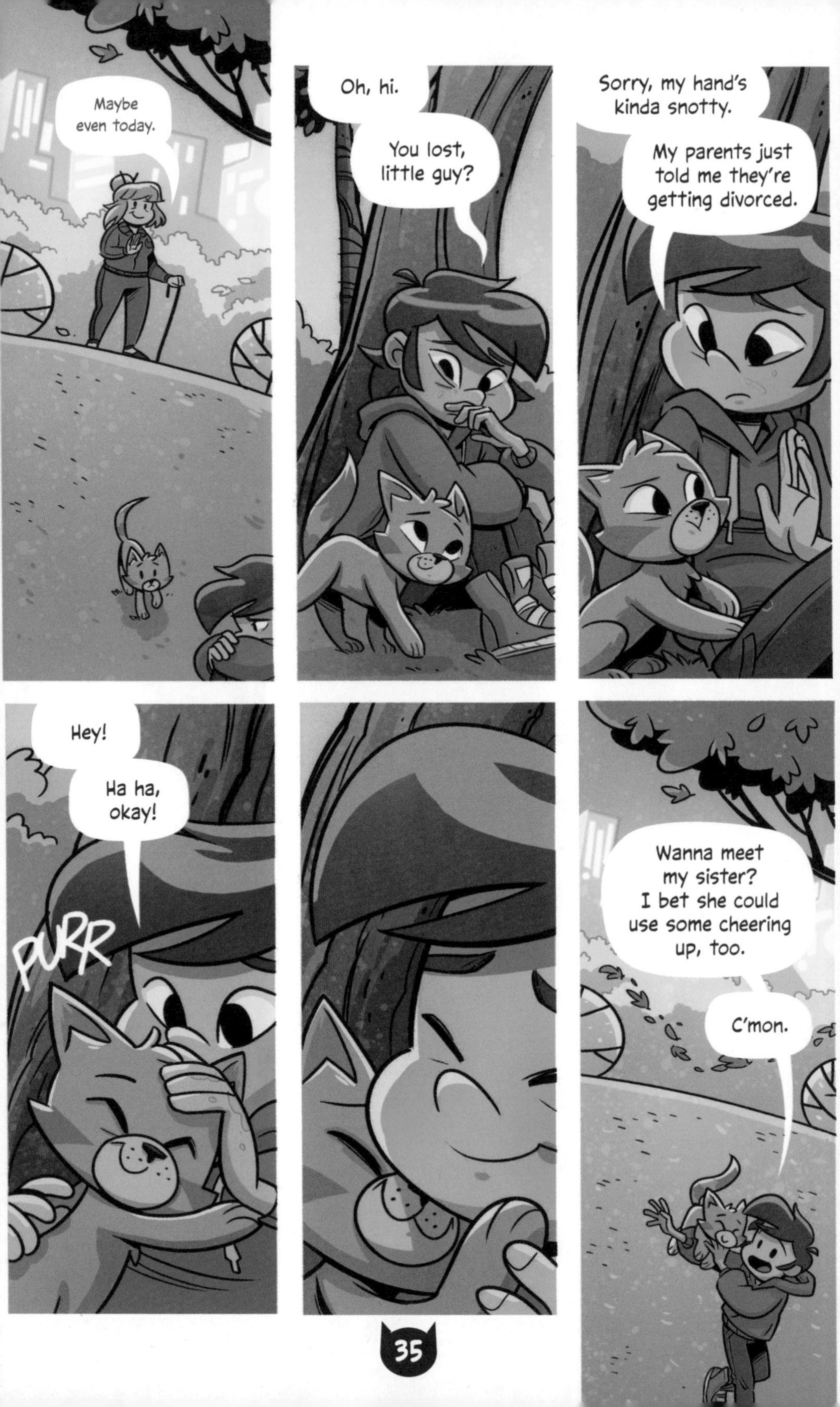
Maybe even today.
Oh, hi.
You lost, little guy?
Sorry, my hand's kinda snotty.
My parents just told me they're getting divorced.
Hey!
Ha ha, okay!
PURR
Wanna meet my sister? I bet she could use some cheering up, too.
C'mon.

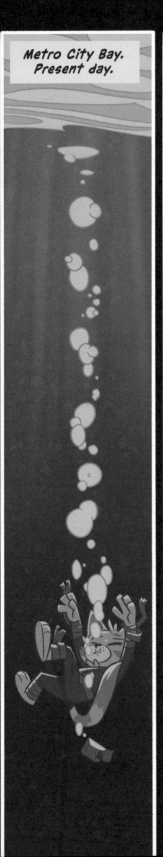

Metro City Bay.
Present day.

SPLASH

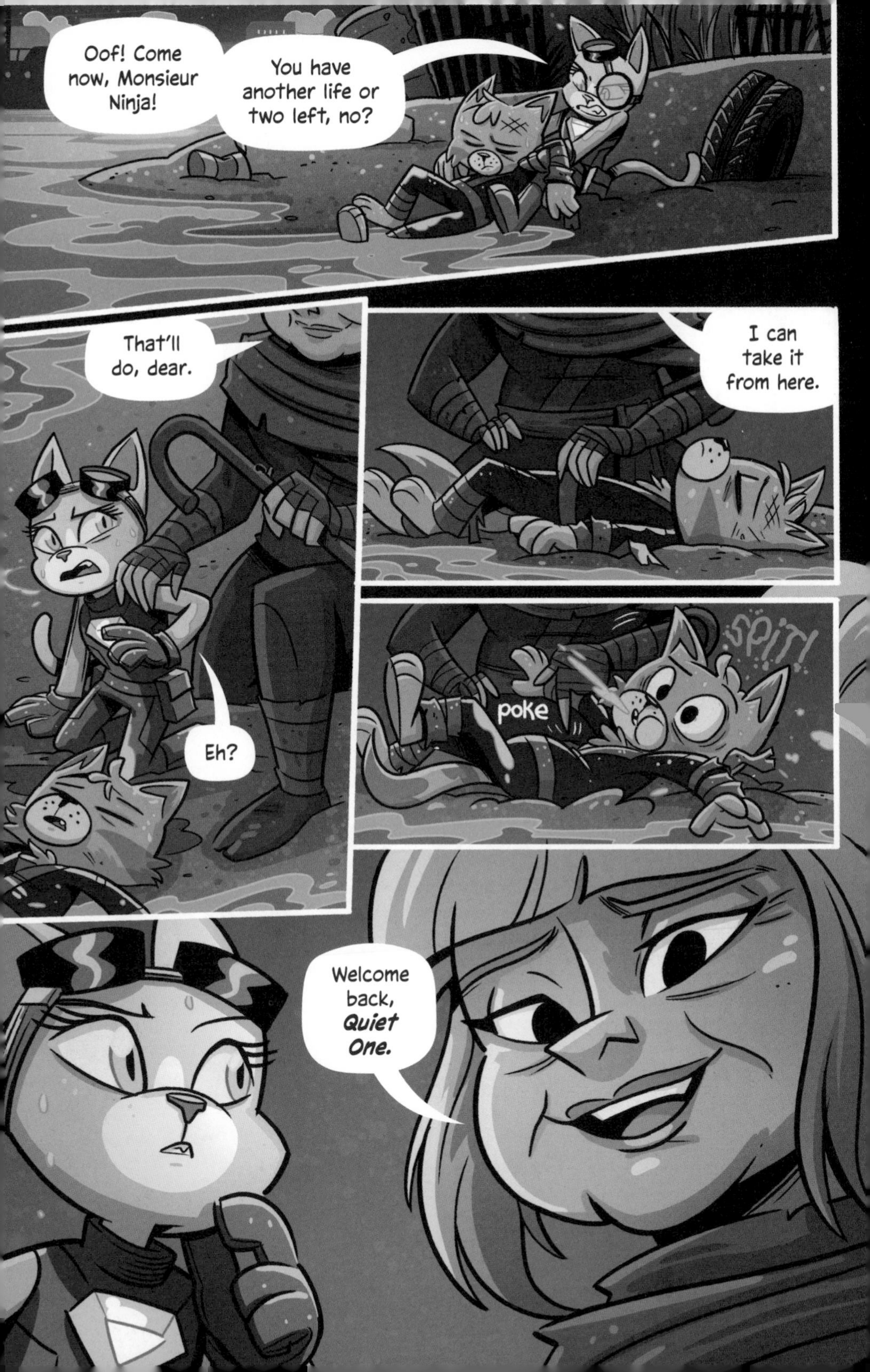

Oof! Come now, Monsieur Ninja!
You have another life or two left, no?
That'll do, dear.
Eh?
I can take it from here.
poke
SPIT!
Welcome back, ***Quiet One.***

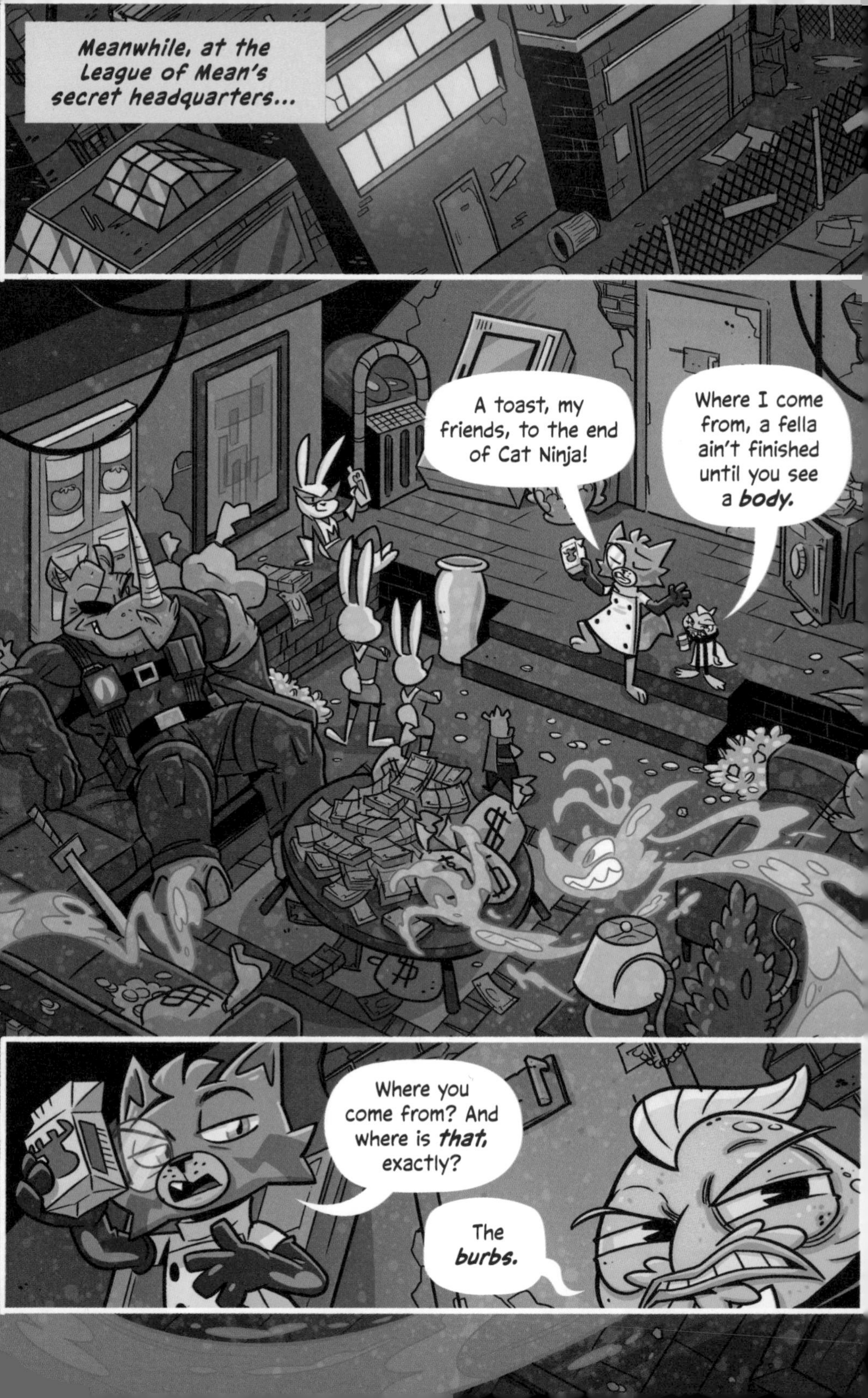
Meanwhile, at the League of Mean's secret headquarters...
A toast, my friends, to the end of Cat Ninja!
Where I come from, a fella ain't finished until you see a ***body.***
Where you come from? And where is ***that,*** exactly?
The ***burbs.***

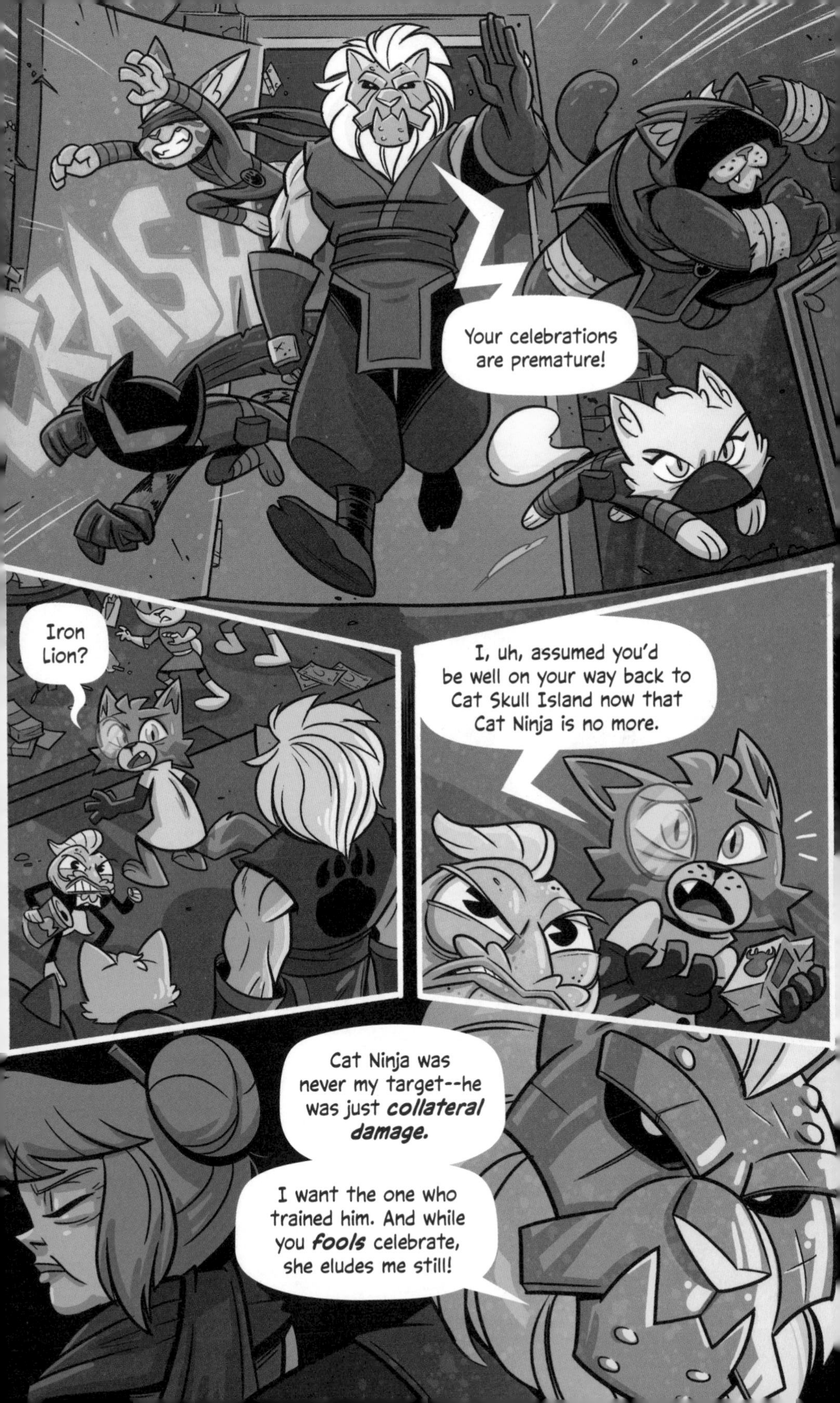
CRASH
Your celebrations are premature!
Iron Lion?
I, uh, assumed you'd be well on your way back to Cat Skull Island now that Cat Ninja is no more.
Cat Ninja was never my target--he was just *collateral damage.*
I want the one who trained him. And while you *fools* celebrate, she eludes me still!

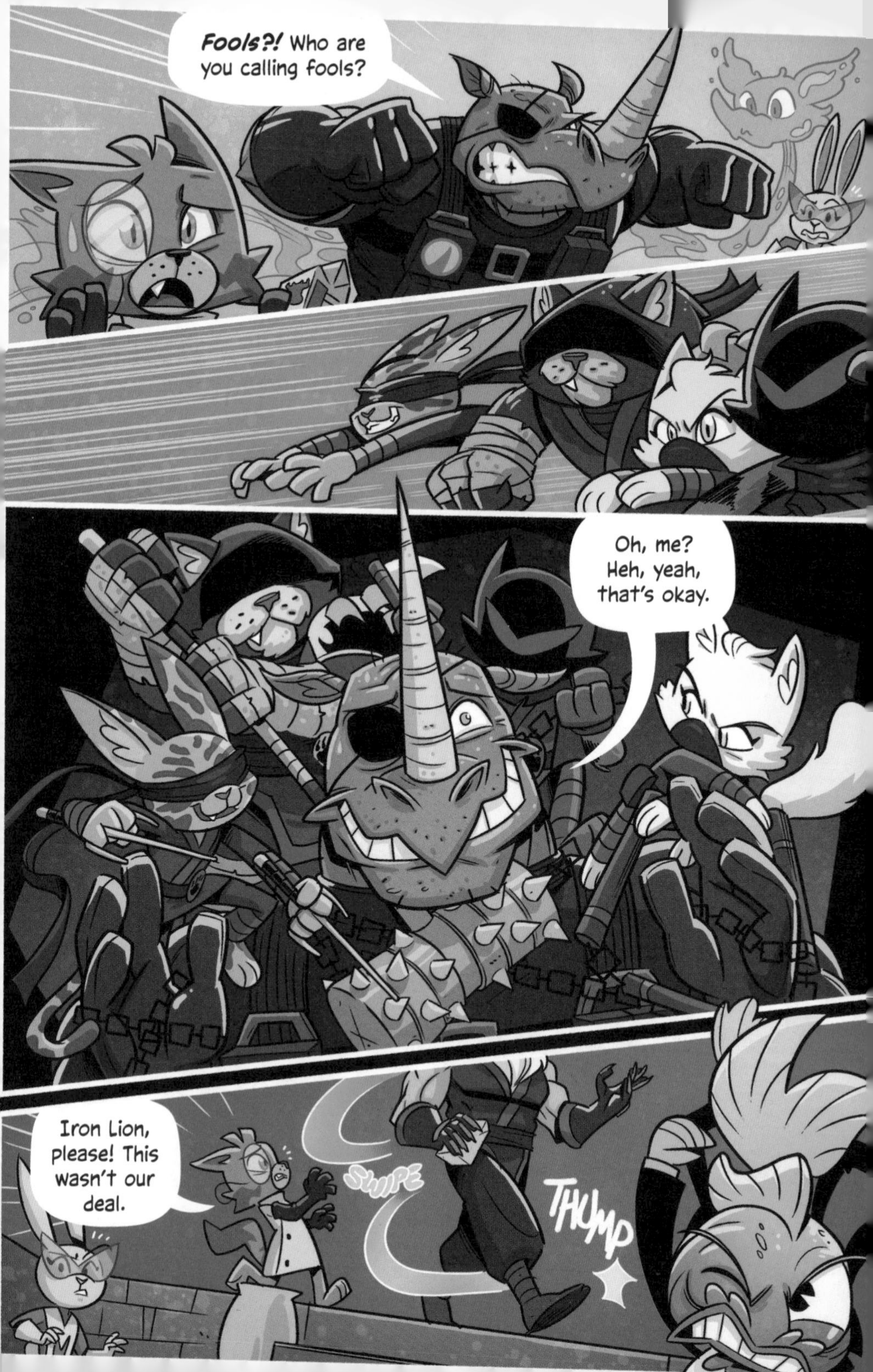
Fools?! Who are you calling fools?
Oh, me? Heh, yeah, that's okay.
Iron Lion, please! This wasn't our deal.
SWIPE
THUMP

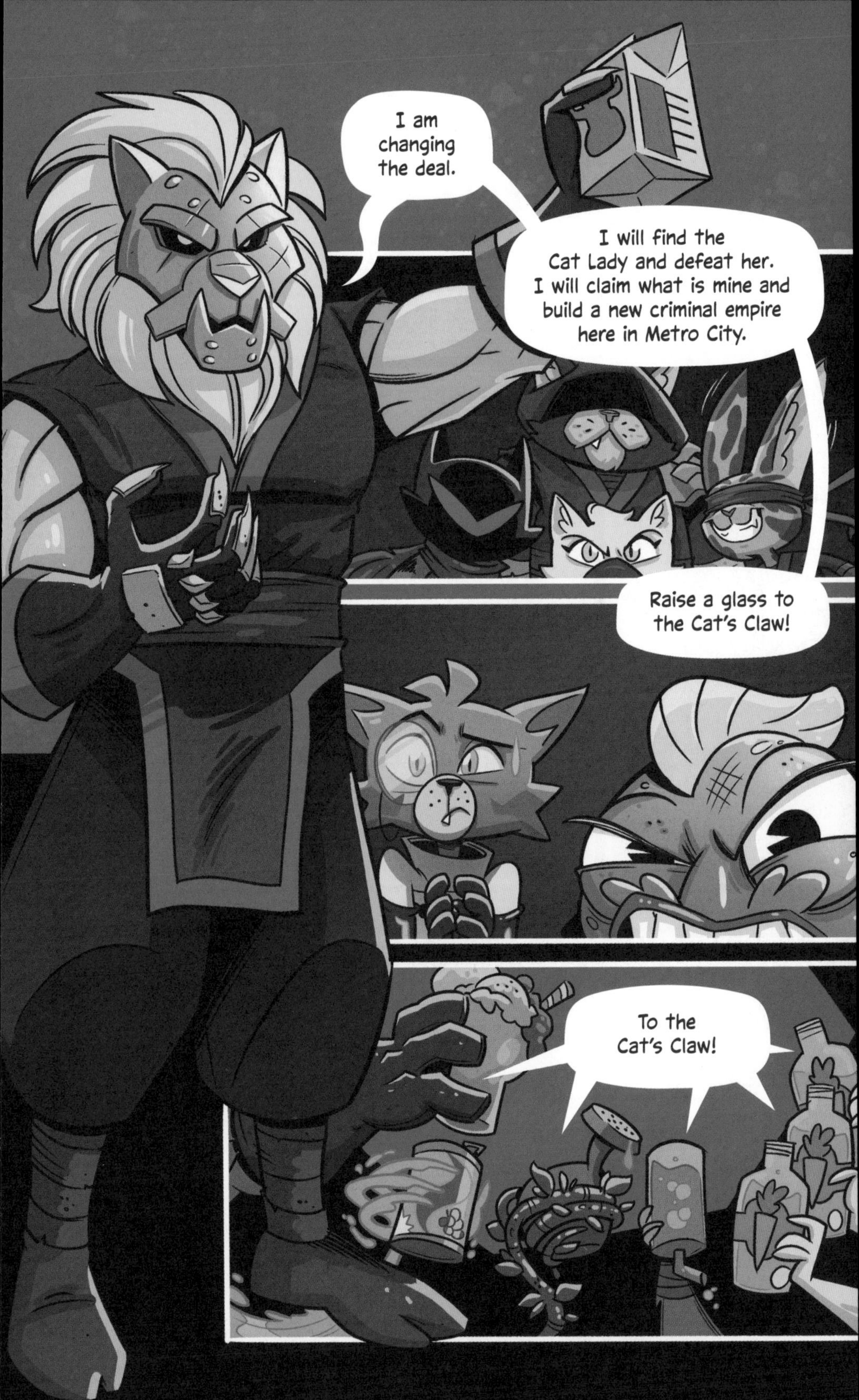
I am changing the deal.
I will find the Cat Lady and defeat her. I will claim what is mine and build a new criminal empire here in Metro City.
Raise a glass to the Cat's Claw!
To the Cat's Claw!

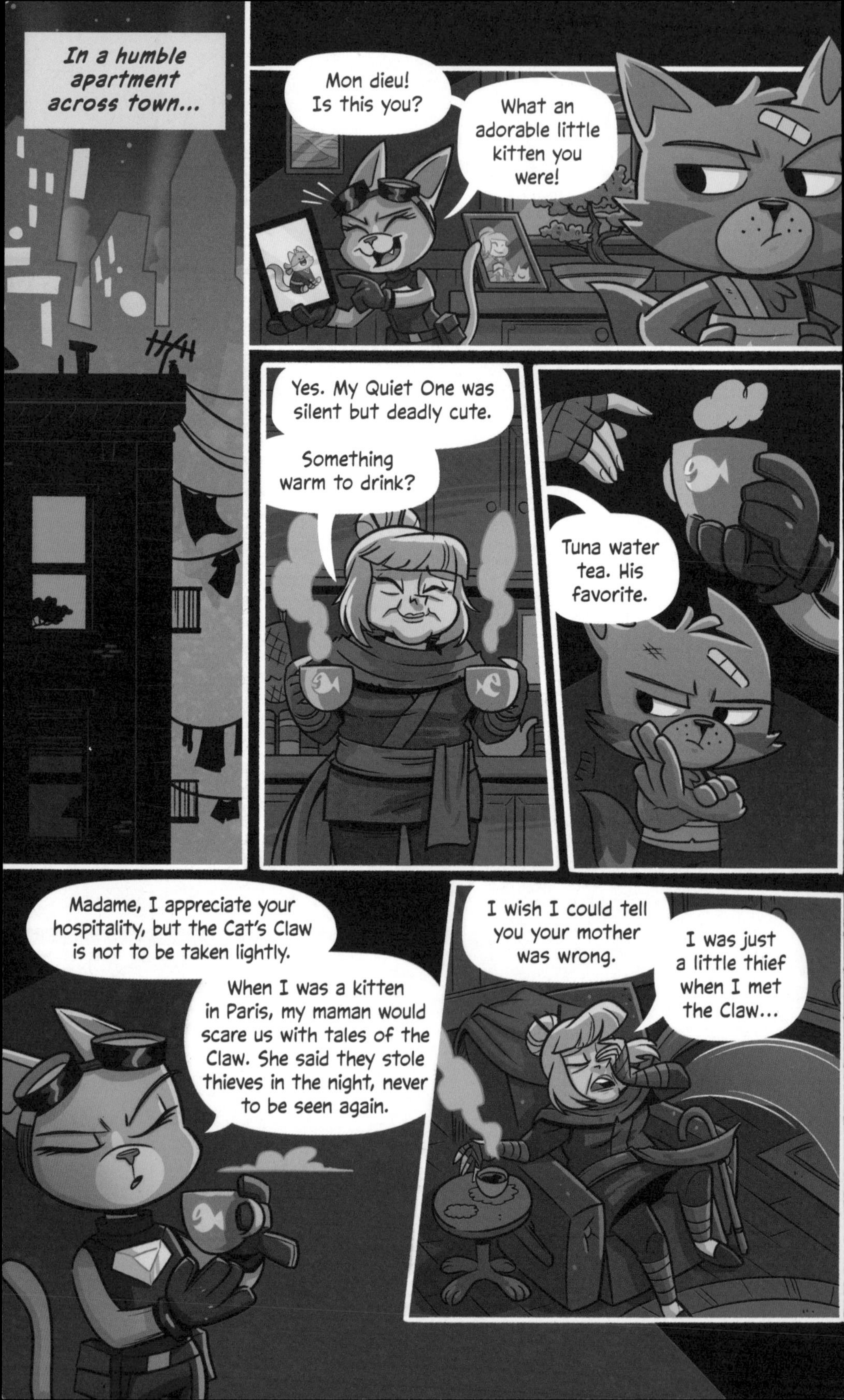
In a humble apartment across town...
Mon dieu! Is this you?
What an adorable little kitten you were!
Yes. My Quiet One was silent but deadly cute.
Something warm to drink?
Tuna water tea. His favorite.
Madame, I appreciate your hospitality, but the Cat's Claw is not to be taken lightly.
When I was a kitten in Paris, my maman would scare us with tales of the Claw. She said they stole thieves in the night, never to be seen again.
I wish I could tell you your mother was wrong.
I was just a little thief when I met the Claw...

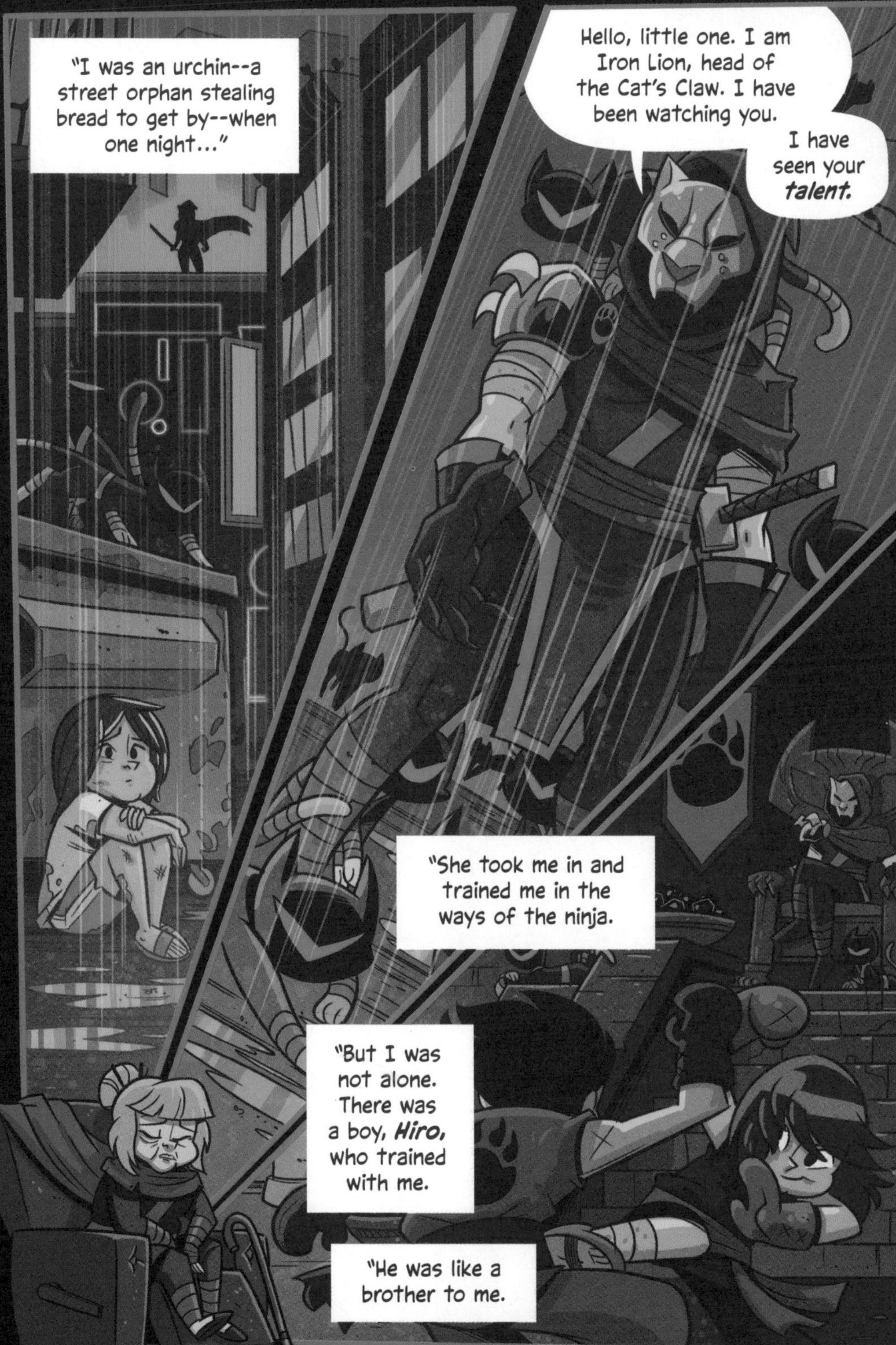
"I was an urchin--a street orphan stealing bread to get by--when one night..."
Hello, little one. I am Iron Lion, head of the Cat's Claw. I have been watching you.
I have seen your *talent.*
"She took me in and trained me in the ways of the ninja.
"But I was not alone. There was a boy, *Hiro,* who trained with me.
"He was like a brother to me.

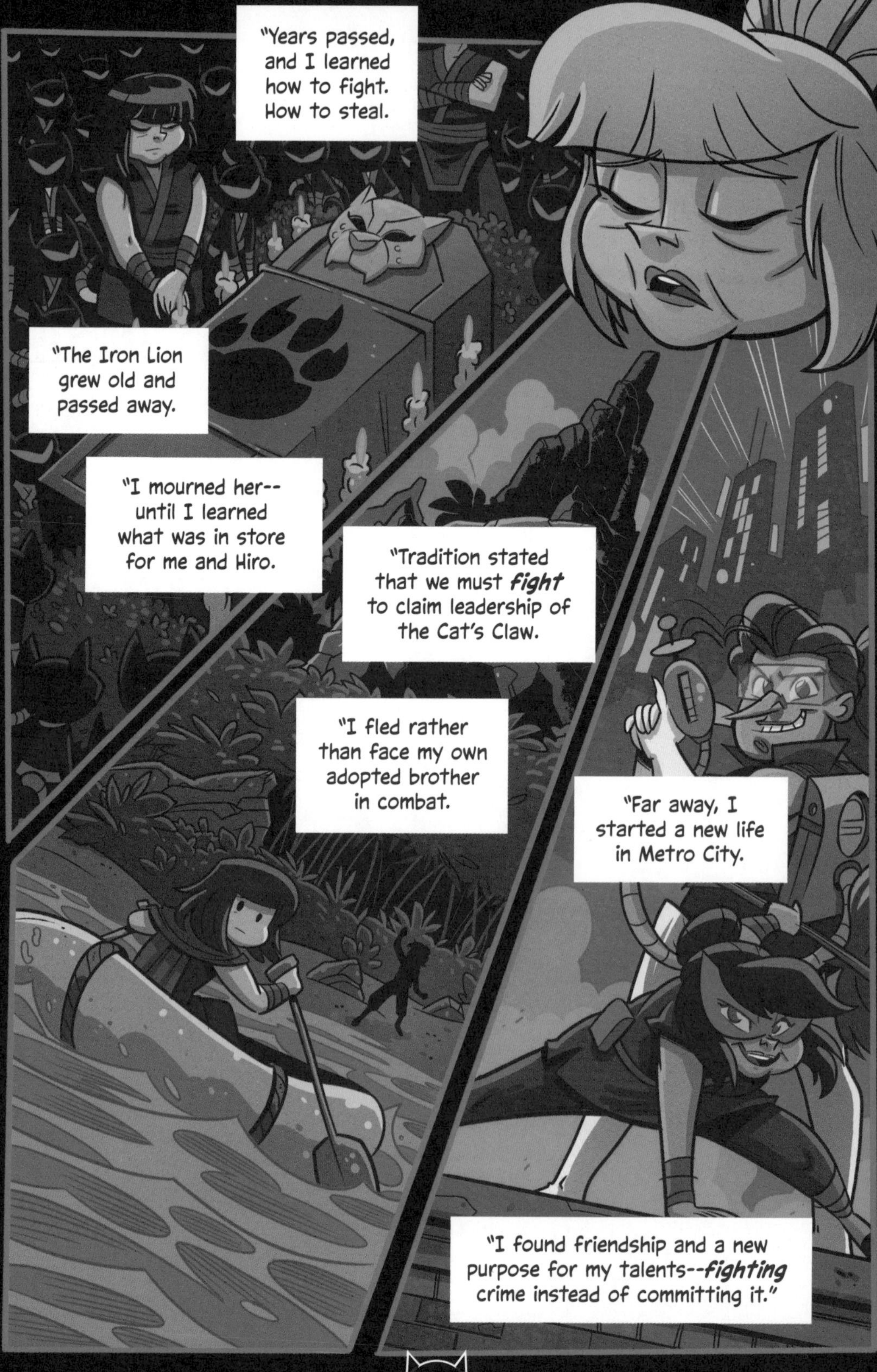
"Years passed, and I learned how to fight. How to steal.
"The Iron Lion grew old and passed away.
"I mourned her--until I learned what was in store for me and Hiro.
"Tradition stated that we must *fight* to claim leadership of the Cat's Claw.
"I fled rather than face my own adopted brother in combat.
"Far away, I started a new life in Metro City.
"I found friendship and a new purpose for my talents--*fighting* crime instead of committing it."

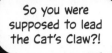

So you were supposed to lead the Cat's Claw?!

It is no wonder they are after you!

Once a member of the Claw, always a member of the Claw. The only way out is *death!*

Yes. And though I have avoided them these many years, it seems Hiro has finally caught up with me.

He never forgave me for fleeing before he could prove himself in combat.

In his mind, I dishonored him. I dishonored the Claw.

He came after you, Quiet One, to get to me.

I am sorry for that.

But he will never hurt you again.

I will face Hiro and give him the fight he craves.

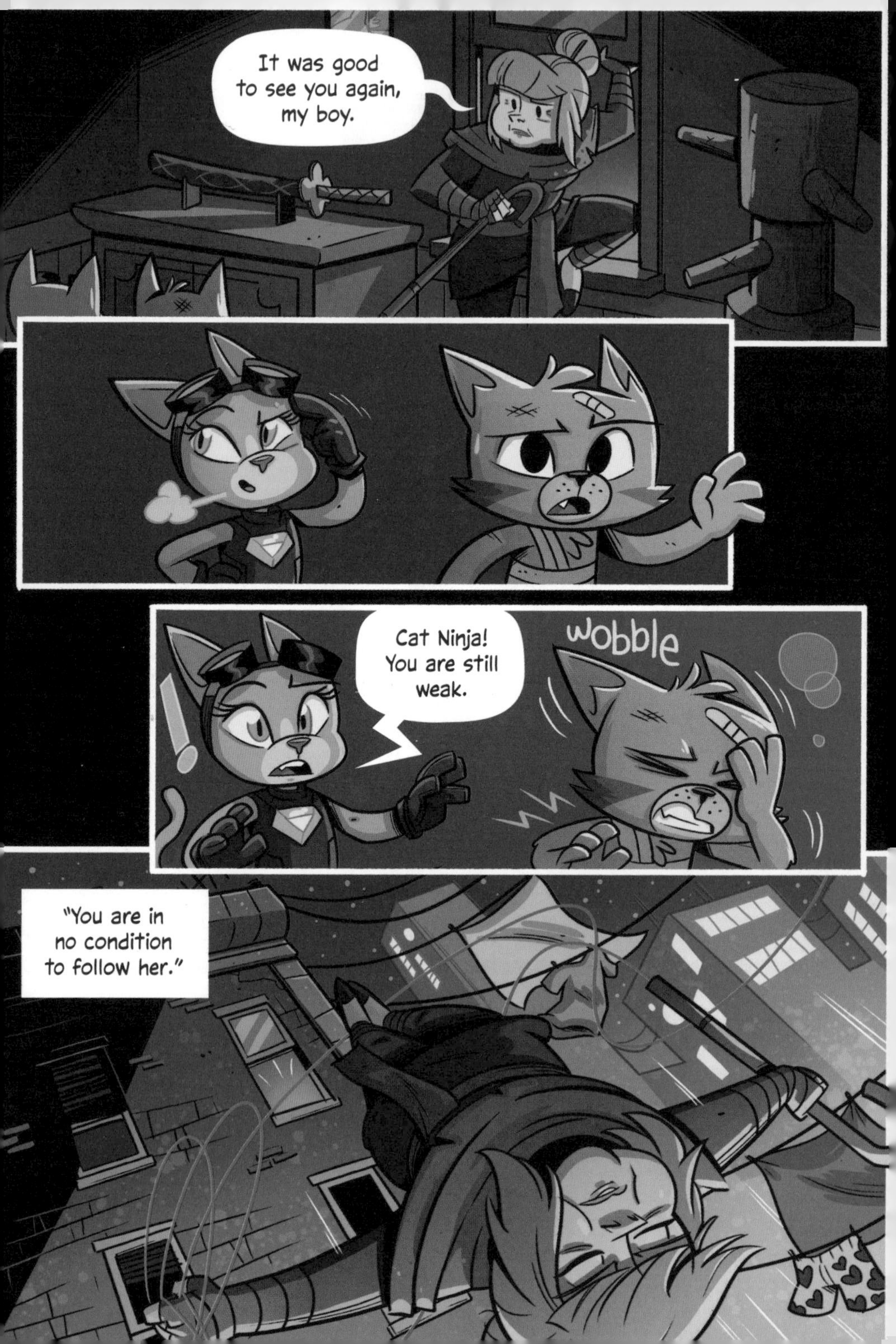
It was good to see you again, my boy.
Cat Ninja! You are still weak.
wobble
"You are in no condition to follow her."

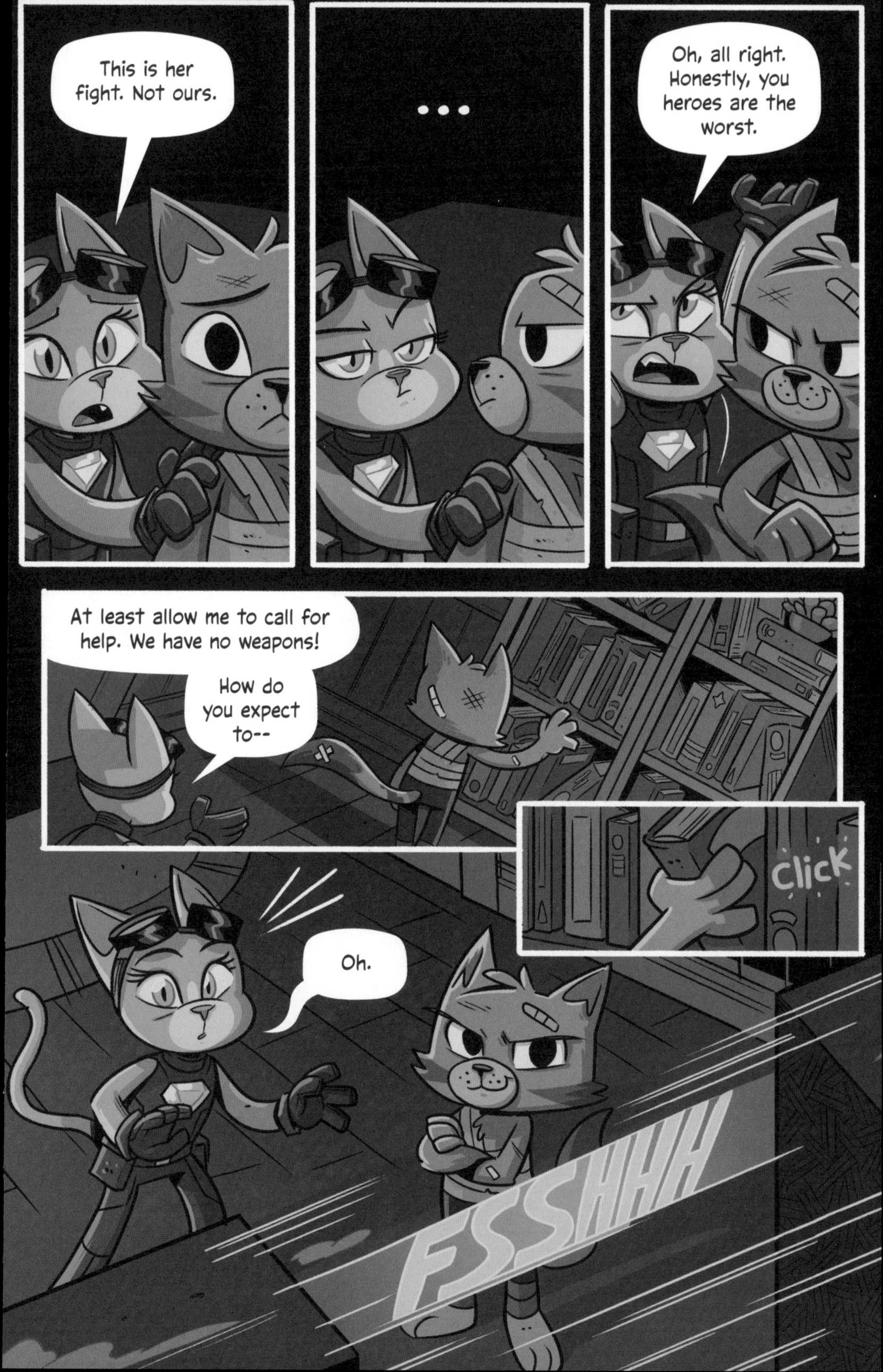
This is her fight. Not ours.
...
Oh, all right. Honestly, you heroes are the worst.
At least allow me to call for help. We have no weapons!
How do you expect to--
CLICK
Oh.
FSSHHH

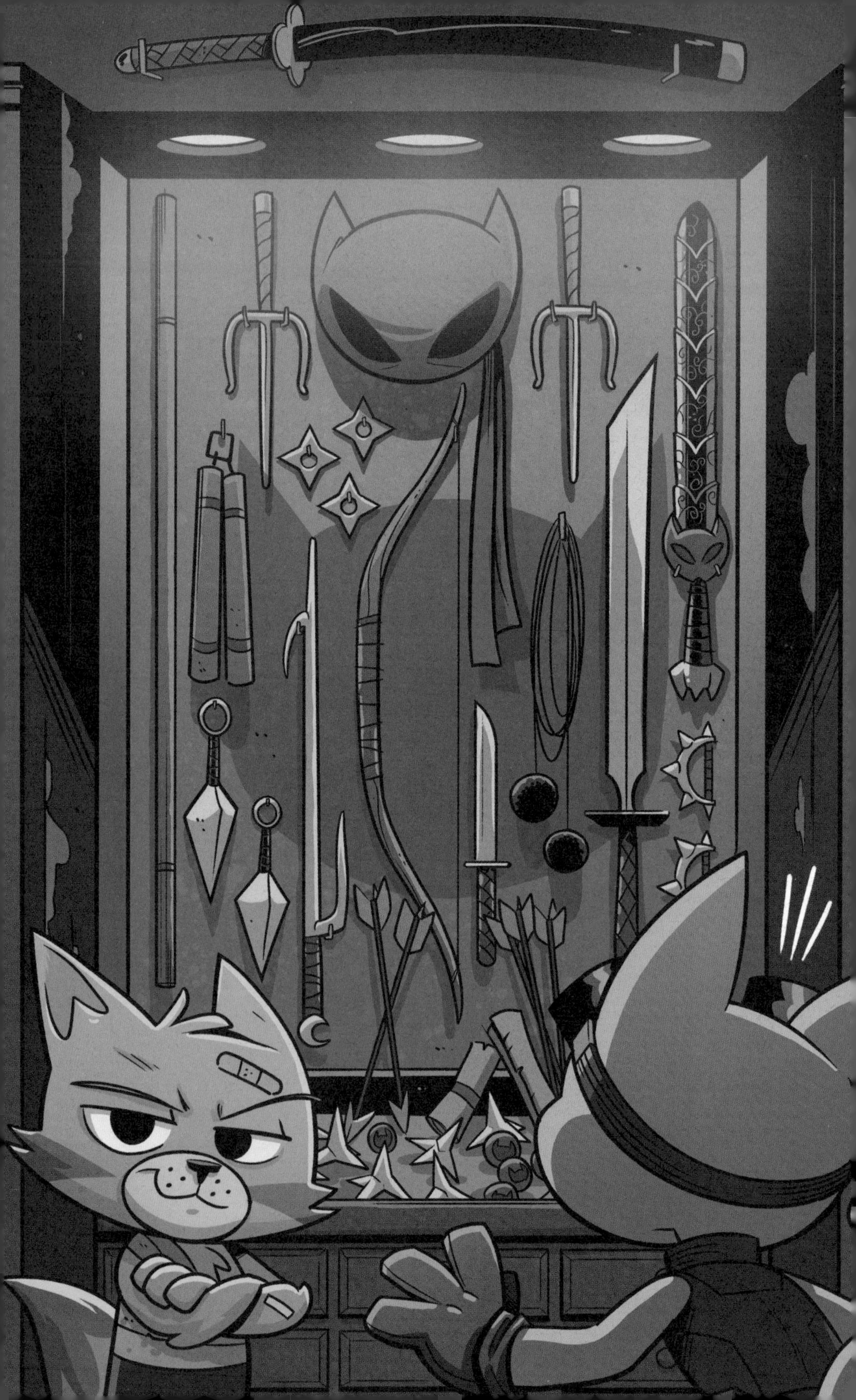

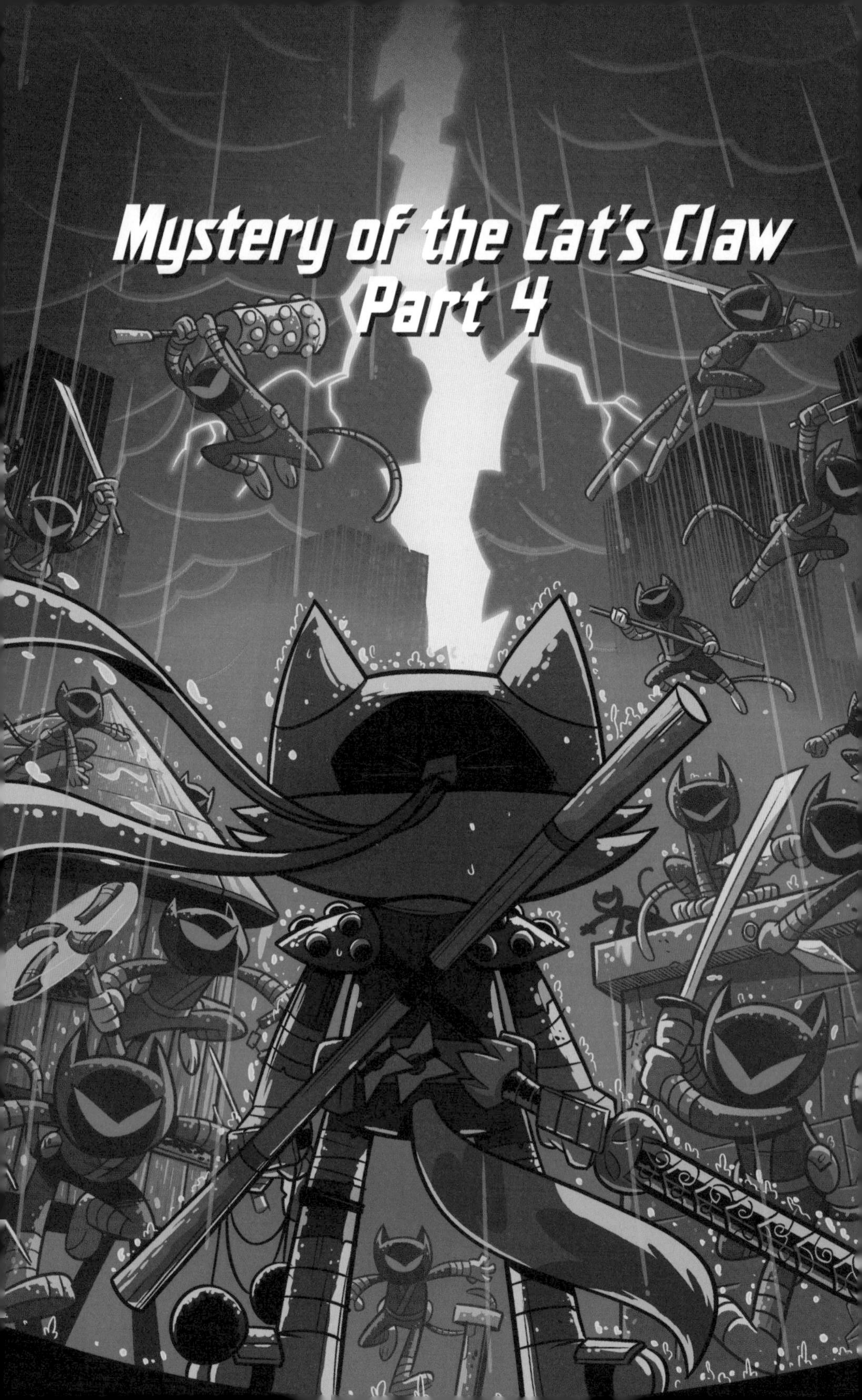
Mystery of the Cat's Claw
Part 4

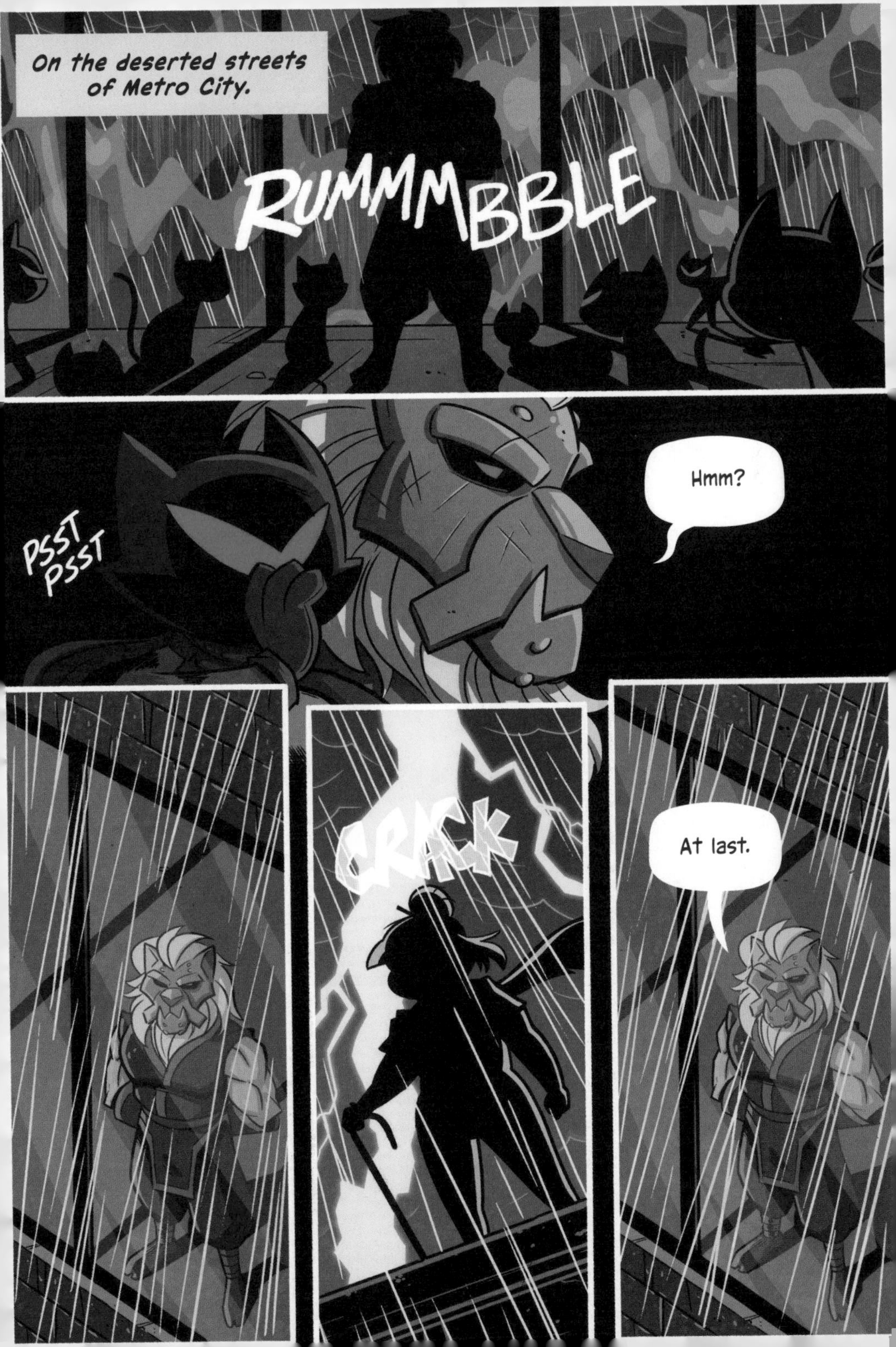

On the deserted streets of Metro City.
RUMMMBBLE
PSST PSST
Hmm?
CRACK
At last.

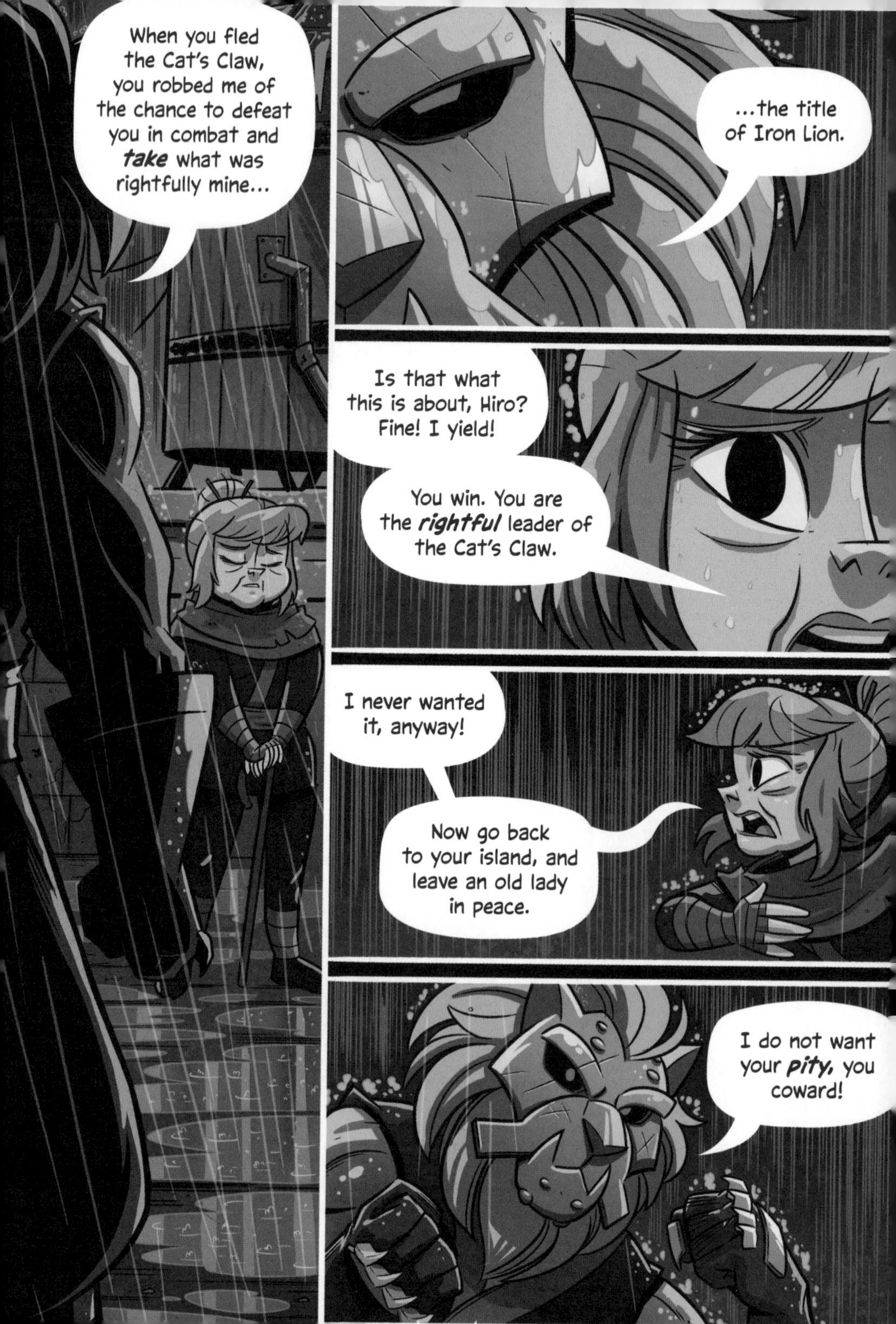
When you fled the Cat's Claw, you robbed me of the chance to defeat you in combat and *take* what was rightfully mine...
...the title of Iron Lion.
Is that what this is about, Hiro? Fine! I yield!
You win. You are the *rightful* leader of the Cat's Claw.
I never wanted it, anyway!
Now go back to your island, and leave an old lady in peace.
I do not want your *pity,* you coward!

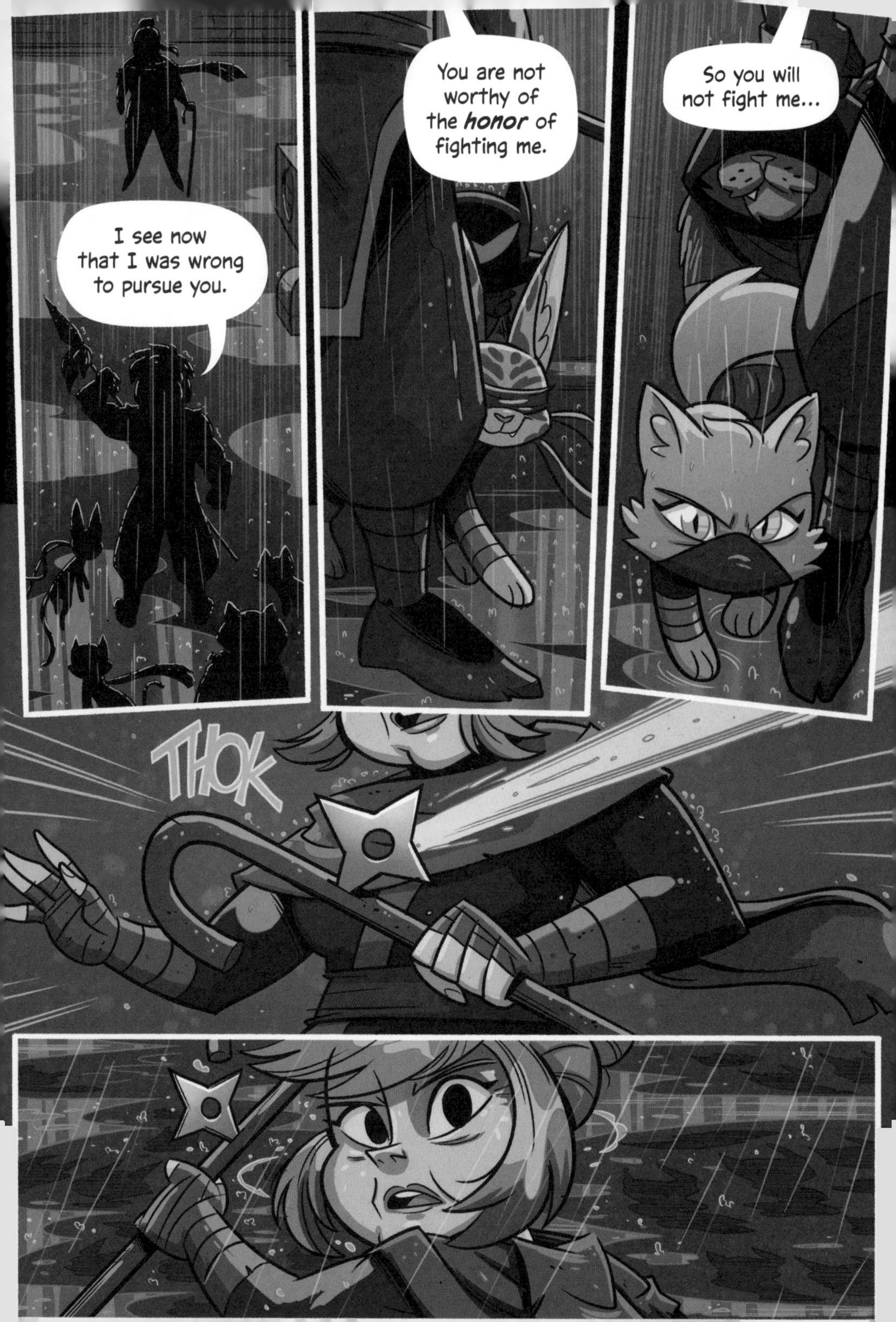
I see now that I was wrong to pursue you.
You are not worthy of the *honor* of fighting me.
So you will not fight me...
THOK

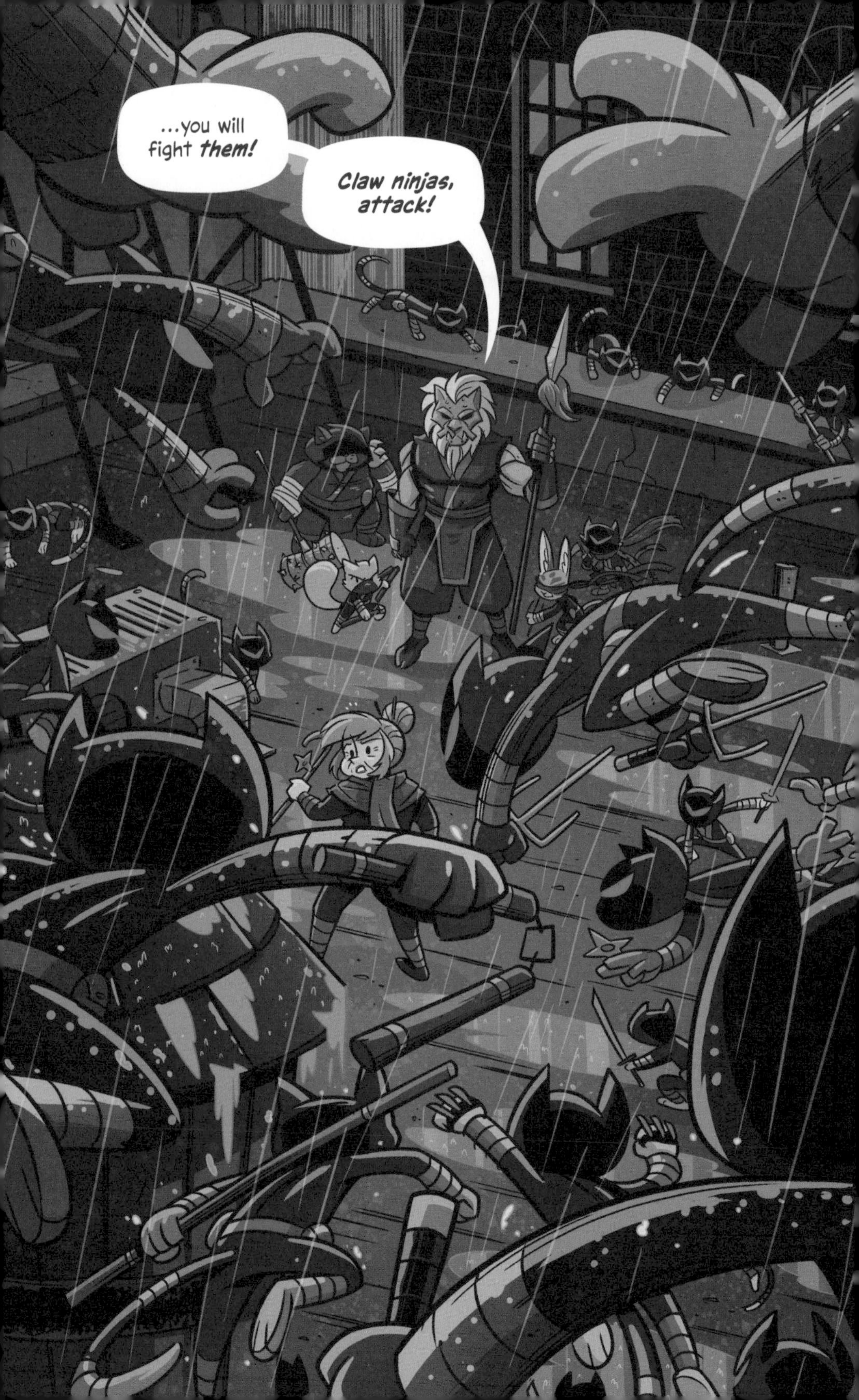
...you will fight them!
Claw ninjas, attack!

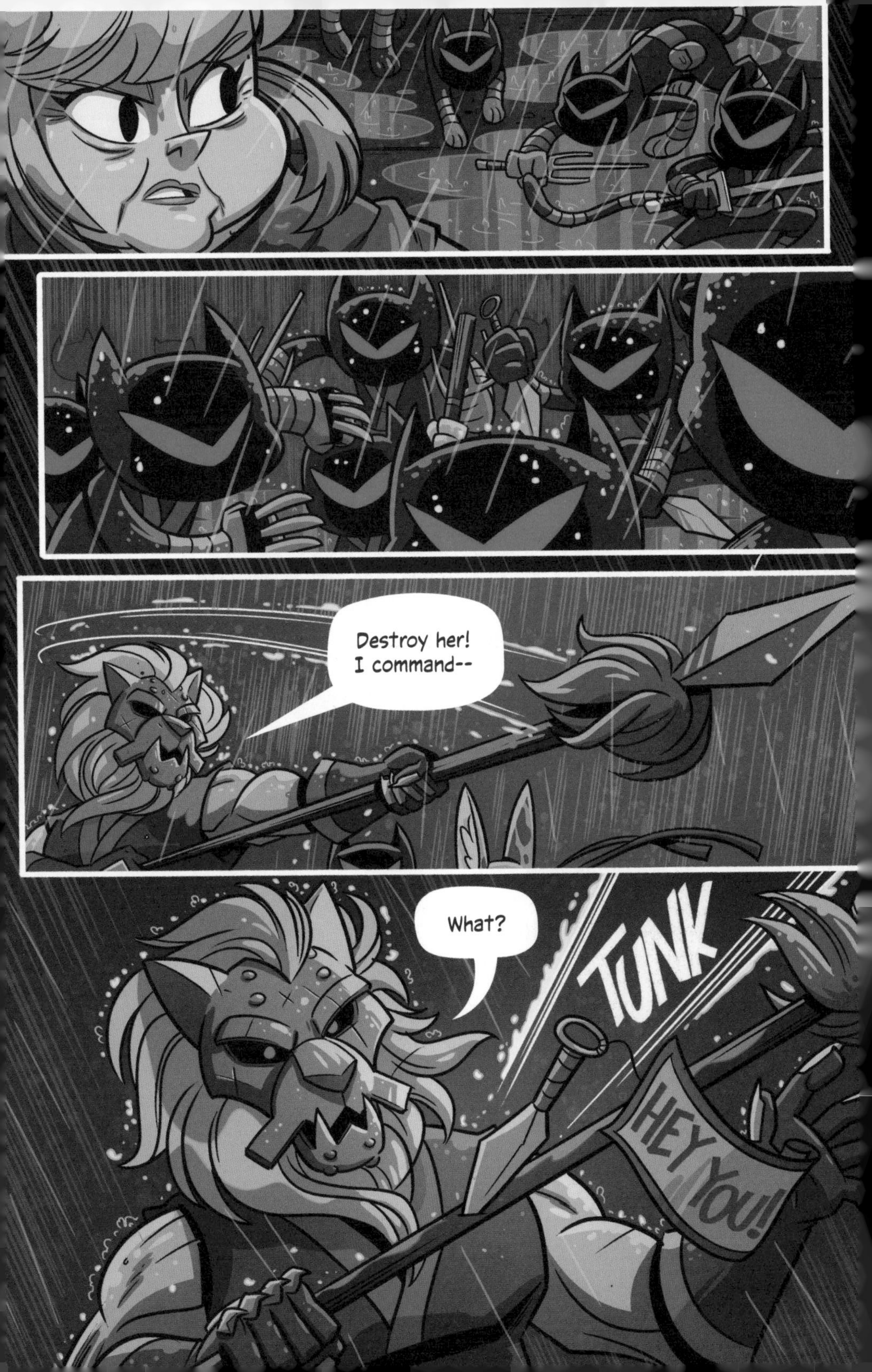
Destroy her!
I command--
What?
TUNK
HEY YOU!

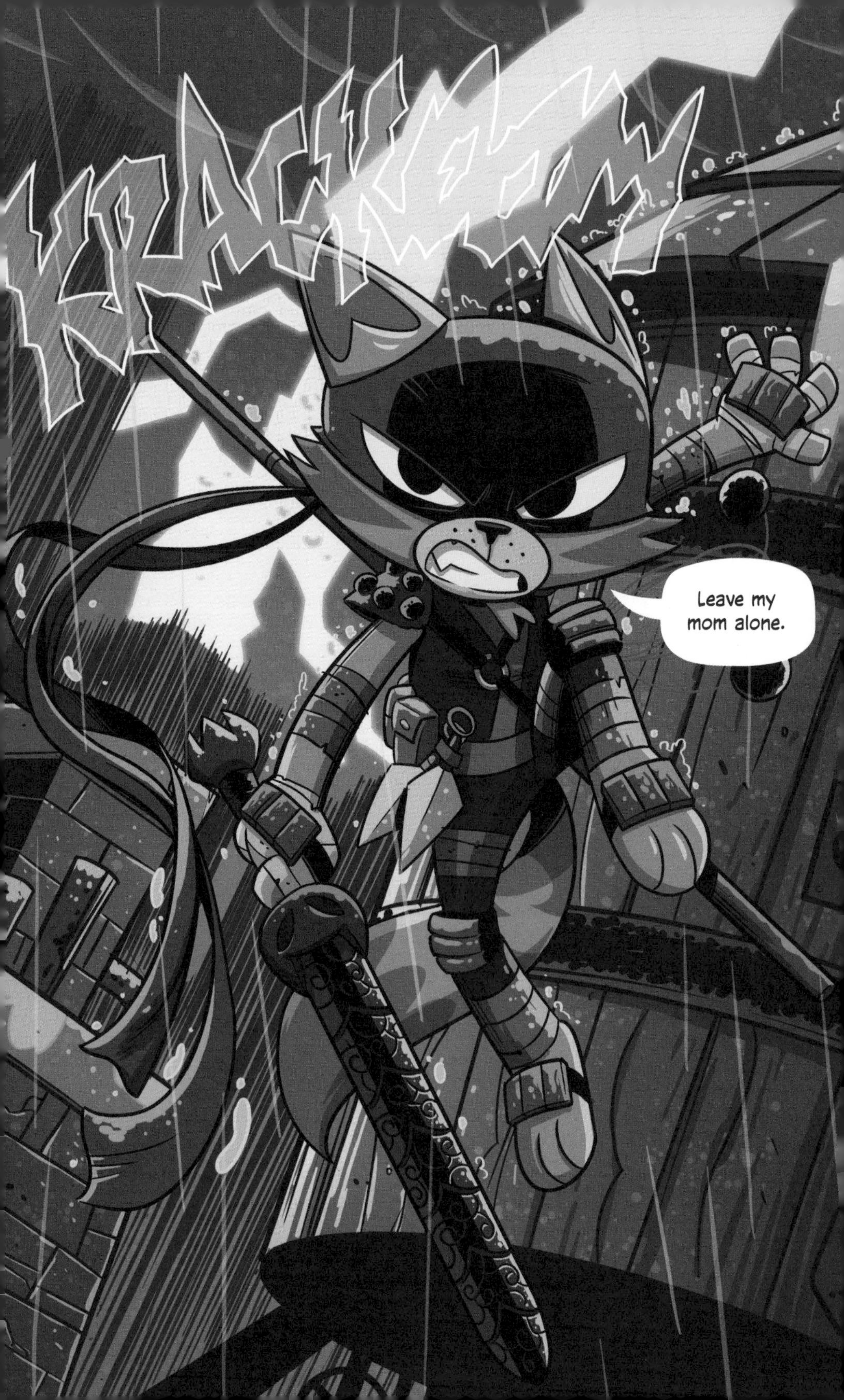
KRACHOOM
Leave my mom alone.

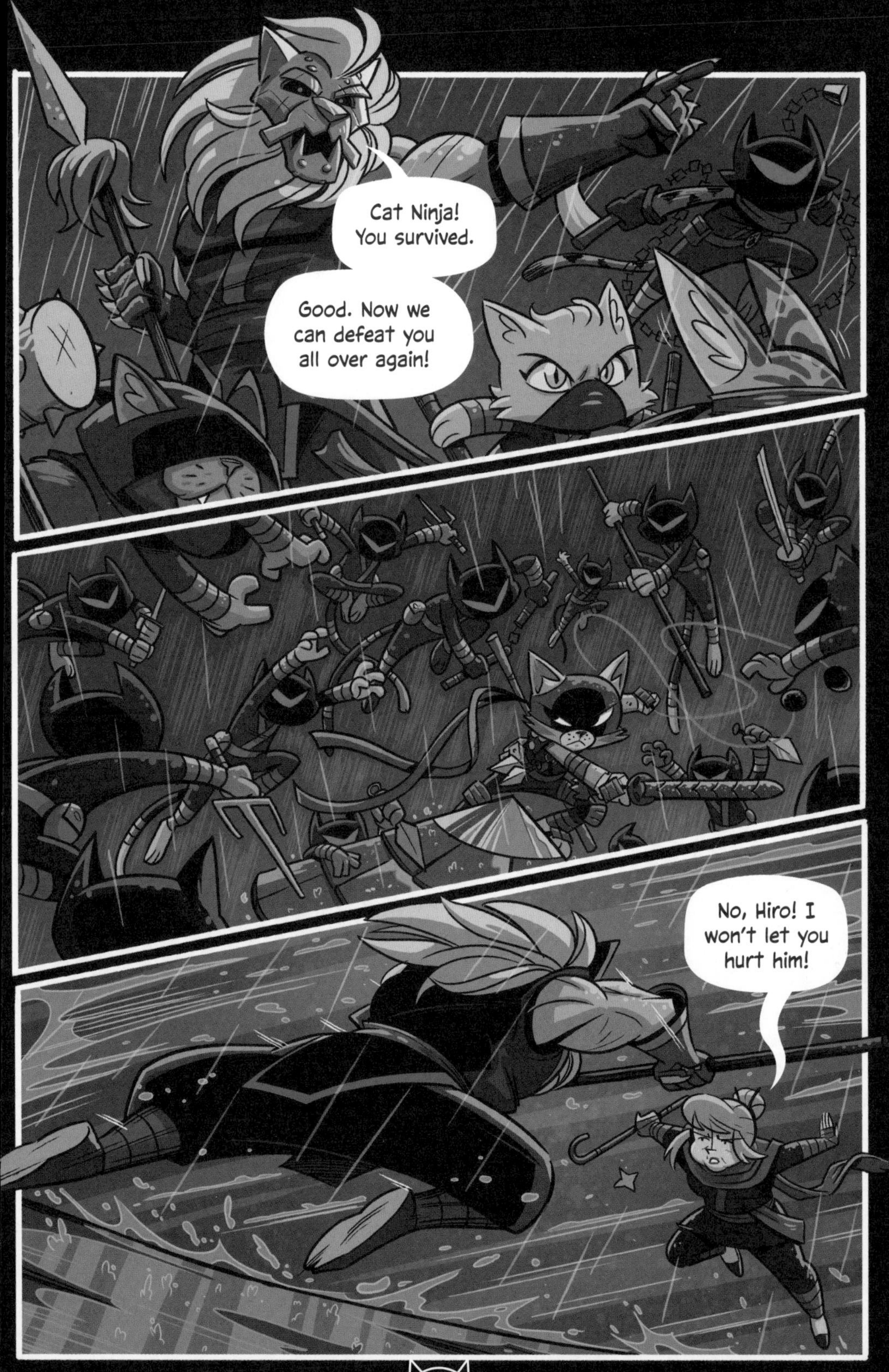

Cat Ninja! You survived.
Good. Now we can defeat you all over again!
No, Hiro! I won't let you hurt him!

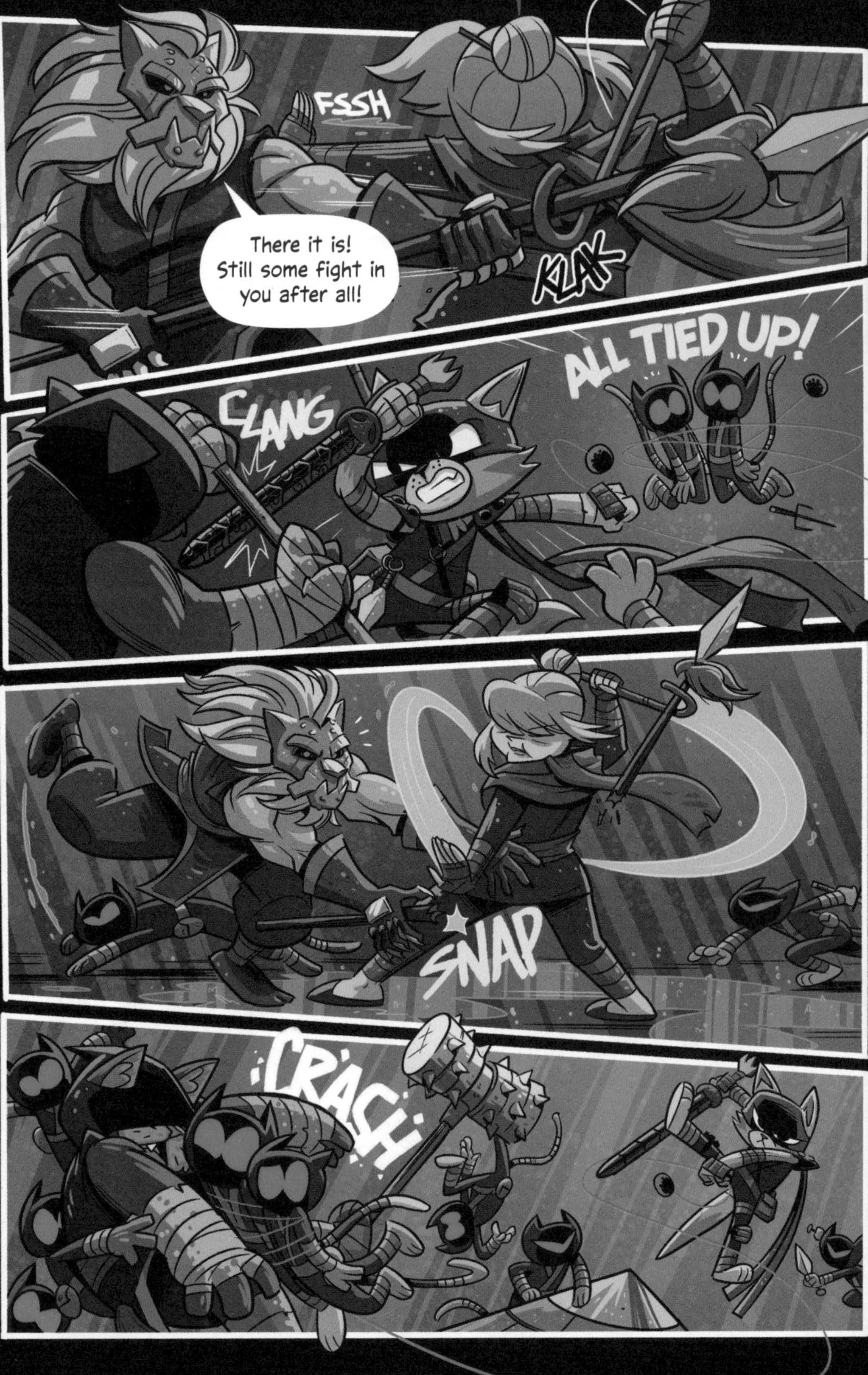
FSSH
There it is! Still some fight in you after all!
KLAK
ALL TIED UP!
CLANG
SNAP
CRACK

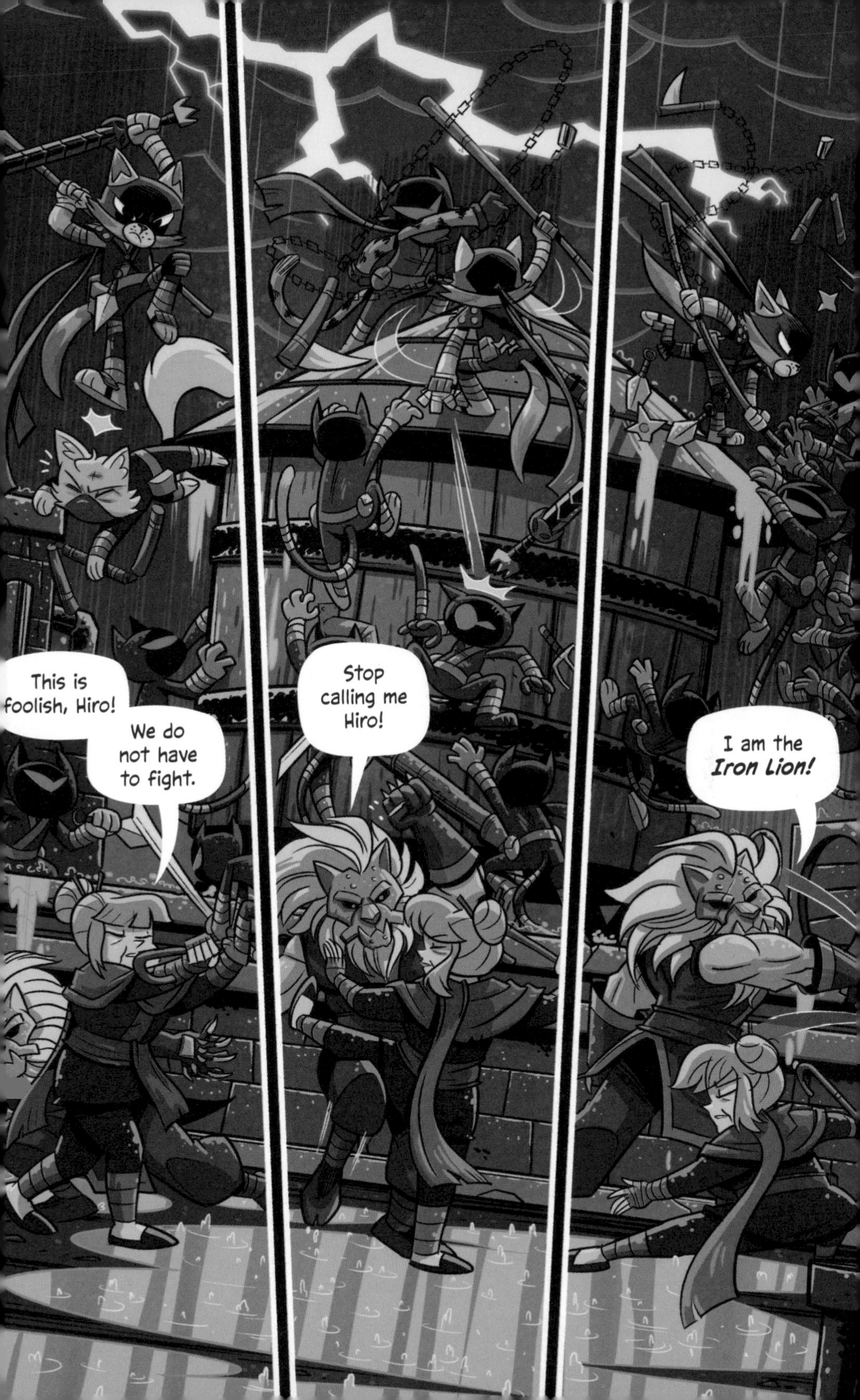
This is foolish, Hiro!
We do not have to fight.
Stop calling me Hiro!
I am the *Iron Lion!*

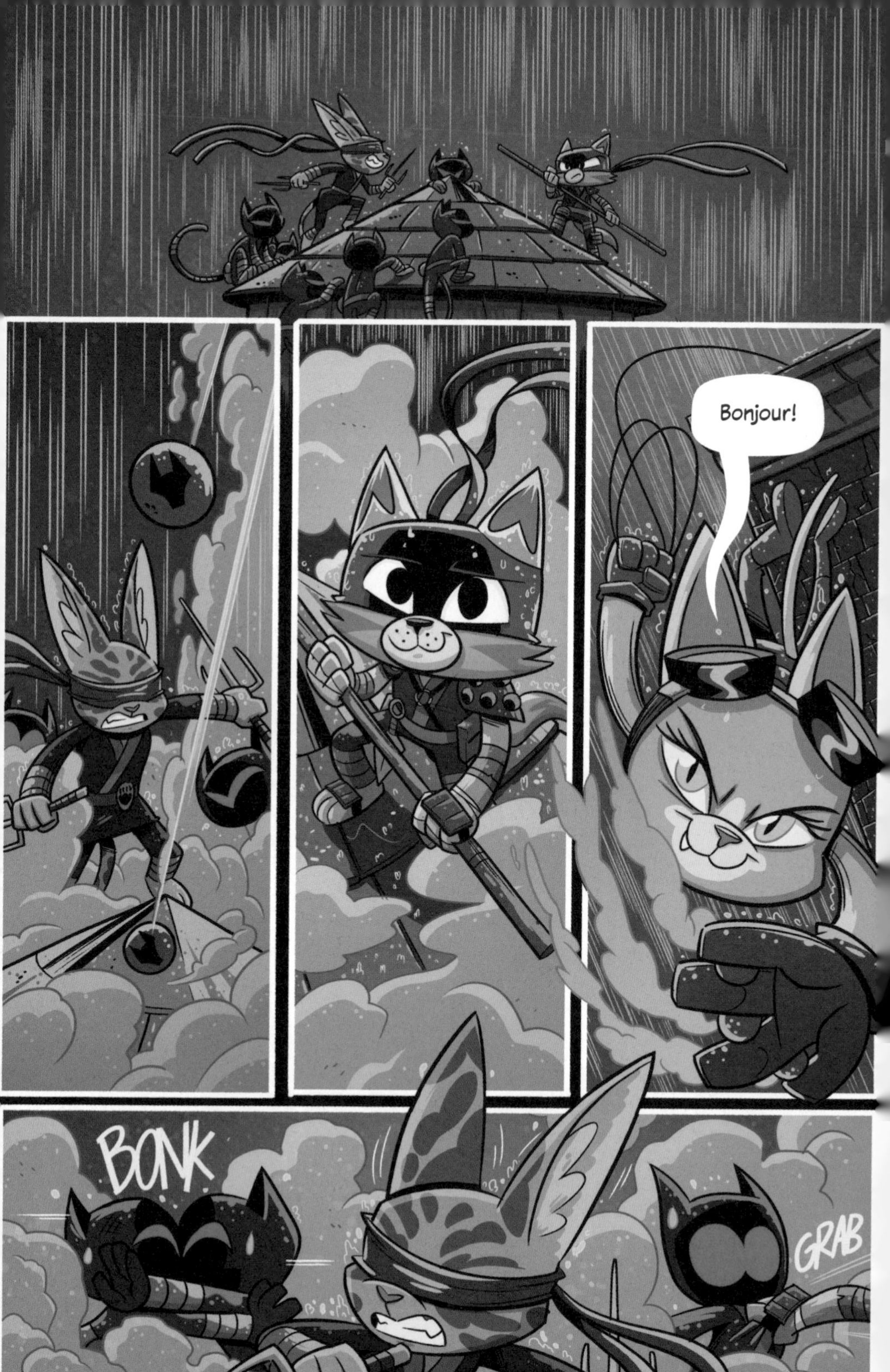
Bonjour!
BONK
GRAB

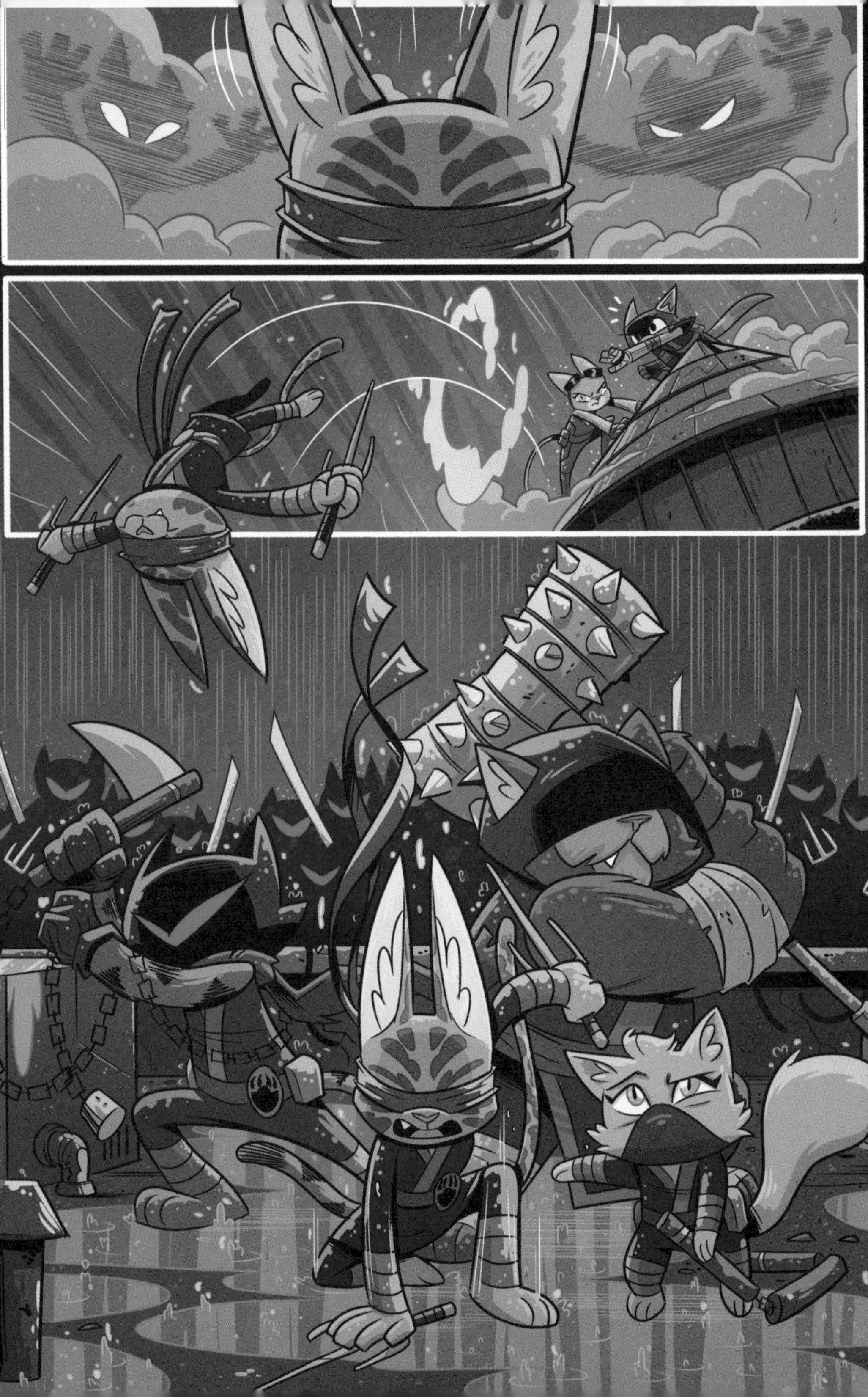

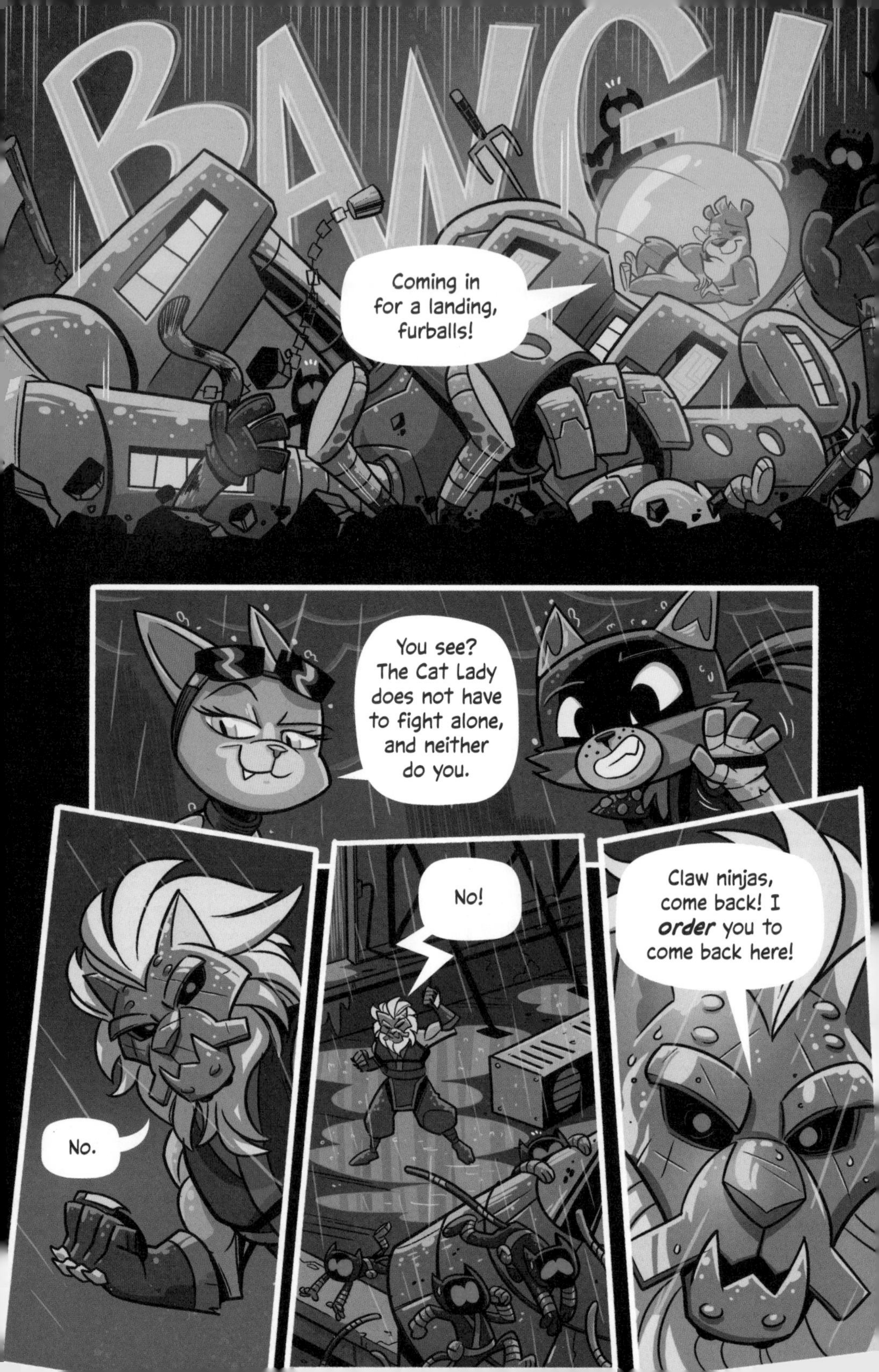
BANG!
Coming in for a landing, furballs!
You see? The Cat Lady does not have to fight alone, and neither do you.
No.
No!
Claw ninjas, come back! I *order* you to come back here!

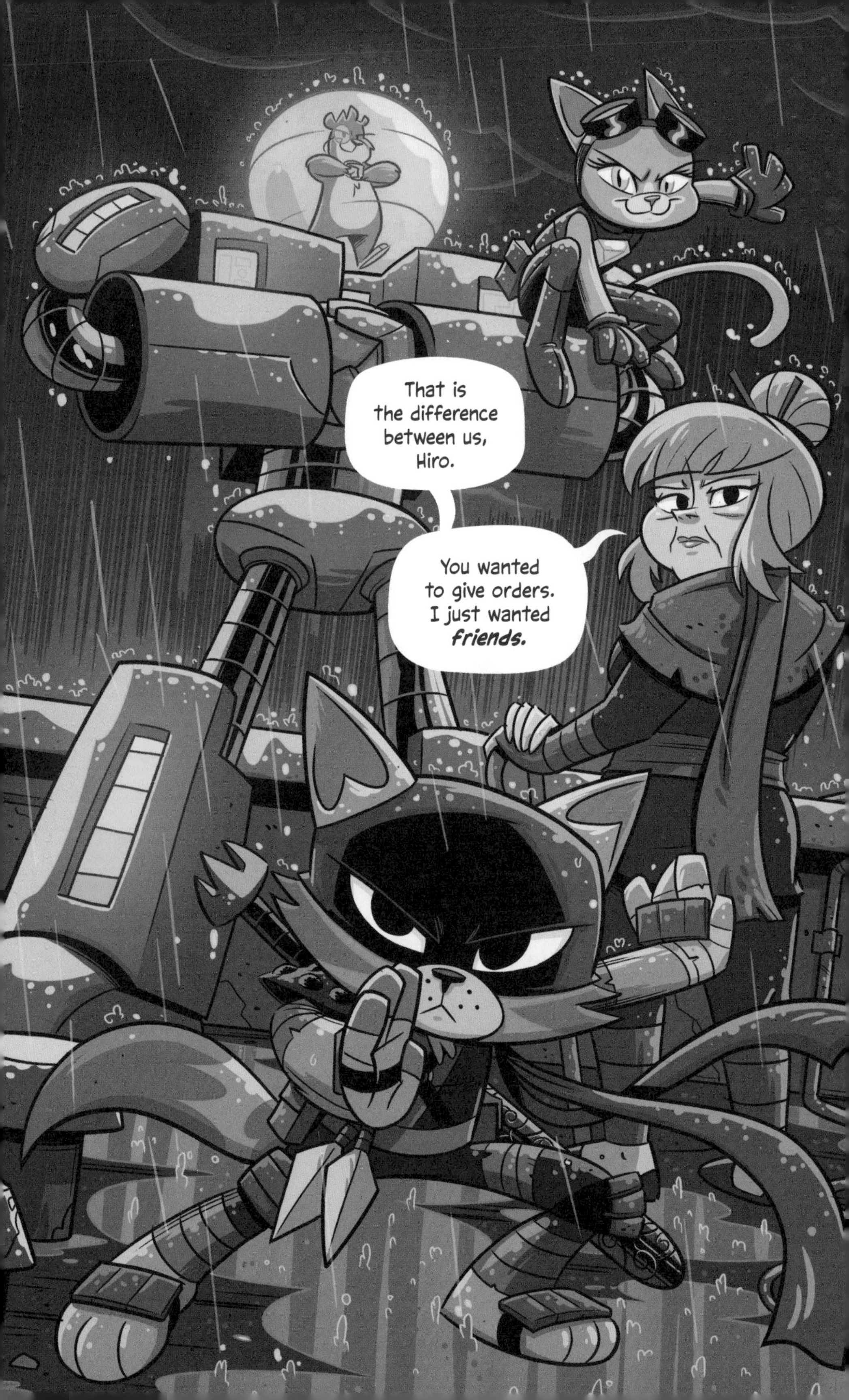
That is the difference between us, Hiro.
You wanted to give orders. I just wanted *friends.*

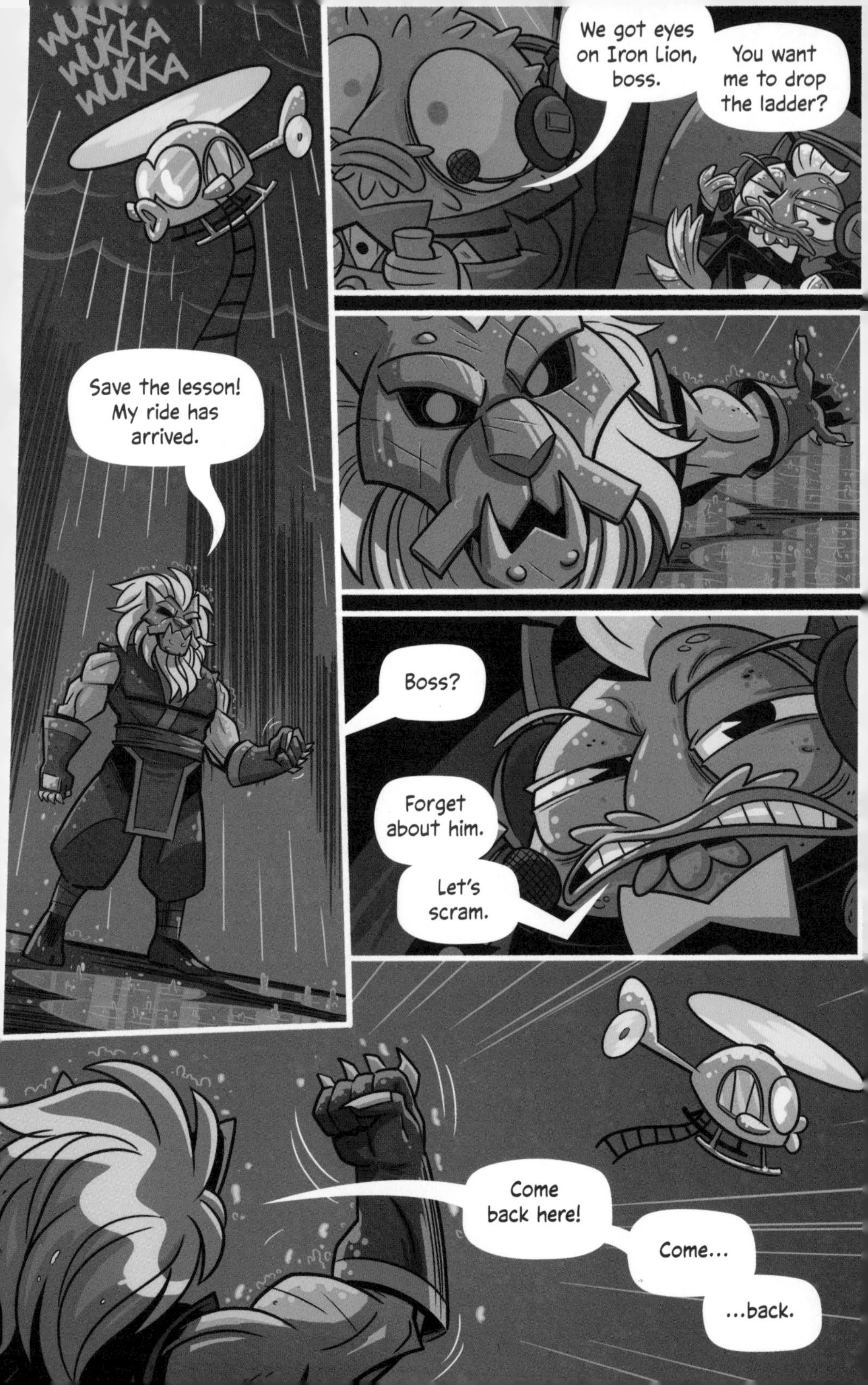
WUKKA WUKKA WUKKA
We got eyes on Iron Lion, boss.
You want me to drop the ladder?
Save the lesson! My ride has arrived.
Boss?
Forget about him.
Let's scram.
Come back here!
Come...
...back.

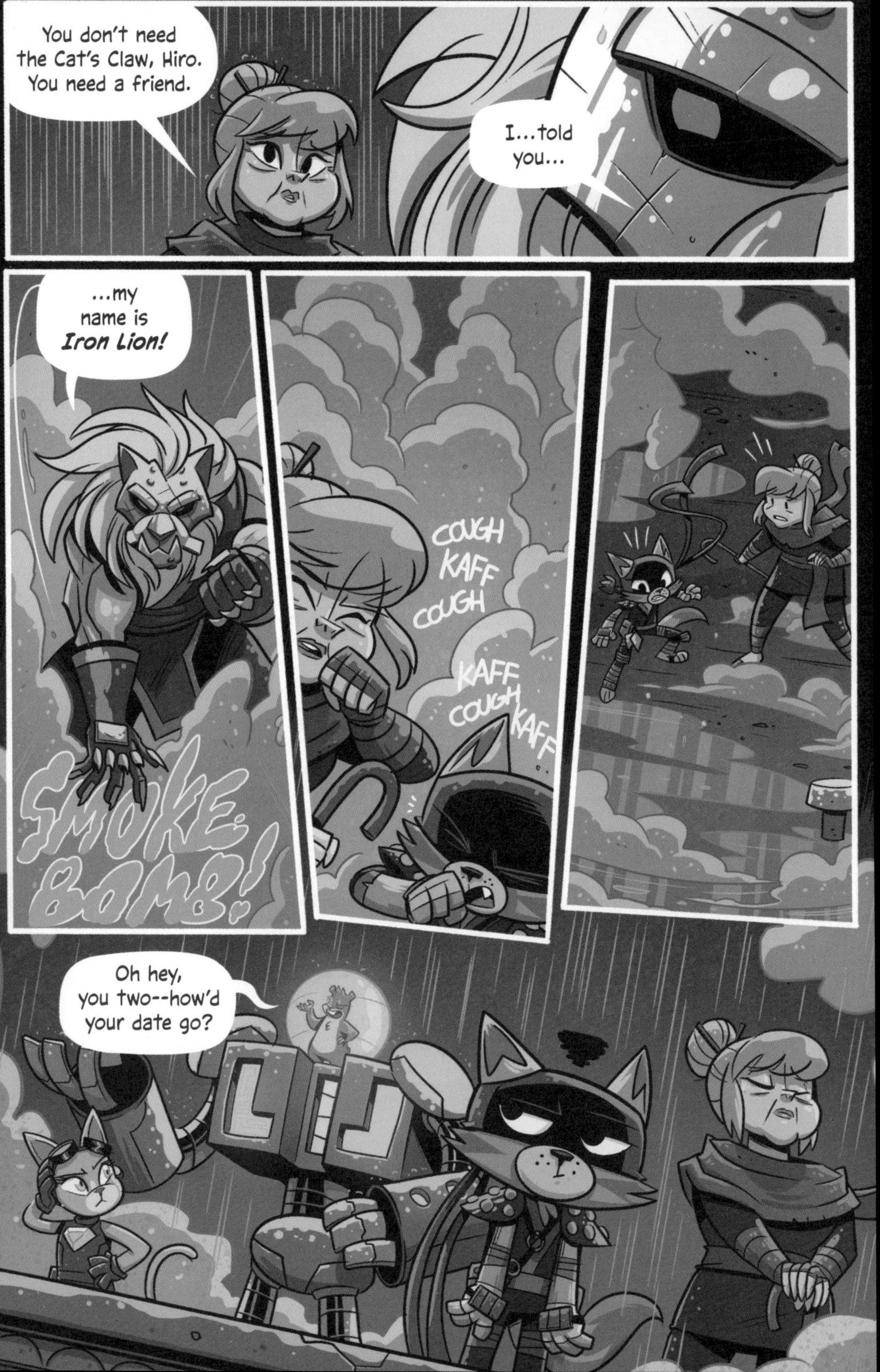
You don't need the Cat's Claw, Hiro. You need a friend.
I...told you...
...my name is *Iron Lion!*
SMOKE-BOMB!
COUGH KAFF COUGH
KAFF COUGH KAFF
Oh hey, you two--how'd your date go?

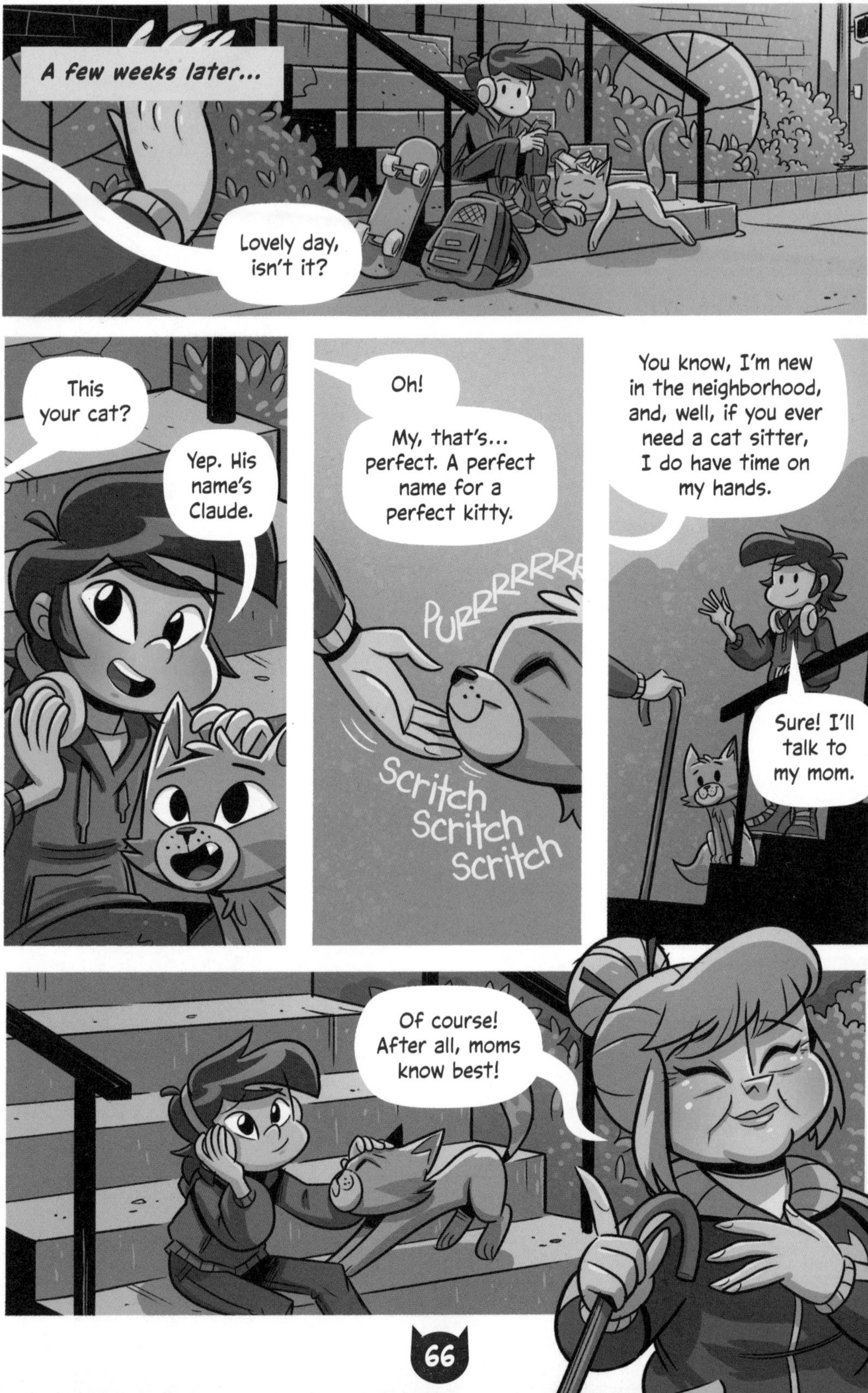
A few weeks later...
Lovely day, isn't it?
This your cat?
Yep. His name's Claude.
Oh!
My, that's... perfect. A perfect name for a perfect kitty.
PURRRRRR
Scritch
Scritch
Scritch
You know, I'm new in the neighborhood, and, well, if you ever need a cat sitter, I do have time on my hands.
Sure! I'll talk to my mom.
Of course! After all, moms know best!

The Fast and the Furriest

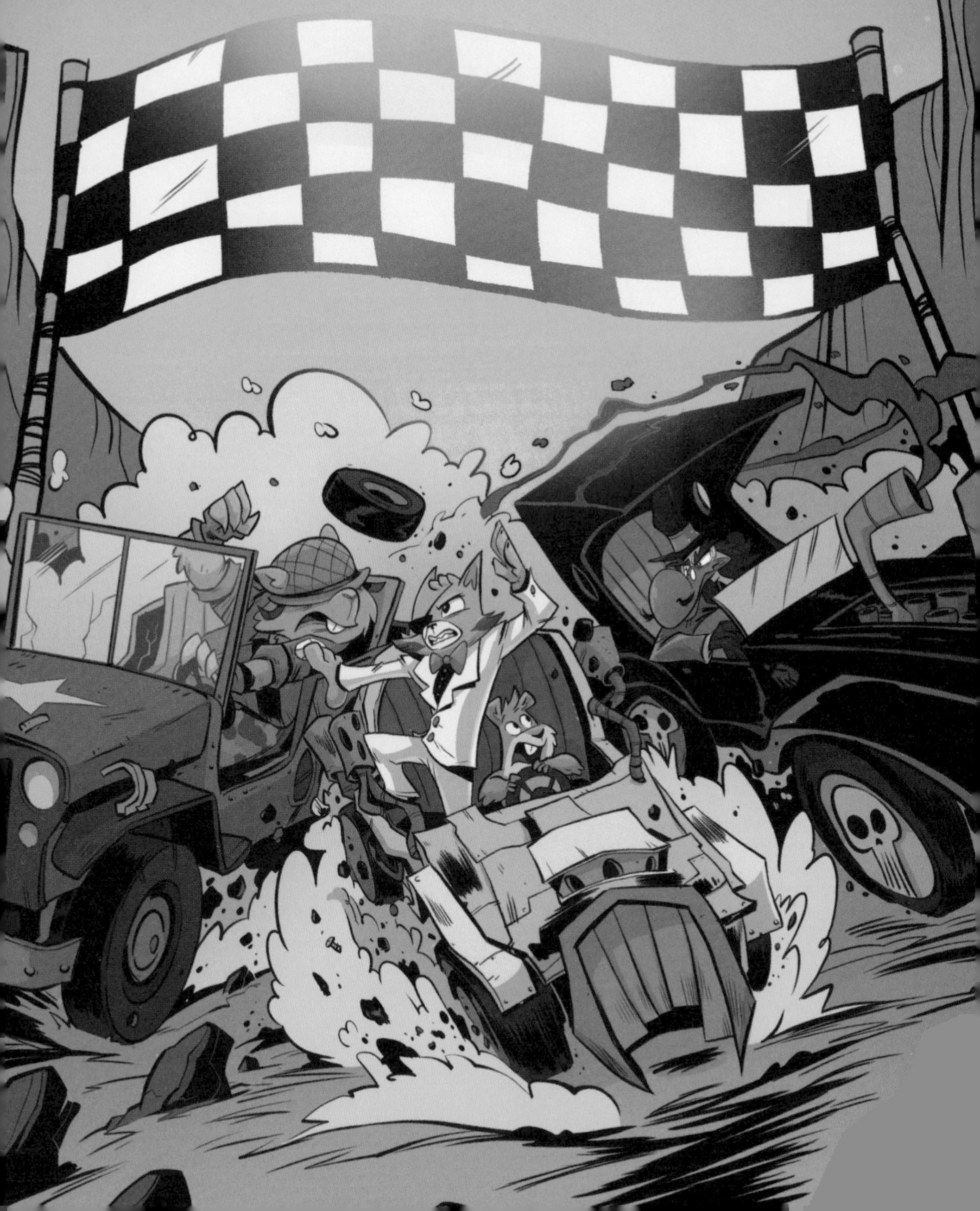

Jadzia Axelrod

Illustrated by
Brett Bean

Colors by
Maarta Laiho

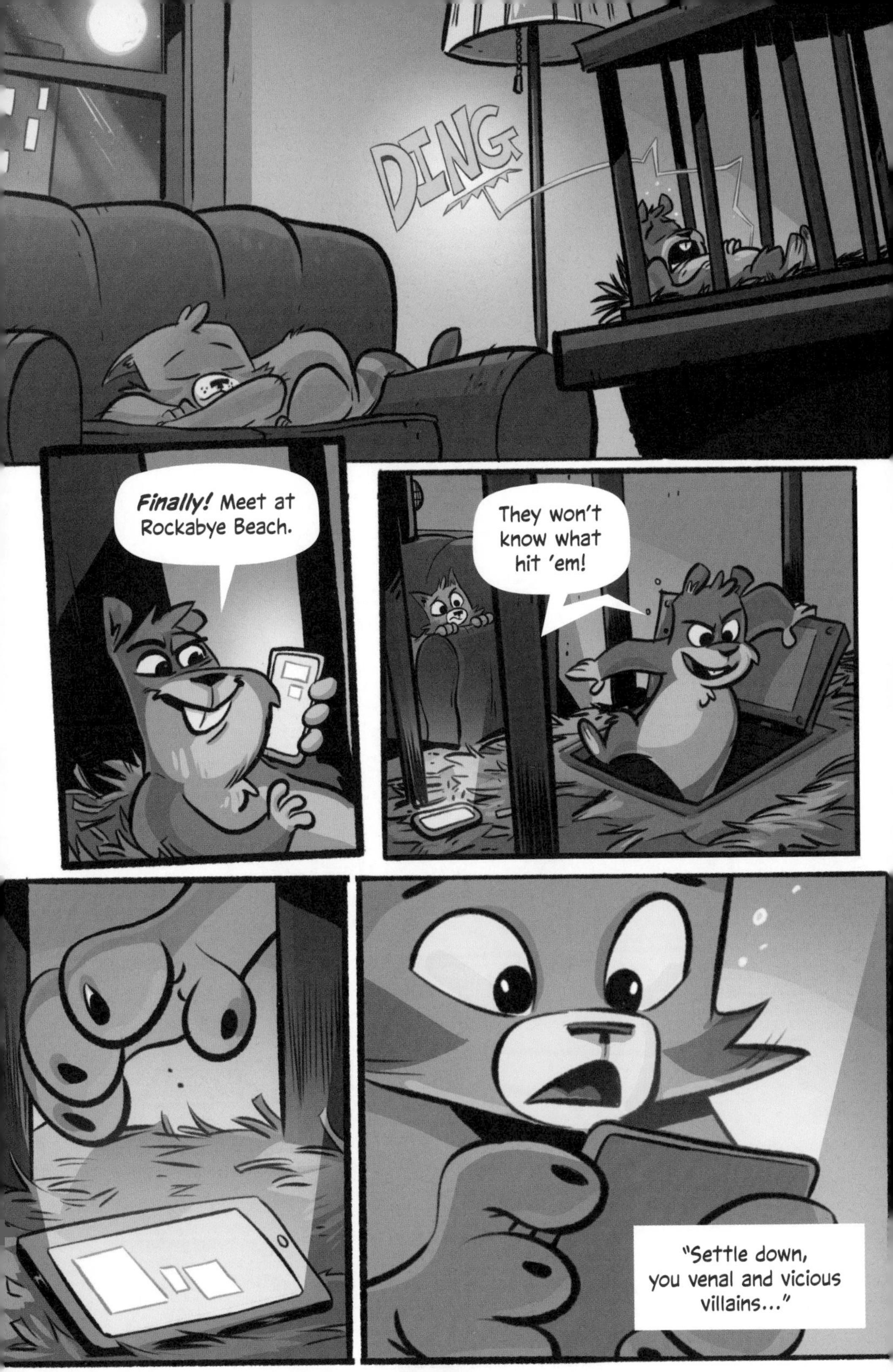
DING
Finally! Meet at Rockabye Beach.
They won't know what hit 'em!
"Settle down, you venal and vicious villains..."

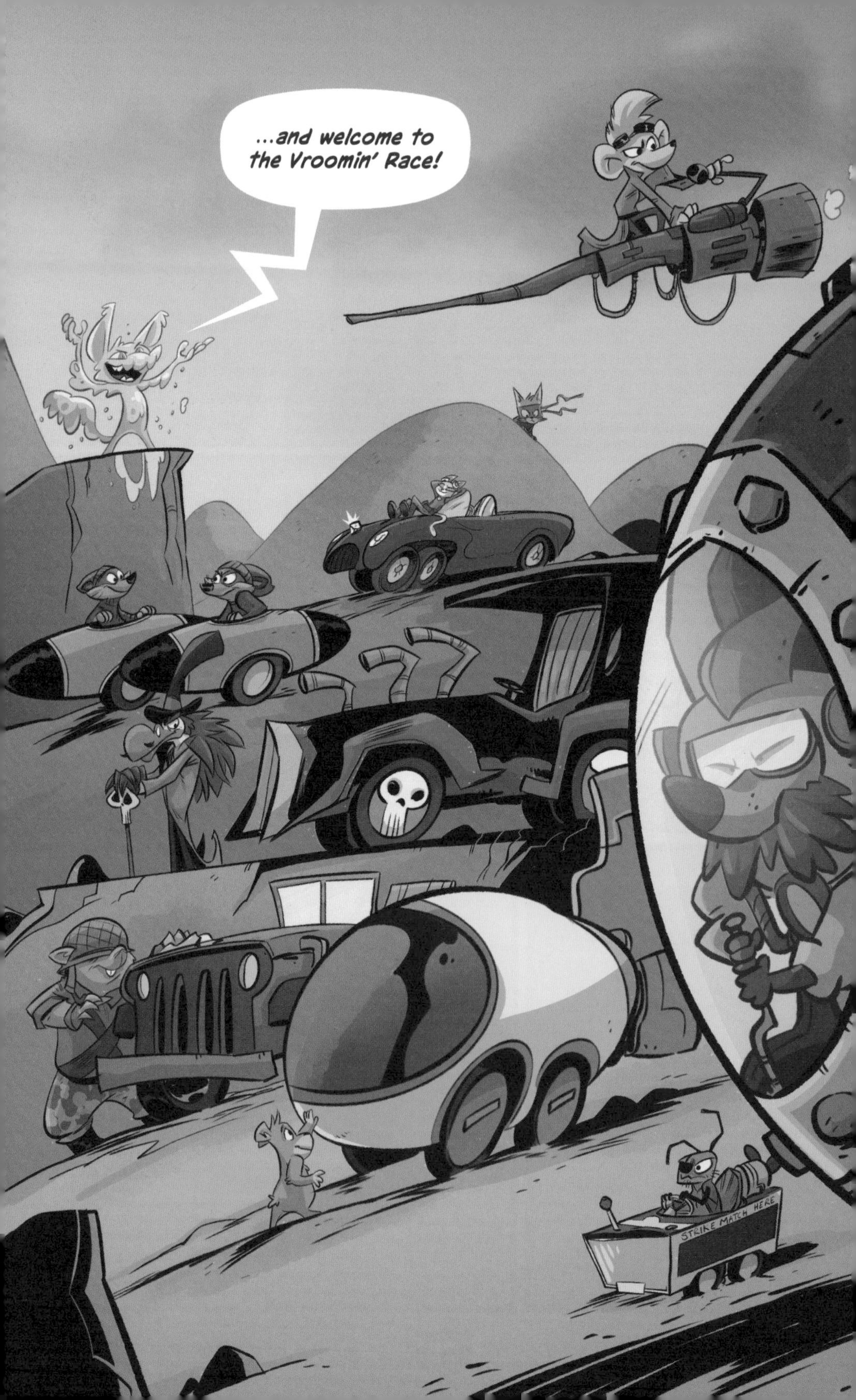
...and welcome to the Vroomin' Race!
STRIKE MATCH HERE

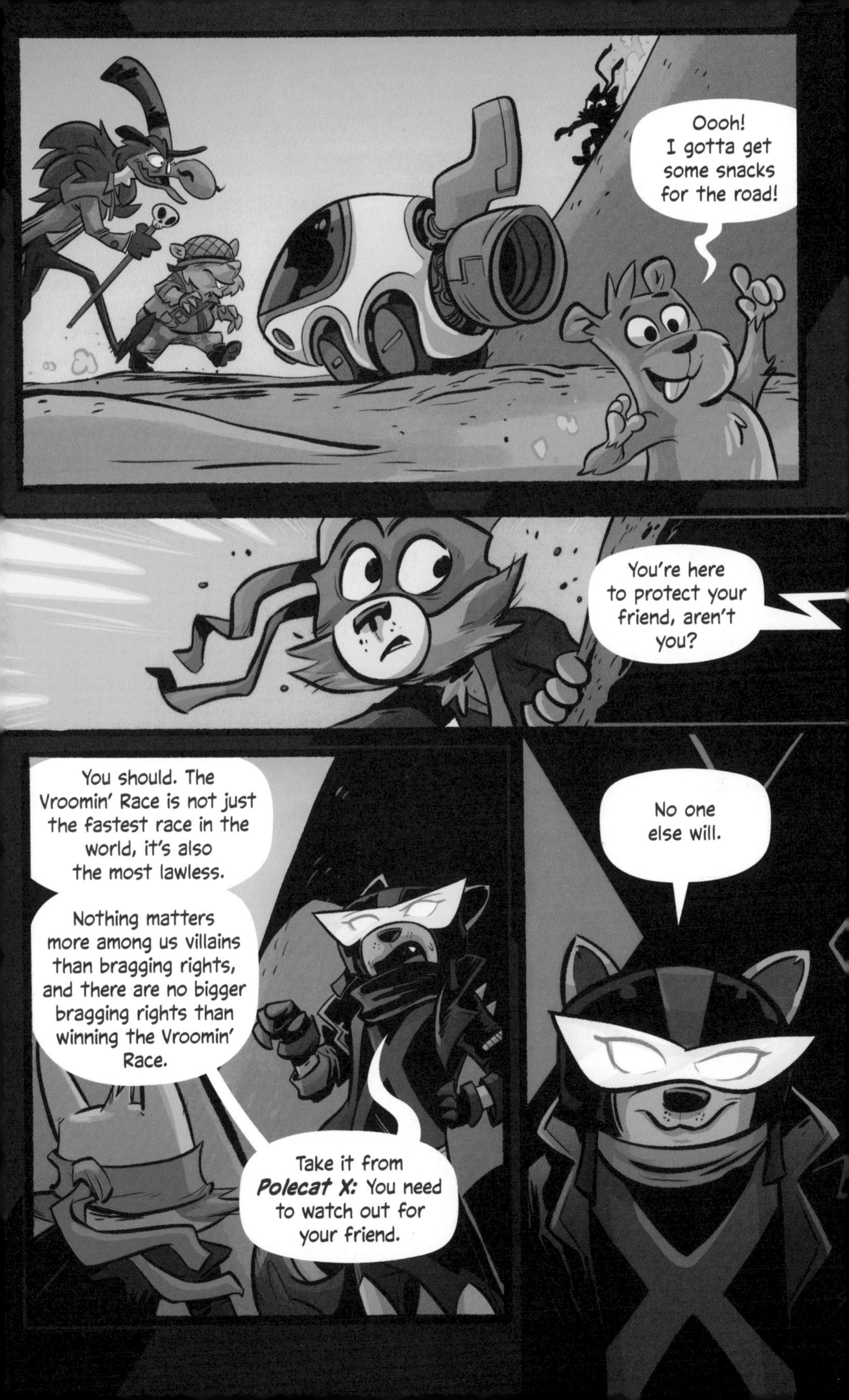
Oooh! I gotta get some snacks for the road!
You're here to protect your friend, aren't you?
You should. The Vroomin' Race is not just the fastest race in the world, it's also the most lawless.
Nothing matters more among us villains than bragging rights, and there are no bigger bragging rights than winning the Vroomin' Race.
Take it from Polecat X: You need to watch out for your friend.
No one else will.

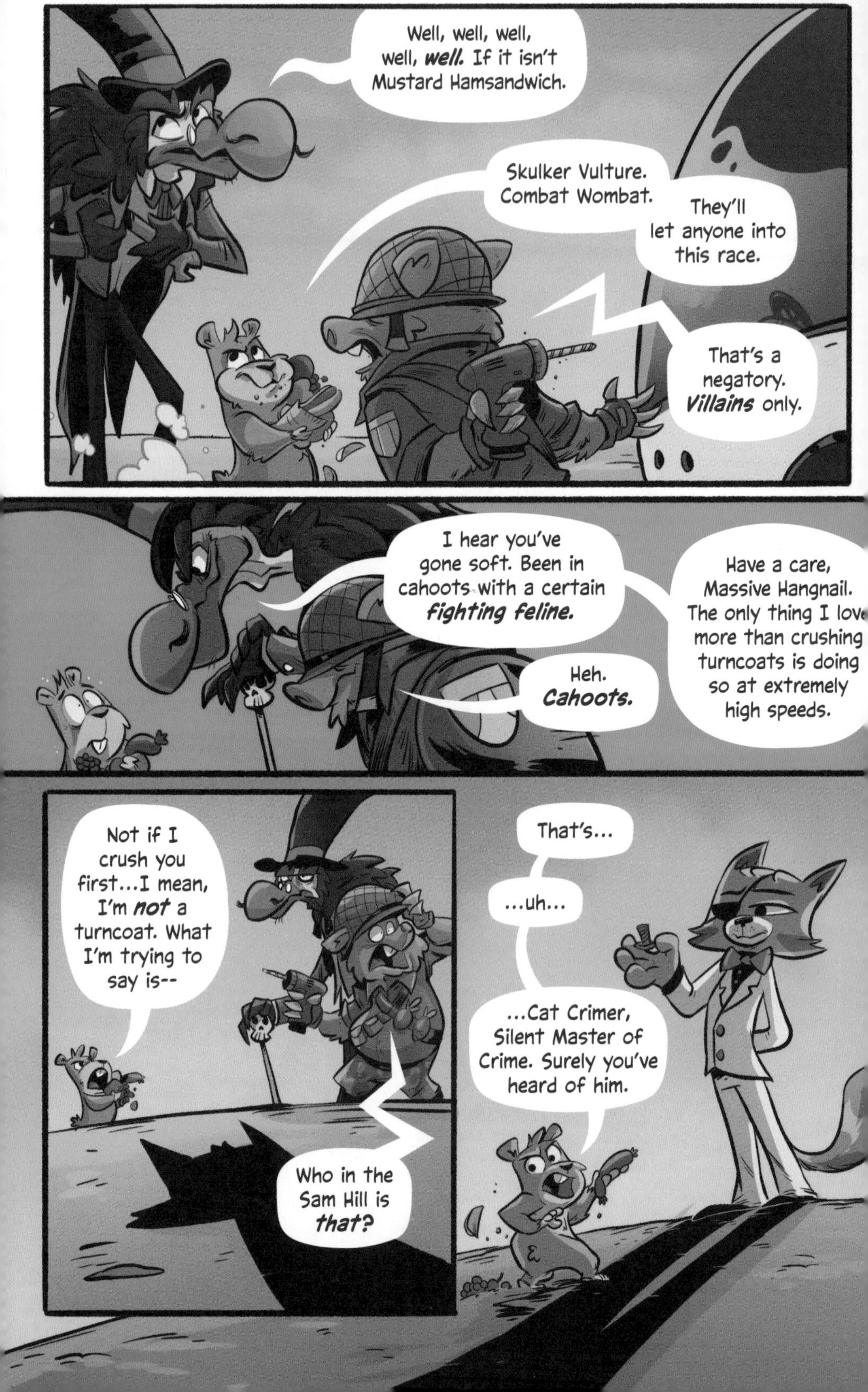
Well, well, well, well, ***well.*** If it isn't Mustard Hamsandwich.
Skulker Vulture. Combat Wombat.
They'll let anyone into this race.
That's a negatory. ***Villains*** only.
I hear you've gone soft. Been in cahoots with a certain ***fighting feline.***
Heh. ***Cahoots.***
Have a care, Massive Hangnail. The only thing I love more than crushing turncoats is doing so at extremely high speeds.
Not if I crush you first...I mean, I'm ***not*** a turncoat. What I'm trying to say is--
Who in the Sam Hill is ***that?***
That's...
...uh...
...Cat Crimer, Silent Master of Crime. Surely you've heard of him.

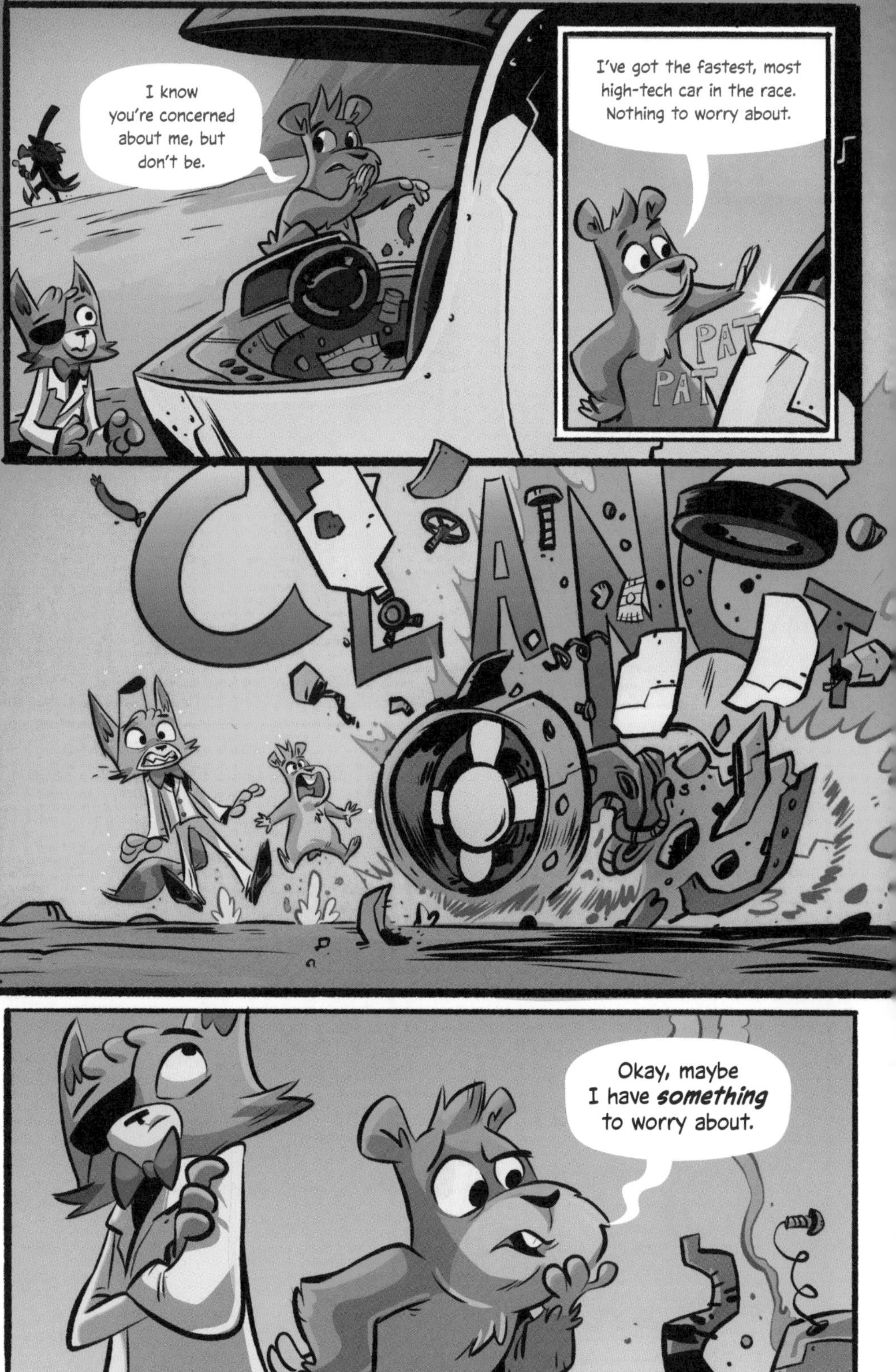
I know you're concerned about me, but don't be.
I've got the fastest, most high-tech car in the race. Nothing to worry about.
PAT
PAT
PAT
CLANG
Okay, maybe I have ***something*** to worry about.

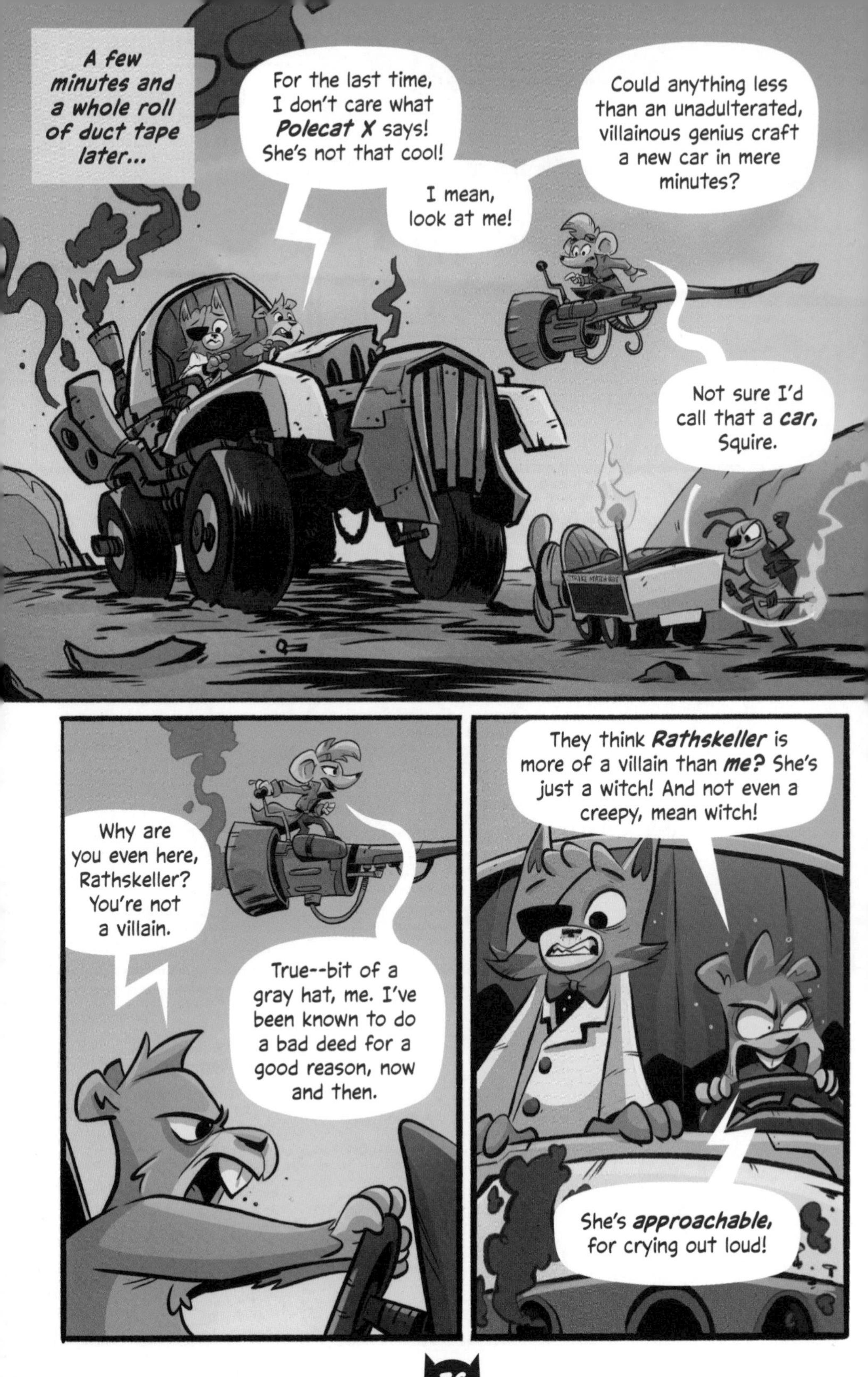
A few minutes and a whole roll of duct tape later...
For the last time, I don't care what Polecat X says! She's not that cool!
I mean, look at me!
Could anything less than an unadulterated, villainous genius craft a new car in mere minutes?
Not sure I'd call that a car, Squire.
Why are you even here, Rathskeller? You're not a villain.
True--bit of a gray hat, me. I've been known to do a bad deed for a good reason, now and then.
They think Rathskeller is more of a villain than me? She's just a witch! And not even a creepy, mean witch!
She's approachable, for crying out loud!

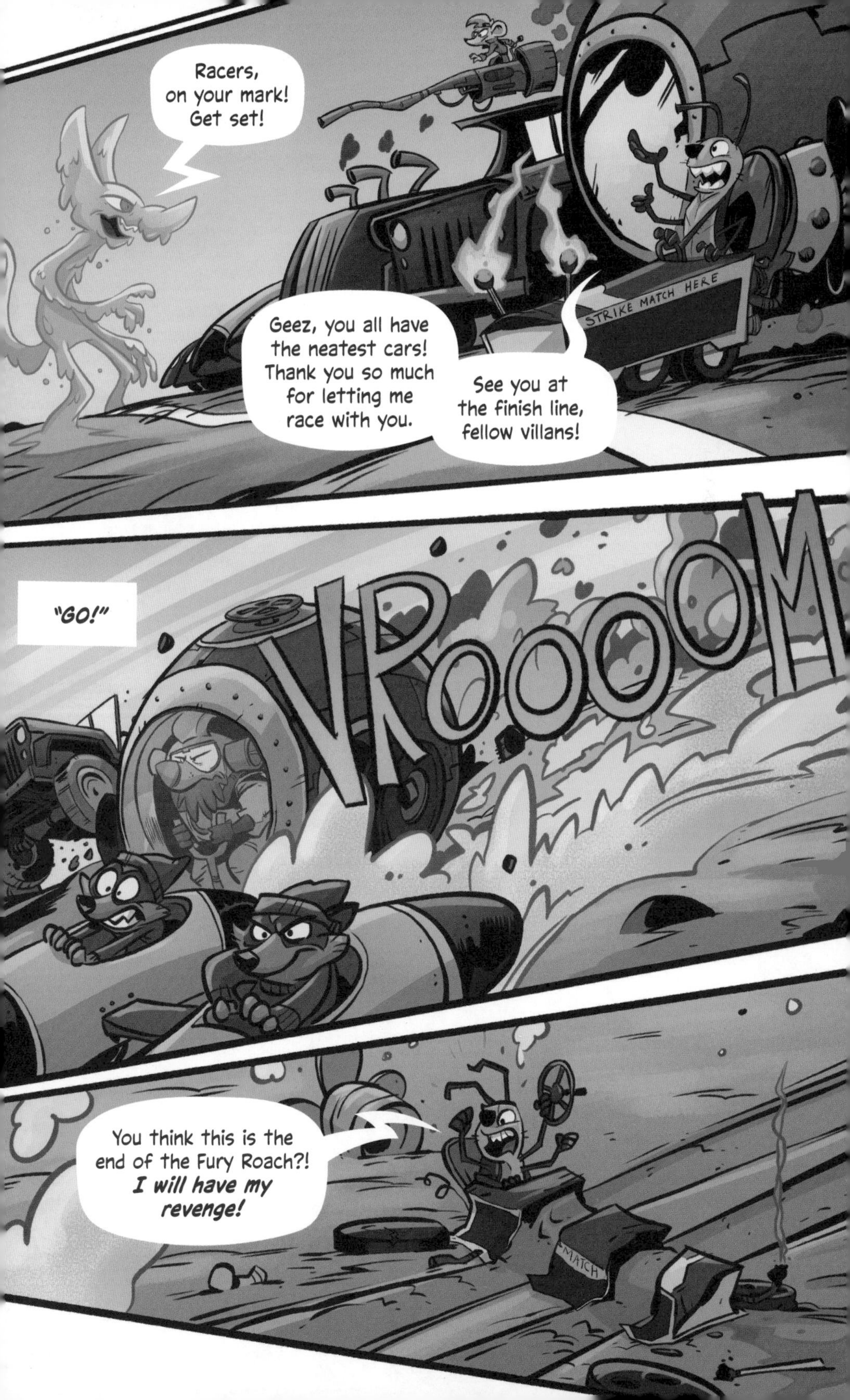
Racers, on your mark! Get set!
Geez, you all have the neatest cars! Thank you so much for letting me race with you.
STRIKE MATCH HERE
See you at the finish line, fellow villans!
"GO!"
VROOOOM
You think this is the end of the Fury Roach?! *I will have my revenge!*
MATCH

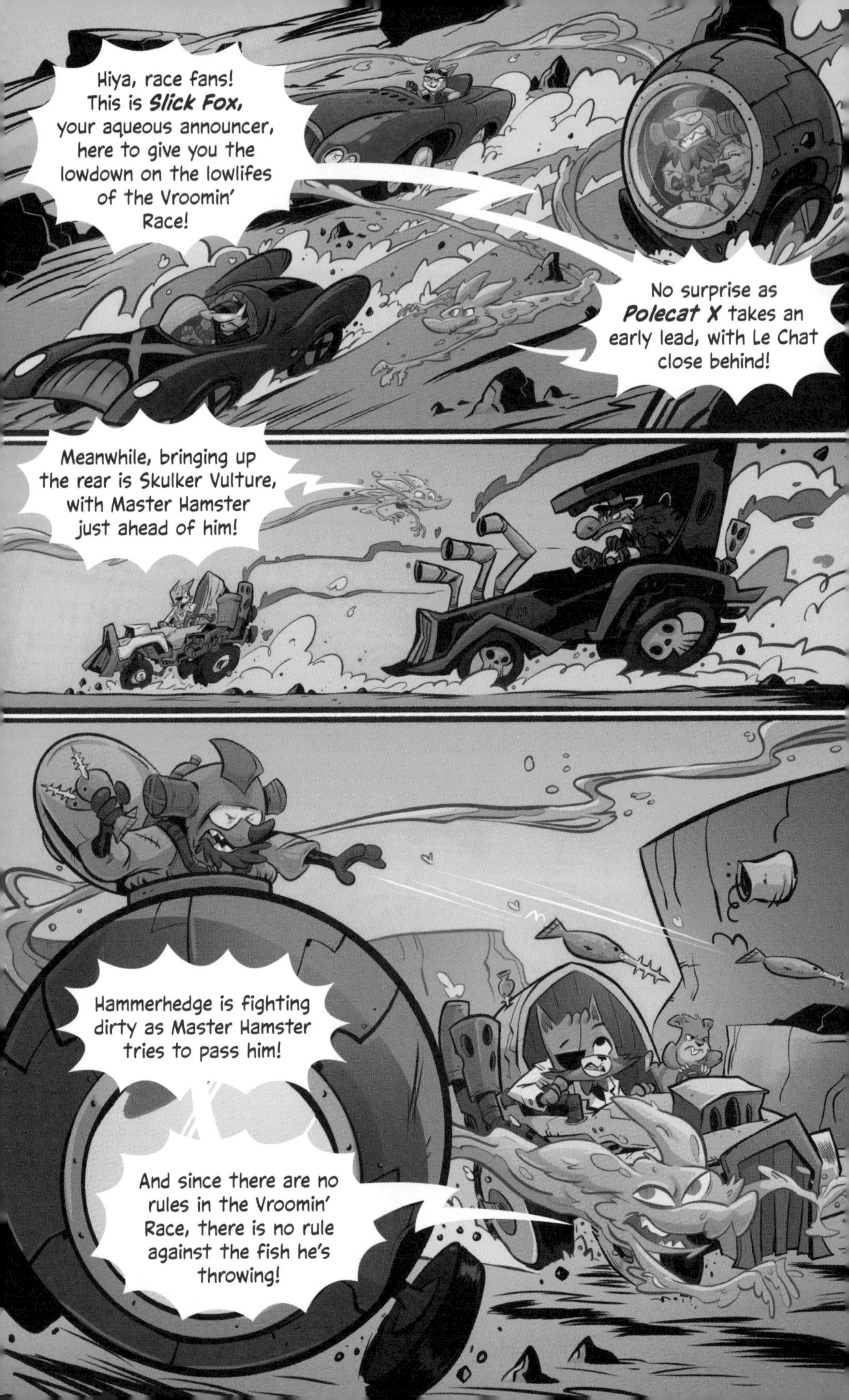
Hiya, race fans! This is **Slick Fox,** your aqueous announcer, here to give you the lowdown on the lowlifes of the Vroomin' Race!
No surprise as **Polecat X** takes an early lead, with Le Chat close behind!
Meanwhile, bringing up the rear is Skulker Vulture, with Master Hamster just ahead of him!
Hammerhedge is fighting dirty as Master Hamster tries to pass him!
And since there are no rules in the Vroomin' Race, there is no rule against the fish he's throwing!

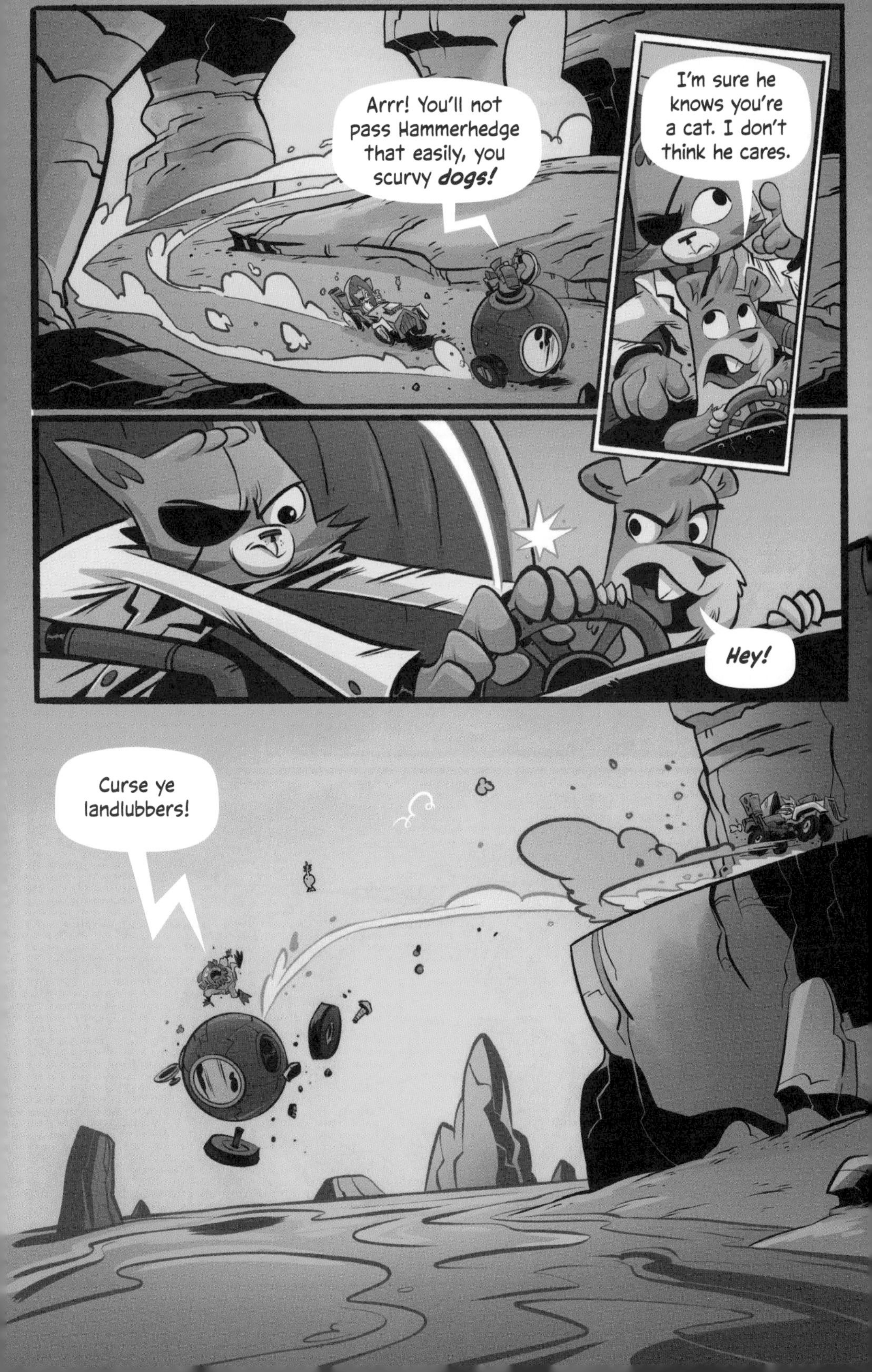
Arrr! You'll not pass Hammerhedge that easily, you scurvy *dogs!*
I'm sure he knows you're a cat. I don't think he cares.
Hey!
Curse ye landlubbers!

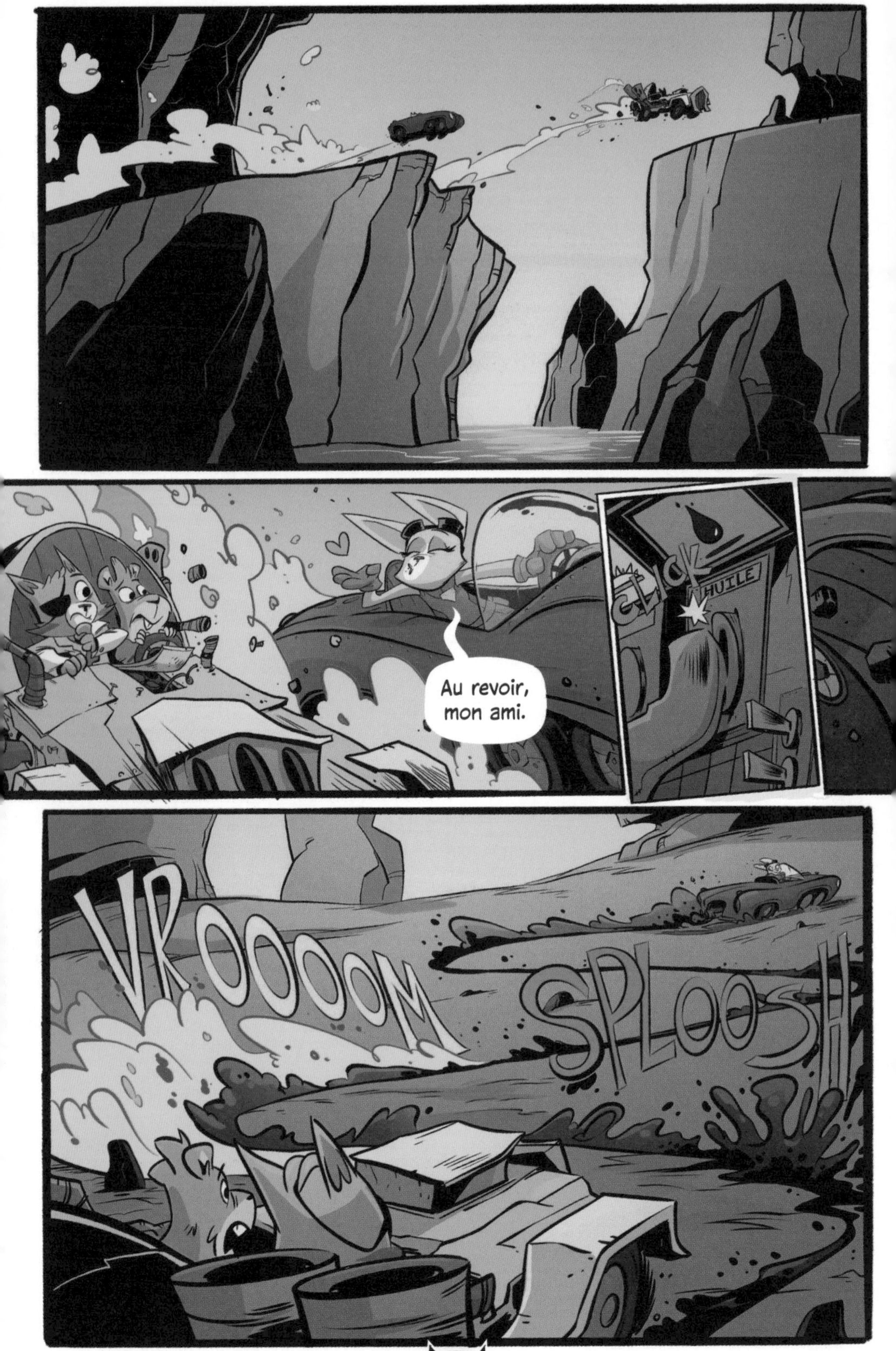
Au revoir,
mon ami.
HUILE
VROOOOM
SPLOOSH

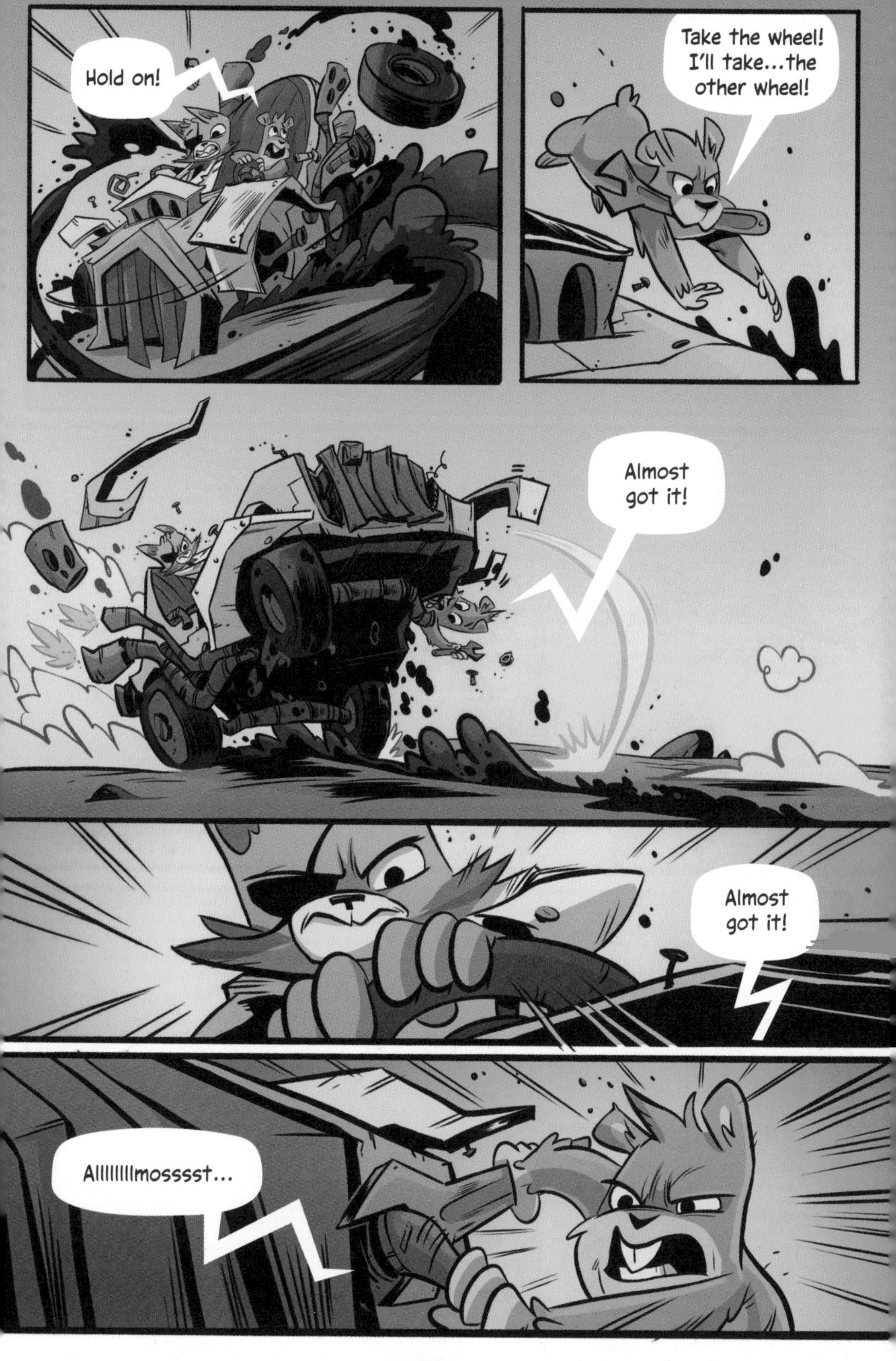
Hold on!
Take the wheel! I'll take...the other wheel!
Almost got it!
Almost got it!
Allllllllmosssst...

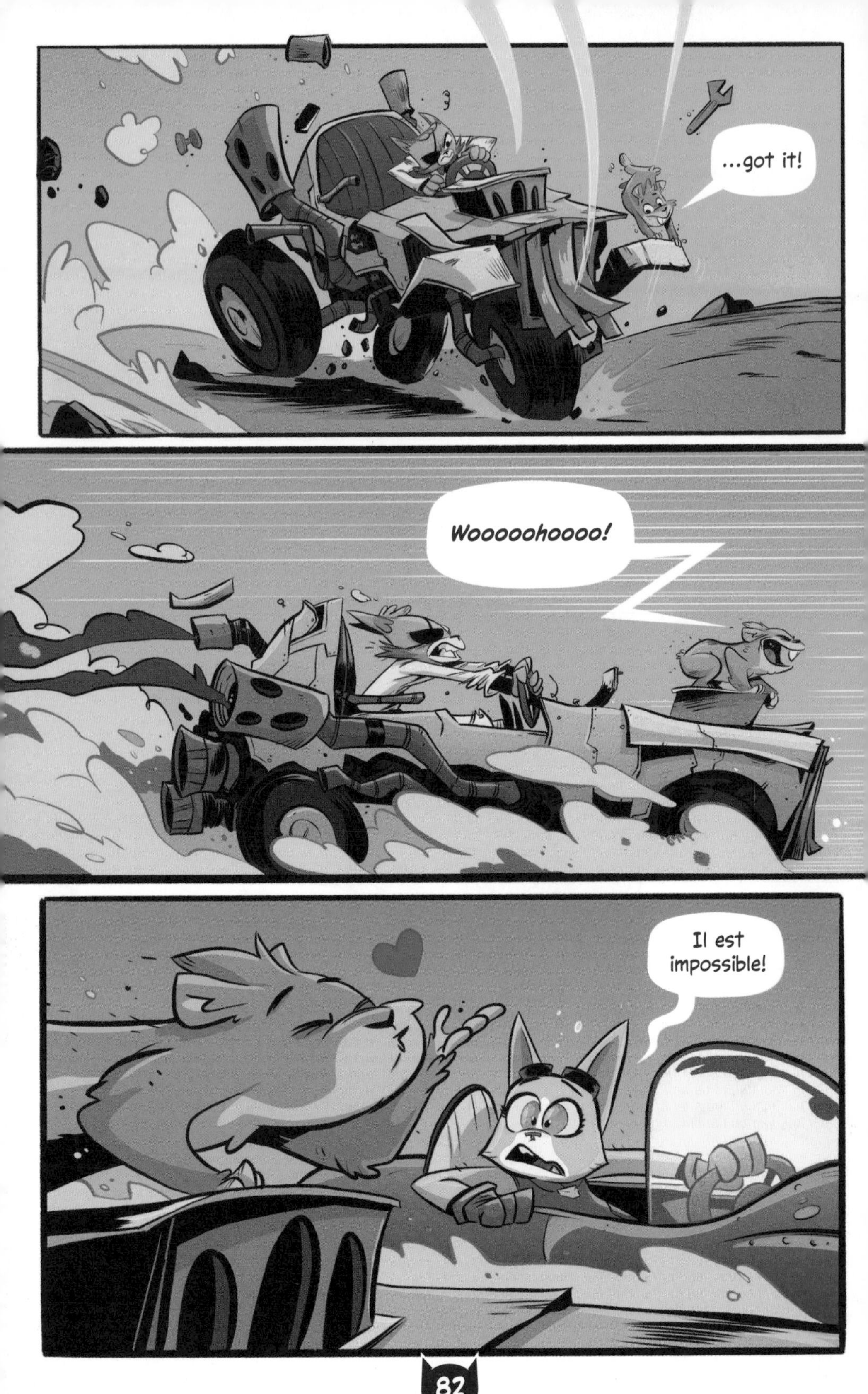
...got it!
Wooooohoooo!
Il est impossible!

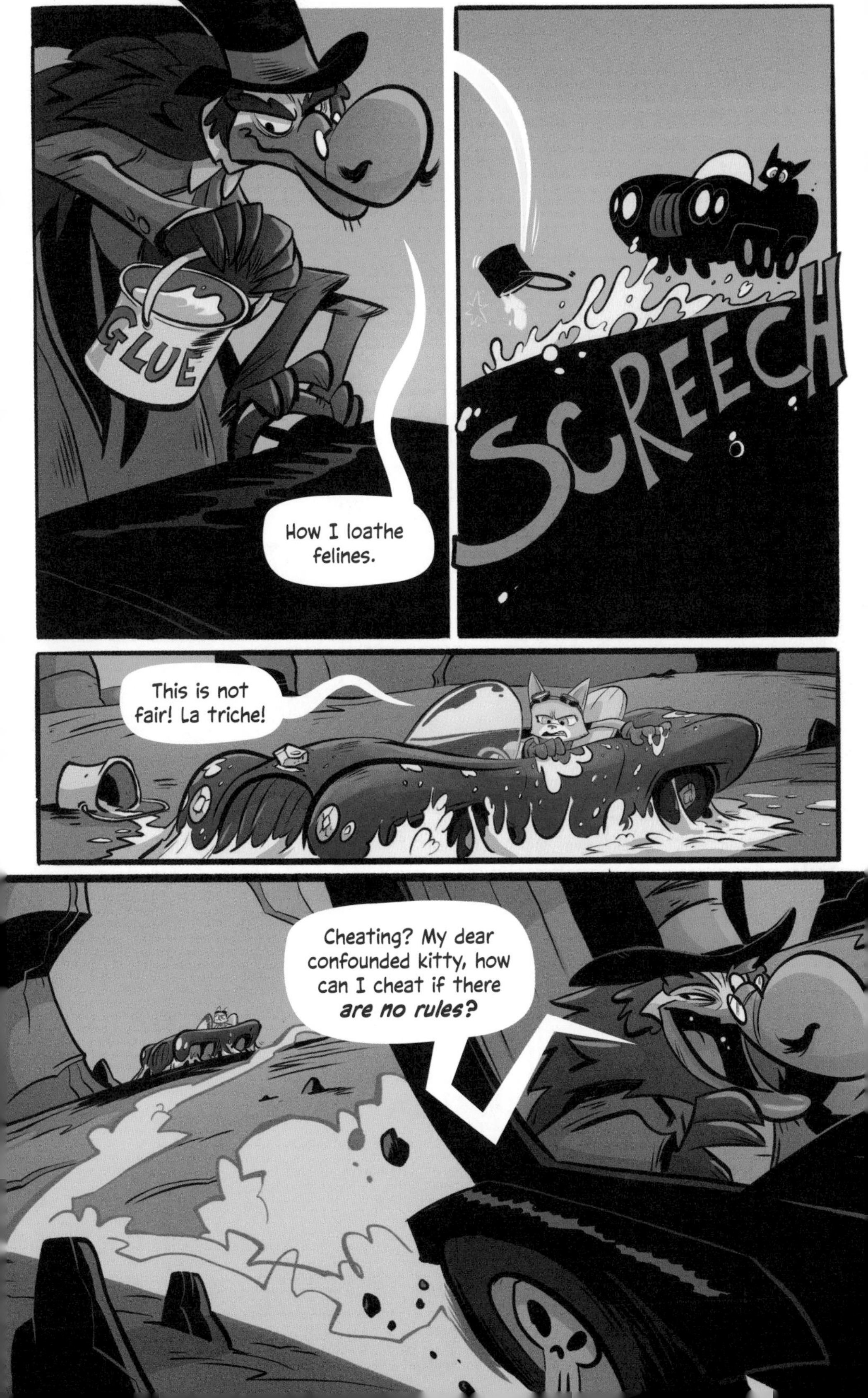
How I loathe felines.
SCREECH
This is not fair! La triche!
Cheating? My dear confounded kitty, how can I cheat if there *are no rules?*

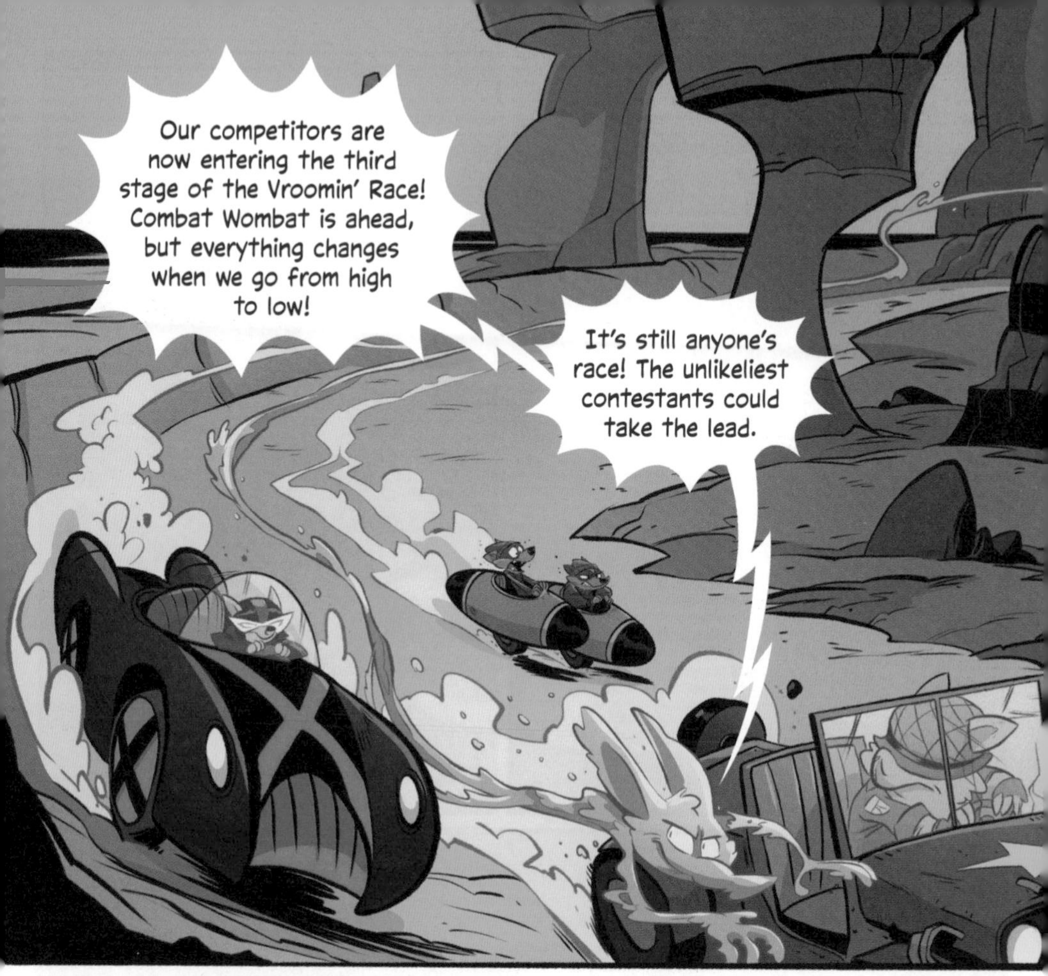
Our competitors are now entering the third stage of the Vroomin' Race! Combat Wombat is ahead, but everything changes when we go from high to low!
It's still anyone's race! The unlikeliest contestants could take the lead.

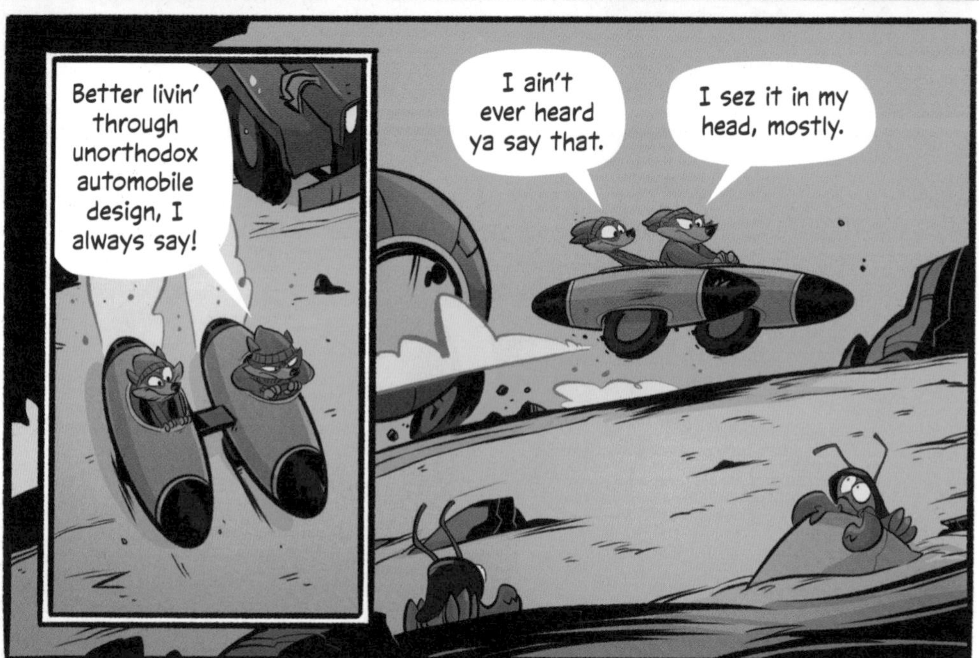
Better livin' through unorthodox automobile design, I always say!
I ain't ever heard ya say that.
I sez it in my head, mostly.

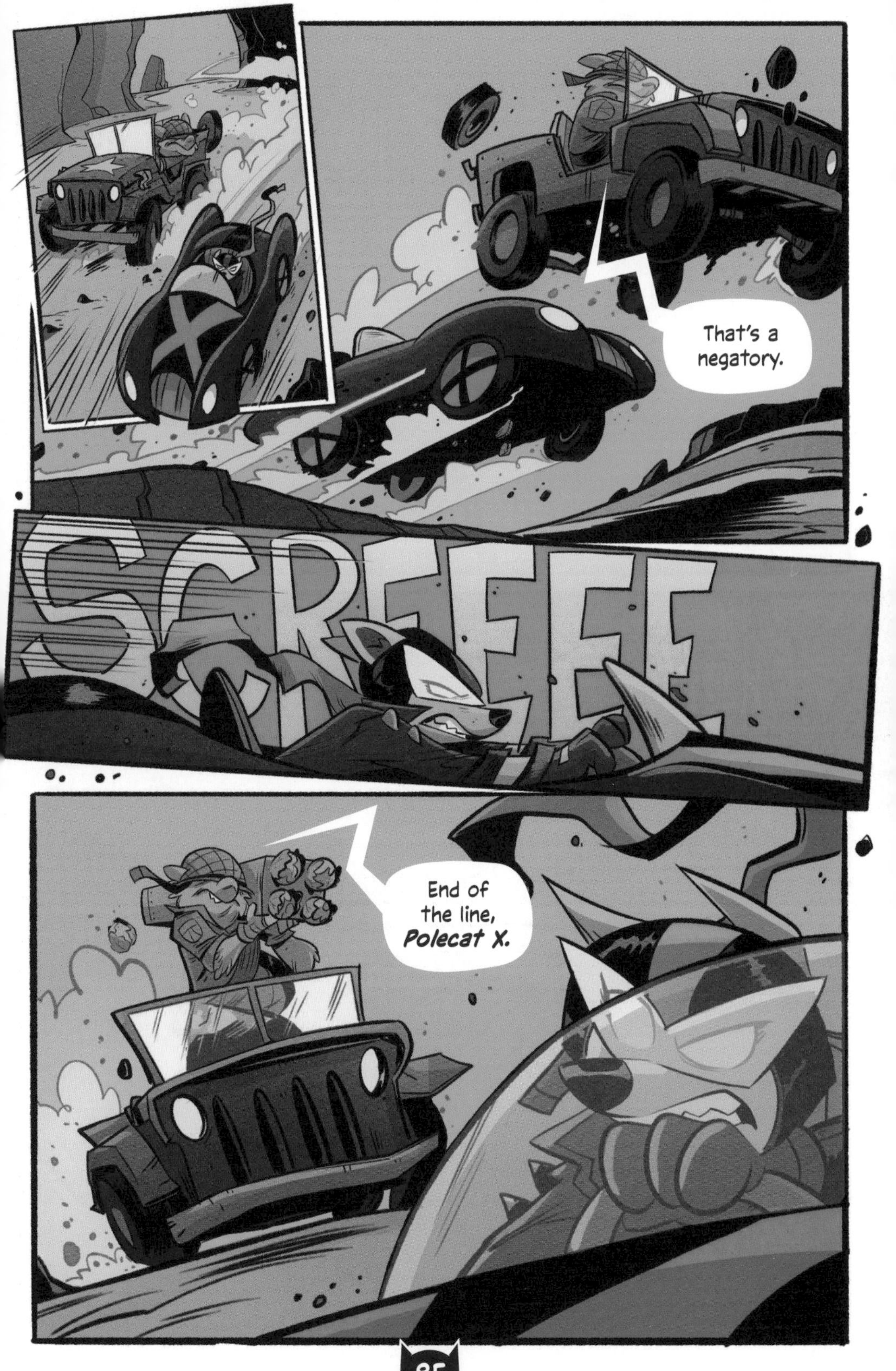
That's a negatory.
SCREEE
End of the line, *Polecat X.*

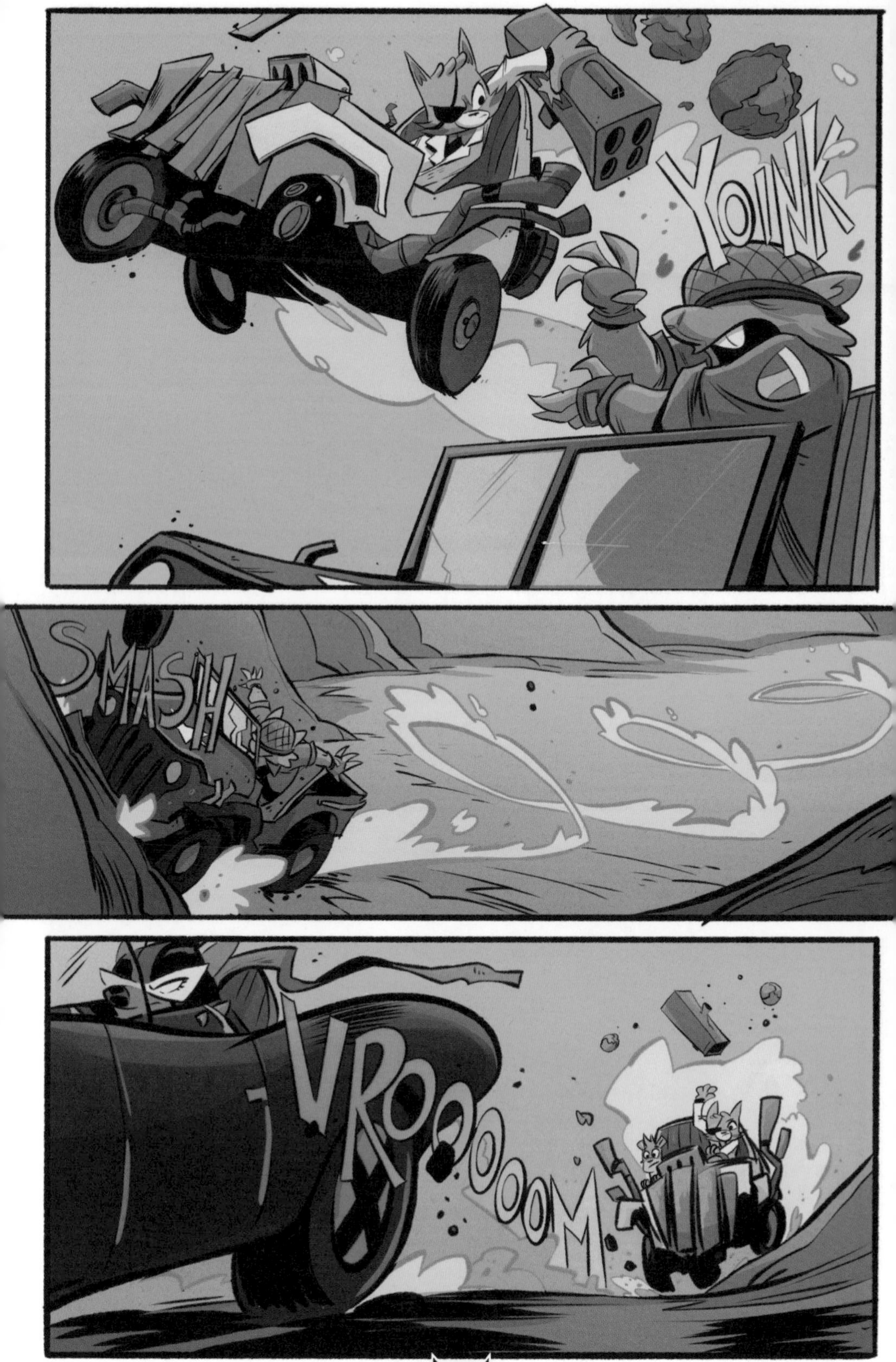
YOINK
SMASH
VROOOOOOM

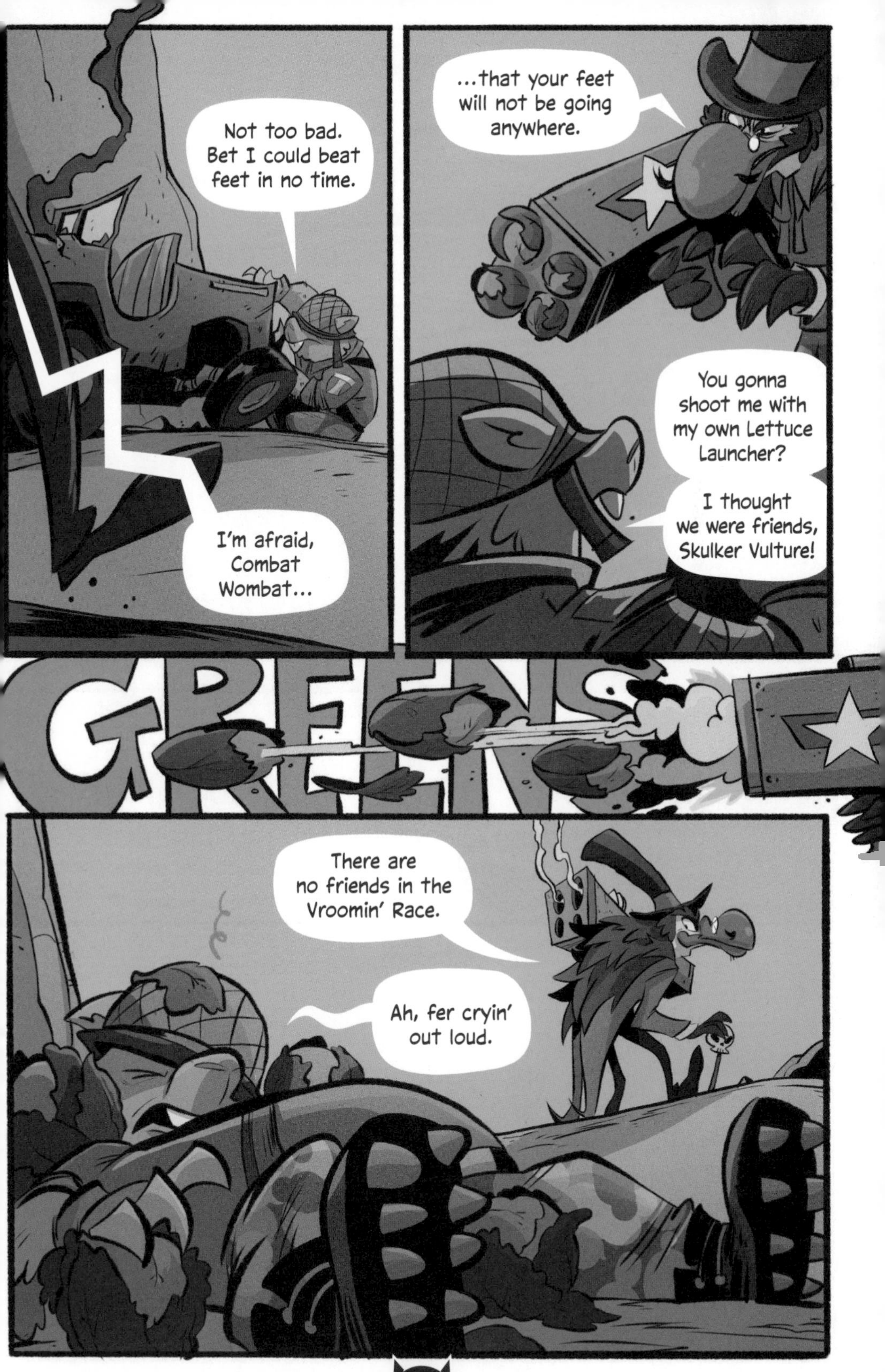
Not too bad. Bet I could beat feet in no time.
I'm afraid, Combat Wombat...
...that your feet will not be going anywhere.
You gonna shoot me with my own Lettuce Launcher?
I thought we were friends, Skulker Vulture!
GREENS
There are no friends in the Vroomin' Race.
Ah, fer cryin' out loud.

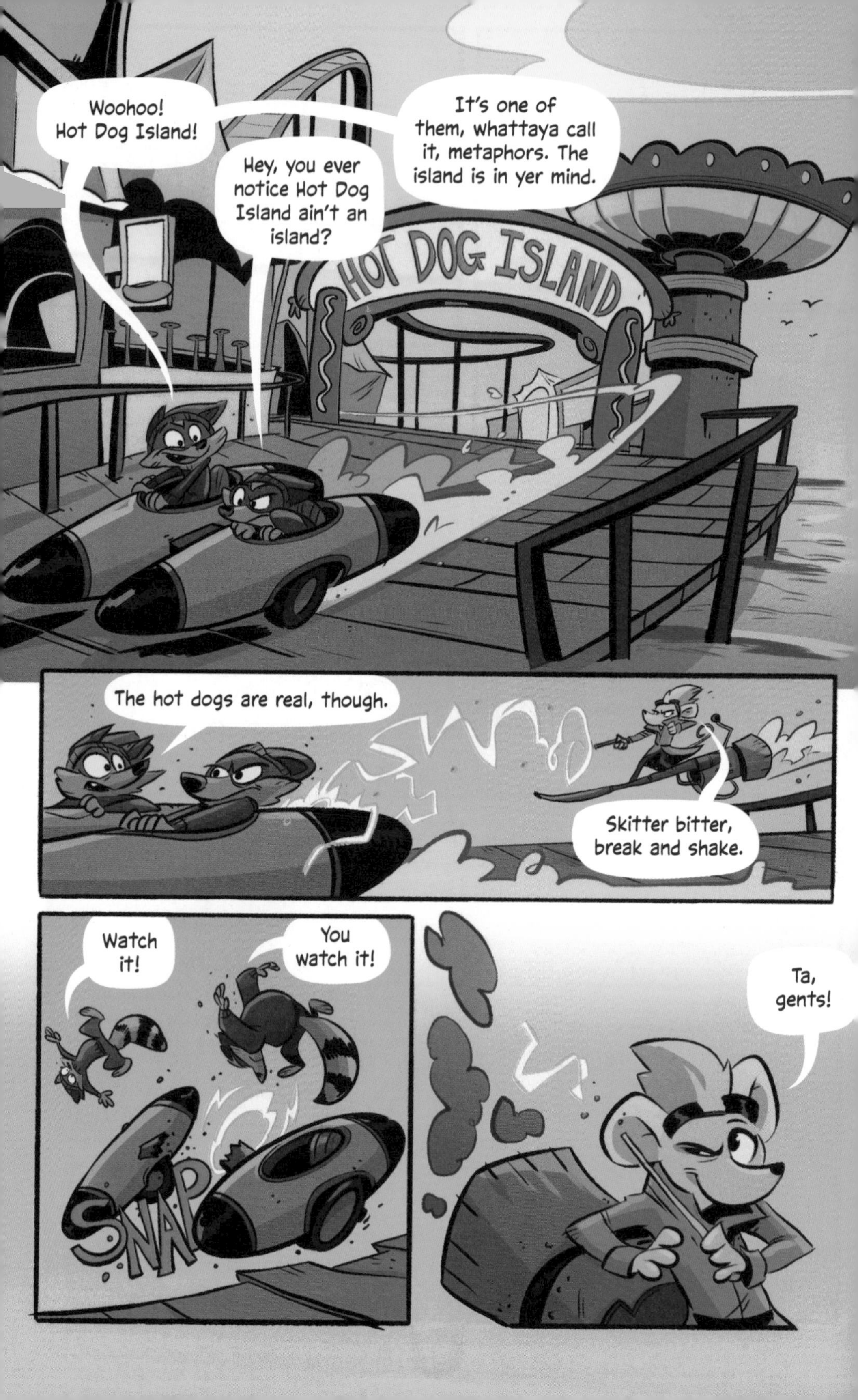
Woohoo! Hot Dog Island!
Hey, you ever notice Hot Dog Island ain't an island?
It's one of them, whattaya call it, metaphors. The island is in yer mind.
HOT DOG ISLAND
The hot dogs are real, though.
Skitter bitter, break and shake.
Watch it!
You watch it!
SNAP
Ta, gents!

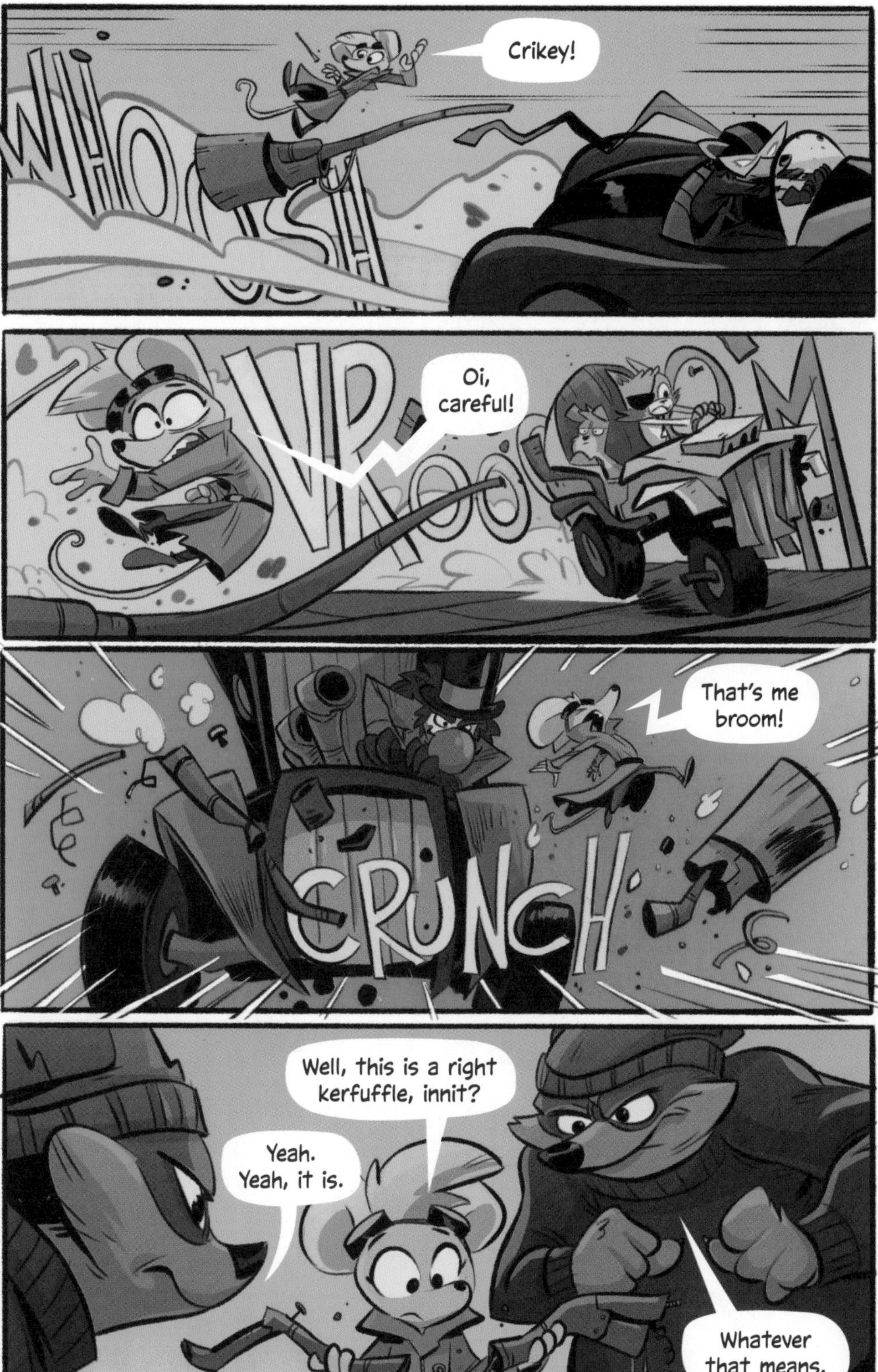
WHOOSH
Crikey!
VROOOM
Oi, careful!
That's me broom!
CRUNCH
Well, this is a right kerfuffle, innit?
Yeah. Yeah, it is.
Whatever that means.

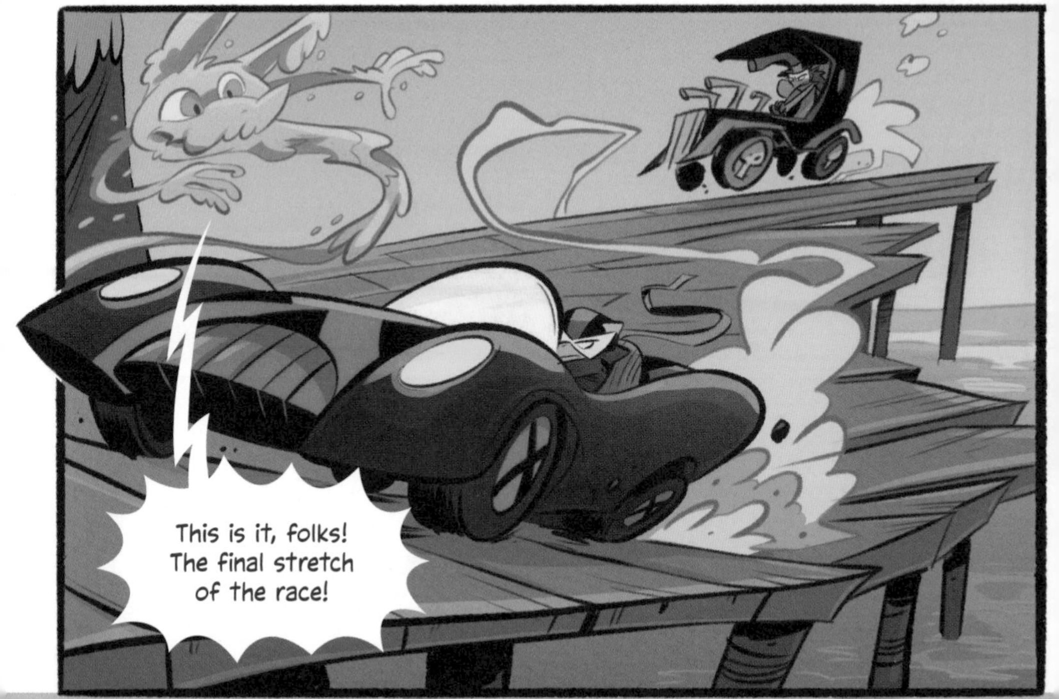
This is it, folks! The final stretch of the race!

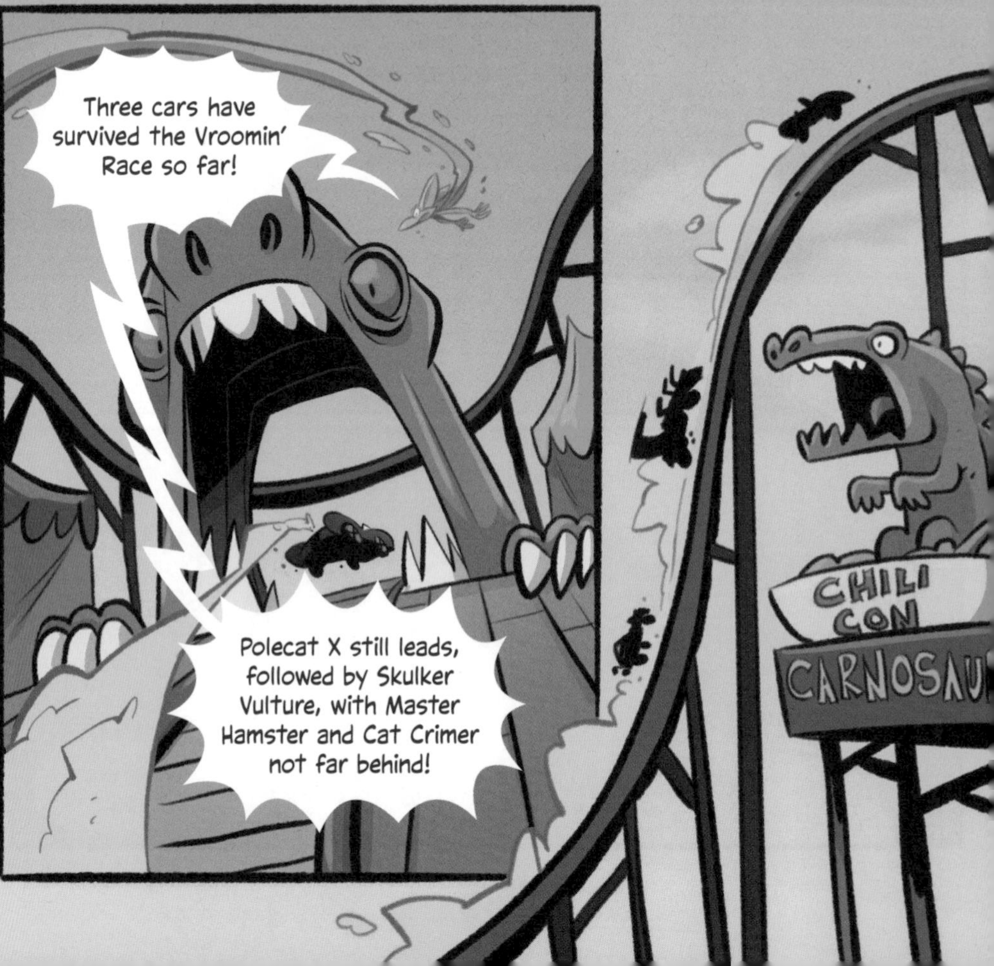
Three cars have survived the Vroomin' Race so far!
Polecat X still leads, followed by Skulker Vulture, with Master Hamster and Cat Crimer not far behind!
CHILI CON
CARNOSAU

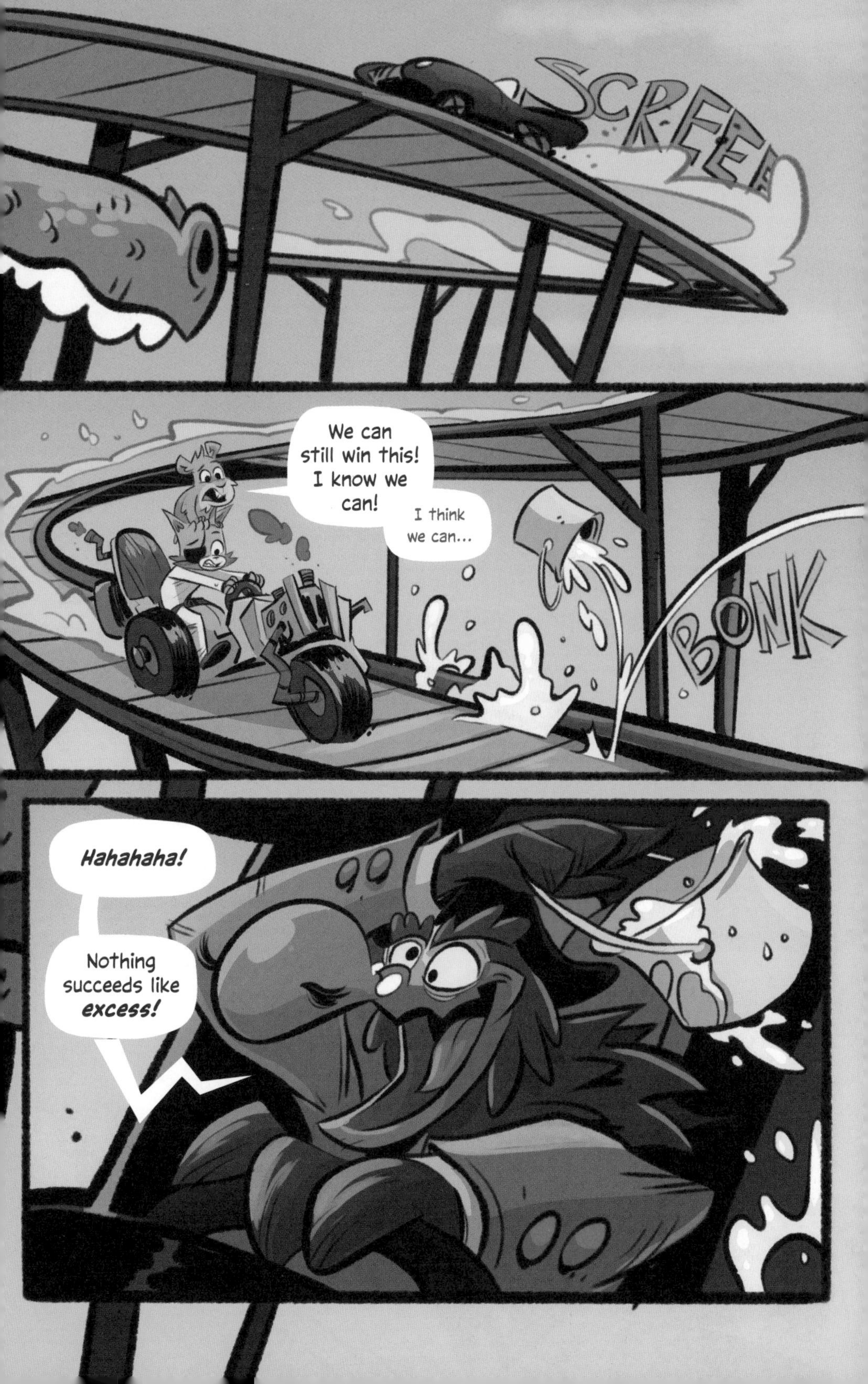
SCREEE
We can still win this! I know we can!
I think we can...
BONK
Hahahaha!
Nothing succeeds like ***excess!***

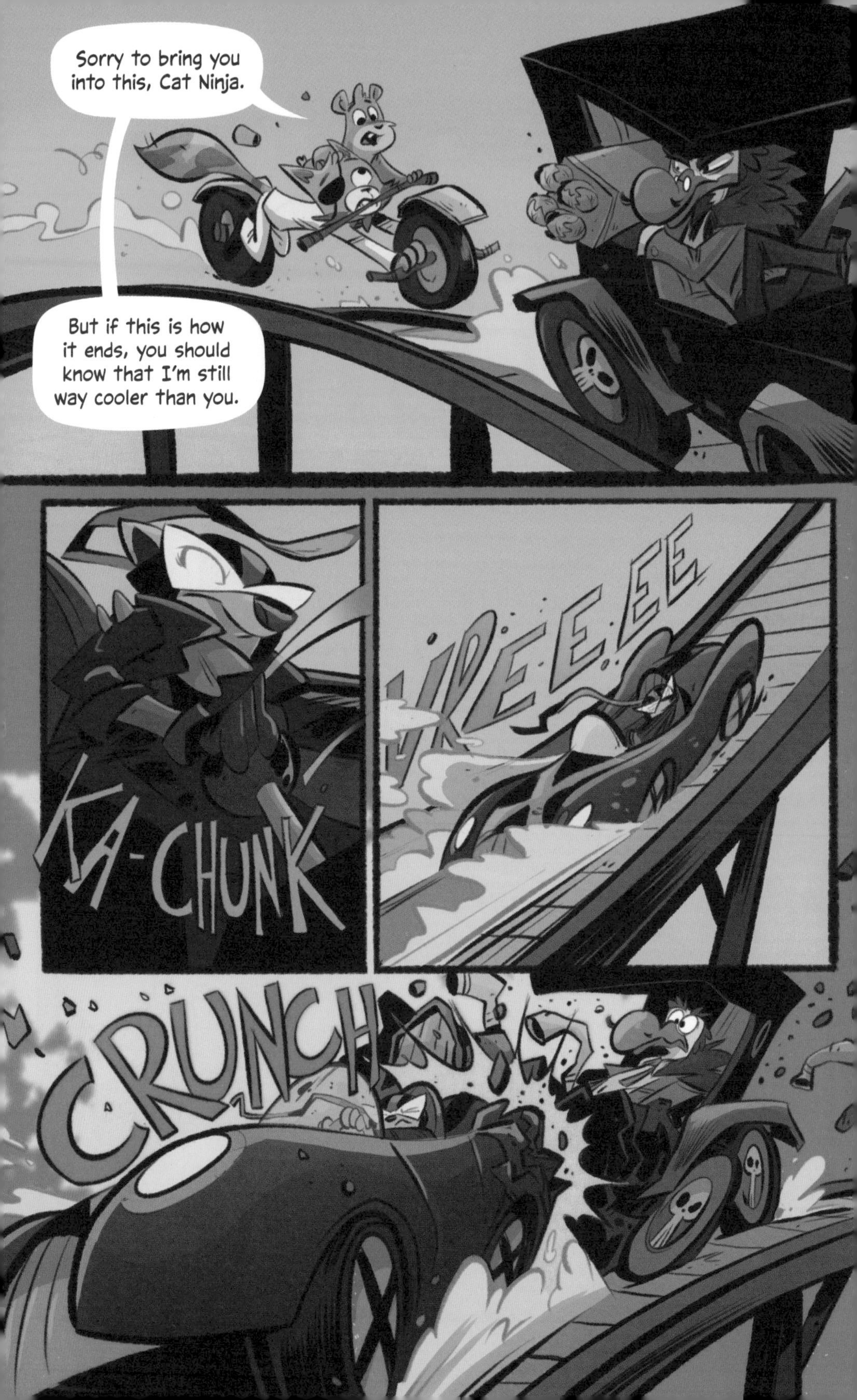
Sorry to bring you into this, Cat Ninja.
But if this is how it ends, you should know that I'm still way cooler than you.
KA-CHUNK
CRUNCH

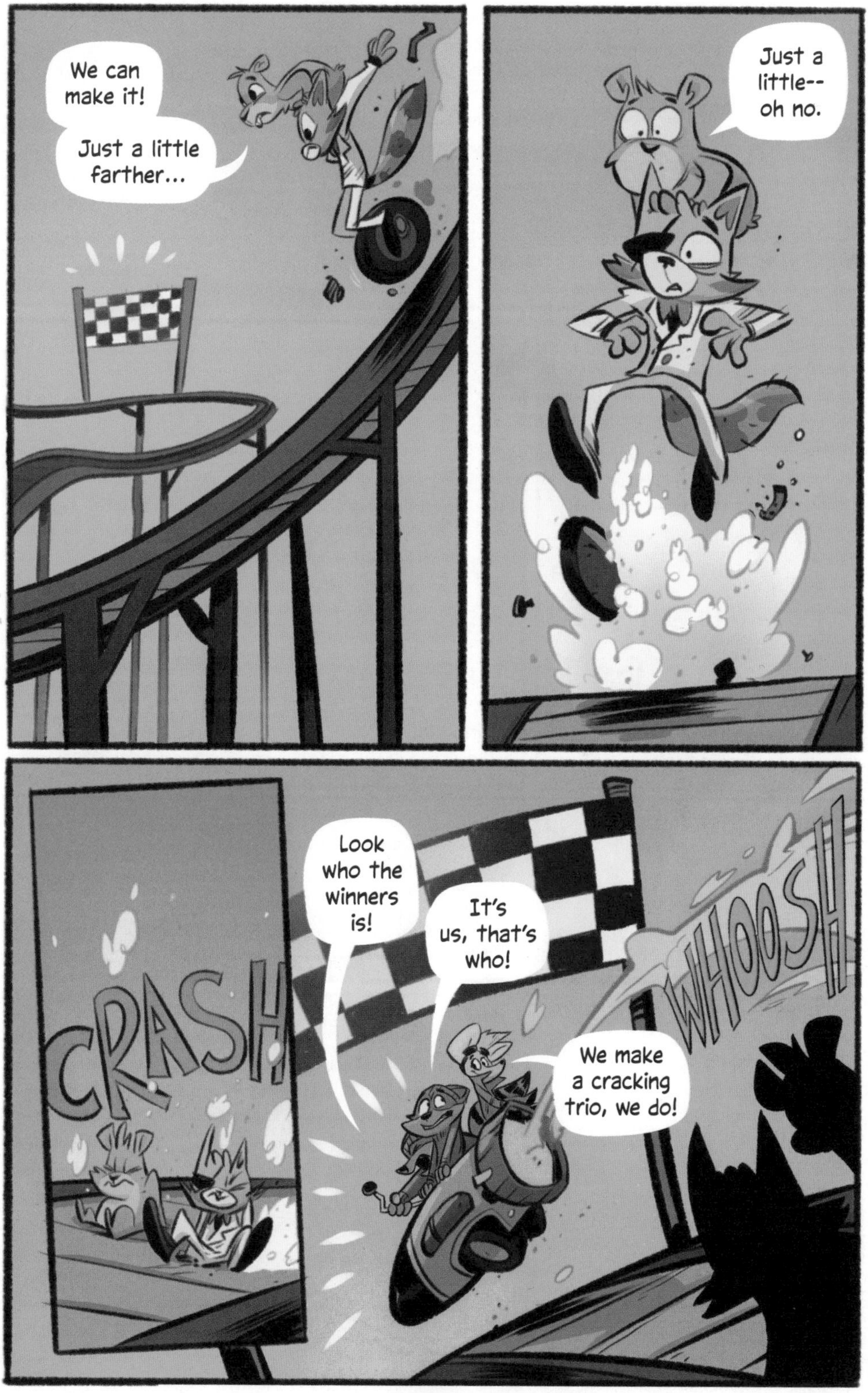
We can make it!
Just a little farther...
Just a little-- oh no.
CRASH
Look who the winners is!
It's us, that's who!
We make a cracking trio, we do!
WHOOSH

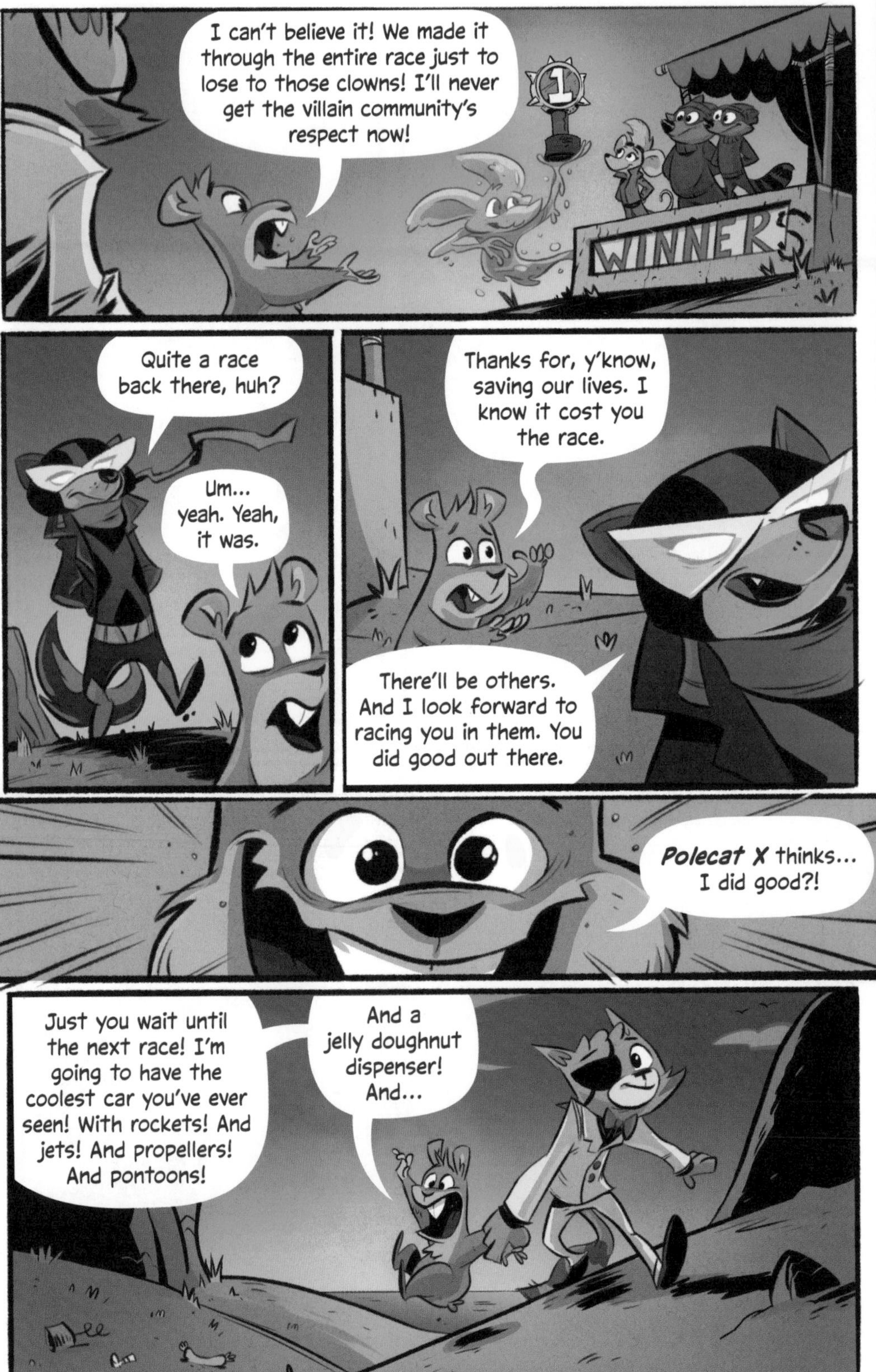
I can't believe it! We made it through the entire race just to lose to those clowns! I'll never get the villain community's respect now!
1
WINNERS
Quite a race back there, huh?
Um... yeah. Yeah, it was.
Thanks for, y'know, saving our lives. I know it cost you the race.
There'll be others. And I look forward to racing you in them. You did good out there.
Polecat X thinks... I did good?!
Just you wait until the next race! I'm going to have the coolest car you've ever seen! With rockets! And jets! And propellers! And pontoons!
And a jelly doughnut dispenser! And...

Bat Ninja

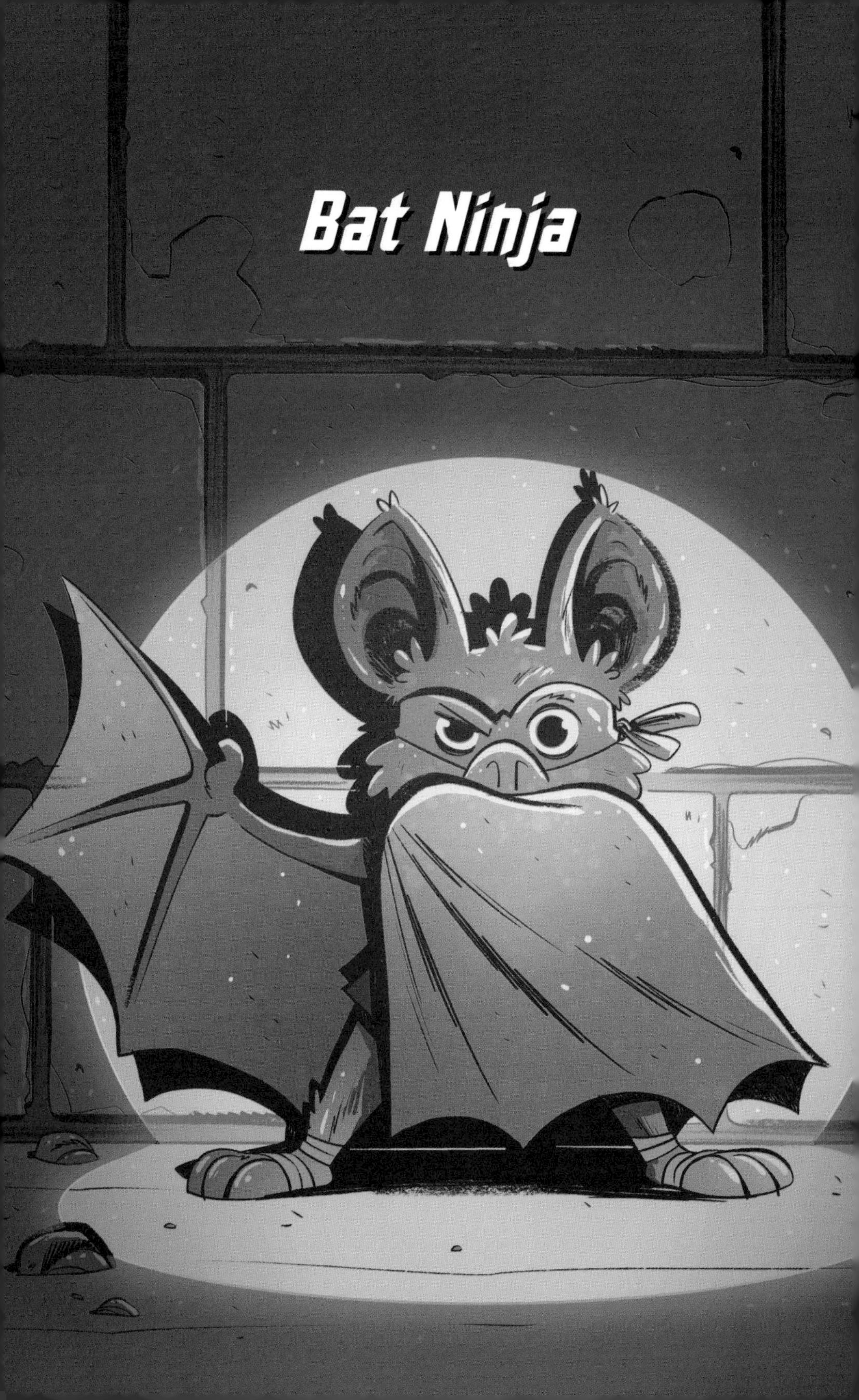

Dan Nordskog

Illustrated by
Eduardo Medeiros

Colors by
Warren Wucinich

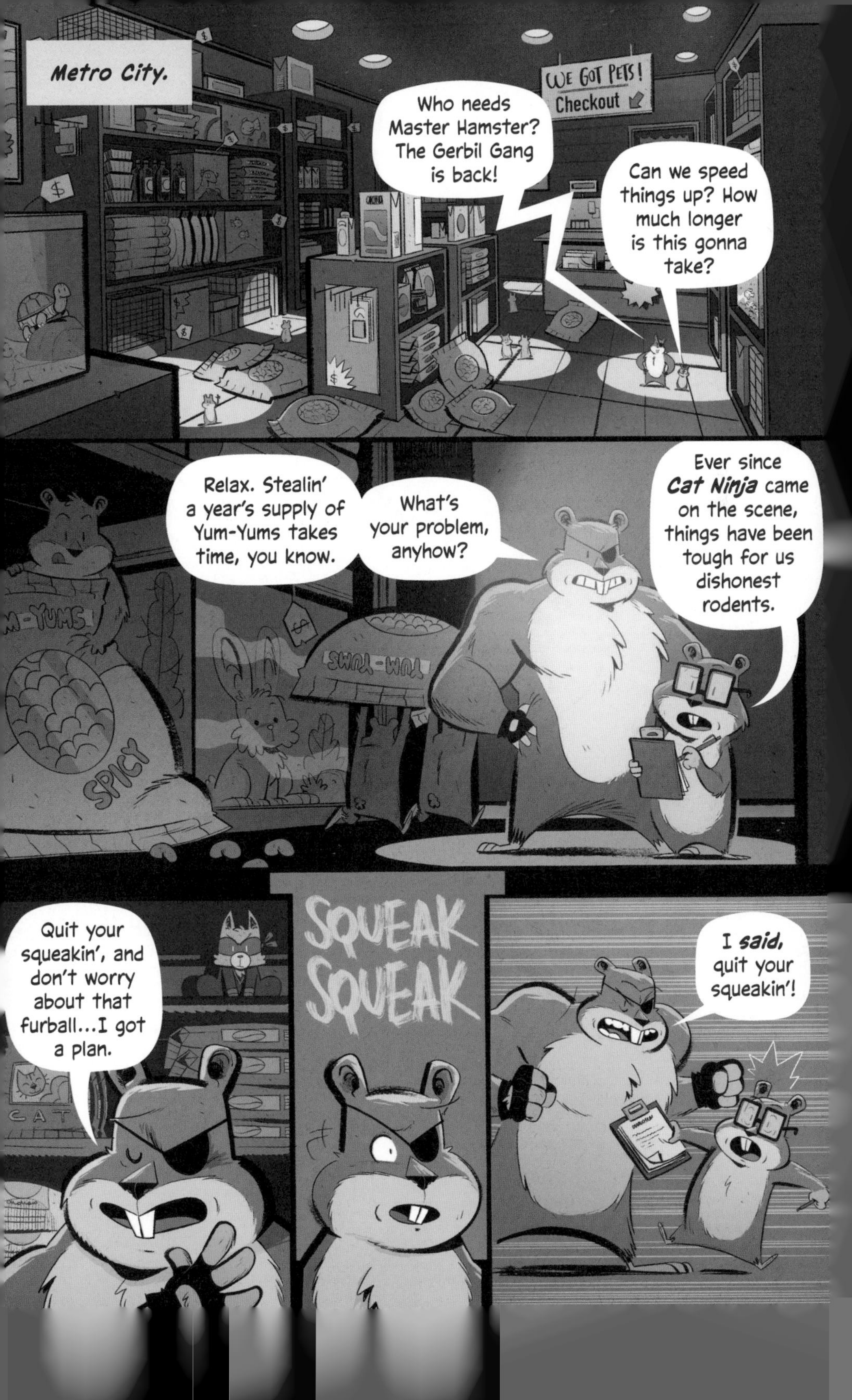

Metro City.
WE GOT PETS!
Checkout
Who needs Master Hamster? The Gerbil Gang is back!
Can we speed things up? How much longer is this gonna take?
Relax. Stealin' a year's supply of Yum-Yums takes time, you know.
What's your problem, anyhow?
Ever since *Cat Ninja* came on the scene, things have been tough for us dishonest rodents.
YUM-YUMS
SPICY
Quit your squeakin', and don't worry about that furball...I got a plan.
CAT
SQUEAK SQUEAK
I *said,* quit your squeakin'!

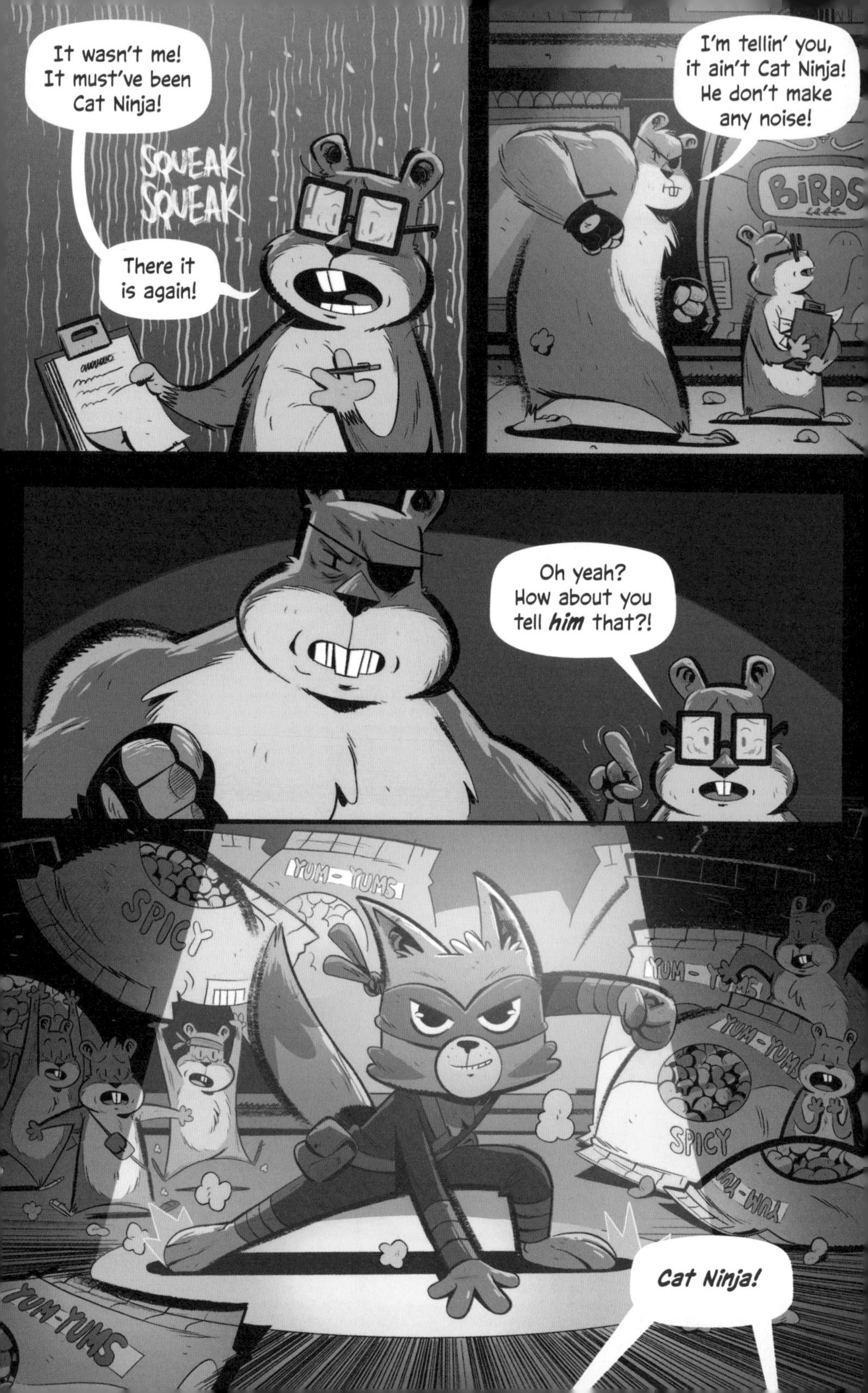
It wasn't me! It must've been Cat Ninja!
SQUEAK SQUEAK
There it is again!
I'm tellin' you, it ain't Cat Ninja! He don't make any noise!
BIRDS
Oh yeah? How about you tell *him* that?!
YUM-YUMS
SPICY
YUM-YUMS
YUM-YUMS
SPICY
YUM-YUMS
YUM-YUMS
Cat Ninja!

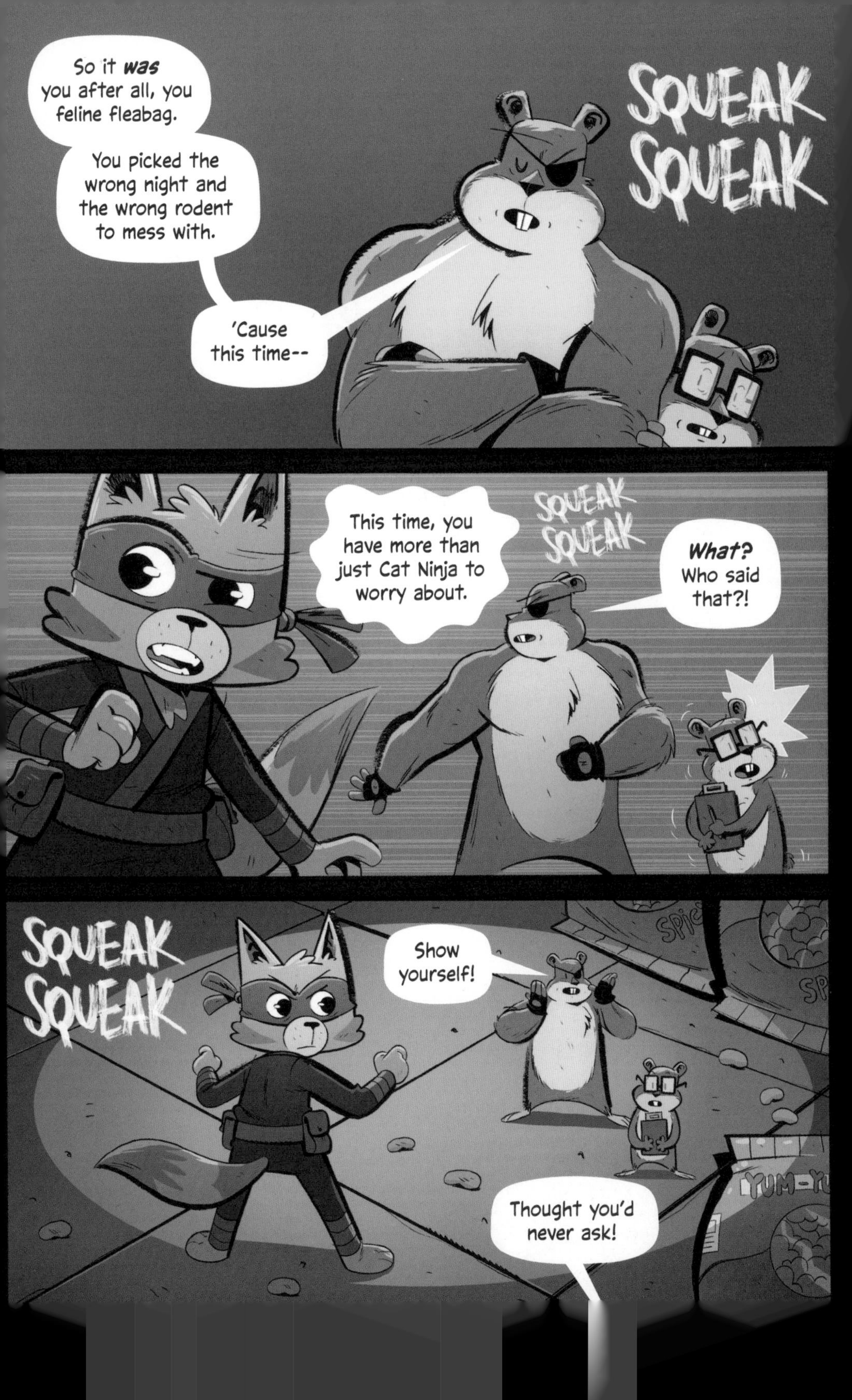

So it *was* you after all, you feline fleabag.
You picked the wrong night and the wrong rodent to mess with.
SQUEAK SQUEAK
'Cause this time--
This time, you have more than just Cat Ninja to worry about.
SQUEAK SQUEAK
What? Who said that?!
SQUEAK SQUEAK
Show yourself!
Thought you'd never ask!

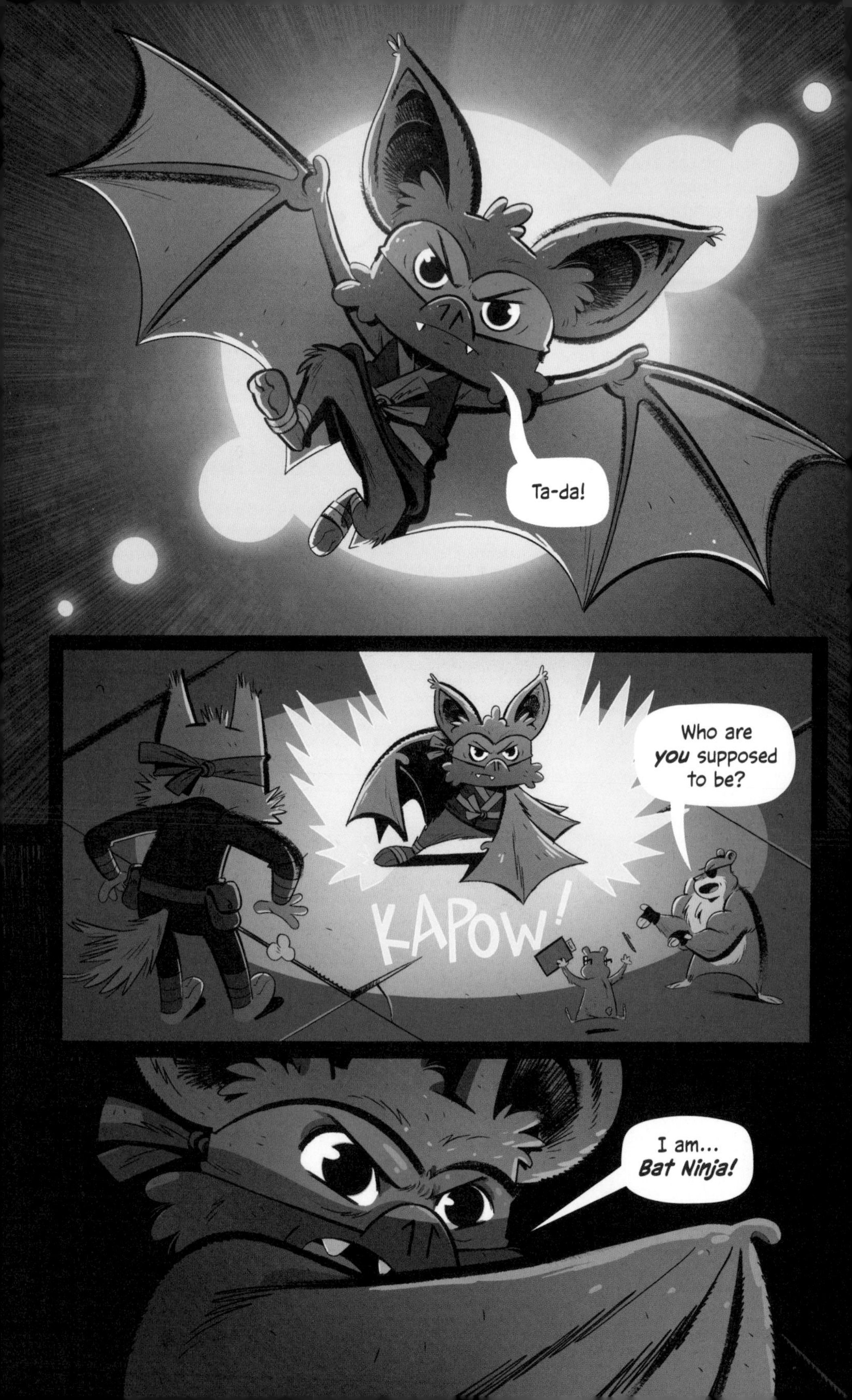
Ta-da!
Who are *you* supposed to be?
KAPOW!
I am... *Bat Ninja!*

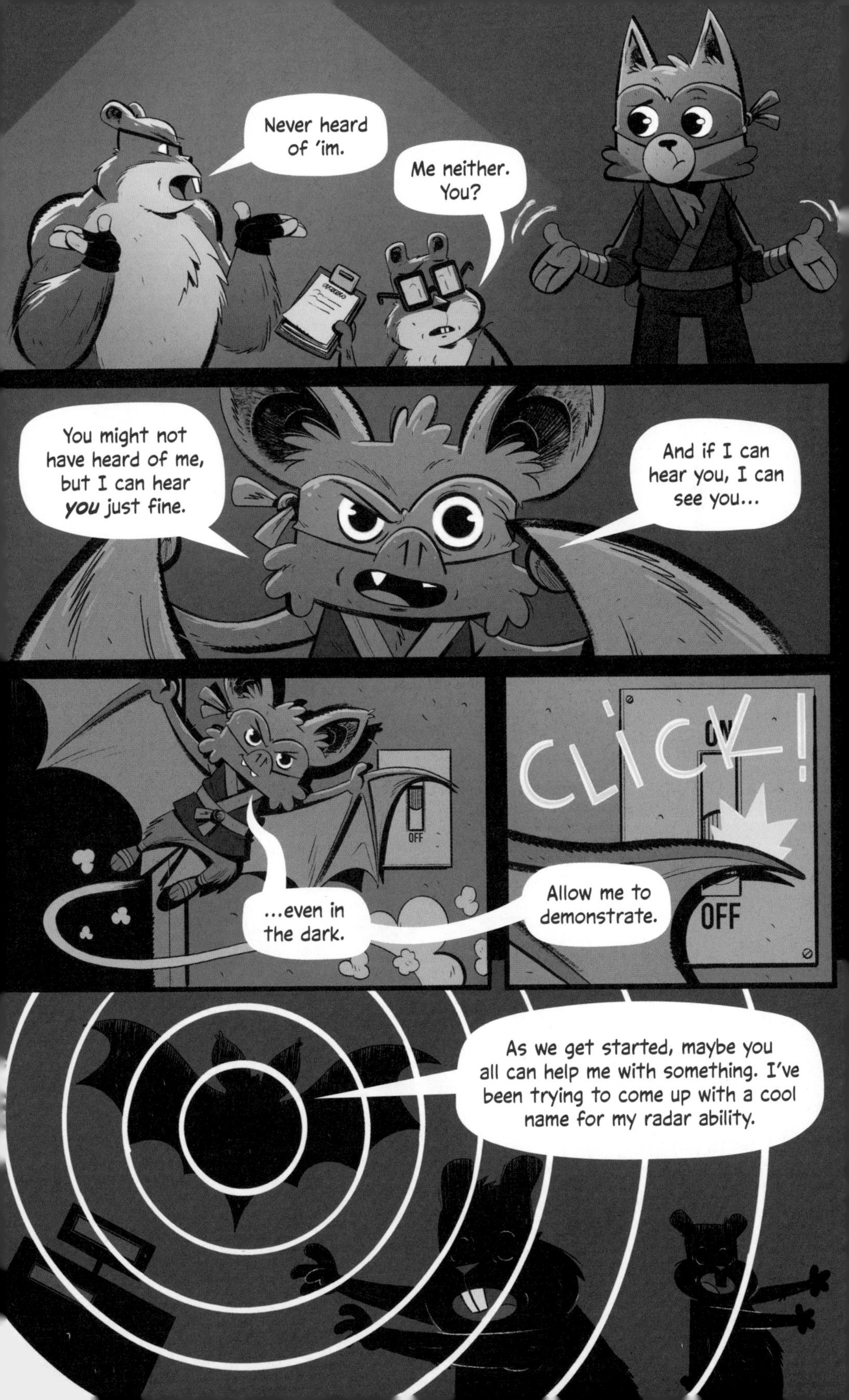
Never heard of 'im.
Me neither. You?
You might not have heard of me, but I can hear *you* just fine.
And if I can hear you, I can see you...
OFF
...even in the dark.
CLICK!
ON
Allow me to demonstrate.
OFF
As we get started, maybe you all can help me with something. I've been trying to come up with a cool name for my radar ability.

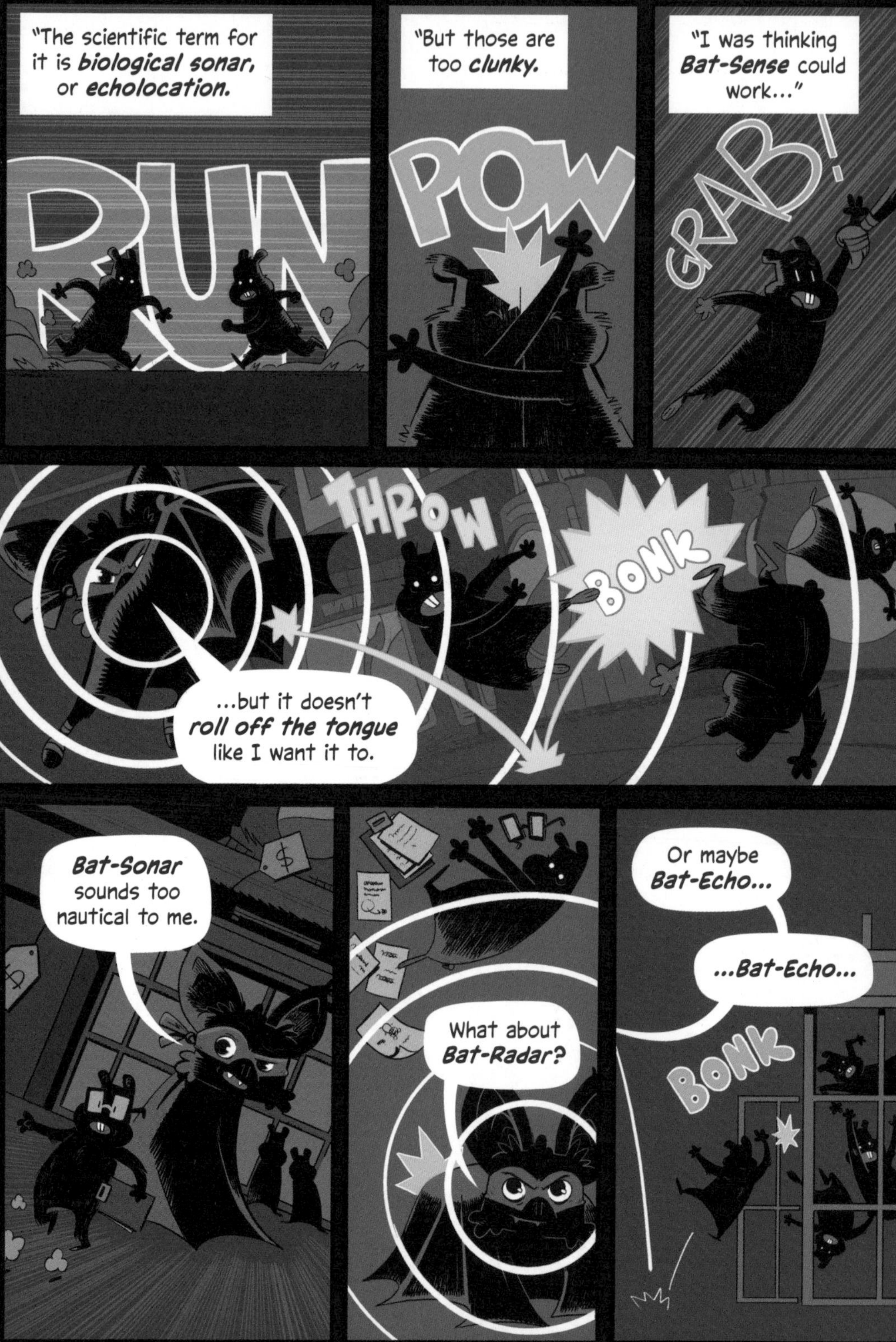
"The scientific term for it is **biological sonar,** or **echolocation.**
RUN
"But those are too **clunky.**
POW
"I was thinking **Bat-Sense** could work…"
GRAB!
THROW
BONK
…but it doesn't **roll off the tongue** like I want it to.
Bat-Sonar sounds too nautical to me.
What about **Bat-Radar?**
Or maybe **Bat-Echo…**
…Bat-Echo…
BONK

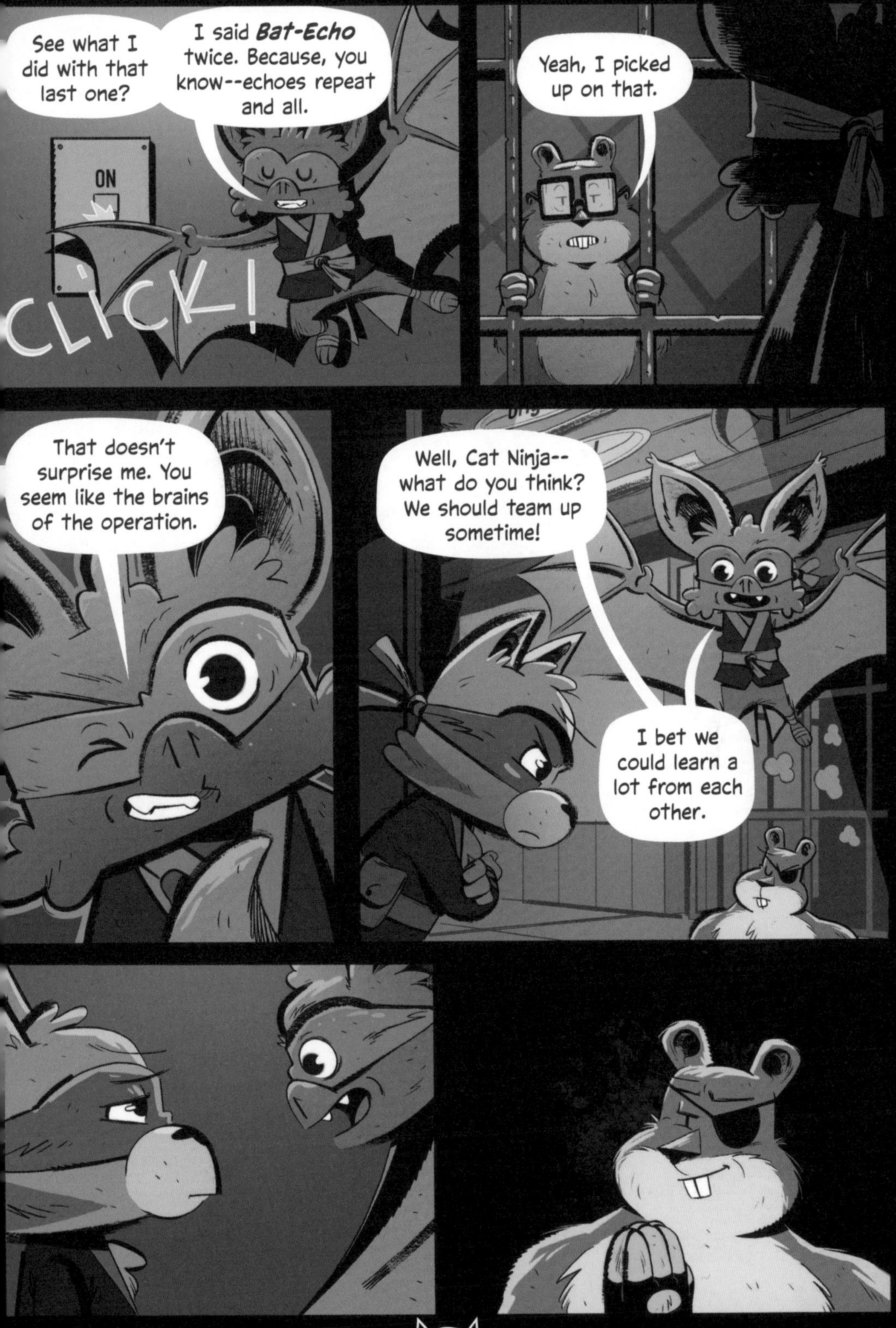
See what I did with that last one?
I said **Bat-Echo** twice. Because, you know--echoes repeat and all.
ON
CLICK!
Yeah, I picked up on that.
That doesn't surprise me. You seem like the brains of the operation.
Well, Cat Ninja--what do you think? We should team up sometime!
I bet we could learn a lot from each other.

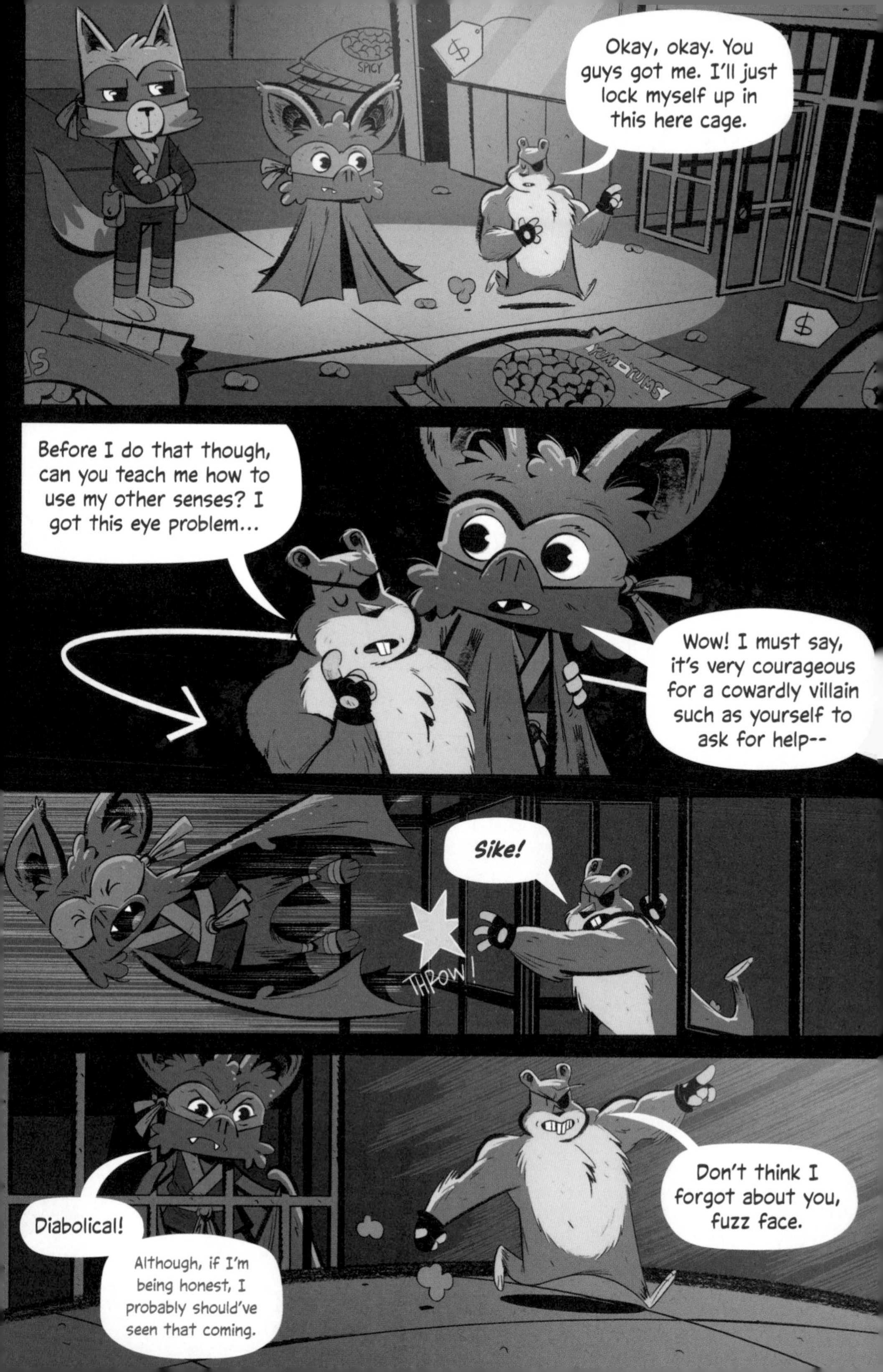
SPICY
Okay, okay. You guys got me. I'll just lock myself up in this here cage.
YUM-YUMS
Before I do that though, can you teach me how to use my other senses? I got this eye problem...
Wow! I must say, it's very courageous for a cowardly villain such as yourself to ask for help--
Sike!
THROW!
Diabolical!
Although, if I'm being honest, I probably should've seen that coming.
Don't think I forgot about you, fuzz face.

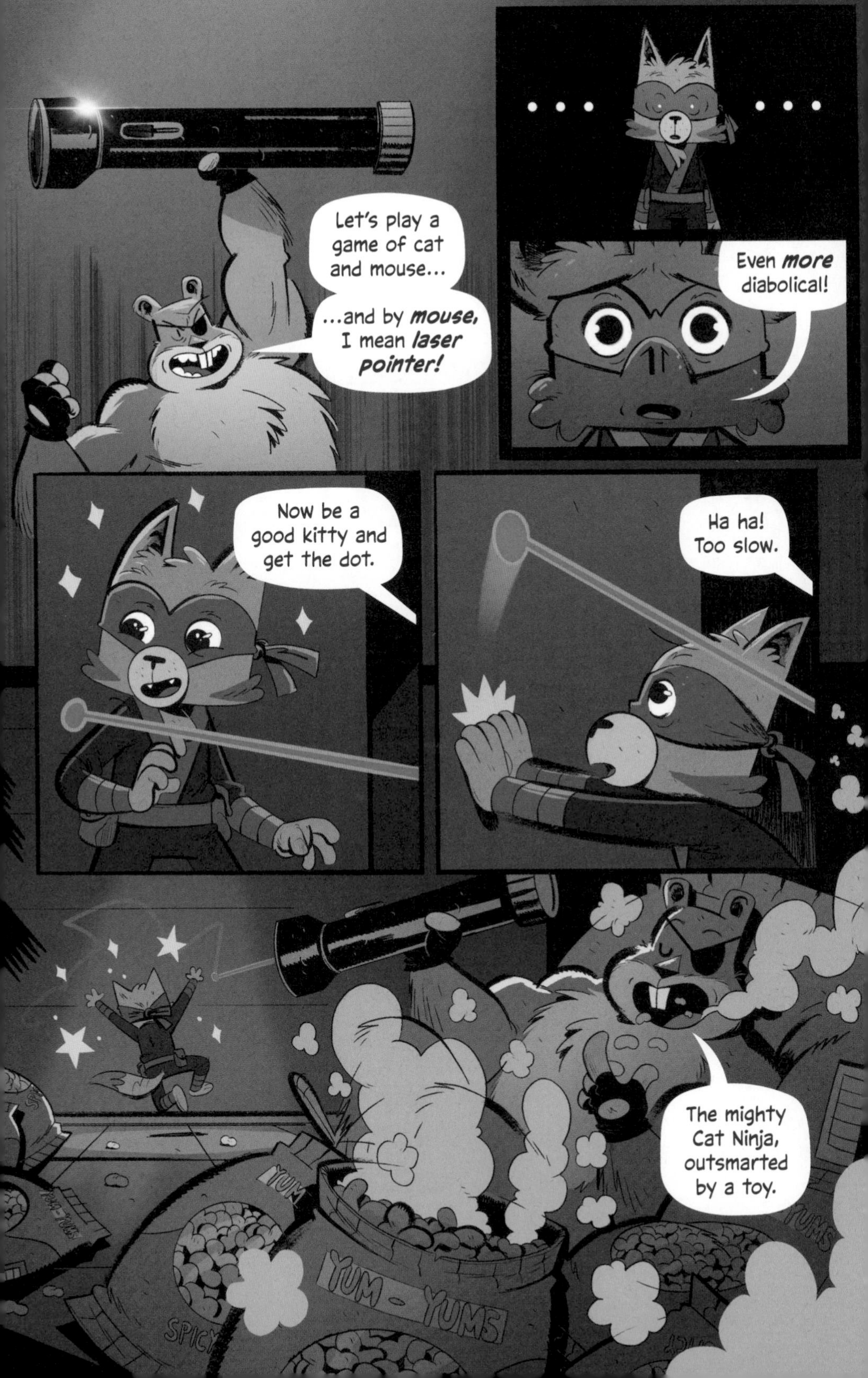
Let's play a game of cat and mouse...
...and by *mouse,* I mean *laser pointer!*
• • • • • •
Even *more* diabolical!
Now be a good kitty and get the dot.
Ha ha! Too slow.
The mighty Cat Ninja, outsmarted by a toy.
YUM-YUMS
SPICY

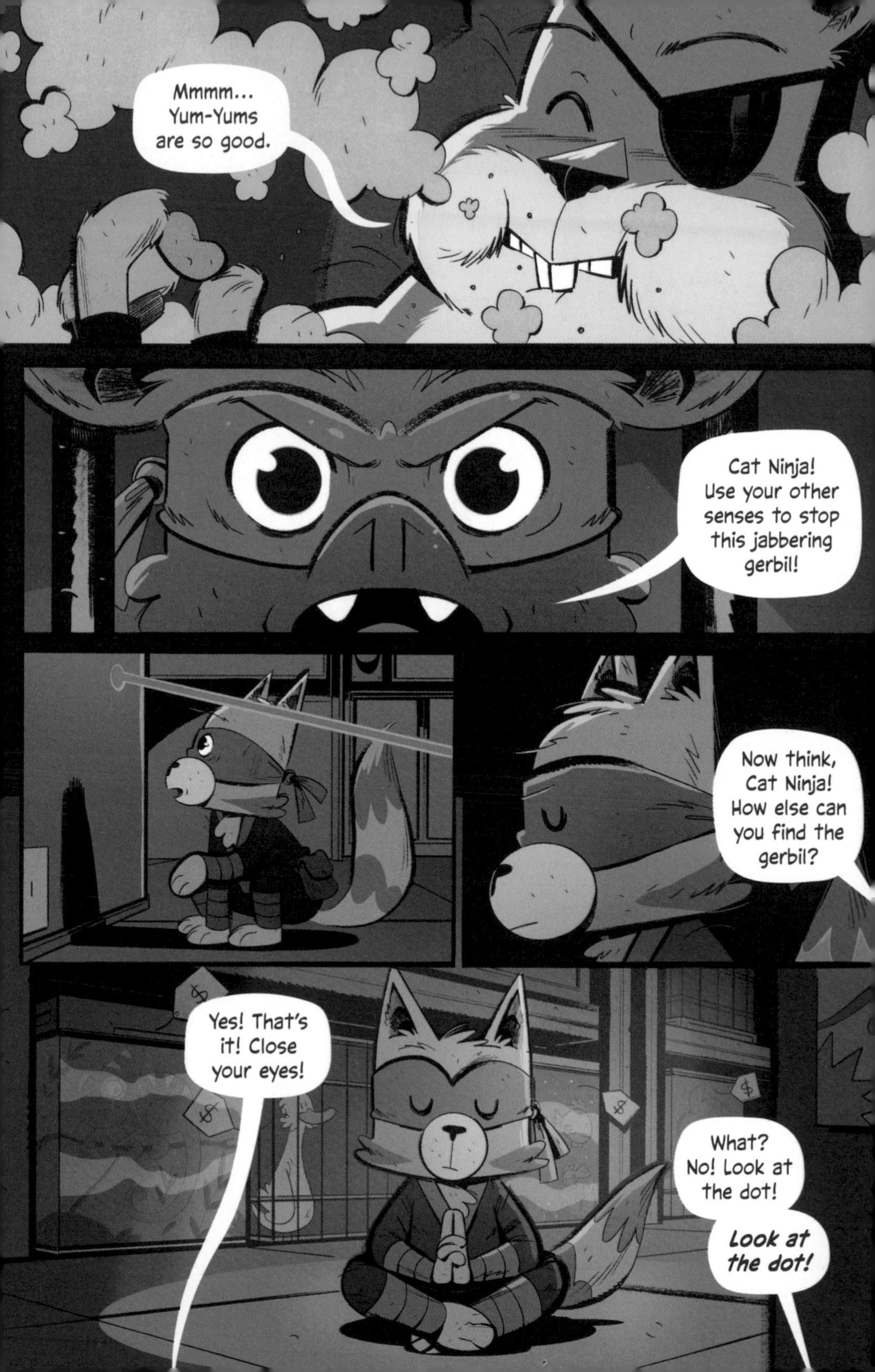
Mmmm... Yum-Yums are so good.
Cat Ninja! Use your other senses to stop this jabbering gerbil!
Now think, Cat Ninja! How else can you find the gerbil?
Yes! That's it! Close your eyes!
What? No! Look at the dot!
Look at the dot!

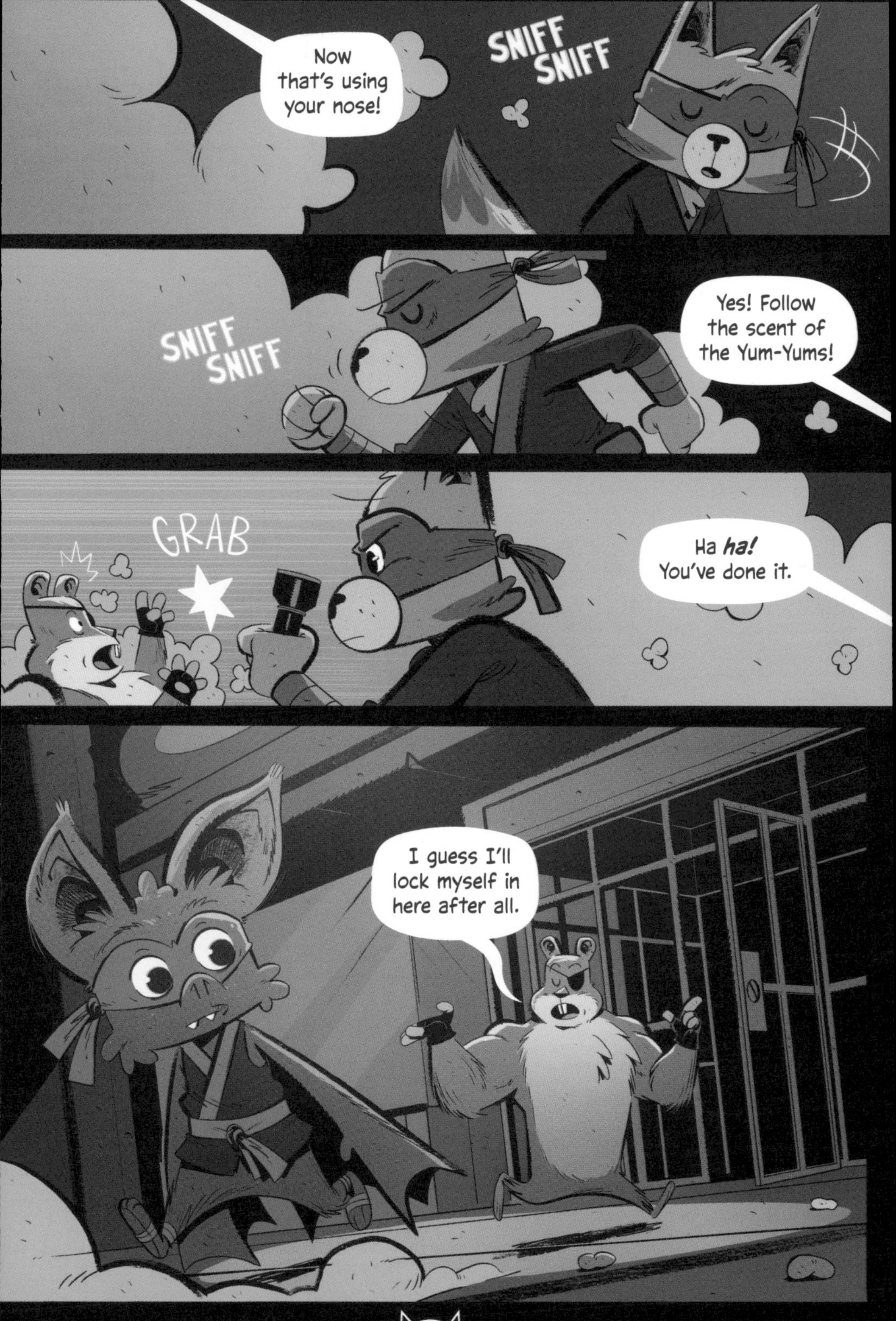

Now that's using your nose!
SNIFF SNIFF
SNIFF SNIFF
Yes! Follow the scent of the Yum-Yums!
GRAB
Ha ***ha!*** You've done it.
I guess I'll lock myself in here after all.

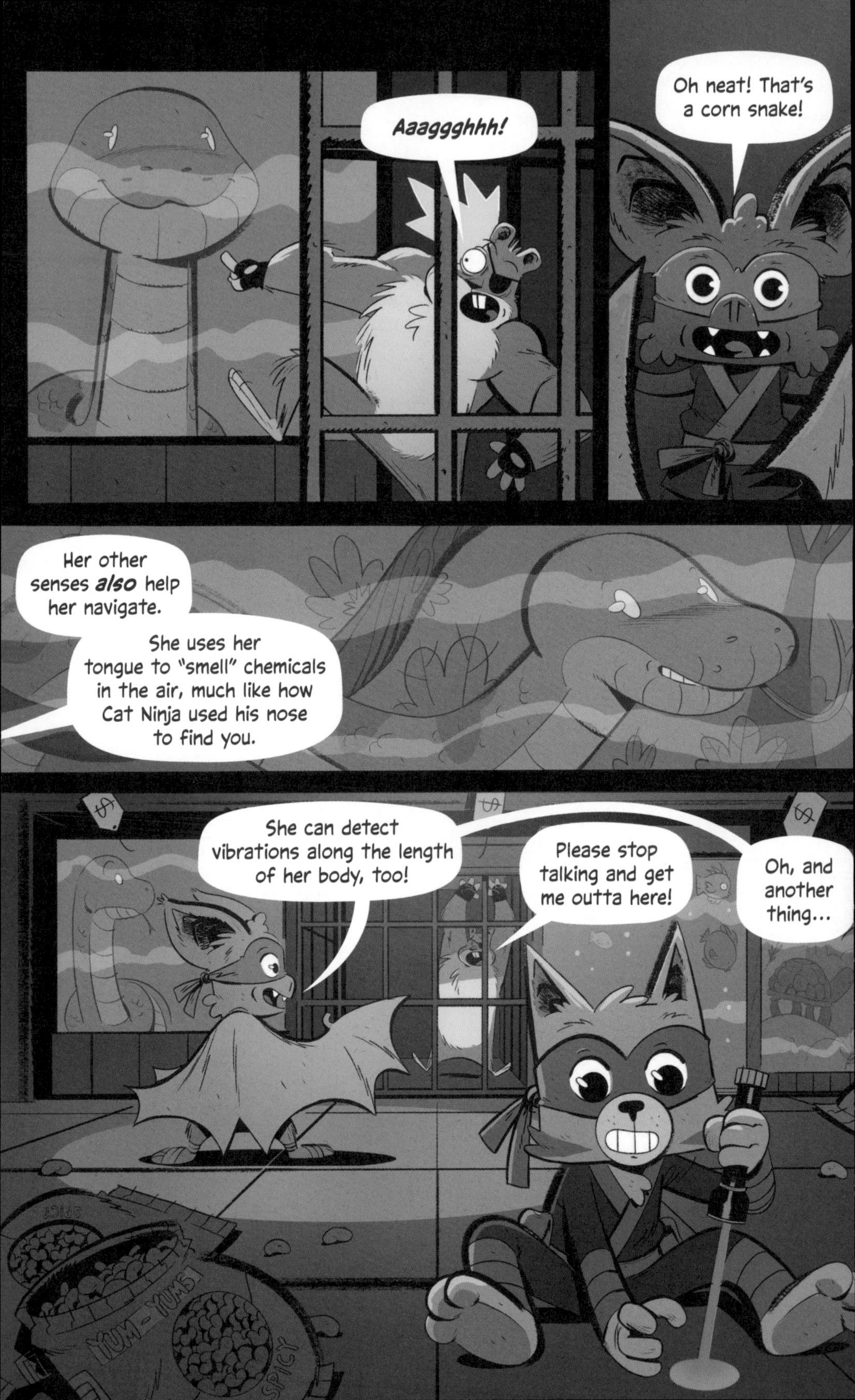
Aaaggghhh!
Oh neat! That's a corn snake!
Her other senses *also* help her navigate.
She uses her tongue to "smell" chemicals in the air, much like how Cat Ninja used his nose to find you.
She can detect vibrations along the length of her body, too!
Please stop talking and get me outta here!
Oh, and another thing...
YUM-YUMS!
SPICY

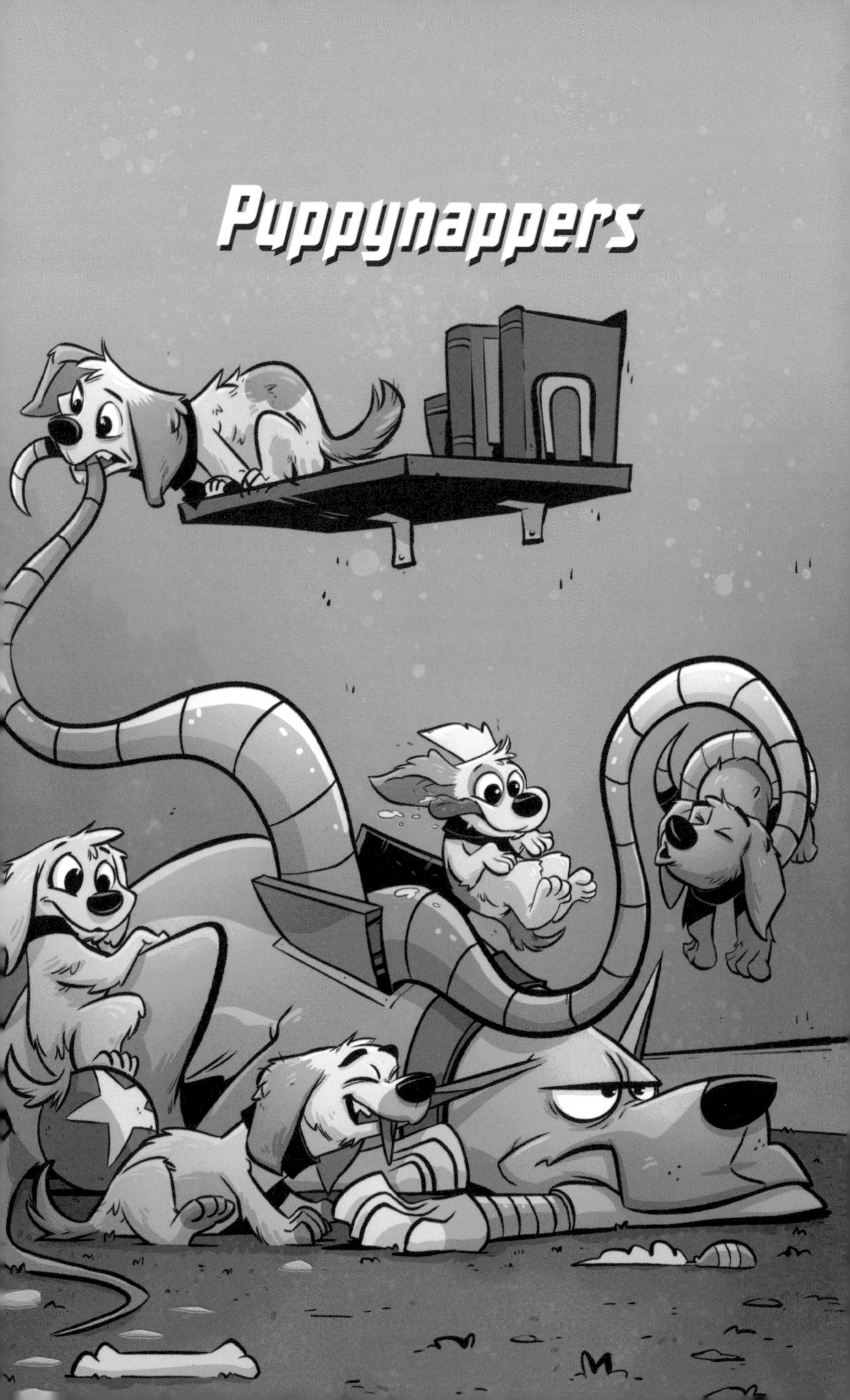

Puppynappers

Kurtis Scaletta

Illustrated by
Brett Bean

Colors by
Warren Wucinich

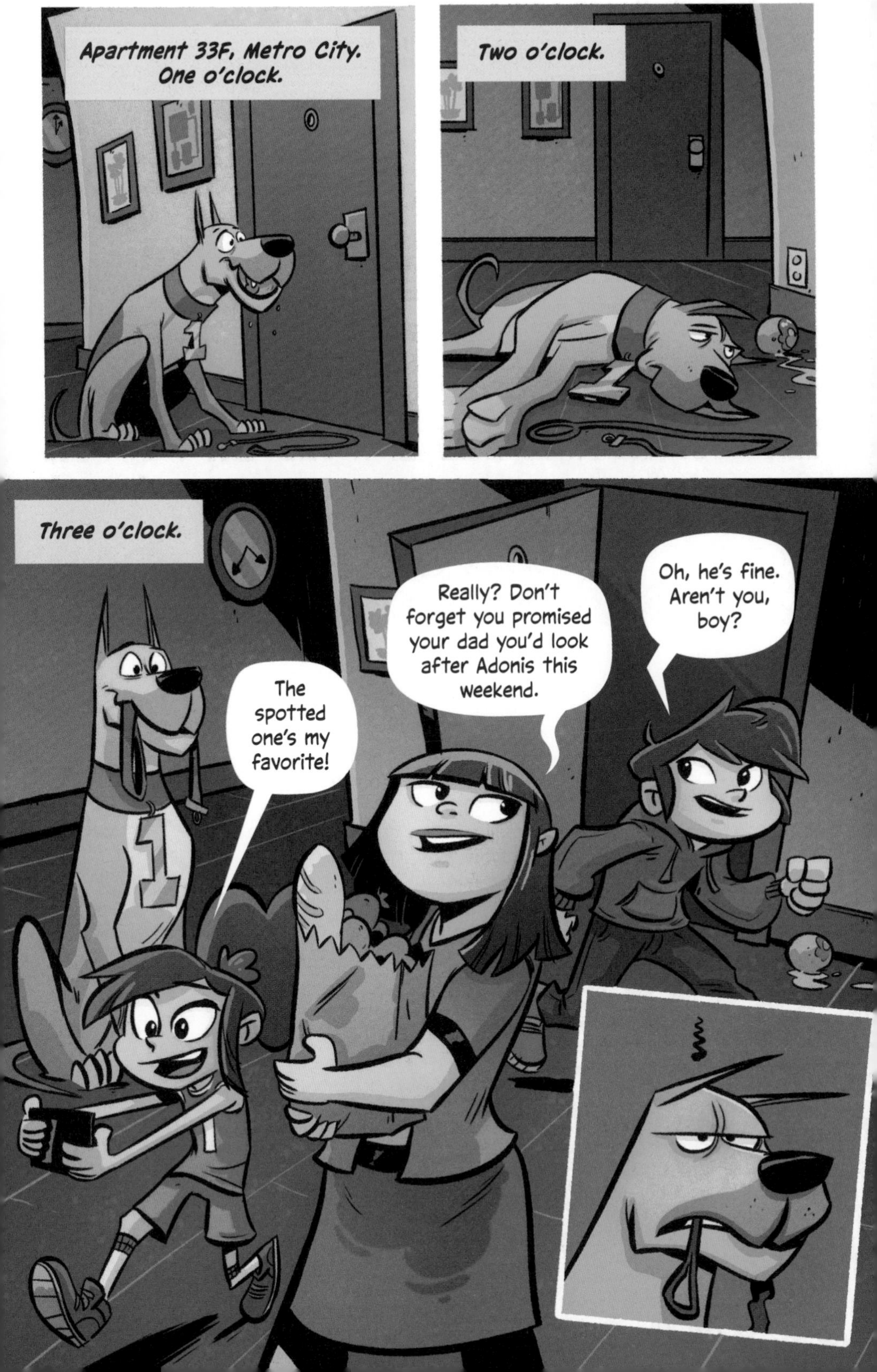

Apartment 33F, Metro City. One o'clock.
Two o'clock.
Three o'clock.
The spotted one's my favorite!
Really? Don't forget you promised your dad you'd look after Adonis this weekend.
Oh, he's fine. Aren't you, boy?

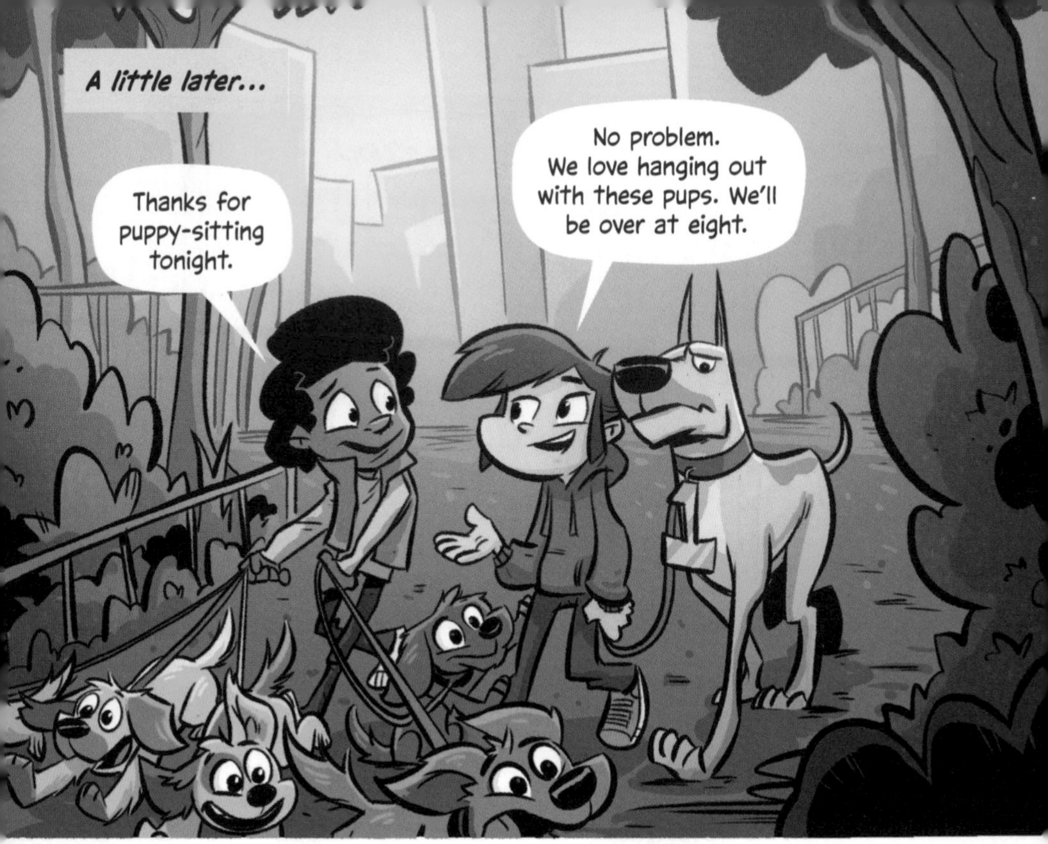
A little later...
Thanks for puppy-sitting tonight.
No problem. We love hanging out with these pups. We'll be over at eight.

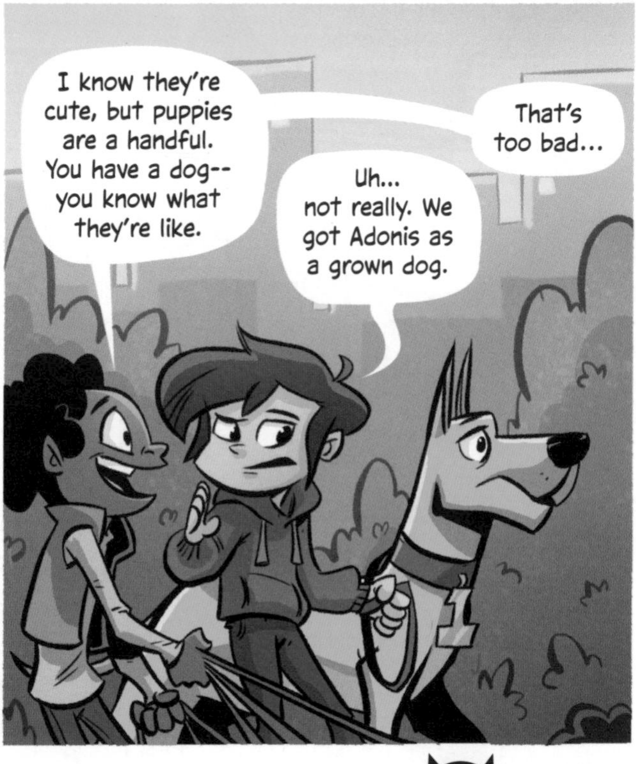
I know they're cute, but puppies are a handful. You have a dog--you know what they're like.
Uh... not really. We got Adonis as a grown dog.
That's too bad...

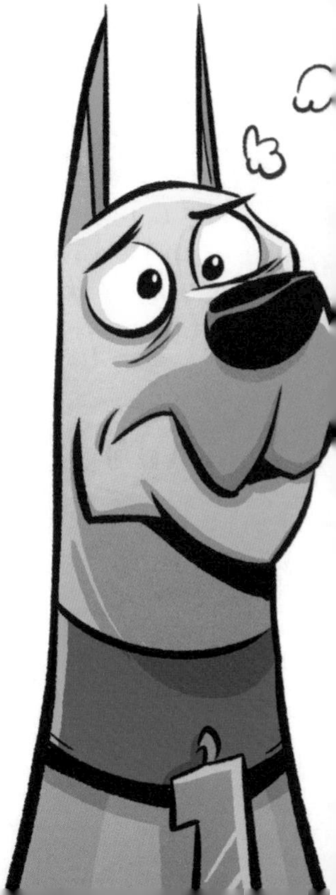

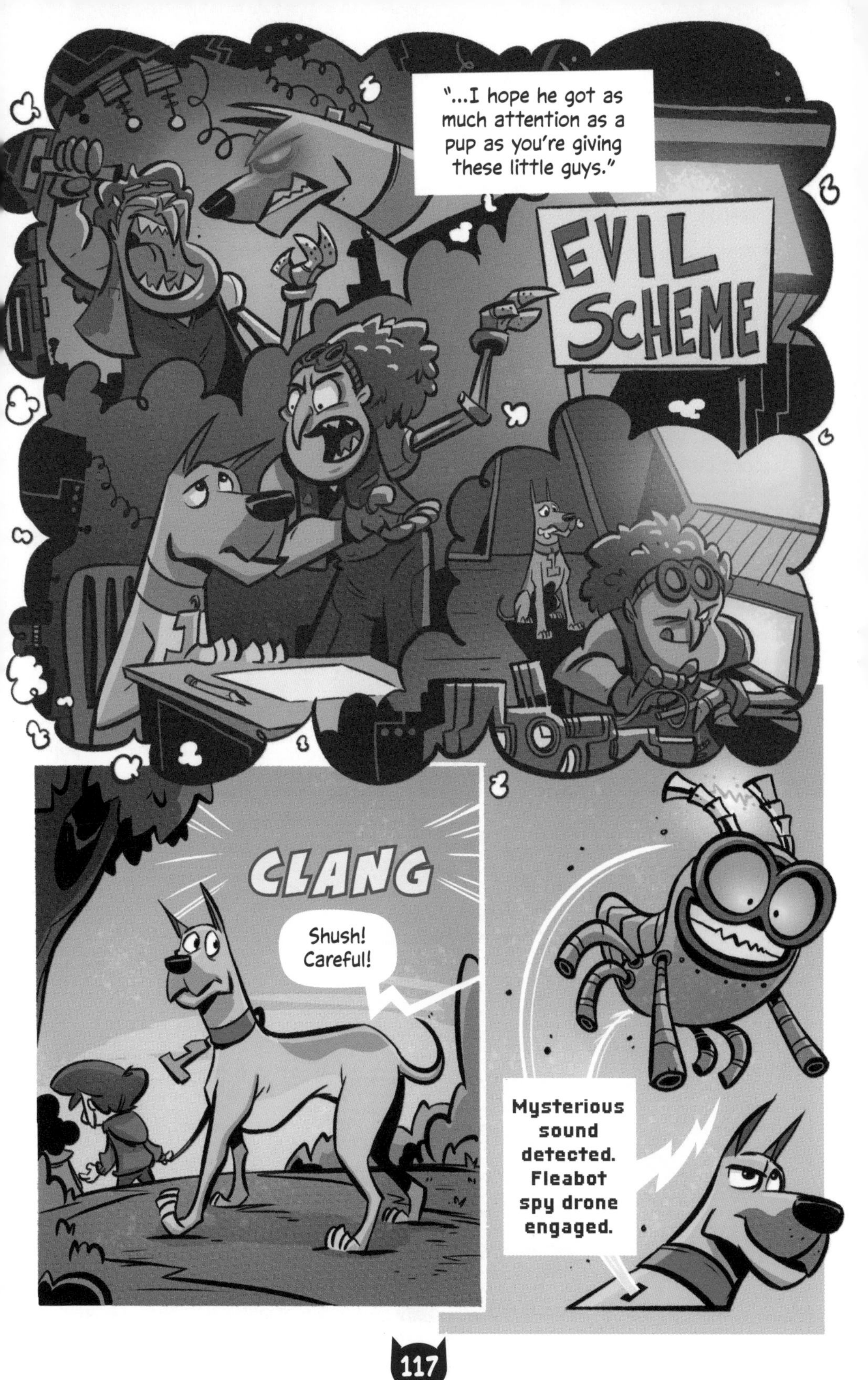
"...I hope he got as much attention as a pup as you're giving these little guys."
EVIL SCHEME
CLANG
Shush! Careful!
Mysterious sound detected. Fleabot spy drone engaged.

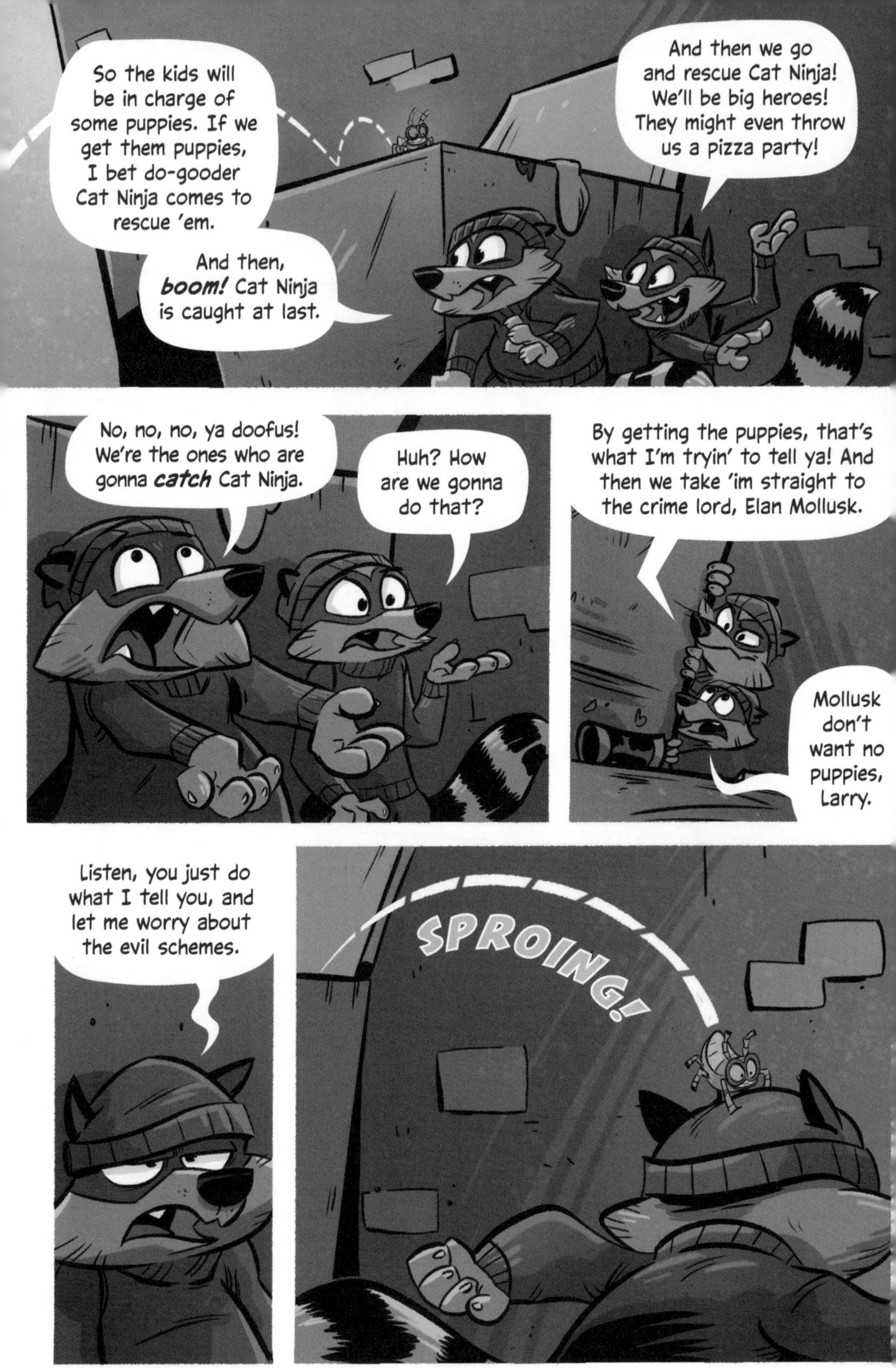
So the kids will be in charge of some puppies. If we get them puppies, I bet do-gooder Cat Ninja comes to rescue 'em.
And then, boom! Cat Ninja is caught at last.
And then we go and rescue Cat Ninja! We'll be big heroes! They might even throw us a pizza party!
No, no, no, ya doofus! We're the ones who are gonna catch Cat Ninja.
Huh? How are we gonna do that?
By getting the puppies, that's what I'm tryin' to tell ya! And then we take 'im straight to the crime lord, Elan Mollusk.
Mollusk don't want no puppies, Larry.
Listen, you just do what I tell you, and let me worry about the evil schemes.
SPROING!

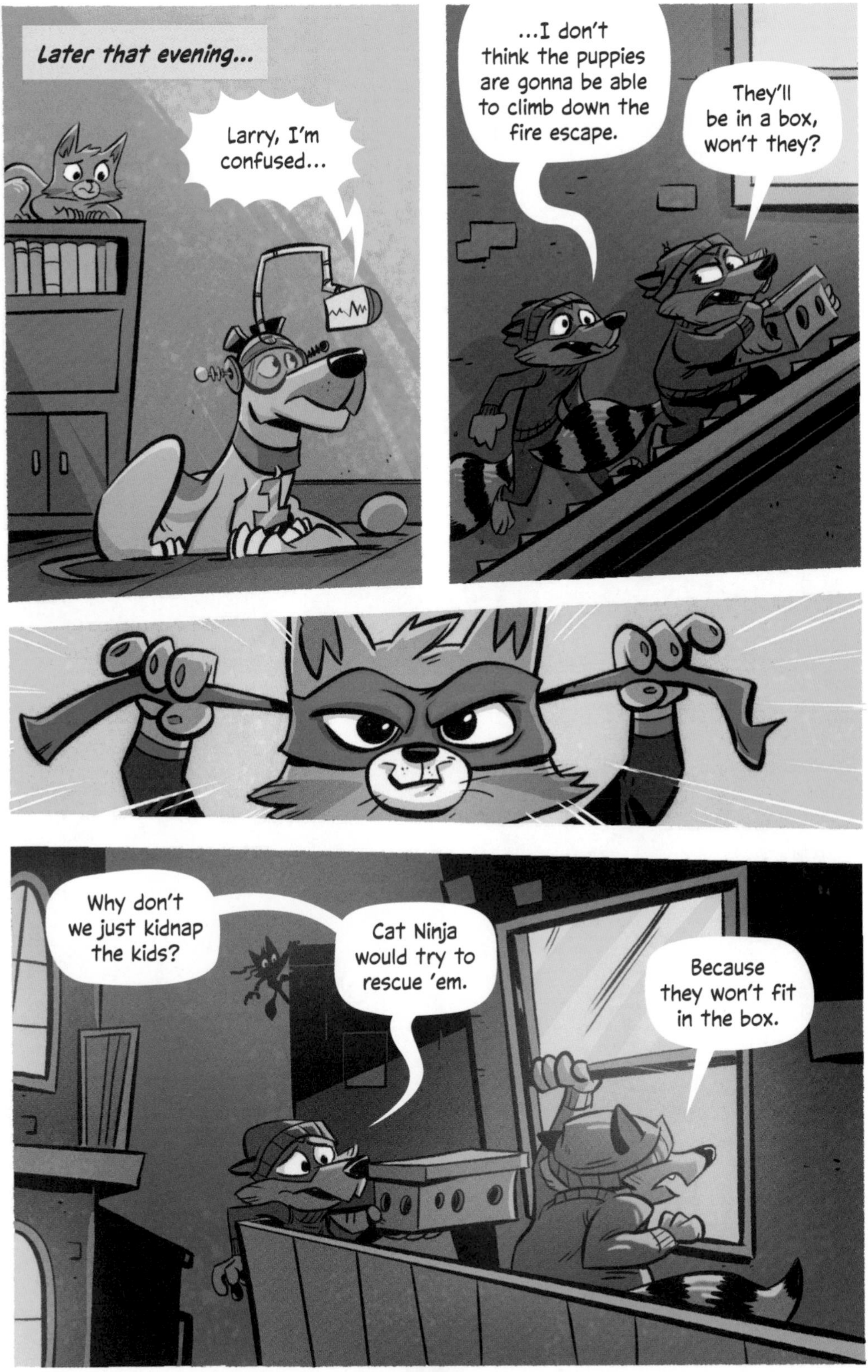
Later that evening...
Larry, I'm confused...
...I don't think the puppies are gonna be able to climb down the fire escape.
They'll be in a box, won't they?
Why don't we just kidnap the kids?
Cat Ninja would try to rescue 'em.
Because they won't fit in the box.

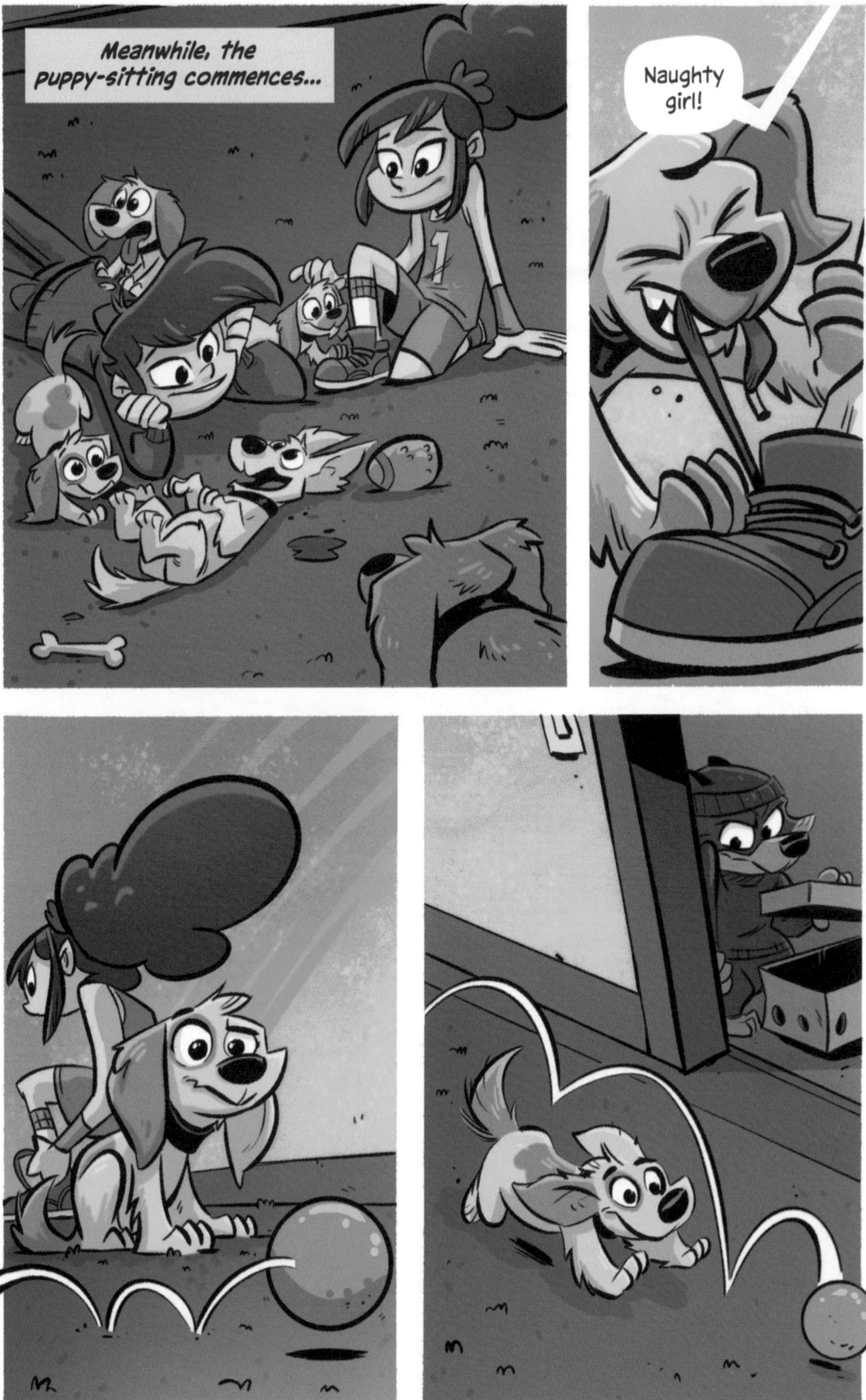
Meanwhile, the puppy-sitting commences...
Naughty girl!

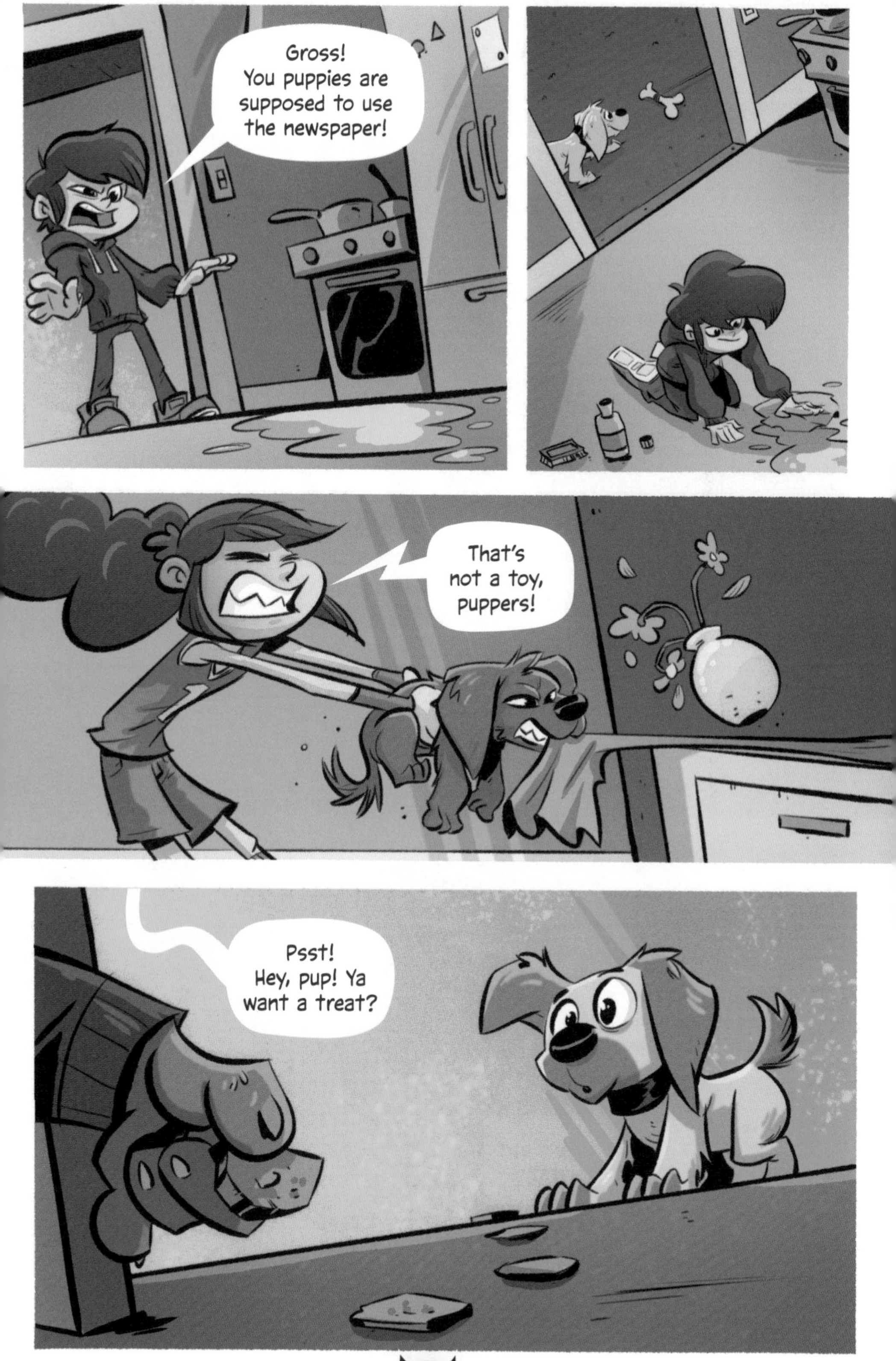
Gross! You puppies are supposed to use the newspaper!
That's not a toy, puppers!
Psst! Hey, pup! Ya want a treat?

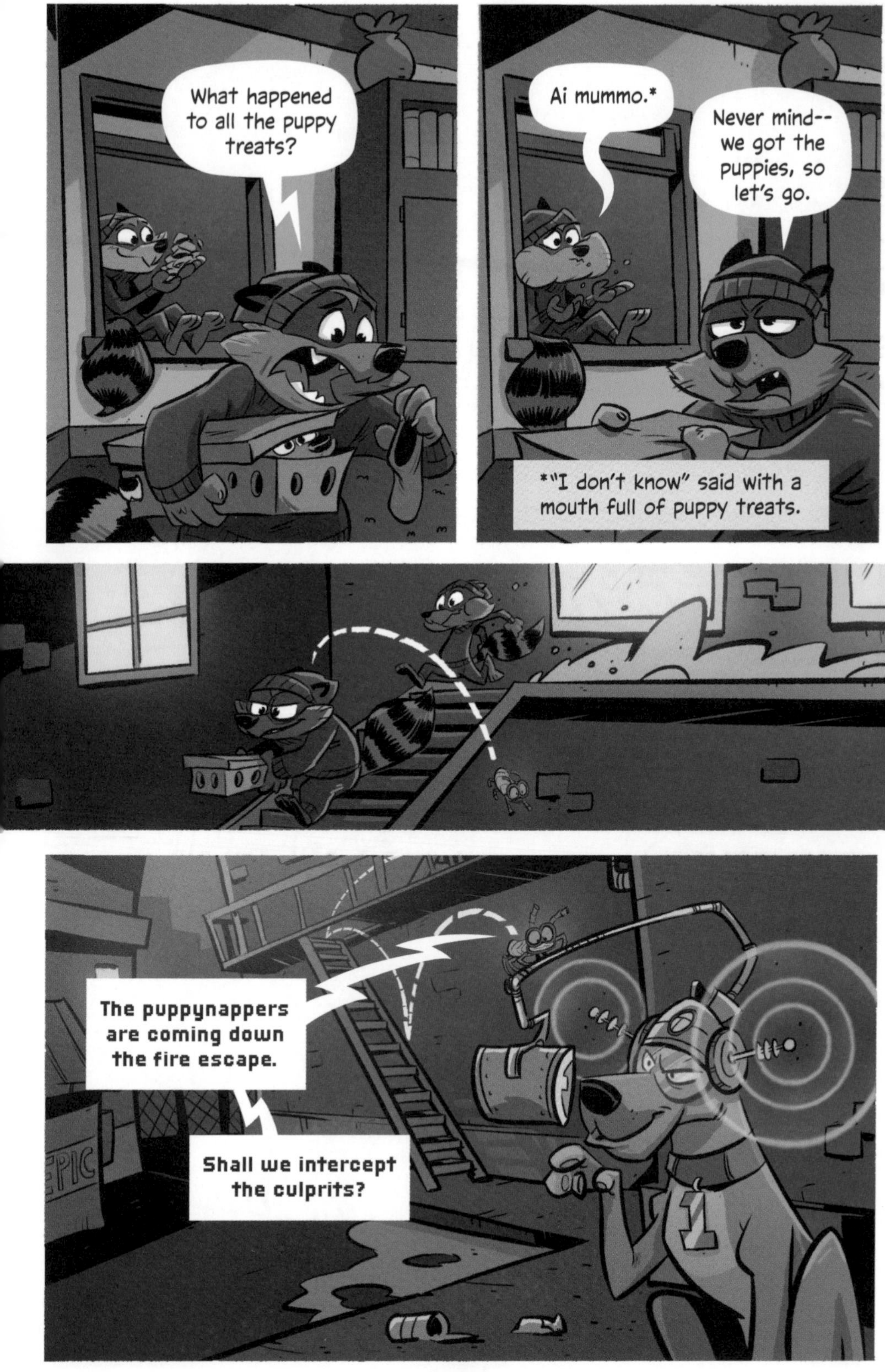
What happened to all the puppy treats?
Ai mummo.*
Never mind-- we got the puppies, so let's go.
*"I don't know" said with a mouth full of puppy treats.
The puppynappers are coming down the fire escape.
Shall we intercept the culprits?
EPIC

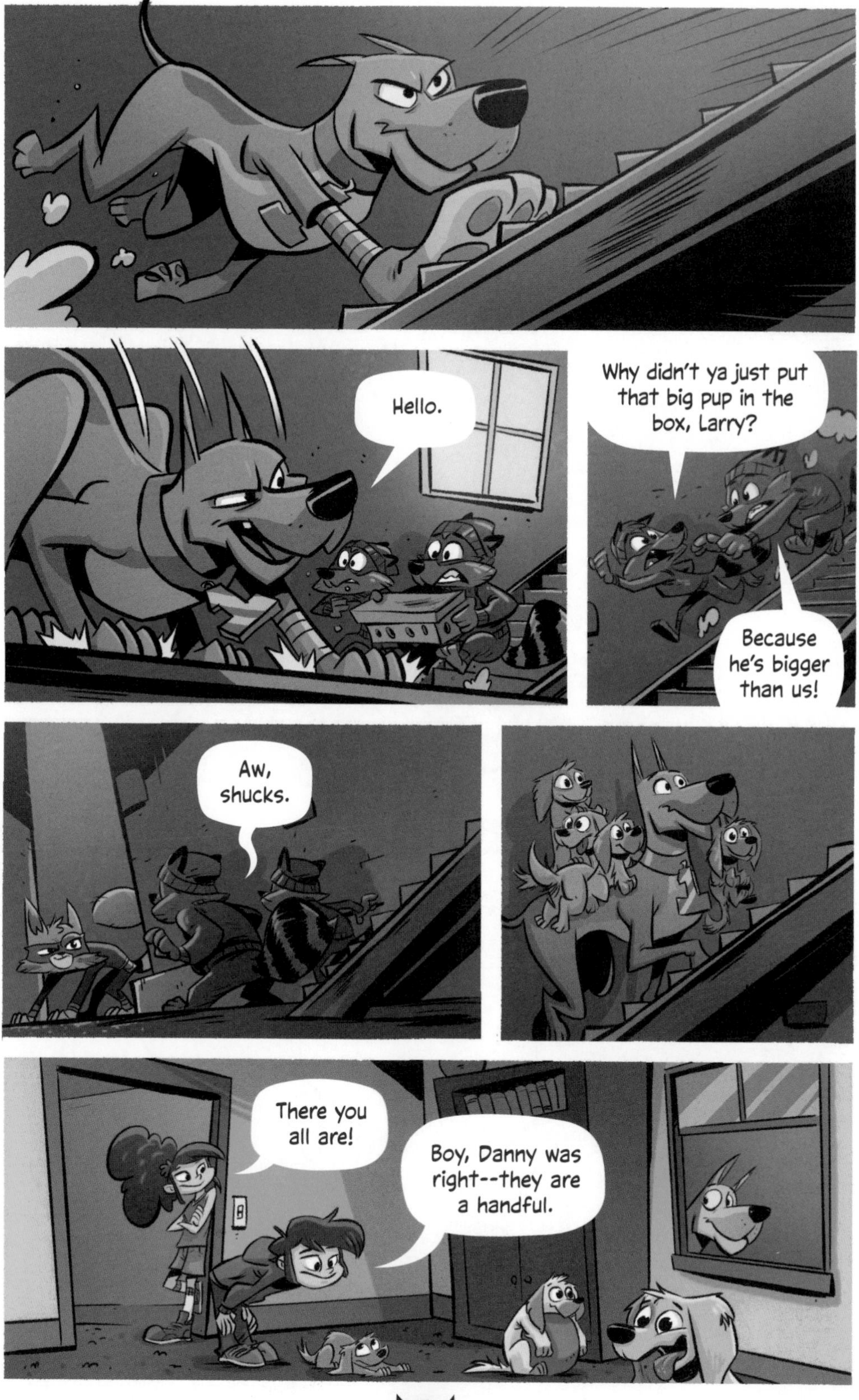
Hello.
Why didn't ya just put that big pup in the box, Larry?
Because he's bigger than us!
Aw, shucks.
There you all are!
Boy, Danny was right--they are a handful.

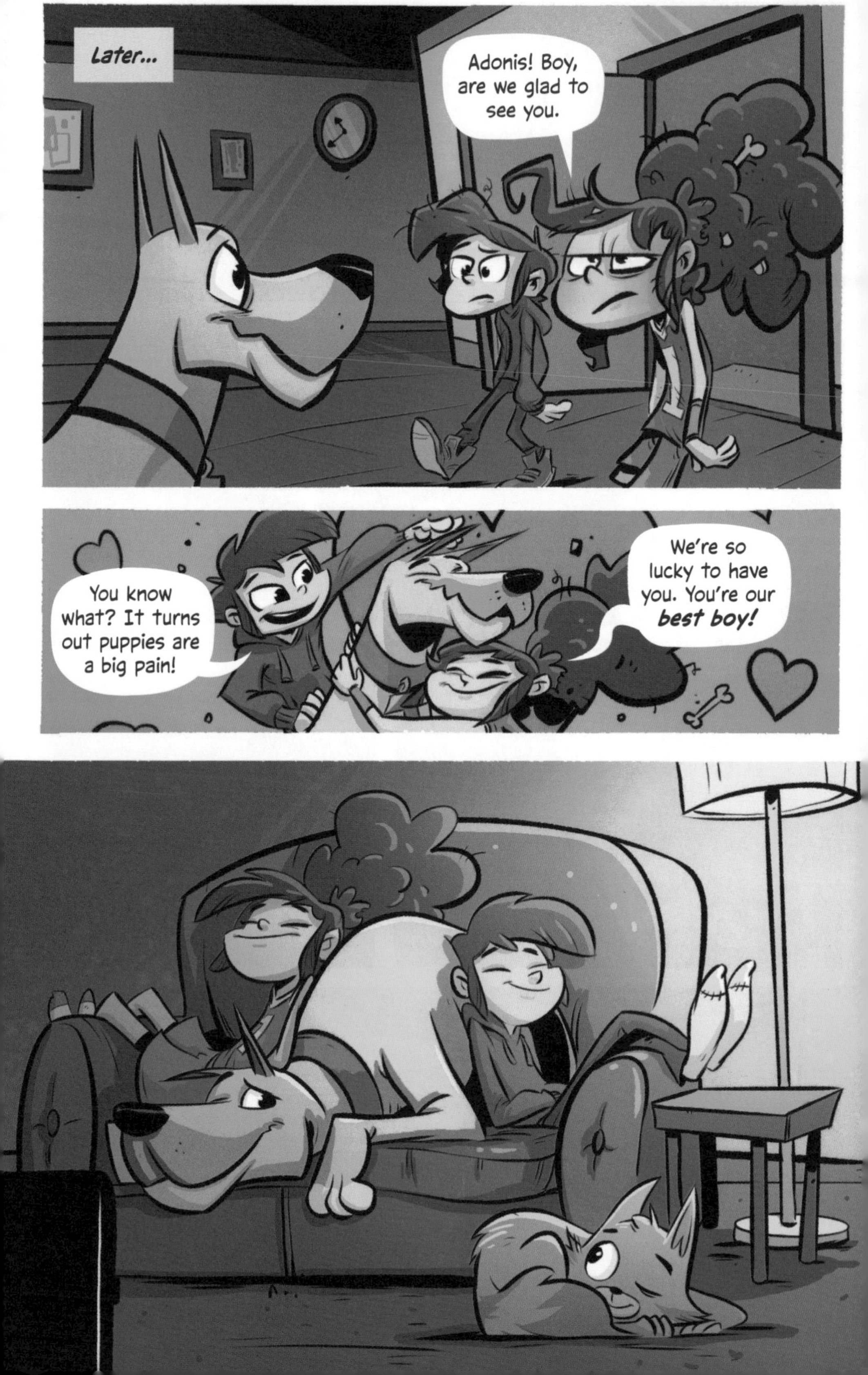
Later...
Adonis! Boy, are we glad to see you.
You know what? It turns out puppies are a big pain!
We're so lucky to have you. You're our **best boy!**

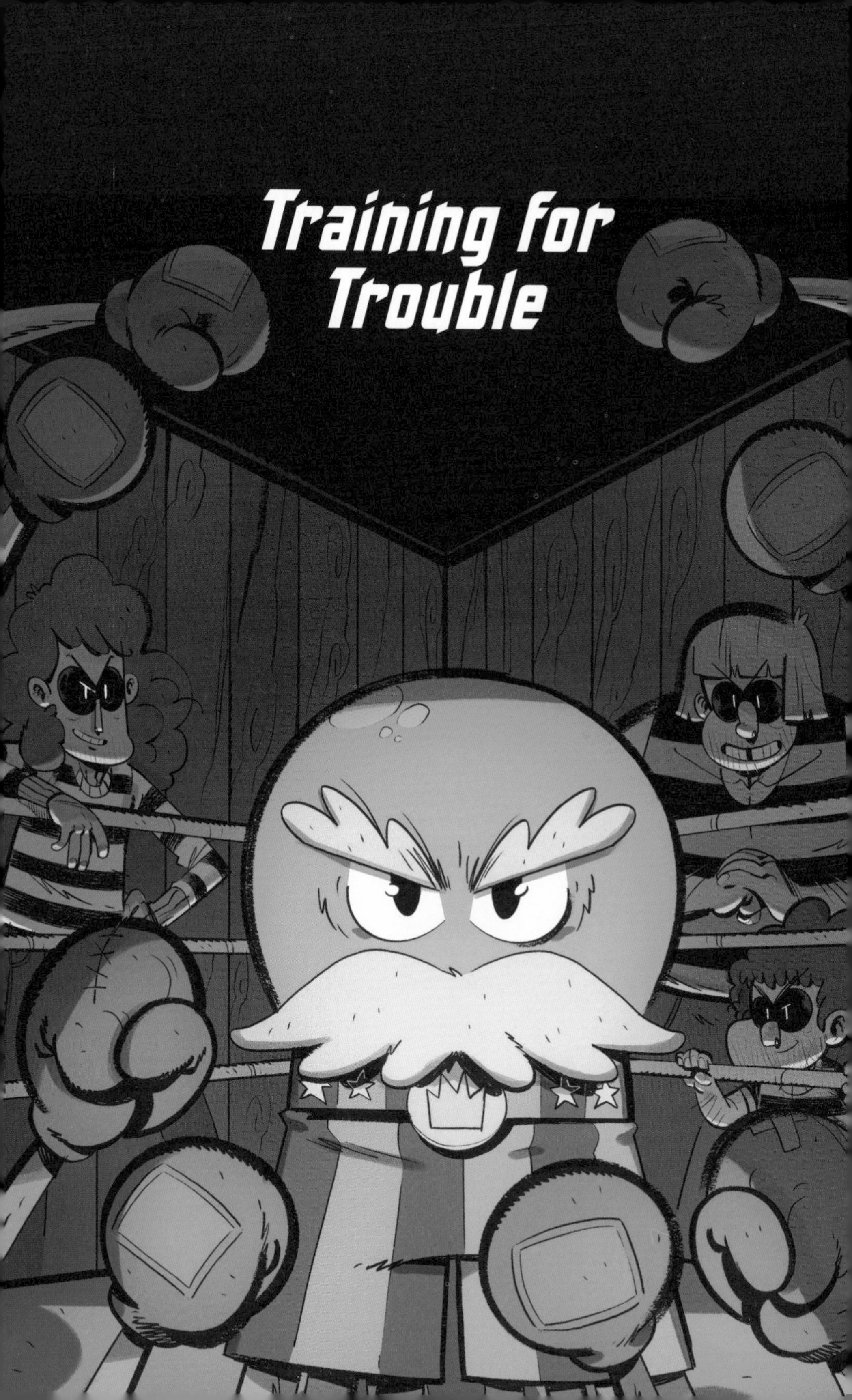
Training for Trouble

Chris Schweizer

Illustrated by
Eduardo Medeiros

Colors by
Cindy Zhi

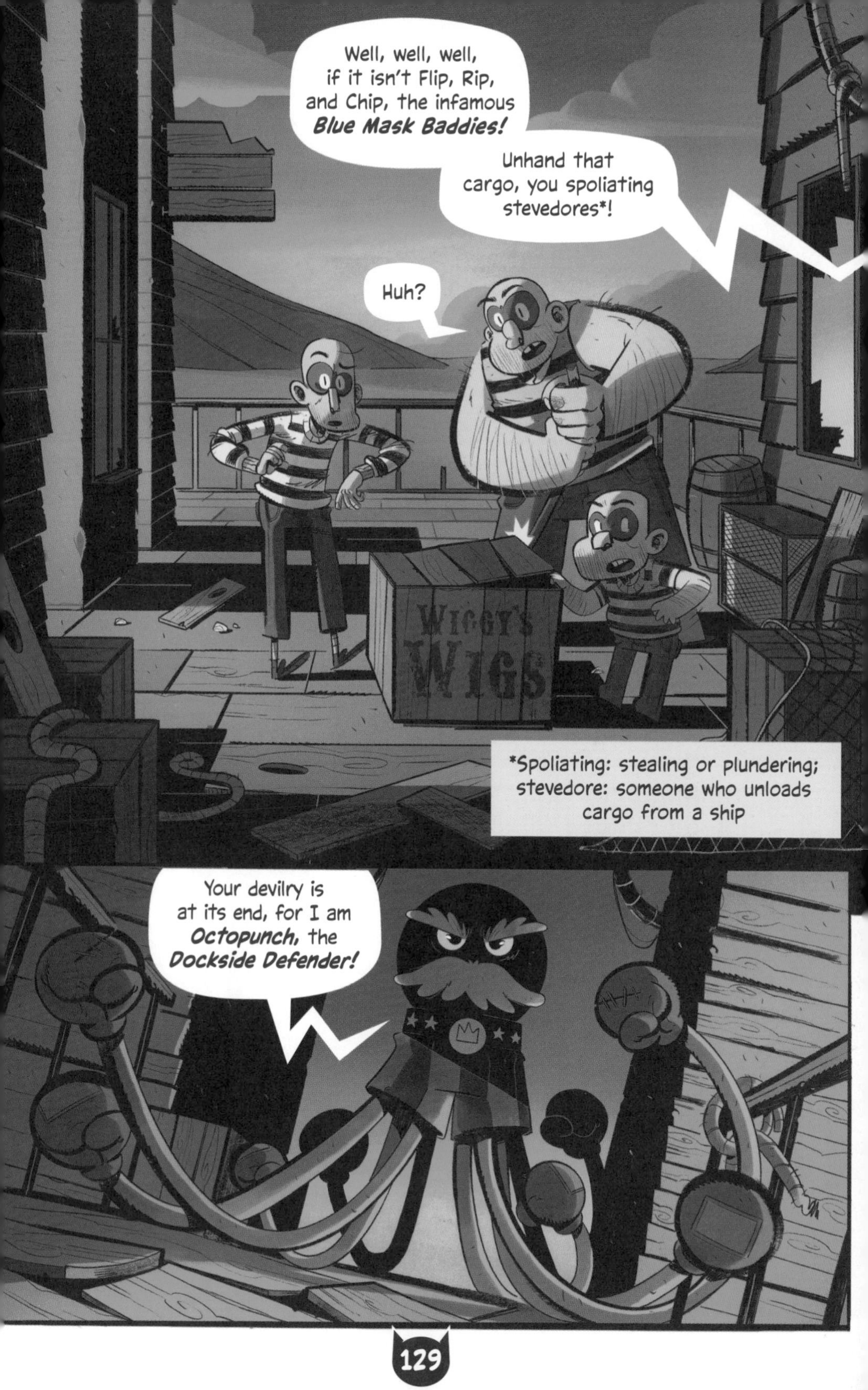
Well, well, well, if it isn't Flip, Rip, and Chip, the infamous *Blue Mask Baddies!*
Unhand that cargo, you spoliating stevedores*!
Huh?
WIGGY'S WIGS
*Spoliating: stealing or plundering; stevedore: someone who unloads cargo from a ship
Your devilry is at its end, for I am *Octopunch*, the *Dockside Defender!*

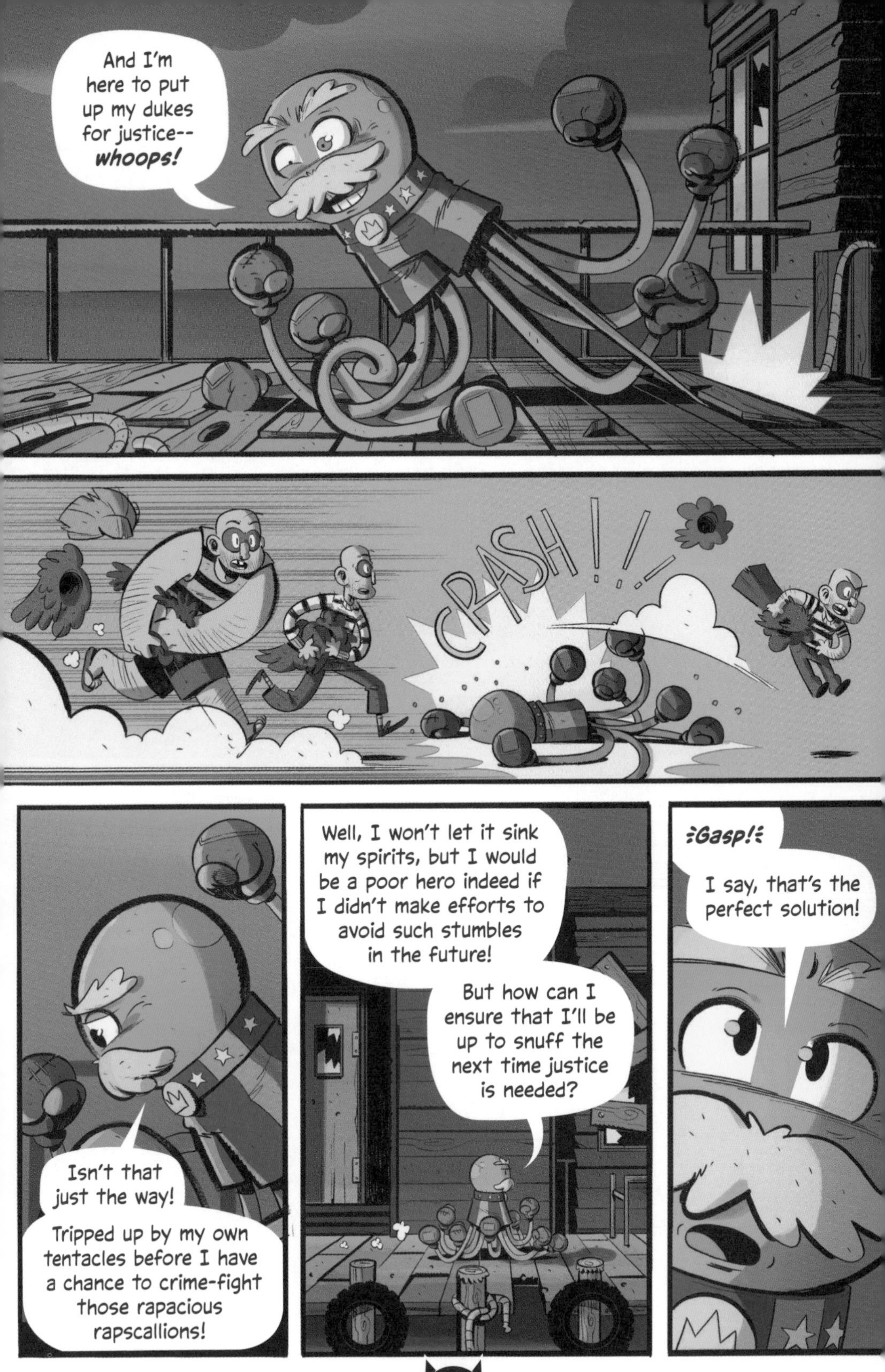
And I'm here to put up my dukes for justice-- *whoops!*
CRASH!!!
Isn't that just the way!
Tripped up by my own tentacles before I have a chance to crime-fight those rapacious rapscallions!
Well, I won't let it sink my spirits, but I would be a poor hero indeed if I didn't make efforts to avoid such stumbles in the future!
But how can I ensure that I'll be up to snuff the next time justice is needed?
Gasp!
I say, that's the perfect solution!

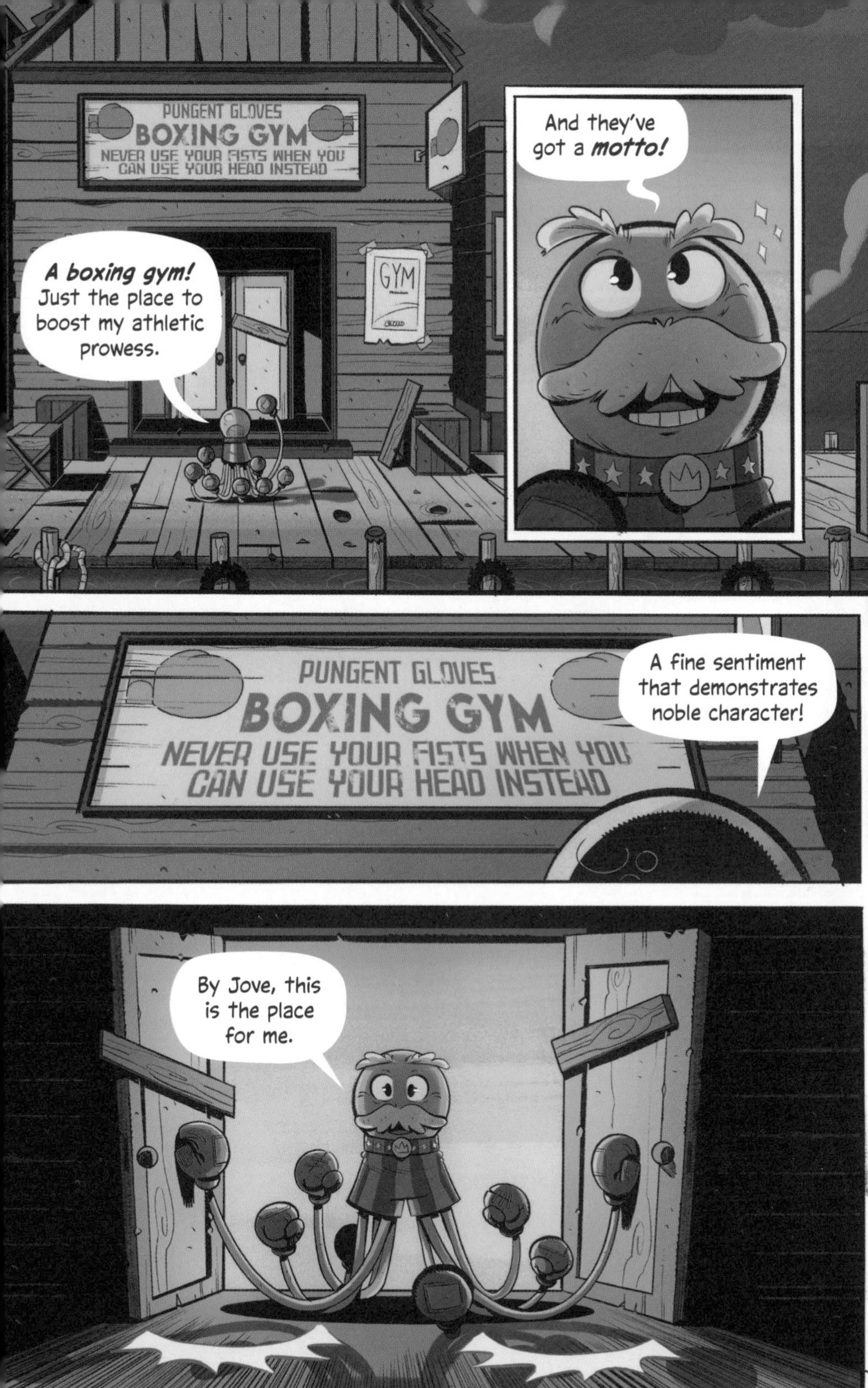
PUNGENT GLOVES
BOXING GYM
NEVER USE YOUR FISTS WHEN YOU CAN USE YOUR HEAD INSTEAD
GYM
A boxing gym! Just the place to boost my athletic prowess.
And they've got a ***motto!***
PUNGENT GLOVES
BOXING GYM
NEVER USE YOUR FISTS WHEN YOU CAN USE YOUR HEAD INSTEAD
A fine sentiment that demonstrates noble character!
By Jove, this is the place for me.

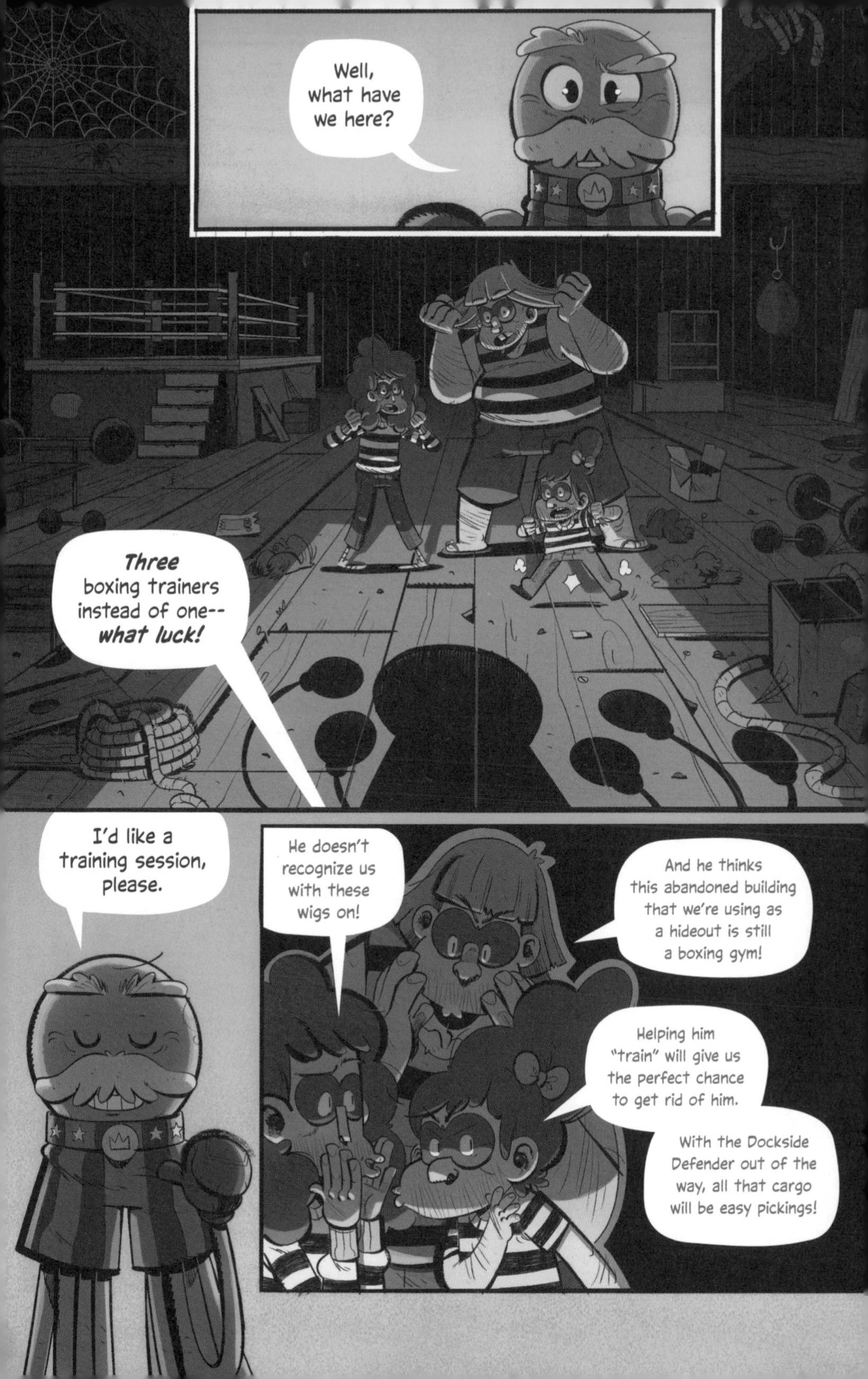
Well, what have we here?
Three boxing trainers instead of one-- ***what luck!***
I'd like a training session, please.
He doesn't recognize us with these wigs on!
And he thinks this abandoned building that we're using as a hideout is still a boxing gym!
Helping him "train" will give us the perfect chance to get rid of him.
With the Dockside Defender out of the way, all that cargo will be easy pickings!

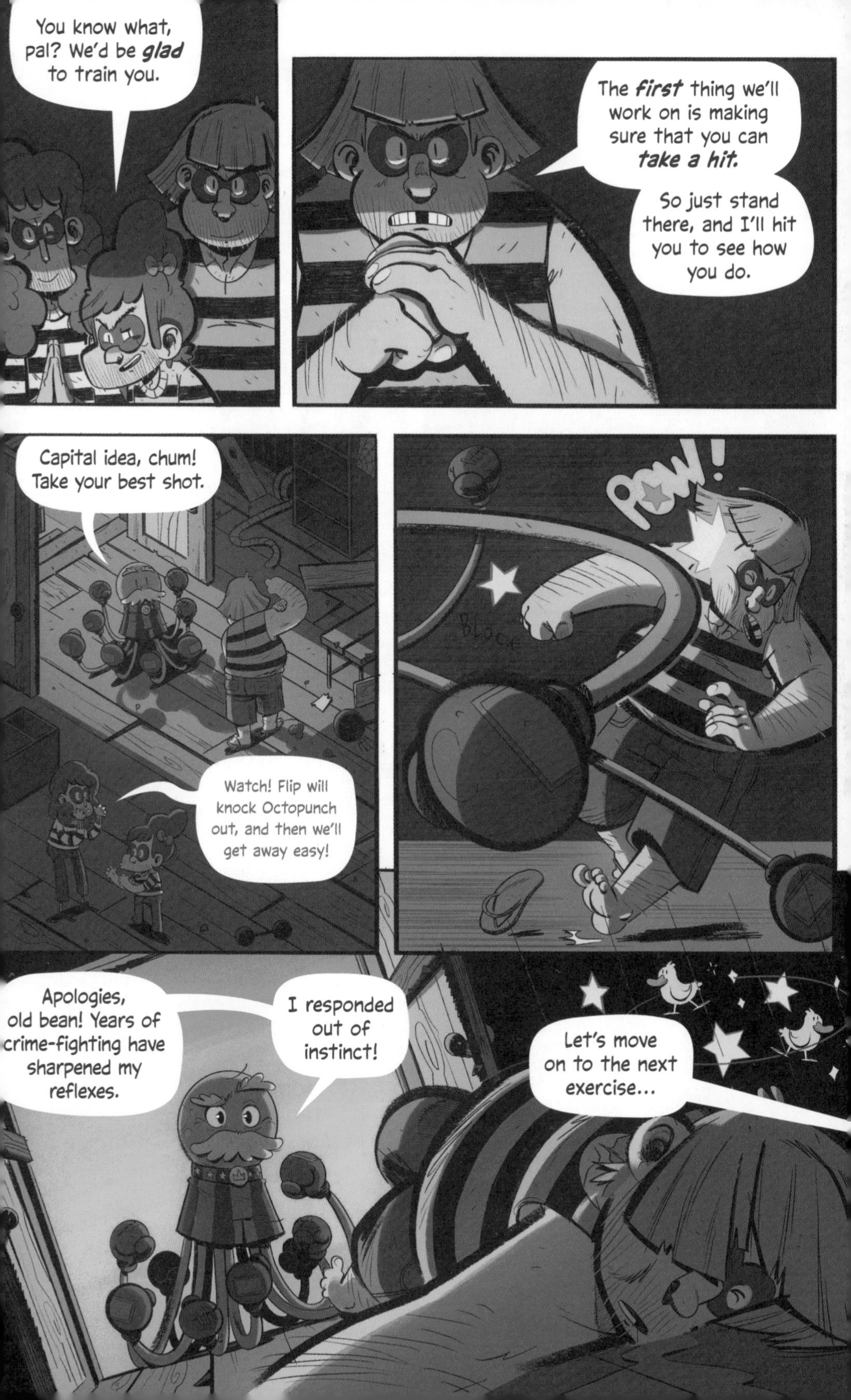
You know what, pal? We'd be *glad* to train you.
The *first* thing we'll work on is making sure that you can *take a hit.*
So just stand there, and I'll hit you to see how you do.
Capital idea, chum! Take your best shot.
Watch! Flip will knock Octopunch out, and then we'll get away easy!
POW!
Apologies, old bean! Years of crime-fighting have sharpened my reflexes.
I responded out of instinct!
Let's move on to the next exercise...

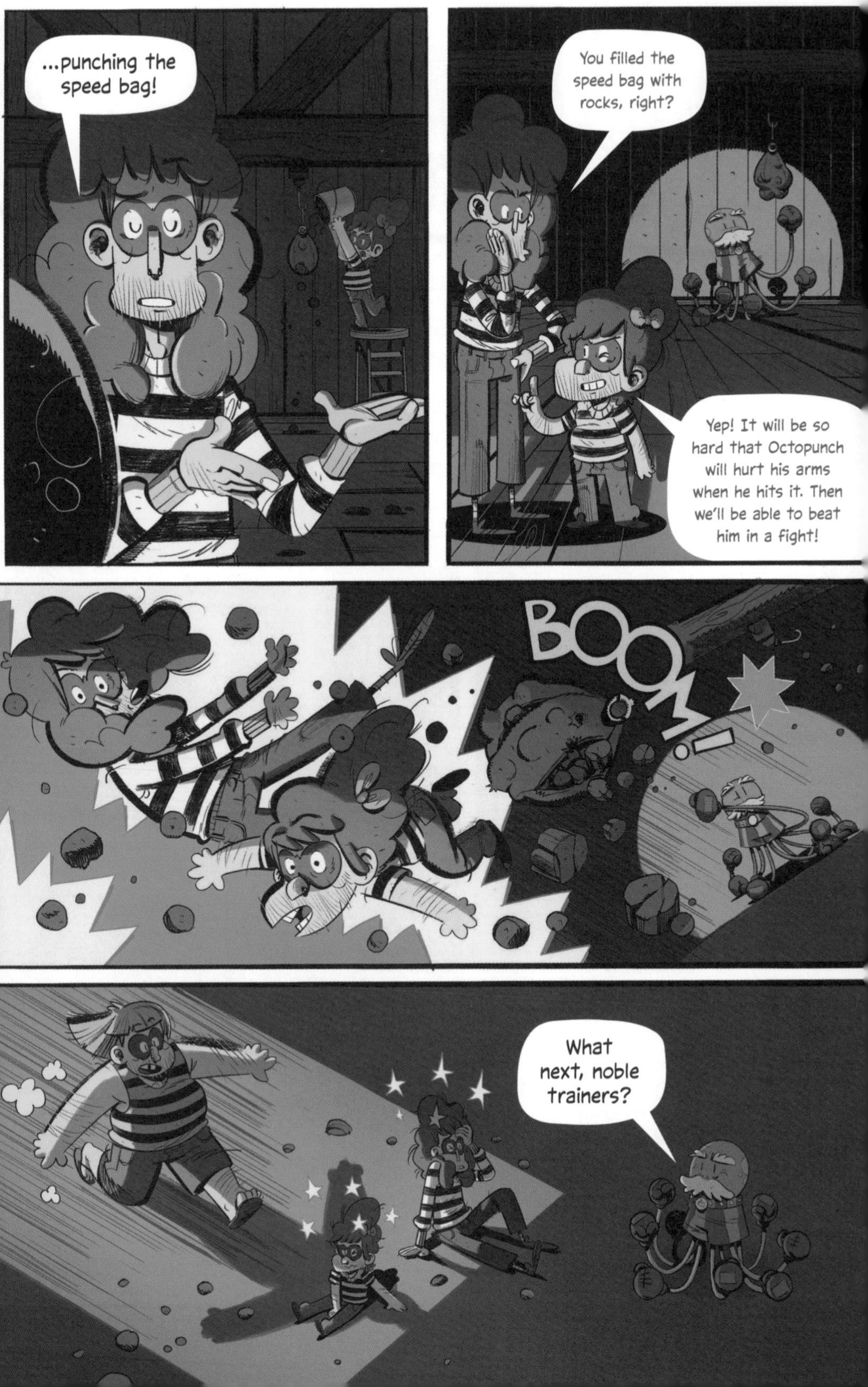

...punching the speed bag!
You filled the speed bag with rocks, right?
Yep! It will be so hard that Octopunch will hurt his arms when he hits it. Then we'll be able to beat him in a fight!
BOOM
What next, noble trainers?

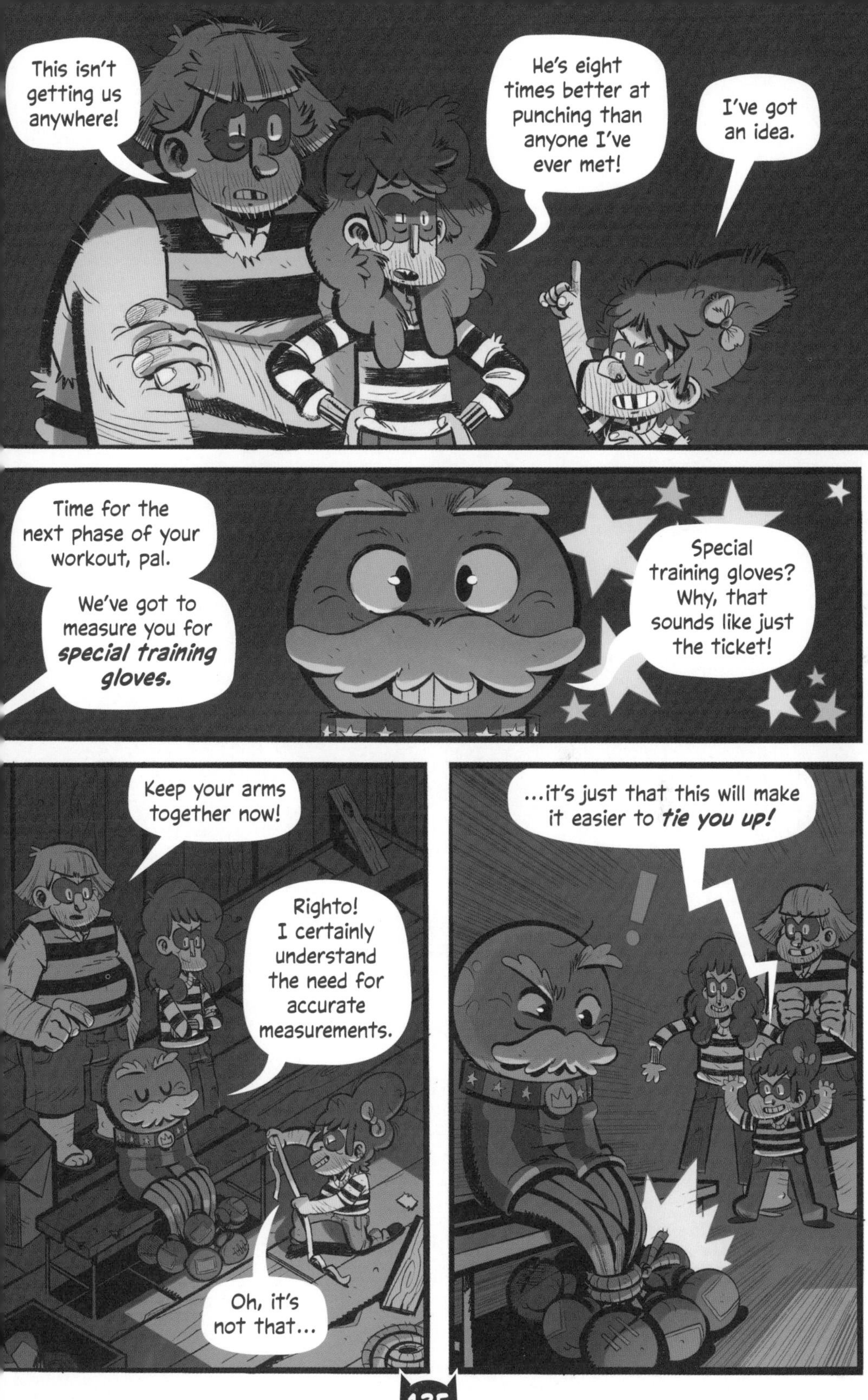
This isn't getting us anywhere!
He's eight times better at punching than anyone I've ever met!
I've got an idea.
Time for the next phase of your workout, pal.
We've got to measure you for ***special training gloves.***
Special training gloves? Why, that sounds like just the ticket!
Keep your arms together now!
Righto! I certainly understand the need for accurate measurements.
Oh, it's not that...
...it's just that this will make it easier to ***tie you up!***
!

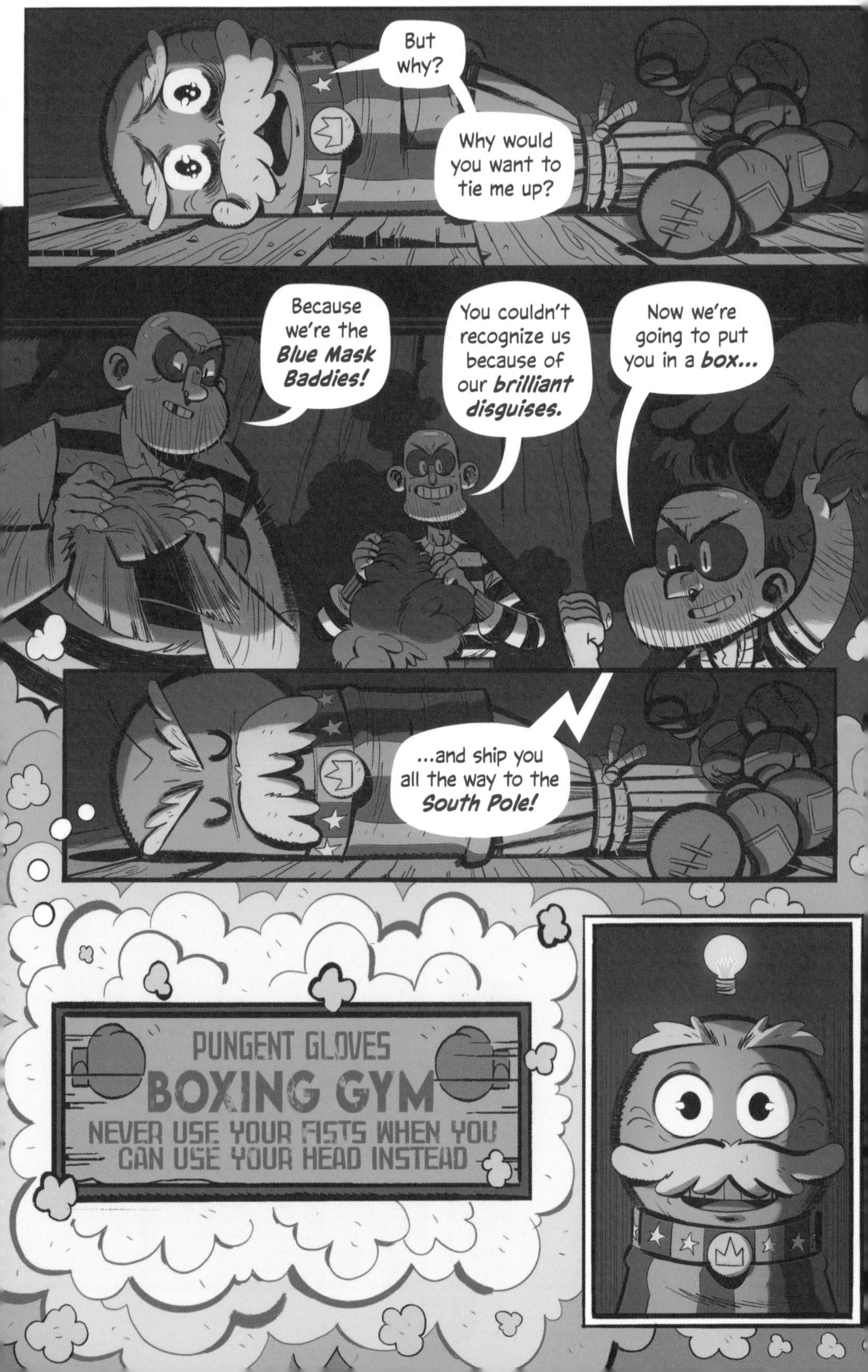
But why?
Why would you want to tie me up?
Because we're the *Blue Mask Baddies!*
You couldn't recognize us because of our *brilliant disguises.*
Now we're going to put you in a *box...*
...and ship you all the way to the *South Pole!*
PUNGENT GLOVES
BOXING GYM
NEVER USE YOUR FISTS WHEN YOU CAN USE YOUR HEAD INSTEAD

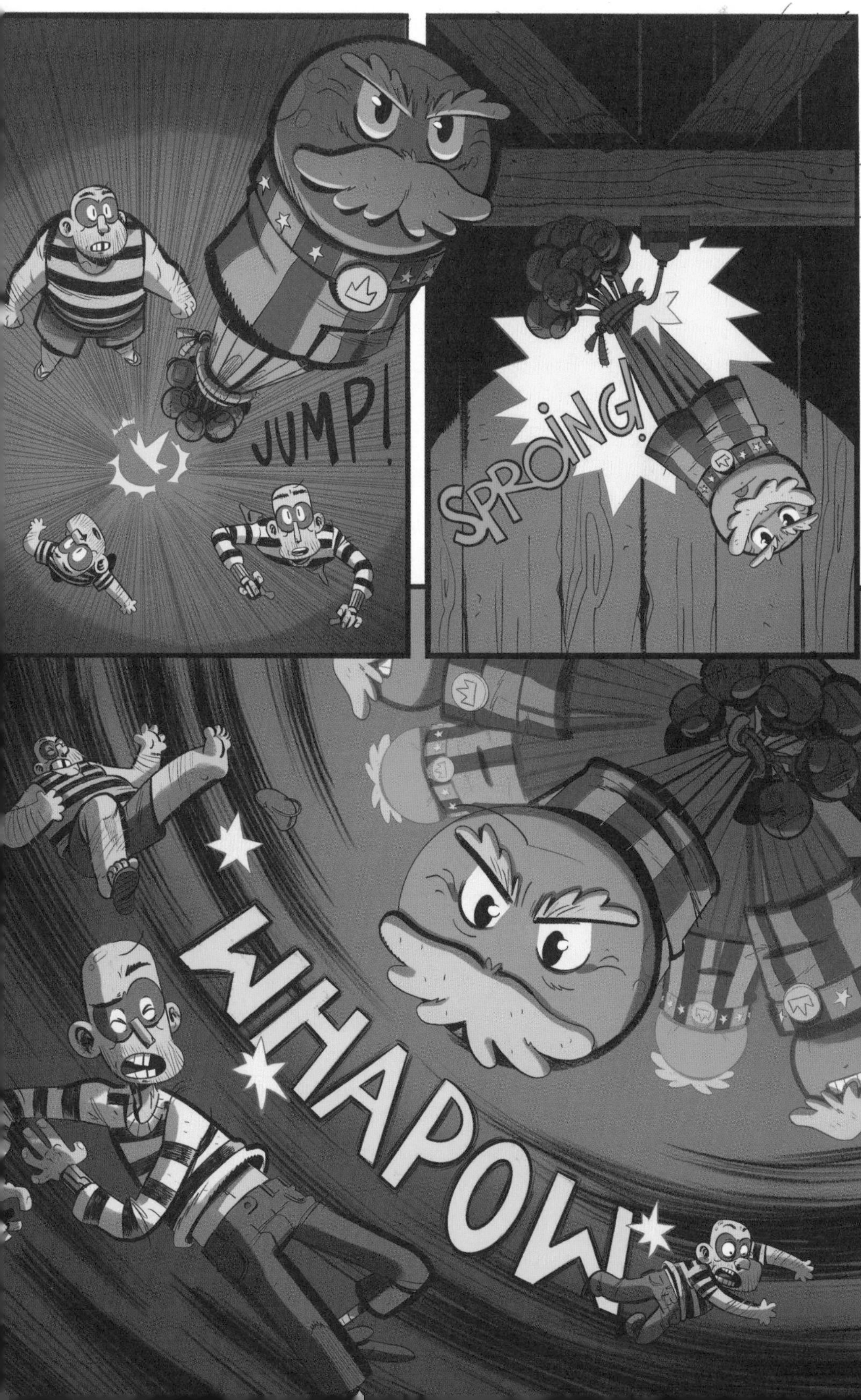
JUMP!
SPROING!
WHAPOW!

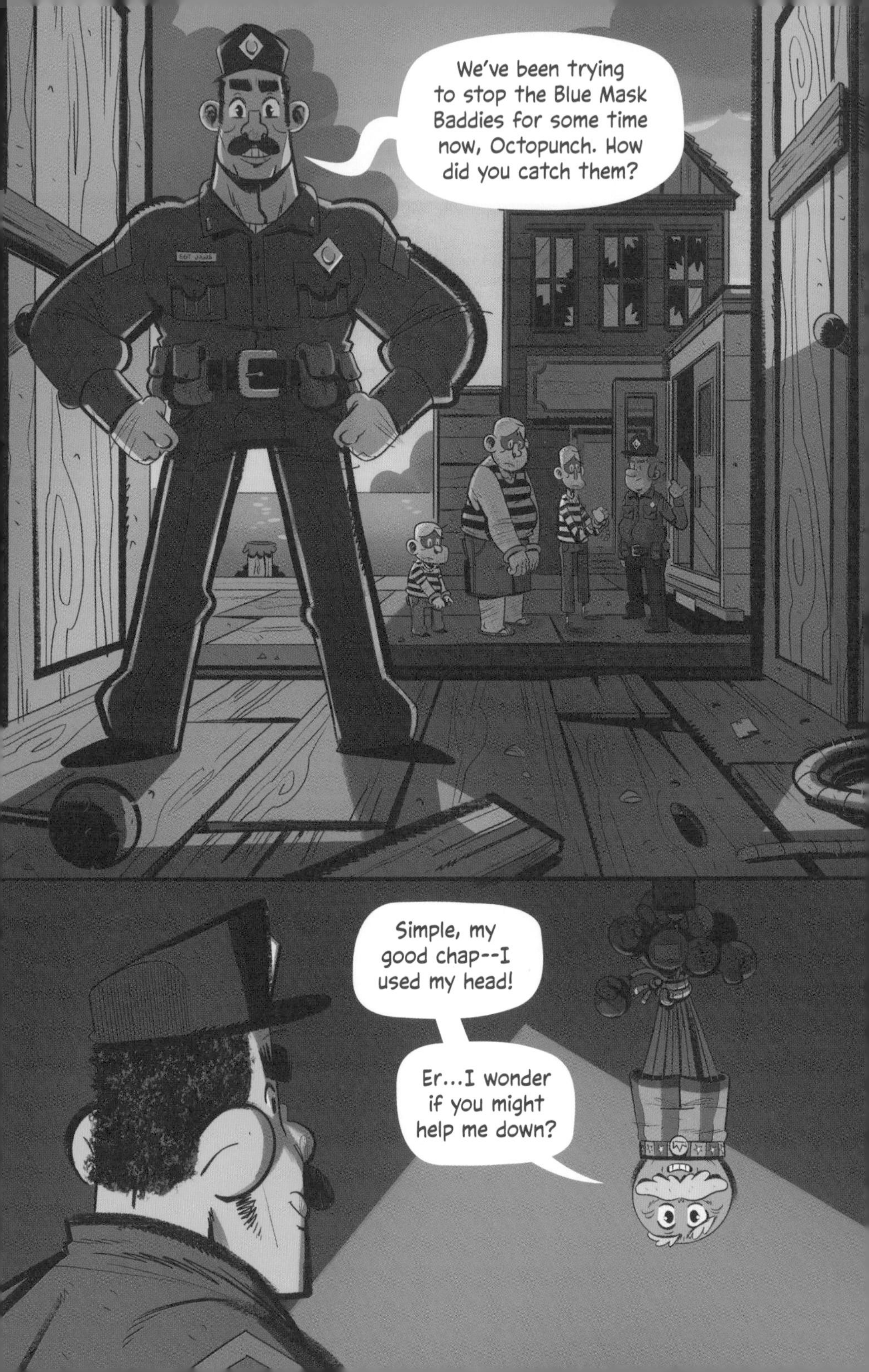
We've been trying to stop the Blue Mask Baddies for some time now, Octopunch. How did you catch them?
Simple, my good chap--I used my head!
Er...I wonder if you might help me down?

T0ast3r

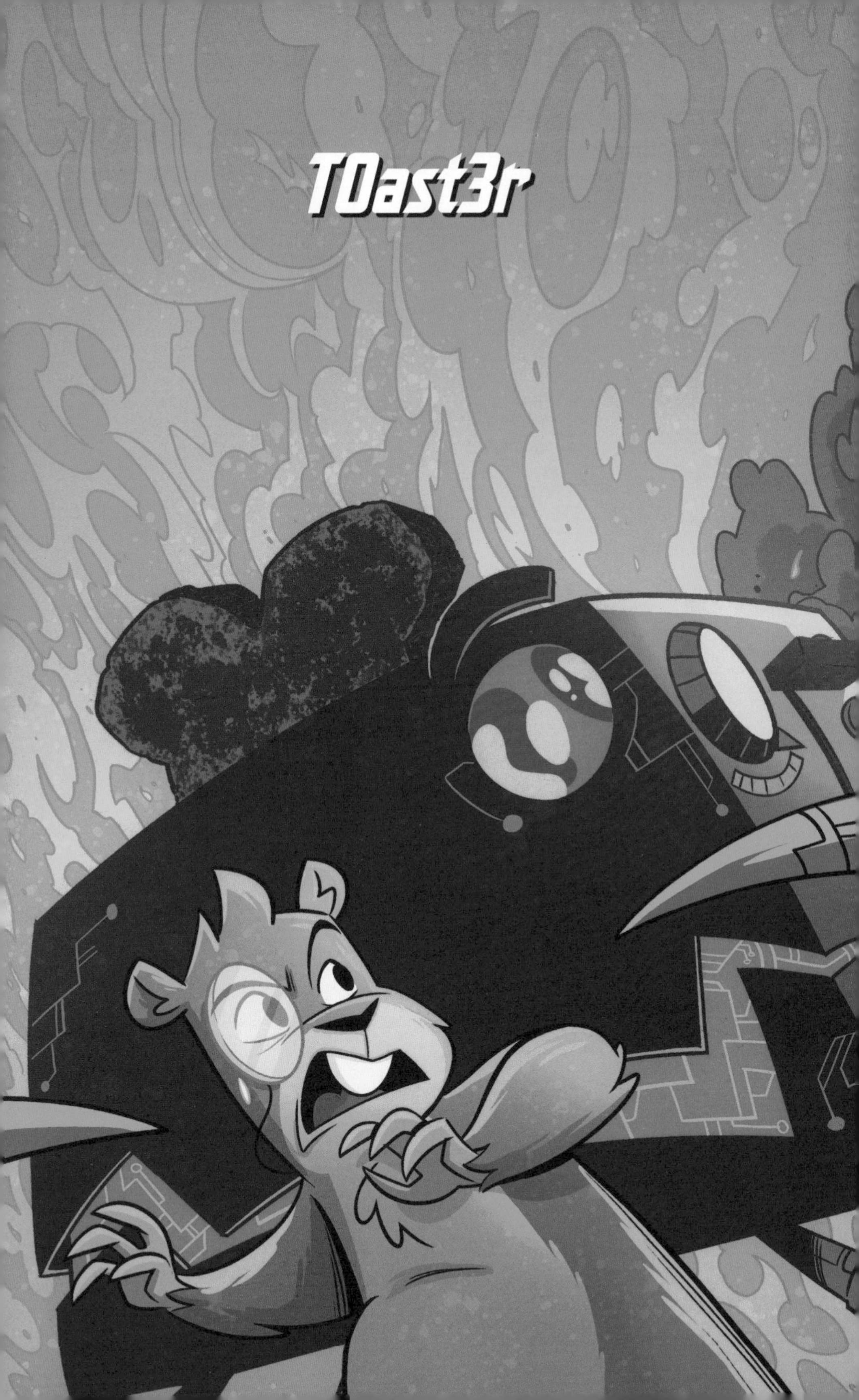

Written and Illustrated by
Chad Thomas

Colors by
Warren Wucinich

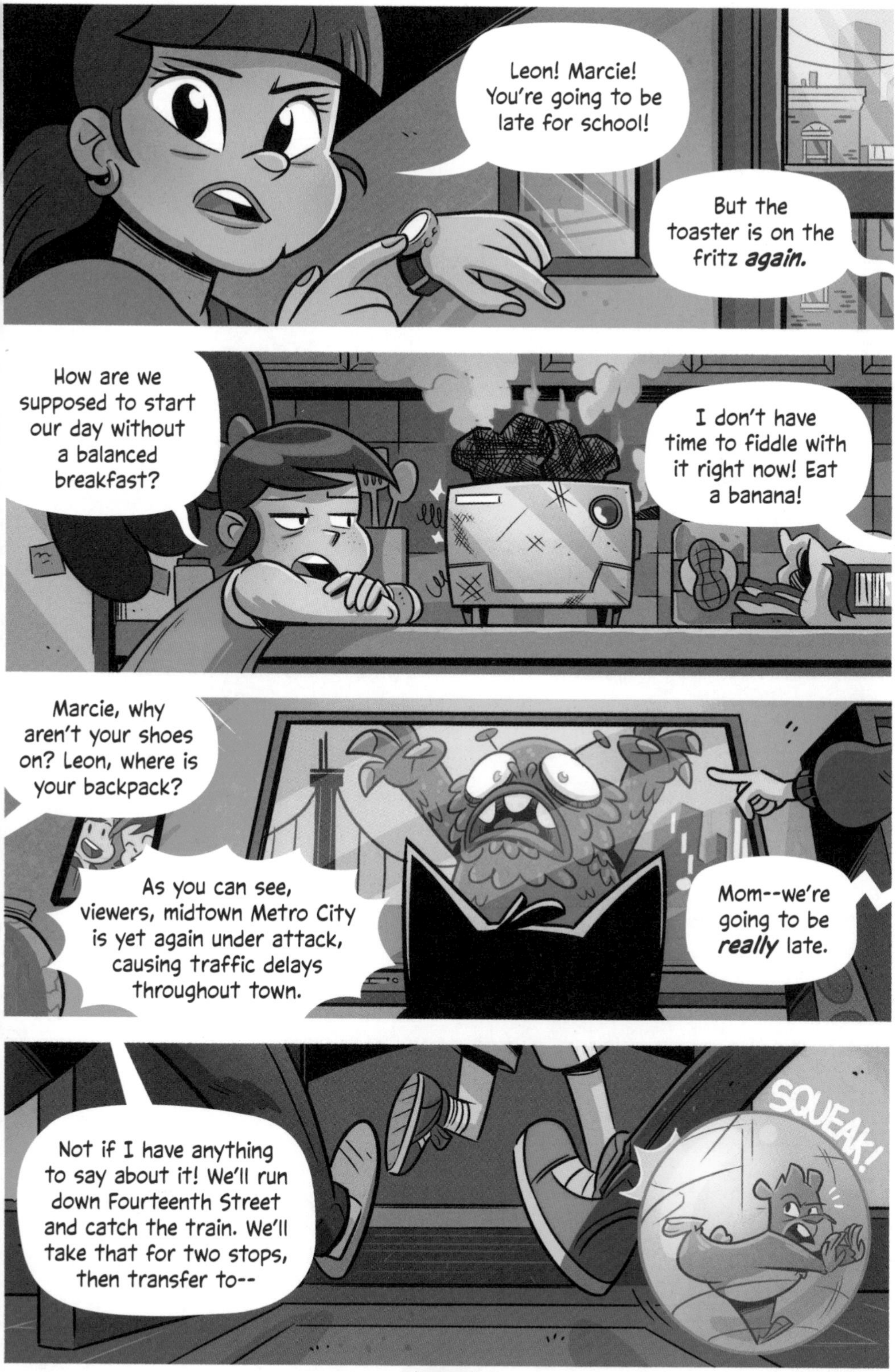
Leon! Marcie! You're going to be late for school!
But the toaster is on the fritz *again.*
How are we supposed to start our day without a balanced breakfast?
I don't have time to fiddle with it right now! Eat a banana!
Marcie, why aren't your shoes on? Leon, where is your backpack?
As you can see, viewers, midtown Metro City is yet again under attack, causing traffic delays throughout town.
Mom--we're going to be *really* late.
Not if I have anything to say about it! We'll run down Fourteenth Street and catch the train. We'll take that for two stops, then transfer to--
SQUEAK!

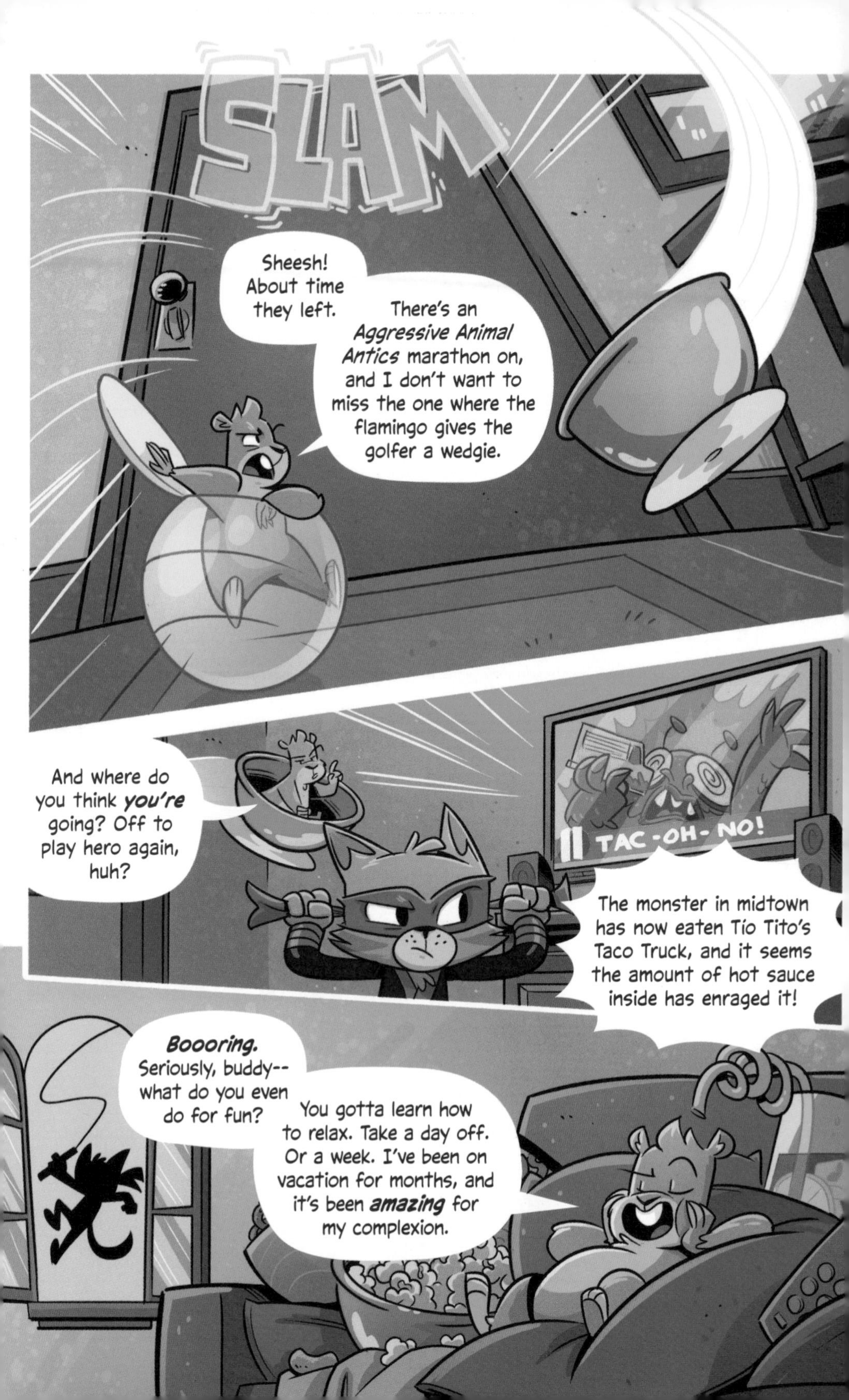
SLAM
Sheesh! About time they left.
There's an *Aggressive Animal Antics* marathon on, and I don't want to miss the one where the flamingo gives the golfer a wedgie.
And where do you think ***you're*** going? Off to play hero again, huh?
TAC-OH-NO!
The monster in midtown has now eaten Tío Tito's Taco Truck, and it seems the amount of hot sauce inside has enraged it!
Boooring. Seriously, buddy-- what do you even do for fun?
You gotta learn how to relax. Take a day off. Or a week. I've been on vacation for months, and it's been ***amazing*** for my complexion.

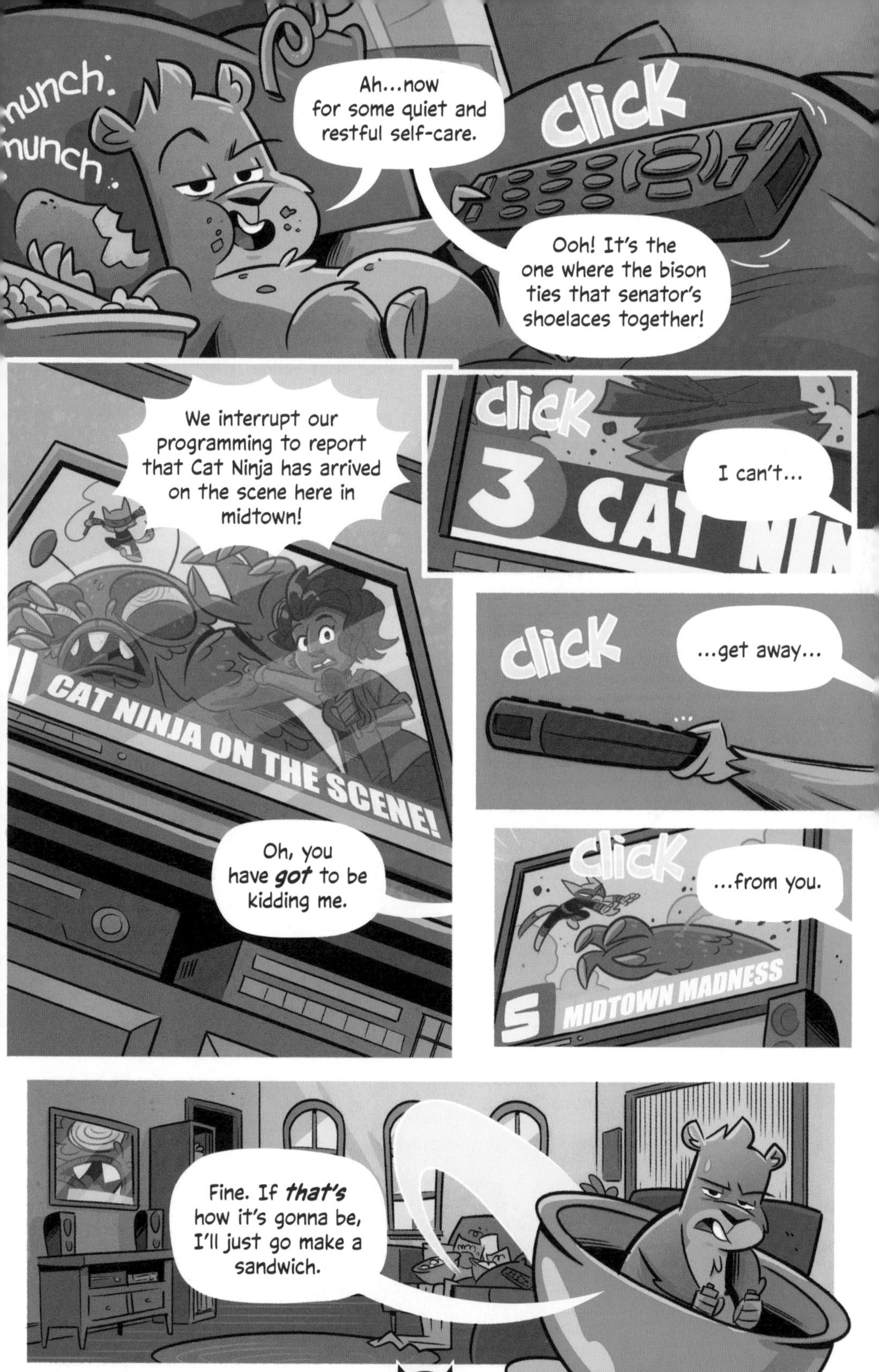
munch
munch
Ah...now for some quiet and restful self-care.
click
Ooh! It's the one where the bison ties that senator's shoelaces together!
We interrupt our programming to report that Cat Ninja has arrived on the scene here in midtown!
CAT NINJA ON THE SCENE!
click
3
I can't...
click
...get away...
Oh, you have got to be kidding me.
click
...from you.
5 MIDTOWN MADNESS
Fine. If that's how it's gonna be, I'll just go make a sandwich.

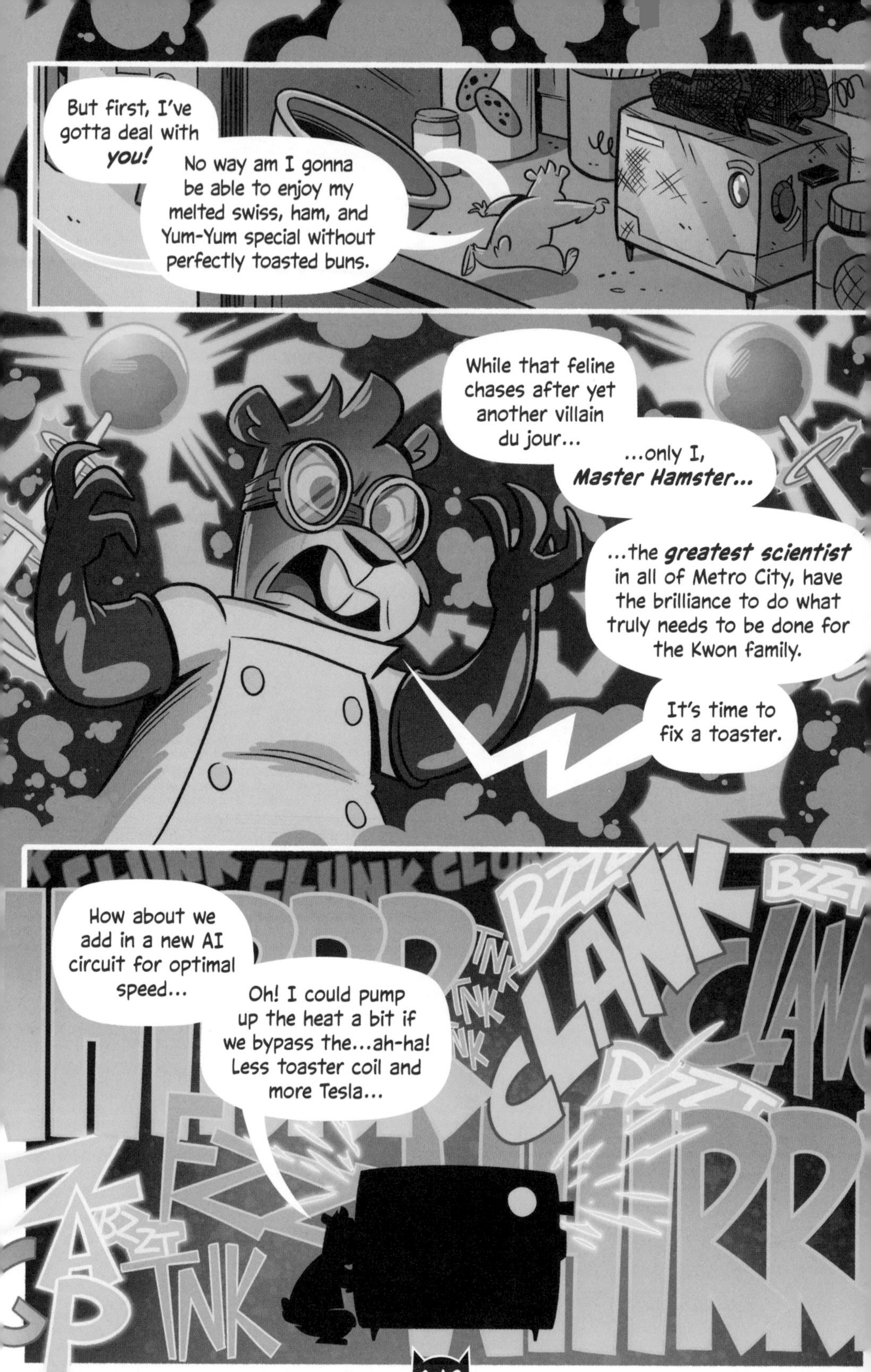
But first, I've gotta deal with *you!*
No way am I gonna be able to enjoy my melted swiss, ham, and Yum-Yum special without perfectly toasted buns.
While that feline chases after yet another villain du jour...
...only I, *Master Hamster...*
...the *greatest scientist* in all of Metro City, have the brilliance to do what truly needs to be done for the Kwon family.
It's time to fix a toaster.
How about we add in a new AI circuit for optimal speed...
Oh! I could pump up the heat a bit if we bypass the...ah-ha! Less toaster coil and more Tesla...
CLANK
BZZT
TNK

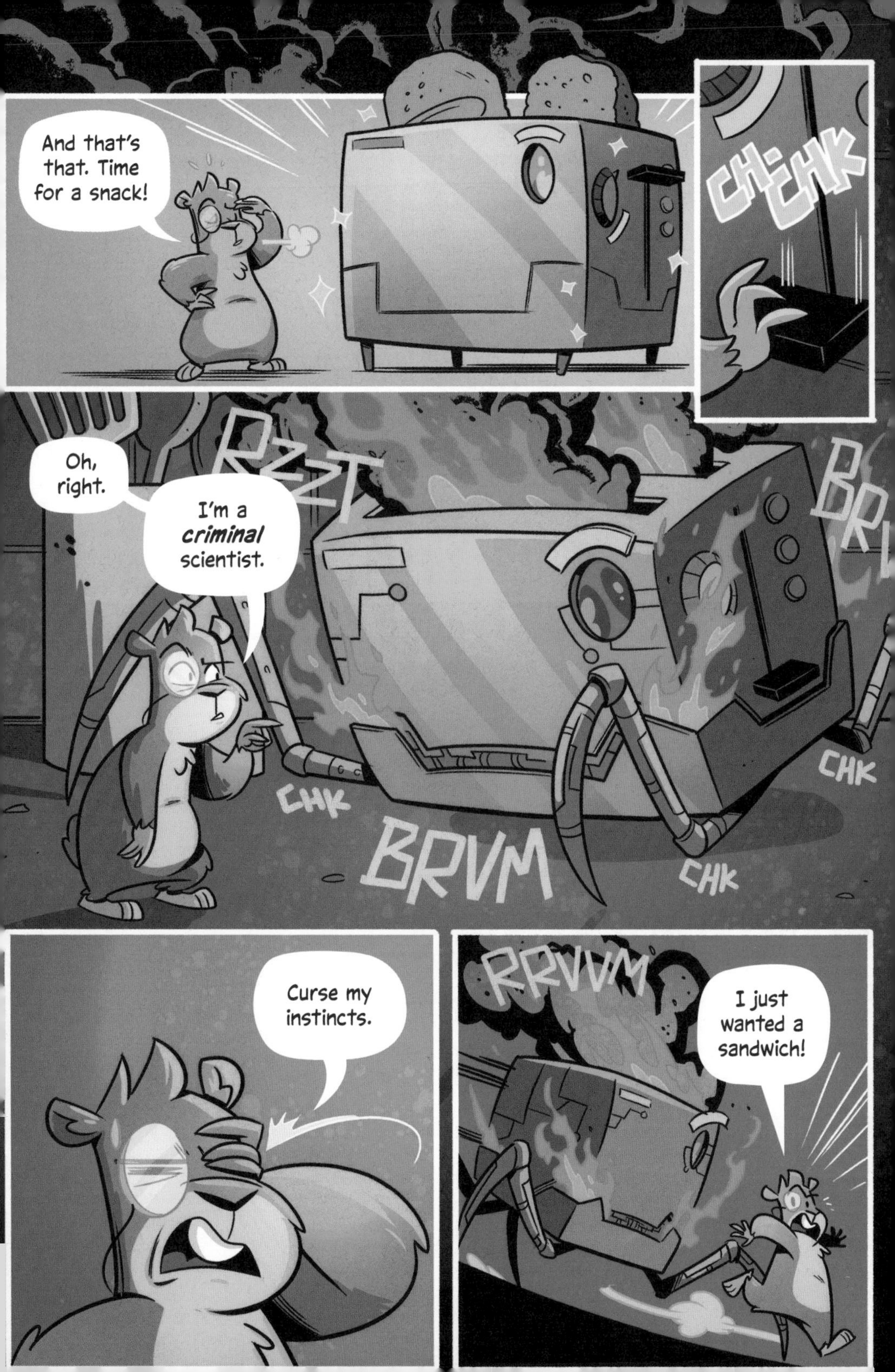
And that's that. Time for a snack!
CH-CHK
RZZT
Oh, right.
I'm a *criminal* scientist.
BR
CHK
BRVM
CHK
CHK
Curse my instincts.
RRVVM
I just wanted a sandwich!

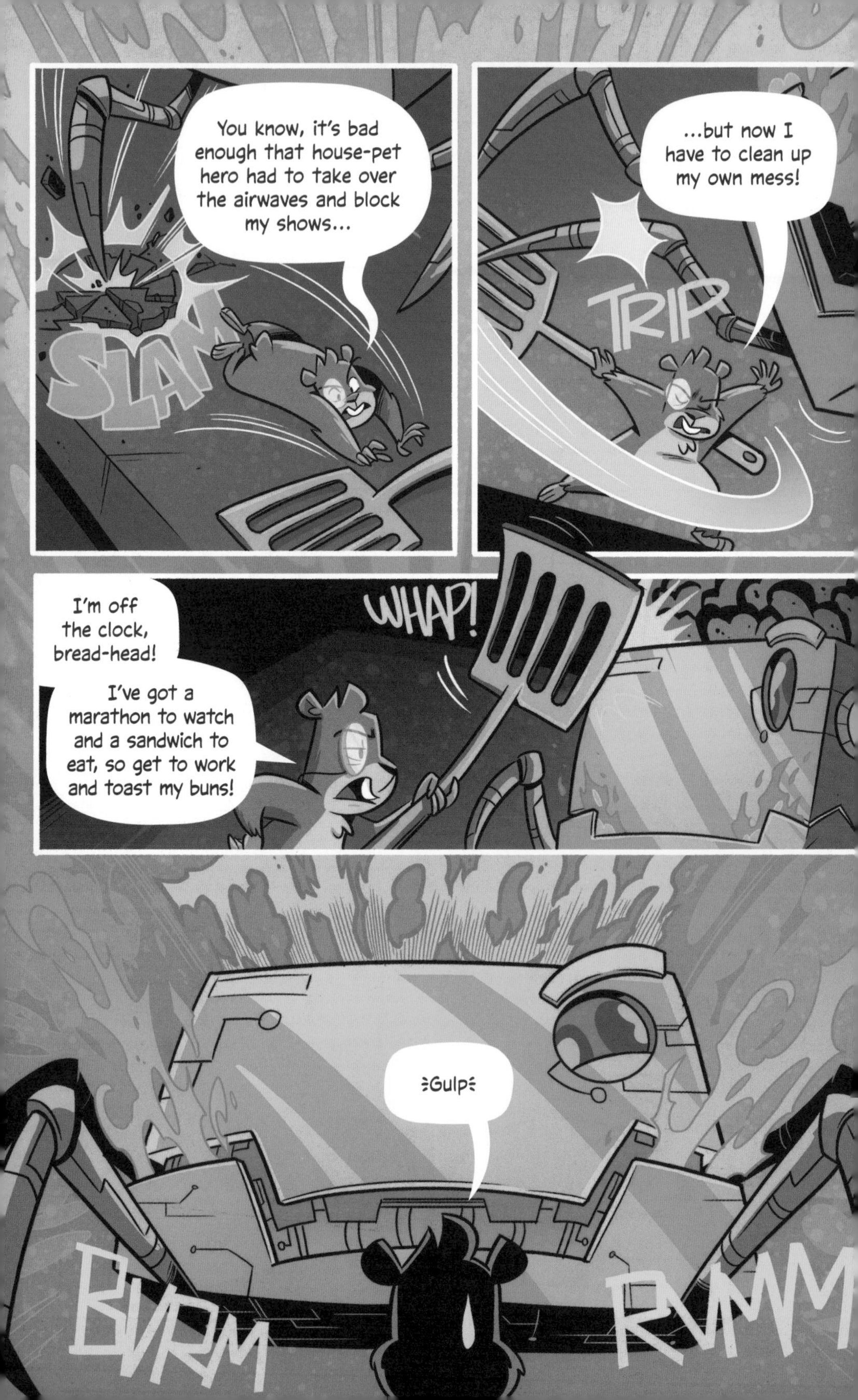
You know, it's bad enough that house-pet hero had to take over the airwaves and block my shows...
SLAM
...but now I have to clean up my own mess!
TRIP
WHAP!
I'm off the clock, bread-head!
I've got a marathon to watch and a sandwich to eat, so get to work and toast my buns!
Gulp
BVRM
RVMM

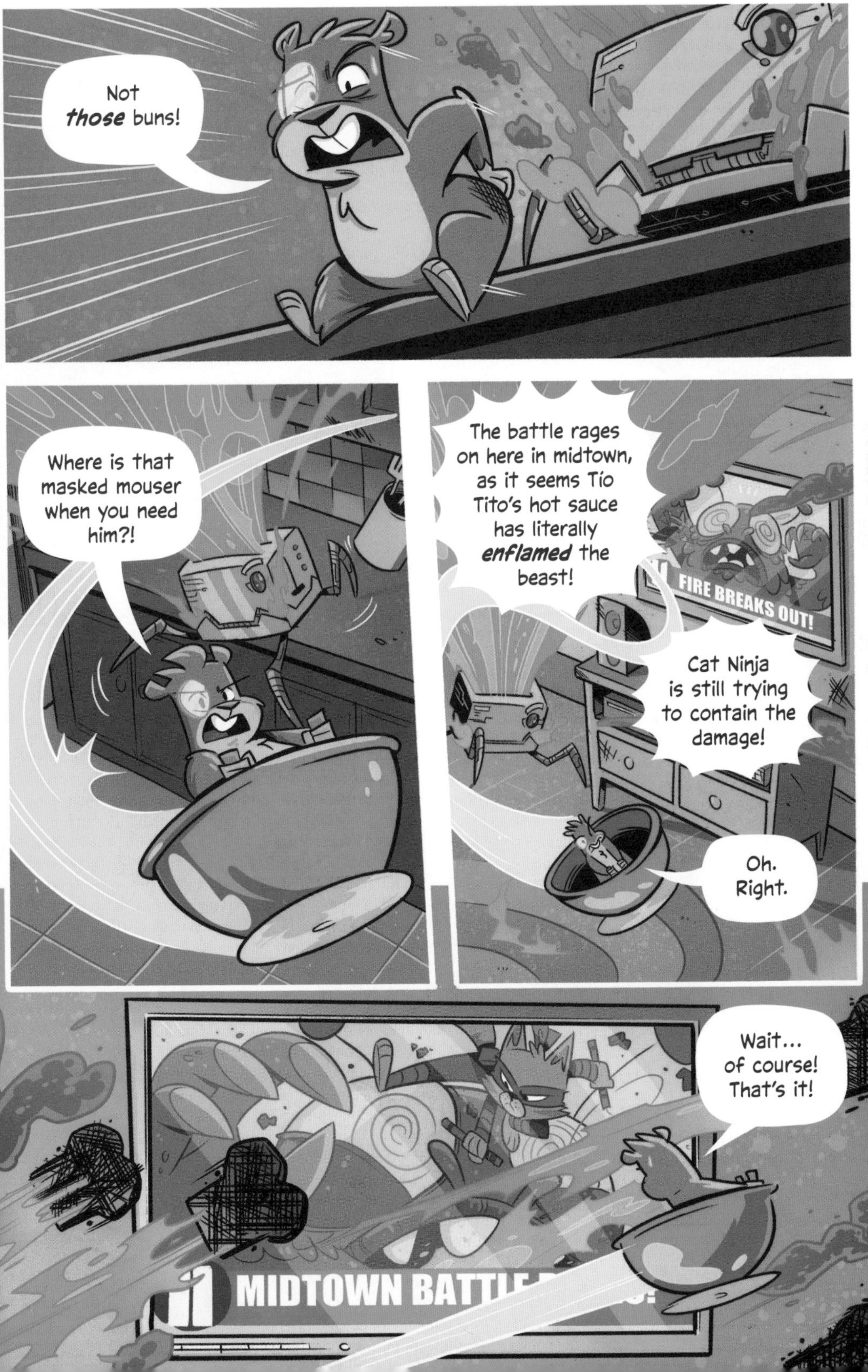

Not *those* buns!
Where is that masked mouser when you need him?!
The battle rages on here in midtown, as it seems Tio Tito's hot sauce has literally *enflamed* the beast!
FIRE BREAKS OUT!
Cat Ninja is still trying to contain the damage!
Oh. Right.
Wait... of course! That's it!
MIDTOWN BATTL

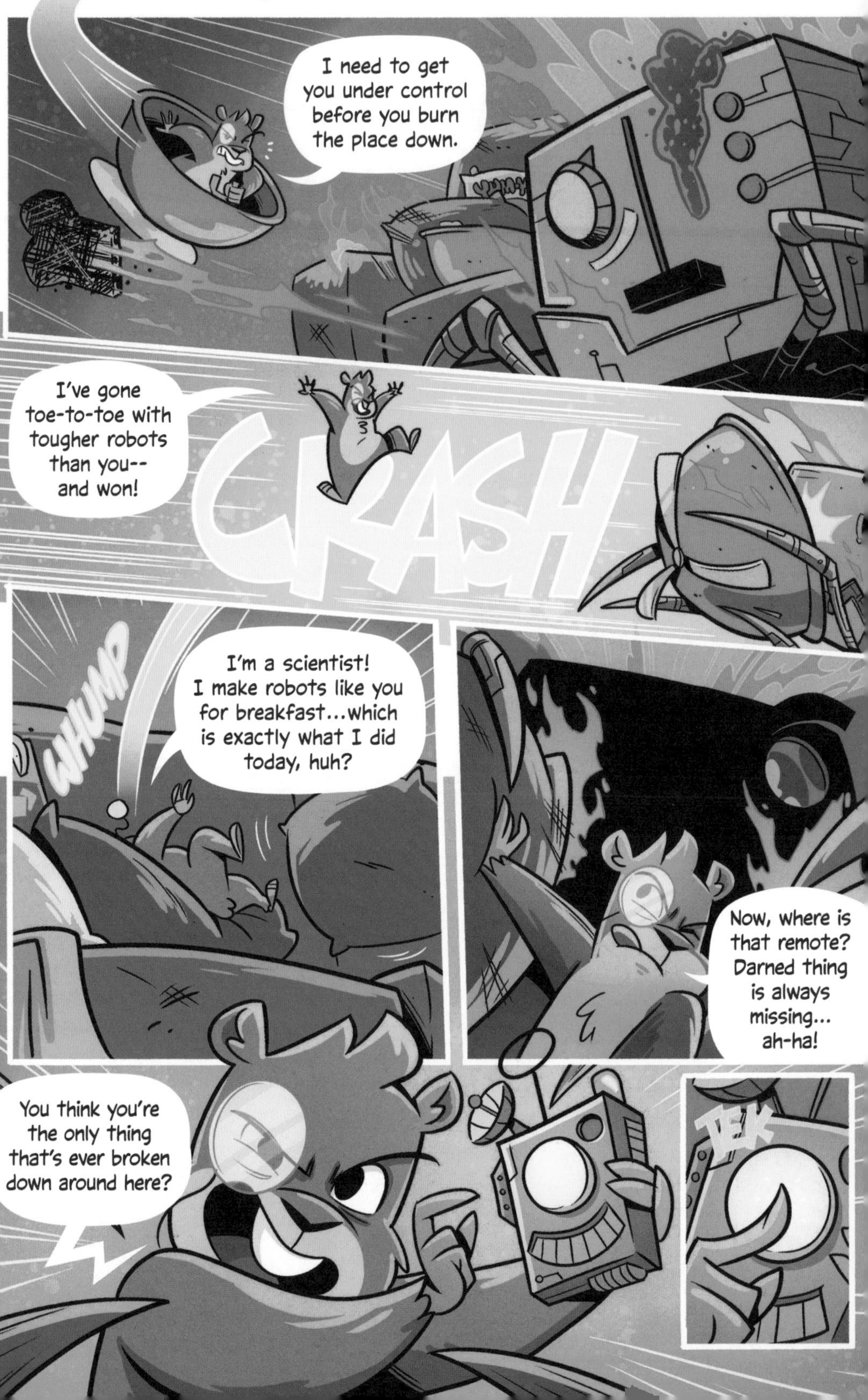
I need to get you under control before you burn the place down.
I've gone toe-to-toe with tougher robots than you-- and won!
CRASH
WHUMP
I'm a scientist! I make robots like you for breakfast...which is exactly what I did today, huh?
Now, where is that remote? Darned thing is always missing... ah-ha!
You think you're the only thing that's ever broken down around here?
TEK

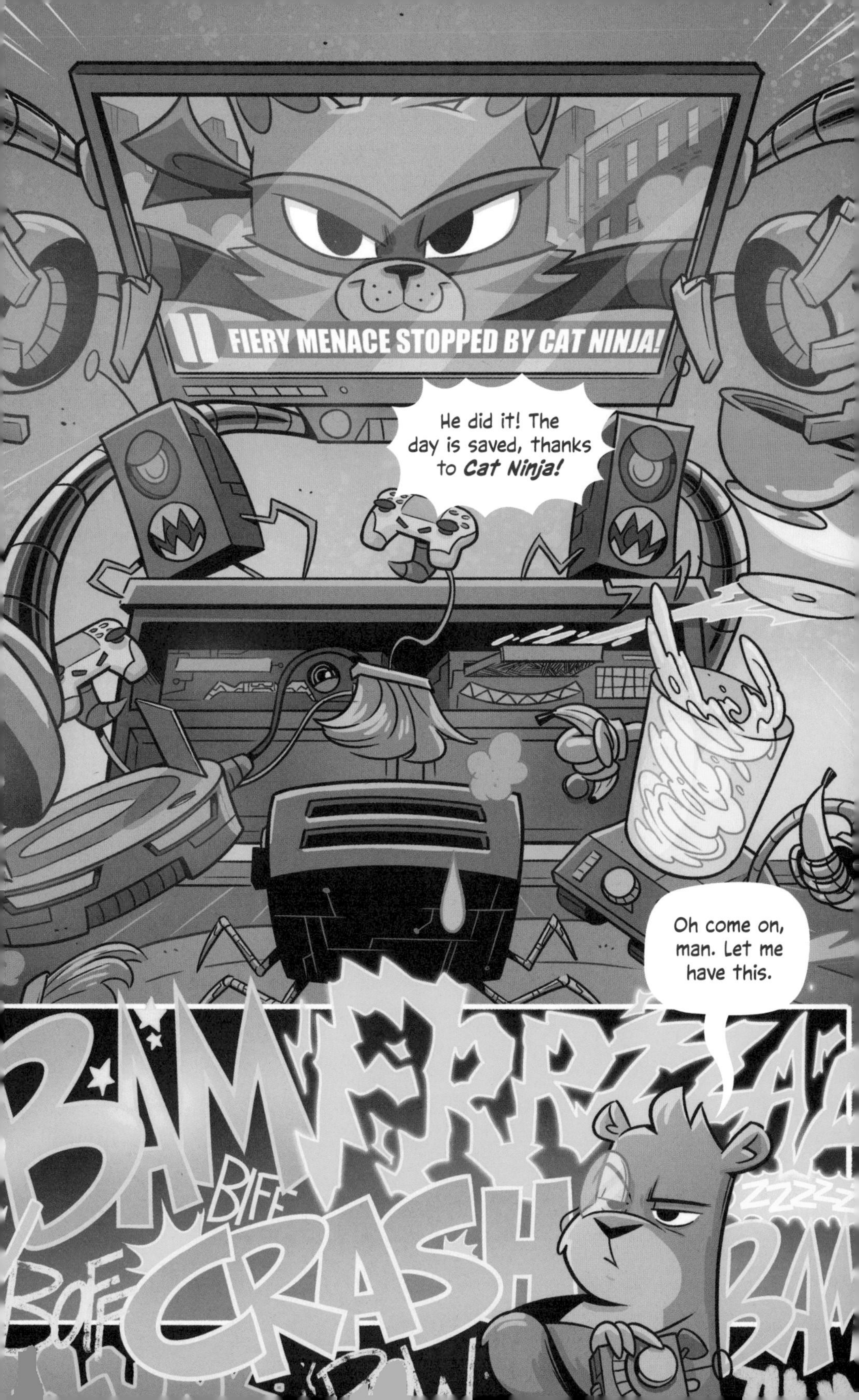
FIERY MENACE STOPPED BY CAT NINJA!
He did it! The day is saved, thanks to *Cat Ninja!*
Oh come on, man. Let me have this.
BAM
BIFF
CRASH
ZZZZZ

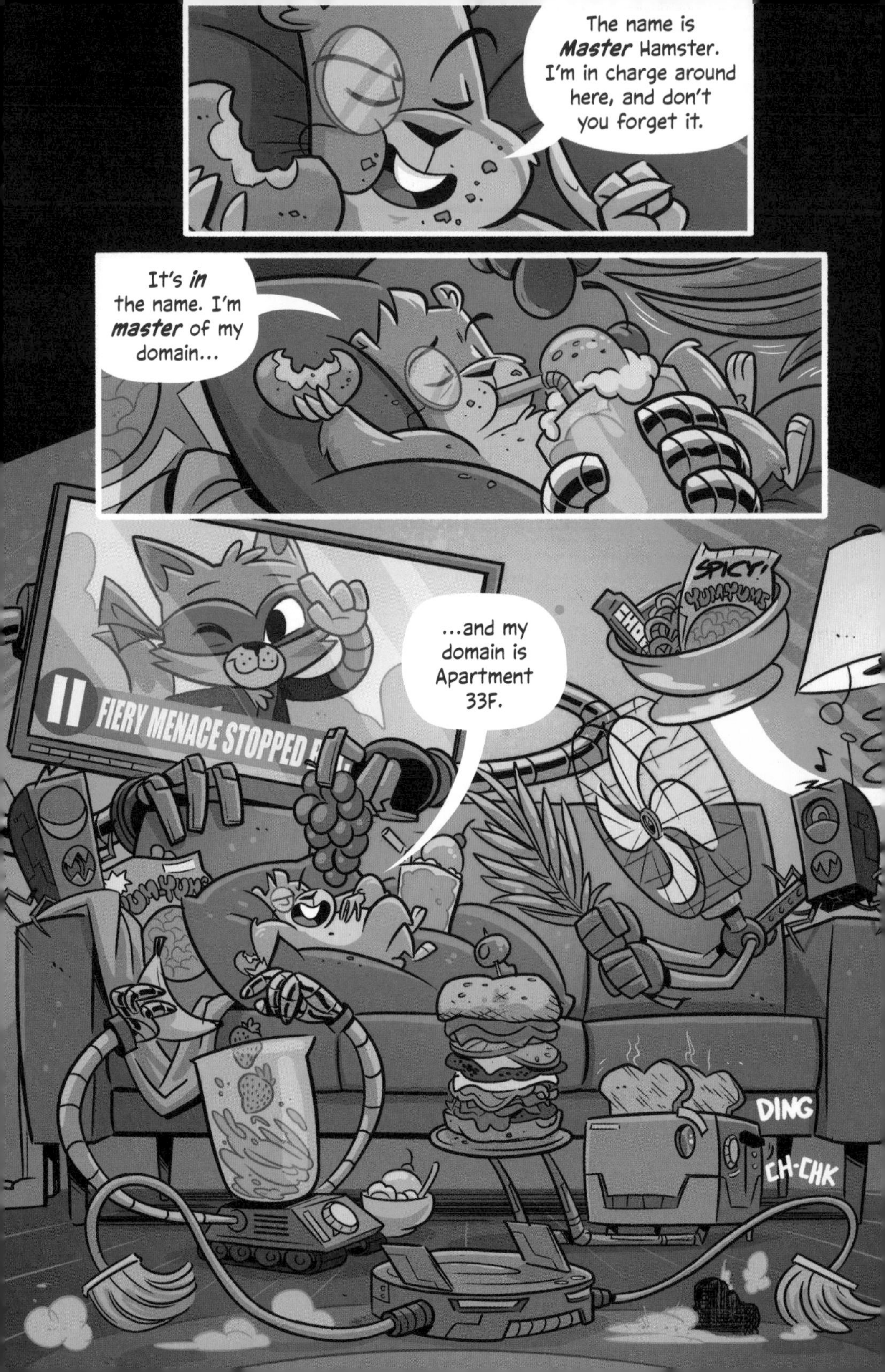
The name is *Master* Hamster. I'm in charge around here, and don't you forget it.
It's *in* the name. I'm *master* of my domain...
FIERY MENACE STOPPED
SPICY!
YUMYUMS
...and my domain is Apartment 33F.
DING
CH-CHK

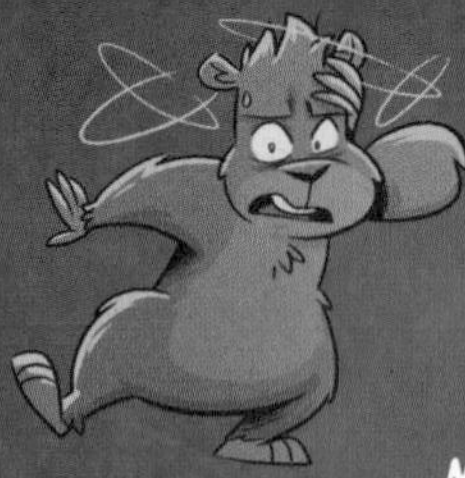

About the Authors

MATTHEW CODY is the author of the award-winning Supers of Noble's Green trilogy: *Powerless*, *Super*, and *Villainous*. He is also the author of *Will in Scarlet* and *The Dead Gentleman*, as well as the graphic novels *Zatanna and the House of Secrets* from DC Comics and *Bright Family* from Epic/Andrews McMeel.

JADZIA AXELROD is an award-winning author, illustrator, activist, gadabout, and circus performer. She is the author of comics and graphic novels for Tor, Quirk Books, and DC Comics. She lives in Philadelphia, where she cooks overly elaborate meals for her wonderful wife and delightful child.

DAN NORDSKOG is a graphic designer, writer, and co-creator of the popular graphic novel series *According to Aggie* for American Girl Publishing. When he's not creating comics, he can be found reading them.

KURTIS SCALETTA has written books about sports, snakes, giant fungi, robots, bees, and video games (among other things).

CHRIS SCHWEIZER is a cartoonist and toymaker who lives in the western coal fields of Kentucky. He's been nominated for three Eisner Awards. He was a kickboxer when he was young but never would have won a fight against Octopunch.

CHAD THOMAS is an illustrator and cartoonist for books such as *TMNT*, *Star Wars Adventures*, and *Mega Man*. He loves his family, comic books, and Star Wars and will let his children beat him in checkers, but never in Mario Kart.

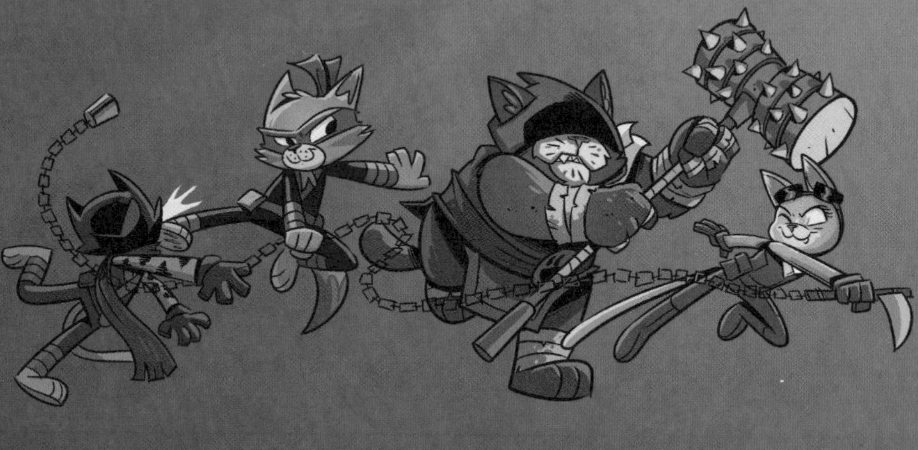

About the Illustrators

CHAD THOMAS is a hero by night, housecat--er, illustrator and cartoonist--by day. He is the artist for numerous titles and seasons within the *Cat Ninja* universe, and his career includes other books such as *TMNT*, *Star Wars Adventures*, and *Mega Man*.

EDUARDO MEDEIROS is a comic book author and artist from Brazil. He has several books published in Brazil and the United States, including *Mondo Urbano* (Devir/Oni Press), *Sopa de Salsicha* (Cia das Letras), *Marvel Strange Tales* (Marvel), *Gotham Academy* (DC Comics), *Open Bar* (Panini Books/Oni Press), *Joker 80th* (DC Comics), and *Funny Creek* (ComiXology). He loves to eat sandwiches and has a lovely 2-year-old son named Gabriel, as well as four dogs and four cats.

BRETT BEAN is the author-illustrator of the graphic novel series *Zoo Patrol Squad* with Penguin Workshop and the illustrator of the *Marvel's Rocket & Groot* (Marvel), Battle Bugs (Scholastic) and Beasts of Olympus (Workshop) series. He also works in film, TV, video games, and board games and has worked with Disney, Activision, Jim Henson's Creature Shop, and more. He lives in Portugal with a bunch of redheads, but you can visit him online at www.brettbean.com.

About the Colorists

WARREN WUCINICH is a comic book creator and part-time carny who has been lucky enough to work on such cool projects as *Invader ZIM*, *Courtney Crumrin*, and *Cat Ninja*. He is also the co-creator of the YA graphic novel *Kriss: The Gift of Wrath*. He currently resides in Boston, Massachusetts, where he spends his time making comics, rewatching '80s television shows, and eating all the pies.

CINDY ZHI is a Sydney-based illustrator and animator who has worked on *Cat Ninja* and is currently cooking up short animated films. When she's not drawing, she can be found hanging out with birds (or watching them through binoculars).

MAARTA LAIHO spends her days and nights as a freelance artist and comic colorist, where her work includes *Lumberjanes*, *Wings of Fire*, and *Hilo*. When she's not doing that, she can be found hoarding houseplants and talking to her cats. She currently lives in Maine.